He reached for his cell phone and scrolled to a number.

The man on the other end of the line didn't answer so much as grunt.

"It's me," Marnin said. "I got it."

"Palmer's computer?"

"A couple of Gage's. Everything from Palmer's was copied over to it. A kid decided to cooperate and told us."

"What about Palmer's?"

"We'd need explosives to get to it."

"Then let's cross that bridge when we come to it. First we need to find out what kind of records Palmer was keeping. We can torch Gage's place if we have to."

"Where should I—"

"Evergreen Security in San Jose. We got an ex-NSA guy down there who can break into anybody's hard drive. Somebody'll meet you in the parking lot."

"I don't know why they're going through all this. Why don't they just wipe the slate clean and start over with a new team? Couple of bodies. Done in an afternoon—and their mistakes buried with them."

"That would be sheer genius. You know the last time somebody got away with killing a federal judge?" He paused. "I'll tell you. Never."

Turn the page for ~~praise for the previous~~ **Graham Gage nov**

FINAL TARGET

"**A**n action packed debut thriller with a unique plot and vivid characters that gives readers a fascinating look into the world of international industrial espionage. I'm looking forward to [Gore's] next."

Phillip Margolin,
New York Times bestselling author of *Supreme Justice*

"**S**teven Gore bursts onto the international thriller scene with a captivating debut.... Lightning paced, deftly plotted, and compulsively readable.... We will be hearing much more from Steven Gore."

Sheldon Siegel,
New York Times bestselling author of *Judgment Day*

"**W**ith his command of storytelling and insider's knowledge, Gore can go up against Nelson DeMille and Daniel Silva and come out a contender."

Library Journal

"**G**ore has effectively introduced the reader to the world of the private investigator.... [He] has crafted a solid thriller."

Salt Lake City Deseret News

"**A** smart, riveting, knock-your-socks-off debut thriller—James Bond for grownups."

Cornelia Read,
author of *The Crazy School*

ABSOLUTE RISK

"*Absolute Risk* continues Gore's winning ways. . . . A truly thrilling thriller."
San Jose Mercury News

"Masterful. . . . Sharp, smart writing and convincing economic detail put this in the front rank of genre fiction."
Publishers Weekly (*Starred Review*)

"Steven Gore, himself an international private investigator before he turned to writing, brings a credibility to his high-octaned action."
Washington Post (online)

"Gore stuffs a lot into his plot . . . but he manages it well, with a winning protagonist and a plausible premise."
Booklist

"Brad Meltzer and Vince Flynn fans will love this."
Library Journal

"A brisk pace and an intriguing plot make the pages turn themselves."
Richard North Patterson,
New York Times bestselling author of *Silent Witness*

By Steven Gore

Graham Gage Thrillers
FINAL TARGET
ABSOLUTE RISK
POWER BLIND

Harlan Donnally Novels
ACT OF DECEIT

STEVEN GORE

POWER BLIND

A GRAHAM GAGE THRILLER

HARPER

An Imprint of HarperCollinsPublishers

This book is a work of fiction. The characters, incidents, and dialogue are drawn from the author's imagination and are not to be construed as real. Any resemblance to actual events or persons, living or dead, is entirely coincidental.

HARPER

An Imprint of HarperCollins*Publishers*
10 East 53rd Street
New York, New York 10022-5299

Copyright © 2012 by Steven Gore
ISBN 978-0-06-178224-4

First Harper premium printing: August 2012

Printed in the United States of America

Visit Harper paperbacks on the World Wide Web at www.harpercollins.com

10 9 8 7 6 5 4 3 2 1

For Hanna Fenichel Pitkin,
who asked the questions many years ago
that Graham Gage struggles to answer

POWER
BLIND

A Decade Before

Yaqui voices chanted in Moki's ears as he loped up Jackson Street, his stride keeping pace with the water drums and rattling gourds. This wasn't really a San Francisco sidewalk beneath his feet, but the Red Rock Trail into the Chiricahuas. Those weren't shrubs grown tight against fences, but tumbleweeds trapped by the Sonoran wind. That wasn't a sprinkler, but a headwater spring feeding desperate patches of peppergrass and sage . . . each alive only by the grace of the weeping earth.

The boy glanced up as he crested the hill, his view of the darkening Pacific framed by six-story cliffs of stucco and brick. A startled pigeon—no, a desert nighthawk—swept across the dying sunset, then spun and dove toward a swallowtail emerging from the Flower World below.

A-la in-i-kun, mai-so yol-e-me,
hu-nu kun, mai-so yol-e-mee

So now he is the deer,
so now he is the deer

Moki pressed his palms against the earbuds, leaving himself deaf to all but the Mexican harps and the violins and the flutes of the Deer Dance singing in his head, the hunt played out in song and shuffling feet from dusk till dawn . . . through the eyes of the hunter, and of the deer.

So now he is the deer.

Moki cut right, startling a coyote that ducked behind a hedge. He smiled to himself. The blur of reddish-brown had merely been a family dog stalking whitetails that no longer grazed the asphalt-covered hills. He raced on, angling across the pavement, dodging a black Hummer charging up the hill, its chrome wheels flashing, its engine growling, its music thumping.

Now down toward the bay. The sidewalk steep and slick. Shorter steps. Touching lightly, almost skipping—but off the beat. He lengthened his stride to catch the rhythm . . . almost . . . moving faster.

That's it.

He heard his uncle's voice soar above the other singers:

A-la in-i-kun mai-so yol-e-me
So now he is—

Screeching tires ripped the air. The Hummer skidded and jumped the curb. His thin arms flailed as he slammed into its side and ricocheted into a retaining wall, his CD player exploding as his head and hands snapped back, the cinderblock scraping his flesh as he collapsed to the ground.

Stunned, dazed, nauseated.

Boots thudding on pavement. Laughter raging down. The stench of spilled beer and wet cigarettes. Throbbing subwoofers vibrating sheet metal and plastic and glass, savage words pounding through the haze from someone else's music, someone else's drums, someone else's life.

Slumping to his side, squinting up in terror, the streetlights blocked by ghostly screaming heads— then punching fists and stomping feet and cracking ribs and spattering blood . . . until . . . at length . . .

The stillness of the weeping earth.

Private investigator Graham Gage turned as a gentle knocking escalated through the threshold of his jet-lagged concentration. He looked up at his receptionist, Tansy Amaro, standing just inside his third story office, then toward his telephone, a call on hold, the blinking light silent, but not unspeaking.

"You didn't need to come up here," Gage said. He reached down and slipped his road-worn passport into a safe anchored to the floor next to his desk. "I'm not talking to him."

"But he sounds awful."

Tansy rubbed her hands together like a mother fretting over a sick child, rather than over a man on the corrupt side of Gage's profession who'd spent his career destroying lives such as hers.

"It's not my problem," Gage said, "and not yours either . . . especially not yours."

Irritation pierced through the mental haze that had thickened around him during his flight across nine time zones from Zurich to San Francisco.

"You think it's ever bothered Charlie—or those punks, or their lawyers—that for ten years your son hasn't even been able to recognize the sound of your voice?"

Tansy lowered her eyes and wiped fine beads of sweat from her forehead. The mid-September inversion layer hovering above the city had overwhelmed the air conditioner and the redbrick walls of the converted warehouse.

She gazed through a casement window at the smog-leadened bay, then looked back at Gage and said, almost in apology, "I've just never been able to hate anyone."

"It's not hate, Tansy. It's thirty years of disgust."

Gage glanced at his watch. It had already been ninety minutes since his flight had landed at SFO. It was time for a cool shower, not for a descent into the miasma of deceit and corruption that had been Charlie Palmer's life—that Gage was certain still remained his life. For never in his career as a police officer, as a detective, and finally as a private investigator had Gage witnessed an authentic rebirth from a near-death experience, even one as cruel as the shooting that had left Palmer splayed on a Sunset District sidewalk six weeks earlier.

Gage was certain that whatever Palmer was seeking in his call, it wouldn't be justice. It would only be—it could only be—revenge. And Gage wanted no part of it.

"Does he know who you are?" Gage asked.

"Why should he know who . . ." Tansy's voice faded. She shook her head. "I don't think so. I'm not sure how he'd know."

Gage pushed himself to his feet. The preceding weeks spent tracking a fugitive through Europe weighed on his middle-aged body as if each sleepless minute could be measured in pounds.

"Put him on," Gage said. "Tell him who you are. But don't let him know I'm listening."

"You can't expect—"

"Let's see what he's learned from living with just a fraction of Moki's misery. Let's see whether he feels any remorse at all for sabotaging the case against those thugs."

"But we never got proof it really was him," Tansy said.

Gage pointed at the speakerphone centered on the conference table and said, "Maybe after all these years we're about to get it."

But Gage didn't think so.

Even if he was right that it had been Palmer who'd terrified the only prosecution witness into fleeing on the eve of the trial of the young men who'd beaten and stomped Moki, Gage doubted Palmer would now confess and make this his day of judgment. For confession would require Palmer to admit to himself who he was and what he'd been: a weapon in the hands of the wealthy and powerful employed to revictimize their victims, slashing through the fabric of their lives, leaving those like Tansy bereft of the truth of their own pasts, and those like Moki deprived not only of justice, but of the joys of a fully lived life.

Tansy sat down and reached toward the on button. She paused, staring at the phone, and then withdrew her hand.

"You don't believe he's learned anything, do you?" Gage said.

Uncertainty washed over Tansy's face. "No . . . I mean yes . . . I mean you can't expect people to change that fast."

Gage knew it wasn't a matter of speed, but of possibility, for Palmer's flaws were of character, not aberrations of circumstance, and one of those was an indifference to tragedy that made him incapable of guilt and impervious to others' sorrow.

Gage tossed a file folder into his briefcase and pulled his suit jacket from the back of his chair.

"You're going to have to roll the dice," Gage said. "Maybe you'll get your answer, and I'll get mine."

Tansy took in a breath and connected the call.

"Mr. Palmer? Mr. Gage isn't available. I really did give him your message."

The strained, wheezy voice of Charlie Palmer answered. "Why . . . would . . . I . . . think—"

"Because I'm Moki Amaro's mother."

Tansy looked up at Gage. His grim expression filled the empty seconds, his gaze fixed on her.

"Mr. Palmer?"

In Palmer's silence, and in each other's eyes, Gage and Tansy heard and saw that they'd each gotten their answers.

Gage shook his head as Tansy lowered hers and reached toward the off button—but she left her hand hovering, as if praying the call wouldn't end in a soundless void.

A quiet sobbing emerged from the speaker. It rose toward a suffocating hysteria that choked off Palmer's voice as he grasped for words.

"I . . . I . . . pl . . . please . . . don't . . . hang up."

Tansy's eyes teared. She covered her mouth, still staring at the phone. She again looked at Gage, silently asking, *Enough?*

Gage wasn't sure it was enough, or if there was anything Charlie Palmer could do or say, or was capable of doing or saying, that would be enough. But gazing down at Tansy and listening to the man's hard breathing at the other end of the line, Gage couldn't escape another truth: that Palmer, too, was part of the fabric of others' lives. He was a father, a son, and a husband. And although Palmer's past meant Gage couldn't trust his plea in the present, in it Gage saw their faces and heard their voices.

Gage laid his coat over the back of a chair and set his briefcase down on the floor.

"What's on your mind, Charlie?"

Gasps and sobs fractured Palmer's next words, then the line disconnected.

"What did he say?" Tansy asked, looking up, her brows furrowed, as though searching for something lost. "I couldn't make it out."

"I think he wants to compose himself," Gage said. "It sounded like he said he'll call back in an hour."

Tansy's eyes kept searching. "Will you wait?"

Gage nodded. "I'll wait."

Sixty-three minutes later, Tansy once again stood at Gage's office door. But this time her fretting hands and her downcast eyes that rose and looked past him toward the unblinking intercom light, told him even before she spoke the words that Charlie Palmer was dead.

Senator Landon Meyer leaned back in his chair on the sixth floor of the Dirksen Building and gazed down through his window and watched the midday traffic passing on Constitution Avenue.

Constitution. His conscience bit at him as he said the word to himself. Who was he to tell the executive branch who it could or couldn't nominate to the Supreme Court? Who was he to violate the separation of powers that once seemed so indispensable to the American form of government?

But in ten minutes he would settle into the rear seat of a limousine, ride to the White House, and do exactly that.

A phrase of St. Augustine's repeated itself in his mind as he surveyed the city:

It was pride that changed angels into devils; it is humility that makes men as angels.

Then he reminded himself, as if in absolution, that the humble don't run for office—or at least they don't win—and the prideful are unable to compromise.

Compromise. Another twinge refocused his mind. There would be no compromise.

Not this morning.

Not with this president.

Not on these nominations.

Landon didn't doubt that under the law he was merely one among equals. *Unus inter pares.* But for causes he thought only a political physicist could discover, he had become the pivotal force in a divided Senate, making him *primus inter pares.* First among equals. And it gave him the power to dictate through these new justices—and through the uniquely American Leviathan the Court had become—what privacy rights Americans would retain, what powers the president would wield in war and peace, and even what latitude would be left to the states to govern their own affairs.

The American Leviathan. That's how he'd described the Court a week earlier while walking with a summer intern down the marble hallway toward the Senate chamber. The young woman had looked up at him with an innocent smile and said how much she loved reading *Moby Dick* as a child, then blushed when she realized the reference was political, not literary. She then said she'd read Thomas Hobbes's *Leviathan* in a government class in college and found it terrifying.

Landon recalled smiling to himself and letting the matter drop, for he'd actually been thinking of the Book of Job, an allusion he suspected she was still too many uncommitted sins away from understanding.

The image faded and was replaced by another, a memory of winter steelhead fishing as a young congressman with Graham Gage on the Klamath River. It was a month after Gage had exposed an opposition push-polling operation that had used the similarity of Landon's wife's maiden name to that of a criminal to accuse her of real estate fraud. Gage, standing in the drift boat, teaching him how to read water, how to deduce the unseen from the seen, pointing toward a submerged rock, sheared off the cliff above and ragged enough to rip through the hull, its presence revealed only by the water churning below it downstream.

Landon now felt the chill that had shuddered through him at that moment, one far deeper than the one inflicted by the raw wind sweeping up the canyon. It was a terror of hidden hazards, deposited solely by chance, upon which his career might someday be wrecked.

Chance.

Landon understood, even as he sat there readying himself to impose his Supreme Court nominees on the president, that his enormous power was an outcome of events that all could have been otherwise. Suppose he hadn't survived the childhood car crash that killed his sister? Suppose he hadn't been elected student body president at Yale? Admitted to Harvard Law School? Elected to Congress? Run against House and Senate opponents who ran aground each election eve on the shores of their naïve mistakes? And, finally, stepped into the chairmanship of the Senate Judiciary Committee only because of the death of a colleague?

It wasn't a secret from Landon why these events now replayed in his mind. It was the subconscious way he'd always reminded himself that the inescapable and all-too-human sin of pride was threatening to mutate into a secular hubris: the dangerous belief that he alone was the source of the power he possessed. It sometimes even tempted him to dismiss the warning of Shakespeare's Brutus that he'd framed and mounted in his office wall on the day he was first sworn in to Congress:

There is a tide in the affairs of men,
Which, taken at the flood, leads on to fortune;
Omitted, all the voyage of their life
Is bound in shallows and in miseries.

Looking up at those words as he did now, Landon had often felt a peculiar unease, a kind of bad faith. A Republican senator elected by the people of California was nothing if not against the tide. Republican governors? Nearly always. Senators? One in a generation: himself—and he knew this was exactly the sort of dangerous material from which hubris was formed.

A beep from his phone startled him. He leaned forward to rise, thinking it was his secretary informing him his driver had arrived. He then noticed the call was on his private line. He picked it up. It was his younger brother, Brandon, a federal judge in their hometown of San Francisco, calling to take vicarious pleasure in something Landon viewed as merely necessary.

"I'm just about to leave . . . Sure, I'll call you later."

Landon hung up the phone. Ultimately, he recognized, it was to his brother he owed what he didn't owe to chance. As a corporate lawyer, it was Brandon's connections that funded his campaigns and later supplied the money he deposited into the political action committees of the Senate leadership to buy himself a seat on the Judiciary Committee.

As much as he had despised it, at Yale they were known as Machiavelli and the Prince. Brandon: dark hair, peering eyes, diminutive face, expert debater. Landon: tall, fair-skinned, strong-jawed. A leader, not an arguer. That they could be brothers had unnerved their classmates, just as it had the families on Nob Hill where they'd grown up. The dissimilarity had always powered an undercurrent of whispering that tugged at them as they walked to their table in the dining room of their parents' country club or swam in the pool. But, fortunately, age, like erosion, had smoothed the stark edges of their contours and softened the contrast.

The phone beeped again. This time it was his driver. Landon rose, and then glanced down at the Supreme Court building across the street. It seemed at this moment like a fist with two fingers missing, mangled and powerless—

But not for long.

As he walked down the hallway toward the elevator, he wondered what the president's reaction would be when he heard the two names. How would a president who had always fled to the center because he'd lacked the courage of his convictions adjust to this reminder that he owed his presidency to contributors who were finally demanding that they receive what they'd been paying for over all these years.

The sun cresting the East Bay hills blinded Gage as the bridge exit into San Francisco looped back toward the waterfront. He descended into the shade of the office towers and condo complexes that had reshaped the shoreline in the quarter century since he had converted the hundred-year-old warehouse into his firm's offices. A minute later, he emerged near the four-lane Embarcadero, its palm-bordered trolley line giving the boulevard the unnatural and uncomfortable appearance of having been harvested from the San Diego harbor and grafted onto San Francisco Bay.

Gage paused at an intersection as a still-groggy runner crossed against the light, then drove south past a scattering of piers and restaurants, and slipped into an alley. He parked along the back wall of his building and walked around to the front, where he spotted his surveillance chief sitting on the concrete steps, staring across the street toward the water.

"Thanks for calling Socorro," Viz said as Gage

approached. "Your and Faith's condolences meant a lot to her."

Hector McBride had been nicknamed by Gage for his godlike ability to catalogue the covert lives of his targets and to condense and evaporate like an omniscient cloud. Despite standing a couple of inches taller than Gage's six foot two, it sometimes seemed the ex-DEA agent could disappear into the sliver of a midday shadow.

But not today. Today his despair surrounded him like a physical presence.

Gage examined Viz's drawn face, and then sat down beside him.

"The problem was Charlie," Gage said, "not your sister."

Viz shrugged. "Still . . ."

"How's she holding up?"

"It's kind of like he died twice. When he first got shot, the doctors said he wasn't going to make it, so she got herself ready. Kind of steeled herself, then she got blindsided."

"Have they figured out what caused his death?" Gage asked.

"A seizure, maybe a heart attack. They're doing an autopsy this morning." Viz glanced up at the hazy sky, then out at the commuter traffic inching toward downtown through a humid alloy of fog and smog. "Maybe yesterday's heat had something to do with it."

Viz leaned forward, knees spread, forearms resting on his thighs, rotating his gray Stetson between his hands, fingers working their way along the inside of the sweatband and his thumb along the brim.

"I'd appreciate you and Faith coming to the funeral. For Socorro's sake. It's going to be pretty lonely. Charlie didn't have any real friends, and his parents aren't well enough to travel from Florida."

"We can even come back to the house afterward, if you think it would help."

Viz nodded, then lowered his head, his unfocused eyes oblivious to his rotating hat.

"Makes you think, doesn't it?"

"About what?"

"About dying too soon—" Viz caught himself, flustered, eyes pained. His own words reminding him of the death of Gage's father three months earlier. "Sorry, I didn't mean . . ."

Gage's mind pushed past the final memory of his father at the moment of his death to their last conversation a day earlier. Sitting by his bedside at the family's southern Arizona ranch, holding his hand as they gazed out the adobe-framed windows at the desert. His father, a family physician, had laughed about being paid in Yaqui corn, Apache chickens, and Mexican tamales in the years after World War II, cried about friends he'd lost in combat when he was young and to disease as he got older, and wondered aloud about the changes the world would see after he was gone.

"My dad told me his only regret was that he wouldn't live long enough to see how everything turned out," Gage said.

Viz pulled away and looked over at him. "But nobody ever . . ."

Gage nodded. "I think that's why he had a little smile on his face when he said it."

"But there's a difference between your father and Charlie." Viz's voice rose, more in frustration than in argument. "A big difference." He set down his hat on the step next to him, as if preparing to plead Palmer's case. "Your dad's life had a kind of completeness. Charlie's was unfinished, and he didn't have a chance to make things right."

"He had lots of chances," Gage said, "he just never took them."

They both knew it was worse than that, for the lens through which Palmer had chosen to view others' lives had filtered those chances out.

Even more, Palmer's kind of life made his the kind of death that brought all his acts and deceits into the present, and into the space between the two of them sitting on these steps.

Palmer had spent his career as part of an underworld of lawyers and private investigators—as clandestine as a secret society and as public as a Hollywood celebrity trial—that exploited victims' shames and terrors and forced them to choose silence over justice.

In the years after he'd left the San Francisco Police Department, Palmer had been the surreptitious hand that had tipped the scales in countless child custody hearings and divorce battles, in sexual harassment complaints, even in disputes over movie rights and royalties. He'd been an expert in the art of leverage, in discovering the embarrassing lapse, the plagiarized high school term paper, the drunken confession on a defunct social networking site, the juvenile petty theft from Victoria's Secret, the videotaped *ménage à cinq* in a college dorm, the used condom in a Las Vegas hotel room, or the empty bottle of Prozac in an aging star's garbage.

He'd also been an expert at avoiding exposure; for those furious enough to expose him also had the most to lose.

And sitting there next to Viz, with him so desperate to redeem the unredeemable, it was unimaginable to Gage that Palmer had found the courage in his final moments to crawl out of the darkness and into a light that would transform his entombed past into a living legacy.

"It's just hard to live with mixed feelings about dead people," Viz said. "He did a lot of bad stuff as a cop and an investigator, but he was also a brother-in-law who tried to do good for his kids." He sighed. "The truth is I'm not sure they have a clue about who he really was."

Viz turned toward Gage and spread his hands.

"But how could they? All they ever saw were movie stars and politicians calling him, begging for his help. And it wasn't like he could ever go to career day at their school and describe what he really did for a living."

"What about Socorro? You think she understands?"

"I'm not sure she's ever seen past what she thought she saw on their first date." Viz shook his head and blew out a breath. "And I hope she never does."

They sat in silence listening to an airplane banking over the city and heading east, the engine roar fading until it merged with the rumble of traffic and the growl of container ships powering across the bay toward the Port of Oakland.

Gage glanced in the direction of the Palmer's Victorian mansion on Russian Hill, beyond the concrete and steel of the financial district and the brick-lined alleys of Chinatown, his mind's eye seeing it standing among oaks and weeping willows.

"Charlie called me a couple of times after he got home from the hospital," Gage said. "I was on the road until that final one."

"That's what I heard from Socorro. It shocked the hell out of me. I always figured you'd be the last on his list. It's not like you two were ever friends. But then I started thinking maybe he got desperate, frustrated because SFPD hadn't found out who shot him."

Gage shook his head. "I don't think that was it. Spike Pacheco told me Charlie didn't seem to care whether or not the guy got caught. He hardly even looked at the photo spreads Spike showed him. It's not SFPD's fault the case dead-ended."

Viz peered over at Gage. "Dead-ended how? On the back burner or off the stove altogether?"

"It's a matter of diminishing returns. There was nothing more Spike could do without Charlie's co-operation."

"Were you going to help him, whatever it was?"

Gage pointed over his shoulder toward the lobby and the reception station. "If Tansy had her way."

Viz smiled. "I'll bet she's still trying to save him."

"Saving a dead man would be a helluva trick."

"I don't know, boss," Viz said. "They say Yaquis can do things other humans can't."

Gage took in a long breath, then exhaled. "Not this time."

"How about at least playing the childhood friend card to get Spike to jump-start the investigation? Big guy like you, little guy like him, must've been a dozen times you saved his ass when you were growing up together. You've got to have something in the bank."

"There's nothing more to go on. The leads have dried up."

"What about the new ones?"

Gage turned toward Viz. "Did Charlie tell your sister something Spike doesn't know about?"

"No." Viz half smiled and then wrapped his hope inside a prediction. "The new ones you're gonna come up with."

"You playing the sister card?"

"When it comes to Charlie, that's the only one I've got."

One of Gage's other investigators walked up the steps. She paused to squeeze Viz's shoulder and express her condolences, then continued into the building.

Gage angled his thumb toward the entrance. "You want some coffee?"

"I better." Viz picked up his hat. "It was a long night. Socorro couldn't sleep, so I stayed up with her."

They rose and walked through the double glass doors. Muffled sounds of printers and copiers and a dozen telephone conversations flowed from the hallways beyond. With clients scattered across the world's twenty-four time zones, Gage's office operated on a 6 A.M. to midnight schedule, with investigators working overlapping shifts. Toxic spills in

India or industrial sabotage in Dubai or securities frauds in London weren't limited to between nine and five, Pacific time.

Viz paused at the vacant reception desk. "Where's Tansy?"

"Moki had an early doctor's appointment."

Viz's face darkened as he looked down at the empty chair. "It's heartbreaking. I don't know how she does it. I've never understood why she didn't send him back to the reservation. I mean it's not like he'll even know she's not around."

"You wouldn't let other people take care of Socorro if something happened to her." Gage pointed at Viz's chest. "You're a lot more like Tansy than you let on."

Viz spread his arms. "Actually, I'm about two and a half Tansys."

"How's that? You gain a few pounds?"

"No. I think she lost a few."

Viz inspected Tansy's blotter calendar on which she kept track of the locations of the investigators as they traveled. The boxes for the first two weeks in September were marked with a code for Gage's name.

"I didn't think to ask about your trip," Viz said, looking back at Gage. "You find the guy who stole the fiber-optic design?"

"In Zurich. Thanks for asking, but I know you've got more important things on your mind." Gage glanced at the calendar. "You need some time off?"

"Just a day or so. Funeral stuff. Their kids are coming up from UCLA tomorrow and they'll stay close by her. I'm not much for sitting around."

"Since when? That's how you spend most of your life. It's part of your job description. I know. I wrote it myself."

"Well . . ." Viz shrugged. "You know what I mean."

"Yeah, I know what you mean."

Gage led Viz down the hallway to the kitchen and poured them both mugs of coffee.

"You think Socorro will want me to look into the shooting?" Gage asked, handing one to Viz.

"I don't know. She's not the sort of person who's going to let her life turn on whether the guy gets caught. She knows how twisted people get who live for revenge." Viz paused, and his eyes went vacant. Then he looked back at Gage. "But still, there's got to be a lot of uncertainty. And it's hard to live with a mystery, especially since whoever it was killed him in the end."

n hour after he'd left the president, Landon Meyer was still light-headed with a kind of breathlessness he hadn't felt since his college rugby days when the world condensed into exhilarating, time-freezing moments. His hands vibrated as he raised the highball glass of bourbon from his desk to his lips.

He'd steeled himself as he was escorted into the Oval Office. President William Duncan sat in an elbowed mahogany armchair. Chief of staff Stuart Sheridan stood by a window facing the Rose Garden. Duncan only stood long enough to shake Landon's hand and to direct him to the couch.

It had never struck Landon more clearly than at that moment that if Brandon was his Machiavelli, then Sheridan was the president's. Except Duncan and Sheridan could have been twins separated at birth. Duncan had been raised in a coal-mining town and wore the weathered face of struggle, while Sheridan had summered in the Hamptons, a childhood of ease. Both were in their late sixties, hair dusted with gray, faces keen and self-satisfied despite the historic reversal of roles in the Supreme Court nomination process that was moments away.

"I think we should skip the niceties," President Duncan said, "and start at the bottom line." He offered a thin smile. "We can make nice later, if necessary."

"I've given this a great deal of consideration, Mr. President—"

Duncan raised his palm. "Skip that part."

Landon felt himself redden as if he was receiving a dressing-down in front of his classmates.

"Mr. President—"

"The names, man. Just the names."

Landon gave him the names.

Duncan and Sheridan glanced at each other, then both grinned at Landon.

The president spoke first. "Let's just call them Starsky and Hutch until we're ready to release it to the press."

Landon leaned forward in his chair.

"That's it? No argument about you not wanting to waste political capital pushing through these nominations? Looking for a middle ground with the Democrats so you won't get pilloried like last time? A black? A woman? An Hispanic?"

Duncan shook his head. "Lame ducks don't need a middle ground—and this is about my legacy." He rose. "I'm not blaming you personally, but for almost seven years Congress has been an evenly divided logjam. My so-called legislative agenda was stillborn. I could've spent my presidency fishing or clearing brush on a Texas ranch and it wouldn't have made much difference. Other than a tiny bit of tort reform and a few defense spending bills, I've accomplished nothing." He spread his arms wide. "Nothing on abortion. Nothing on debt. Nothing on Social Security. Nothing on Alaska drilling. Nothing on nuclear power."

"I'm not sure that's true," Landon said. "What about economic—"

"Diddly-squat. Extending NAFTA was diddly-squat, even less than diddly-squat—and the jury is still out about whether it helped us or hurt us."

Sheridan approached them and then sat down and interjected himself into the conversation.

"The lesson since the days of Earl Warren," Sheridan said, "is that if you can't win in Congress, drive your agenda through the Court." He clenched his fist. "Just when the Democrats think they've won, we'll crush them."

Duncan grabbed the conversation back.

"I'm willing to let my presidency rise and fall on whether we—you—can push Starsky and Hutch through the Senate. Let *Newsweek* call mine a failed presidency. I want to give history something different to write about: how my domination of the Court controlled the country for a hundred years after I was dead."

Landon glanced over at Sheridan, expecting a *Sieg heil* salute.

"Starsky and Hutch are young enough to serve forty years each." Duncan smiled again and threw up his hands. "Shoot, man, that's almost half a century right there, and it'll take another half century for anyone to undo what they accomplish."

"But they're only two. I'm not sure you'll get another opportunity to make an appointment, so we'll only have a majority for—"

"Twenty years is long enough to cast the die. Think of what Earl Warren did. The country still hasn't recovered from that disaster. We'll have a super majority: Starsky, Hutch, Robins, Ardino, Thompson, and Sunseri. Even if one gets weak-kneed, the rest can deliver—and nothing is off-limits."

"Getting these nominees through the Senate will require a lot of money and a lot of horse trading, Mr. President. More than I think you—"

"Damn right it will." Duncan's face hardened. His voice pounded. "Trade them everything else. Let them turn all of Montana into a giant national park, let them double capital gains taxes, let them table the abortion bill until the year 3000, let them hand out condoms to sixth-graders—I don't give a damn . . . but get . . . their . . . votes."

Duncan walked to his desk and picked up a photograph of Ronald Reagan.

"If Reagan had been a Democrat, conservatives would have condemned him as one of the worst presidents in history. At the time, the highest deficits in U.S. history, tax rates through the roof, nothing on abortion, nothing on prayer in schools, drug war a complete failure, a balance of trade that left us drowning, welfare programs never bigger, Castro more powerful than ever. He can't even take credit for the collapse of the Soviet Union. It did itself in.

Nobody in his administration had a clue about what was going on over there."

Duncan stared at the photo. "But what he did was to articulate a unity of vision about what America was." He opened a side drawer of his hand-carved mahogany desk and slid the photo inside. "All that morning-in-America stuff." He turned back toward Landon. "The difference between Reagan and me is that I finally have a way to make the country actually match mine."

The bourbon glass rattled as Landon set it down on the silver coaster on his deceased father's Georgian walnut desk. He could still see the dent where the old man had smashed the telephone handset when he learned Nixon had resigned—an act his father thereafter called the most sickening example of presidential cowardice in U.S. history. He even threatened to quit the Republican National Committee and devote the tens of millions of dollars he raised every year to creating a third party.

Landon rested his elbows on the blotter, then pressed his splayed fingers together. He stared through them into nothingness, thinking about the New Hampshire primary five months away, and about Duncan's last words:

"Get this done, Landon, and you'll own the primaries. I'll do whatever it takes to get you the nomination." Then the self-deprecating smile that once charmed the nation, but now only made him look weak. "You can even hold the goddamn sword while I fall on it."

Landon took in a long breath and exhaled. He'd

been so swept up in the moment, in the grand images Duncan had painted, he'd failed to notice Duncan hadn't a clue why he'd chosen these particular nominees.

He smiled to himself as he imagined the president's fury when he finally realized he'd picked them to ensure not Duncan's legacy—but his own.

Viz drove them in silence from the cemetery south of San Francisco past the granite and marble City Hall and up the south side of Russian Hill. Gage's wife, Faith, and Socorro sat in the backseat, once best friends now reunited by the death of the man who'd kept them apart; a husband's fear of exposure having imposed a life of isolation on his wife.

From the front passenger seat, Gage watched the cacophony of architecture passing by—Italianate, Spanish Mission, Beaux Arts. It struck him that they had nothing in common but the arbitrary whims of a long-dead Barbary Coast elite made wealthy by gold and gambling, prostitution and corruption, each family attempting to impose its architectural will on an untamed city. Observing them now, Gage wondered whether that was the reason Charlie had insisted on buying the mansion in which they lived: an instance of glory-by-proxy, just as with his Hollywood clients.

Viz pulled his Yukon to the curb and shut off

the engine. Gage reached for the door handle while gazing up at the Palmers' four-story Victorian, now restored to a perfect balance of yellow and blue, with accents in red; the colors stark and brutal in an afternoon sun that also shone down on a freshly turned grave.

A blur of motion and then a flash of blue against green caught Gage's eye. He jabbed a finger toward the bushes at the side of the house.

"A guy just went over the fence." Gage swung open his door. "Black hair. Levi's. About five-ten. Heading north."

Gage looked back at his wife and Socorro, then at the trailing car containing Socorro's son and daughter.

"Don't let anyone go inside," Gage said. He then realized there might be confidential client files in Charlie's home office. "And don't call the police yet." He turned to Viz. "You circle around. I'll try to cut through the block."

Viz sprinted up the steep street while Gage ran down a neighbor's driveway and into the backyard. He spotted vertical scrape marks on the weathered wood fence, then called Viz on his cell.

"Looks like he's trying to get out to Union Street."

Gage pulled himself over. A bullmastiff crouched at the opposite gate, barking at the memory of the burglar. The dog's eyes followed his ears around toward the crunch of Gage's dress shoes hitting the rock garden, mouth foaming, licking its lips. Gage slipped off his suit coat and wrapped it around his forearm, knowing a trained dog would go for his arm, while an untrained one would follow its instincts toward his throat. He knew he'd have to sacrifice the arm in either case.

A raspy female voice yelled from his left, "Get the hell out of my yard."

Gage kept his eyes fixed on the dog, now poised for the attack, snarling, seeming to be begging for her command.

"A burglar just ran through here," Gage said. He then glanced toward the open kitchen window and caught a glimpse of a tree stump of a woman with a bleached-blond flattop. "How about you control your dog so I can get after him?"

"Stallone! Sit."

Stallone sat, still blocking the gate.

Gage's cell phone rang.

"I'm out . . . on Union." Viz's breathing was explosive. "I missed him . . . Jumped into a new Lexus SUV . . . and took off."

"You get the plate?"

"Too far away . . . didn't even get a good look . . . at the guy . . . Where are you?"

"In the backyard of the house just northeast of your sister's. A dog got in my way."

"Need help?"

"The owner is coming out. I'll meet you on the front steps of Socorro's. Let's search the place before anyone else goes in and then check with the neighbors."

Gage and Viz found Socorro setting a steamer of tamales on the cooktop when they walked into the kitchen after their fruitless neighborhood canvass. She was tall and slim; the pale brown skin of her mother combined with the gentle Irish features of her father.

"Anything missing?" Viz asked her.

"Not that I could see." Socorro covered the pot and set her hot pads on the counter. "I'm not sure the burglar even made it past the living room." She turned toward Gage. "Charlie once told me about criminals who read the obituaries and do break-ins during funerals." She shrugged. "I guess that's what it was. I'm glad we got back in time so he didn't get anything."

Gage pointed upward. "Did you check Charlie's office?"

"It's always a mess. I'm not sure you'll be able to tell anything. Faith and I glanced in. His computers are still there."

"Mind if we look?"

"Of course not. But why his office? We keep the valuables in a safe in the bedroom. I already looked. It's untouched."

Gage didn't want to worry her with his suspicion it was Charlie's work, not their personal possessions, that had been the target, so he said, "Just to be thorough."

Gage and Viz walked down the hallway to the front staircase, passing Faith sitting with the Palmer children in the living room. They climbed three flights to reach Charlie's attic office. A month-and-a-half-old newspaper lying open on his desk told them the room had remained as Charlie had left it hours before he was shot. The shredder bin was overflowing. The bookcases were stacked with files and books both lined up and piled sideways.

"What was the guy searching for?" Viz asked as they surveyed the room.

Gage didn't have an answer.

"You think it has something to do with what Charlie wanted from you?"

"Has Socorro told you what it was?"

"She hasn't wanted to talk about it yet."

Gage sat down at Charlie's desk, then jiggled the computer mouse, waking up the monitor. In a few clicks Gage found the list of recently accessed documents.

"Looks like the guy wasn't your everyday burglar," Gage said. "He was opening files starting about an hour ago."

"And your everyday burglar doesn't drive a new Lexus SUV."

Gage's gaze shifted back and forth between the laptop and desktop computers, and asked, "Why didn't he just grab them and run?" But then he answered his own question. "He'd have to turn them off and he was afraid he couldn't get back in because he wouldn't know the passwords."

Viz pointed downward. "And a lot of the files are stored on a server Charlie has hidden behind a wall in the basement. It would've taken the burglar hours to find it."

Gage felt a moment of unease, almost of dread, for Socorro and her children. The ghosts of Charlie's past had not died with him, but had instead mutated into flesh and blood and had invaded their lives, and would again, unless—

He pointed at the computers.

"Let's copy everything onto one of our laptops

so we can access the files later, then pack them up, along with the server, and take them to the office. And we better make a show of it so if the crook didn't get what he was searching for, he won't be coming back thinking there's something left to find."

Viz locked his hands on his hips. Mouth tight. "It pisses me off. How could he do this to his family? They've got to live in fear for who knows how long because of the shit he pulled."

Gage glanced at a twenty-five-year-old photo on the bookshelf of Charlie in his SFPD uniform. Even as a rookie, he had the dead eyes of a snake and a predator's grin.

"Your sister should've divorced him years ago," Gage said. "At some point the illusion of first impressions must've worn thin enough to see through."

"Even if it did—which I doubt—she'd never divorce him," Viz said. "She's too damn Catholic for her own good."

Gage rose from the chair. "How come you're not?"

"By the time I was twelve, I was bigger than any two priests in the parish put together. They couldn't scare me anymore."

Gage expected Viz to smile, but he didn't.

"I even coined my own two-word catechism. It came in real handy in Afghanistan."

"What's that?"

"Fuck eternity."

After Gage and Viz returned downstairs, Socorro asked Gage to walk with her into the screened-in back porch. They sat in wicker lounge chairs facing a lawn enclosed by mature oaks, pistache, and weeping willows, their trunks wrapped with ivy and surrounded by flowering shrubs. Years ago it had seemed like a refuge from the chaos of San Francisco, but Gage now realized that to Socorro it must have felt like a prison exercise yard.

"Charlie called me the other day," Gage said.

"I know. I dialed the phone for him. I was surprised. He always seemed afraid of you."

"Afraid of me?"

As Gage turned toward her, he noticed in the corner the small table on which she had written a series of children's books before her twins were born. It was covered with flowerpots and planting soil.

"I hadn't even talked to him since the last time I was in this house, and that was over twenty years ago."

"I think it started as jealousy," Socorro said. "He applied for homicide, but got turned down, but they handed you the gold badge without you asking. Even now, everyone in the department still sees you as a legend and Charlie as just a guy who once dressed in blue."

Gage shook his head. "His father was the legend, not me, and that wasn't easy in a town that hates cops."

"As far as Charlie was concerned his father was a failure. Officer Friendly who spent his whole career walking a beat and never even put in for a promotion."

An image came to Gage of the last time he'd seen Charlie. It was also the last time he'd seen Charlie's father. Both smiling, in uniform, standing behind a head table, the son saluting the father.

"That sure wasn't the impression I got at his father's retirement dinner," Gage said.

"What else could he say? The whole department was listening." Her eyes blurred as though reliving the event, maybe even the same moment that had come back to Gage, then she focused on him again. "Even after Charlie went out on his own and the movie crowd made him their rescuer and confidant, he knew the world—or at least the part he cared about most—would never see him as any better than second best."

Gage felt himself being straitjacketed into a conversation he didn't want to be involved in and wondered whether he was listening to the voice of grief forgiving all sins or the obliviousness of a too-kind heart. As he looked over at her, he recalled Faith once saying Socorro had the soul of a Ha... grandmother, living a life framed by tran... weddings, births, anniversaries, and de... ..., but otherwise shut off from the world. She'd never gone with Charlie to celebrity parties, because, in their serial marriages and public funerals, they trivialized what she believed was sacred.

"I still don't see how that adds up to fear," Gage said.

"I don't either. But somehow that's what it turned into." Socorro fell silent, then shrugged and said, "I guess that's one of many things I'll never understand."

When Gage returned from bringing Socorro a cup of tea from the kitchen, he found her staring out toward the silent tulip leaf fountain centered in the garden, her brows furrowed in concentration.

"There was something I was going to ask you." Socorro closed her eyes and rubbed her temples. "The world's been turned upside down. Sometimes my mind just goes blank, especially about things that just happened." She shook her head as if trying to jar loose the thought. "I know what it was. Who is Moki Amaro? Charlie fell apart when he heard the name."

"The son of my receptionist."

"Did Charlie do something to him?"

"It depends on your point of view. Law can be rough."

Gage knew this also wasn't a conversation he wanted to get into, not with a grieving widow, and not with his own regret for having failed to find a way to shut Charlie down decades earlier. He wondered whether part of what had restrained him over the years was that breaking Charlie would have also broken her.

Gage decided to circle back. "You know why Charlie called me?"

She took a sip of her tea and set the cup on the table between them.

"He wouldn't say. He even asked me to leave the room if you came on the line, but I left the phone on speaker and listened just outside the door."

"You think he wanted me to assign one of my people to finish up his cases? I'm sure there are clients who still need their work completed."

The words were a lie in the form of a question, for Gage knew whatever Palmer wanted, it wasn't that. But Gage didn't have a clue what it was. Was it help? Or protection? And for whom? Himself? Or her? Or, even more burdensome, maybe he wanted Gage to do exactly what he was doing: protecting her from the truth about him.

"He always used to joke that you were too straight for your own good," Socorro said. "I guess that means despite everything he trusted you."

Gage pointed up in the direction of Charlie's office. "Viz and I were thinking it would be a good idea to pack up his files and computers and move them to my building."

Socorro's eyes welled up and she shook her head.

"I'm not sure I'm ready to face the emptiness. When I walked in the other day I still expected to see him sitting at his desk, staring at his monitor, even though he hadn't been up there since before he got shot."

"We'll bring everything back when we're done," Gage said. "Set it up just the way it was."

She sighed. "Thanks for understanding. His work was as much a part of him as his clothes in our closet." She wiped at the tears with a tissue. "Maybe it's better if you take it all. I wouldn't be able to make sense of it anyway."

"I'll send over our computer guy, Alex Z."

Socorro smiled, still wiping her eyes, the skin surrounding them raw and red. "The cute rock-and-roller with the Popeye tattoos and silver earrings who makes the girls in San Francisco go gaga?"

Gage nodded. *San Francisco Magazine* had recently done a feature on club scene bands, with Alex Z's picture on the cover.

Her smile broadened. "I think I better make sure my daughter isn't home when he comes by. I don't want to take a chance of her going weak in the knees like all the rest of the girls."

"Don't worry. He's got a girlfriend."

"Then he can drop by anytime." She touched her lips. "That was the first time I've smiled since Charlie was shot. It felt strange. I guess I'm out of practice."

"You've had a tough time. The kids, too."

Socorro's eyes settled on the gas barbecue standing on the brick patio.

"In some ways he was a good father, other ways not. I'm not sure what they'll think about him after the grief passes. A few months ago, Charlie Junior told me his father's clients appeared to trust him more than respect him. Junior found it very troubling."

Socorro looked over at Gage, as if for an explanation. It seemed to him she'd used the words of her son as a proxy to ask questions she was afraid to ask for herself, as though she was trying to protect herself from the abyss by looking at its reflection in a mirror held by another.

Gage felt a wave of sadness for the courage she'd lost during the years she'd spent in a world walled off by Charlie. This wasn't how he remembered her when she was young and fearless, backpacking with Faith in the Sierras and talking long into the night, no subject off-limits, no thought stifled or left unfinished.

He avoided responding to her veiled question by changing the subject.

"Did Charlie have any ideas about who shot him?" Gage asked.

Socorro shook her head. "He just said a man stuck a gun in his back and demanded money. Charlie spun around swinging, but missed and lost his balance. Then the man pulled the trigger. Charlie never got a good look at his face. Just a tall, thin, white guy."

"Do you know what he was working on that day?"

"A tax fraud case, something to do with yacht donations."

"Which side?"

"The broker and the appraiser. A lawyer down in Beverly Hills figured out his clients could get bigger tax deductions for donating their boats to charities than they'd make back by selling them, if the appraisals were pumped up two or three times. Charlie didn't think the case had anything to do with him getting shot, but is it possible?"

Gage shook his head. "People don't go to war over tax cases. The penalties are too light."

"I think that's all he was doing that day. He was winding down his practice even before he was shot. With the twins graduating from college in the spring, he could retire."

Socorro stared down at her hands folded together on her lap.

"It doesn't seem real," she finally said. "Everything feels hollow. Even the cars driving by seem to echo in my ears." She dabbed at new tears. "Hardly anybody called, even after the *Chronicle* article. I guess Charlie was just hired help to the people he worked for."

"People pretend, but there isn't much loyalty in the legal community," Gage said, knowing the people who hired Charlie to do the dirty work would now want to pretend they never had their hands in the grime.

"Judge Meyer was the only ex-client who called."

Gage felt his body tense. Brandon Meyer had Charlie on speed dial during their years working as San Francisco's stable boys cleaning up after clients with more money than morals. Apparently, their connection hadn't broken when Meyer grabbed on to the coattails of his brother, Landon, and hoisted himself onto the federal bench a decade earlier.

"What did he say?" Gage asked.

"That he was sorry to hear about Charlie and

something about whether Charlie had learned any-thing new since they'd last talked."

"About what?"

Socorro glanced over her shoulder toward the inside of the house, then lowered her voice. "I shouldn't have said that. I'm not supposed to tell anyone."

"I won't pass it on."

She took in a breath, then nodded. "Brandon was mugged a week or two before Charlie was shot. His wallet was stolen. Charlie was looking into it."

"Did Charlie tell that to Spike? After all—"

Socorro shook her head. "Charlie was positive the two robberies weren't related. The man who mugged Brandon was Hispanic. Brandon was too embarrassed to report it himself because it hap-pened in the Tenderloin. He cut through one night on his way from the Federal Building to a law office on Van Ness. He thought it would play badly in the media, him getting mugged a few yards away from drug dealers and prostitutes. I can't blame him." So-corro shuddered. "I'm afraid even to drive through there."

"Had Charlie done anything to find the wallet?"

"He'd hung up some posters offering a reward, just using Brandon's initials, and searched around in garbage cans and dumpsters."

Gage nodded. "I wondered what had happened to Brandon. I had a meeting at the U.S. Attorney's office a couple of months ago. I saw him in the courthouse lobby. He gave me that limp-wristed wave he does. He had a bandage above his left eye. I heard he was telling people he had surgery."

"More like stitches."

"Was he sure it wasn't some angry defendant or plaintiff coming back to get even?"

"Charlie wondered about that, too. But I doubt Brandon would remember one face out of the thousands that have passed through his court."

That was true. Brandon might not have remembered the face, but Gage was certain the person wearing it would've reminded Brandon who he was before or after he swung his fist, otherwise there was no point.

"Any other condolence calls?" Gage asked.

"None work-related." She sighed. "I guess Charlie was old news."

Not that old, Gage thought, that somebody wouldn't risk a daytime burglary to search Charlie's computers.

Viz joined them on the porch, standing behind his sister's chair, resting his hands on her shoulders. When her attention was drawn toward a barn swallow flitting past, Viz caught Gage's eye, then tilted his head toward the house. Gage nodded.

"I'll think I'll stay here for a few days," Viz said.

"You don't have to do that," Socorro said, glancing up at him. "I'll be okay."

"I know I don't have to. But I want to. I'll keep you company. Maybe I can help you catch up on chores you put off while you were taking care of Charlie."

"I guess I could use some help there. I hated Faith to see the house in such a mess."

"Trust me," Gage said, "she didn't notice. You should see her office at UC Berkeley. The head of her department tells people it looks less like a professor's office and more like one of the archeological sites she works at."

Faith and Gage walked hand-in-hand up the sidewalk to where Gage had parked his car before Viz had driven them and Socorro to the cemetery.

"Viz was right," Gage said. "She doesn't have a clue who Charlie really was."

Faith looked up at him through clear hazel eyes framed by her slim face and auburn hair.

"Do you think it's willful?" Faith asked.

"Probably not. I suspect there was just an unbridgeable chasm between them."

Faith glanced back toward the house. "I'm wondering whether she decided at some point in their marriage it was emotionally safer to be oblivious. I got the feeling talking to her that she's spent the last twenty years hiding inside of her children's books where lessons were taught by stubbed toes and missing bracelets and grandmothers' stern looks—"

"And not by a gunshot that cuts a husband down in the street."

Gage pressed the remote on his key chain and unlocked the car.

"It hasn't even crossed her mind yet," Gage said, as he opened Faith's door, "that there might be a connection between the shooting and the burglary."

T he big man is pissed," the caller said, in a voice both sarcastic and frustrated.

"I don't give a rat's ass," the Texan answered. "I did the best I could in the time I had. There was no way I could haul out every damn computer in the place. He had a couple in his office, one in his bedroom, and a server somewhere in the house I couldn't even find."

"He wants you to go back in."

"There's nothing there."

"What do you mean, there's nothing there?"

"Just what I said. A rental van showed up a few hours later. A couple of guys cleaned out the place and took it all to Graham Gage's office."

"Damn."

"I made some calls. Palmer was the brother-in-law of a guy who works for Gage. Got the job through his sister."

"Go get it. Take somebody with you this time."

"What? You said he wanted me to do it alone.

If he'd let me take somebody in the first place we wouldn't be in this mess."

The man laughed. "Let's say our leader has engaged in a soul-searching reconsideration."

"What is it about these suits? They think it's just a little harmless chess game, until something goes sour and they panic like schoolgirls in a high wind, their little dresses flapping up in their faces."

"What'll I tell him?"

"Tell him two people, twice as much money—in cash and in advance."

"Where?"

"Same place."

"Leave a hundred grand in a paper bag?"

"I'll be watching. Nobody's walking away with my money."

"And keep an eye on Gage. If he gets too far into this thing, we'll need to do some damage control."

Thanks for coming over."

Gage settled into a wingback chair across from Judge Brandon Meyer in his eighteenth floor chambers in the Federal Building. In the orange glow of the setting September sun, the judge's angular features and dark eyes made him seem lizardlike as he sat perched behind the expanse of his desk.

Looking past Meyer, Gage spotted a worn paperback on the credenza, its spine shadowed under the day's legal newspaper. He smiled to himself when he saw that it was *Longarm: Frontier Justice*, one of a series popular among judges who needed to excite themselves with fictional gunslinging before striding onto the bench, and was handed off from judge to judge as furtively as child pornography or balloons of cocaine.

"How many people do you have over there now?" Meyer asked.

"Twenty, plus support staff."

Gage watched Meyer adopt a nostalgic expression.

"I remember when it was just you, and Faith helping out with the books. Now you've got people working on cases all over the world."

"And I remember when you were prosecuting petty thefts and DUIs at the Hall of Justice. Now international corporations fight their battles in your courtroom."

Meyer forced a sigh. "Seems like a generation ago."

"It was."

Meyer had been a San Francisco County prosecutor, and then a white-collar defense attorney whose strengths were stealth and strategy, not knowledge of the law, and whose temperament, Gage had recognized from the beginning, would never transition from the mercenary to the judicial. Even a decade later, no one in the Federal Building viewed his appointment to the bench as anything more than his brother's reward for funneling money to swing-state Republicans.

"Landon appreciated your work on his last campaign," Meyer said.

"I didn't work on his campaign."

Meyer drew back. "He told me he hired you to find a mole on his staff who was sabotaging his computer network."

"I didn't work on the campaign. I only made sure he could continue campaigning. There's a difference."

Meyer made a weak effort to suppress a smirk, and then said, "A believer in the purity of the process."

Gage felt a wave of revulsion. Justice depended

on that kind of belief and a commitment to act on it, and a judge should respect the process more than anyone—but he knew an argument with Meyer would be futile, so he just said:

"Something like that."

Meyer shrugged. "I never understood your relationship with my brother. He'd spend fifty-one weeks a year talking policy, but come back from a week fishing with you up at your cabin thinking he was some kind of political philosopher instead of a politician."

"It was just him trying out some ideas," Gage said, "not me imposing any on him, and it was also a long time ago."

"Well, it stuck." Meyer smirked, again. "You know what he took to read on the flight to the trade meeting in Beijing last month?"

"I've hardly talked to him in years, and then only about campaign—"

"Thomas Hobbes and St. Augustine." Meyer pulled on the edge of the desk to tilt his chair forward, then pushed himself to his feet, his face screwed up in preparation for the snide follow-through. "As though the solution to the debt crisis can be found in the goddamn *Leviathan* or in the pathetic musings of a sexual compulsive. He would've been better off with Calvin and Hobbes instead of Hobbes and Augustine."

Meyer scowled and scratched the back of his neck as though chagrined at having taken a wrong turn into an intellectual cul-de-sac.

"You want something to drink?" Meyer asked.

"No, thanks."

"You mind?"

Gage shook his head.

Meyer walked over to the bookcase on the opposite wall, then poured two fingers of Scotch into a highball glass. He took a sip as he returned to his chair.

"Socorro told me you're wrapping up Charlie's practice," Meyer said.

"There's not much left."

"Why you?"

"His brother-in-law works for me, Hector McBride."

"The giant who was with the DEA?"

"Same one. Socorro and Faith were friends as undergrads at Berkeley."

"I heard McBride turned down a promotion and resigned on the same day." Meyer smiled. It seemed almost genuine. "Of course, I never understood in the first place how somebody as huge as Mount Rushmore could do undercover work. Why'd he leave?"

"He figured out the drug war was just a succession of losing battles. He joined the army after 9/11 and went off to Afghanistan, then came to work for me." Gage tilted his head toward Meyer's courtroom. "I heard you're done with criminal cases, too."

Meyer assumed a sympathetic pose. "I never relished sentencing poor Mexican kids to ten or twenty years for trying to feed their families by packing a few kilos of cocaine across the desert, so I grabbed at the chance to get out."

He completed his lie with a smile so insincere it almost made Gage wince.

Veteran judges like Meyer referred to handing out enormous sentences as "pulling the trigger," but it didn't really count unless the judge opened fire on a defendant who really didn't deserve it, like the desperate and the destitute, and Gage knew Brandon Meyer always charged into his courtroom with his safety off.

"Why'd the other judges let you off the hook?" Gage asked.

"I'm not, completely. I still have to deal with white-collar crime, mostly high-tech, but the bulk of my calendar is civil." Meyer lowered his voice as though he might be heard in the hallway. "You know a lot of the judges around here. They don't like to work too hard, and those big civil firm lawyers file lots of motions."

Meyer was as smooth and as deceptive as a chameleon. He and Gage both knew he didn't read briefs, or at least nothing he ever did in court suggested he had. He relied on law clerks to give him summaries as he walked from his chambers into the courtroom. In any case, Meyer didn't decide motions based on their legal merits, but rather on who he wanted to win the case.

A client in Japan had taught Gage the word for Meyer's game: *tatemae*. It meant saying aloud what both parties knew wasn't true—and Meyer was the master. Nearly everyone who entered the Federal Building played *tatemae* with judges, cushioning their egos and swaddling their insecurities, because almost everybody wanted something, and judges were the only ones who had it.

Gage didn't want anything.

"What did you want to talk about?" Gage asked.

Meyer took another sip from his highball glass, then set it down on a marble coaster and leaned back in his chair. Gage imagined his shoes dangling four inches above the carpet.

"I understand Socorro told you about the mugging," Meyer said.

Gage nodded.

"I don't expect you to follow up on it. It's low-end work. I'm sure it's been decades since you searched a dumpster. But I'd prefer you didn't tell anyone about it."

"There's no reason to. But if anybody calls in response to Charlie's posters, I'll have one of my people follow up on—"

Brandon raised his palm. "No need for you to do that. Just pass on any names or phone numbers. I'll take care of it."

"I don't expect to hear anything," Gage said. "It's been a couple of months."

"You're right. I think it's a dead issue."

Meyer rose again, signaling the end of the meeting.

Not quite.

Gage remained in his seat.

"A man with a brother running for president should be more careful about where he goes walking at night." Gage smiled. "Remember what happened to Reiman in Oakland last month."

A news photographer, responding to a West Oakland car fire, took photos of San Francisco judge Hal Reiman slipping into Rocky's Adult Videos and strolling out a few minutes later with an Asian teenage boy. The photographer followed them to a grimy stucco motel a block away. The photographer's final shot caught the judge and the kid walking into a second floor room.

"The difference, my friend, is that I was just passing through," Meyer said.

Gage stood up. "But a photo might make it seem like you'd reached your destination."

lex Z's head bobbed and his shoulders rocked to his band's newly recorded tracks in his second floor office in Gage's building as he probed the copies he'd made of Charlie Palmer's hard drives.

Gage tore off a page from his yellow legal pad, folded it into an airplane, wrote *Ready?* on a wing, and sent it flying over Alex Z's head. The multi-tattooed data analyst glanced up as it bounced off the wall and onto his keyboard, then lowered the volume and turned toward Gage. Mid-twenties. Shaggy hair. Earrings both numerous and, on this day, mythological.

"I didn't want to scare you by yelling," Gage said.

"Thanks." Alex Z held up a finger. "And you gave me an idea for a song."

"Glad to help." Gage pointed at Alex Z's earlobes. "What's with the Greek mythology theme?"

"I'm thinking of changing the name of the band from Cheezwiz to Zeus's Deuces. Some lawyer at Kraft sent a letter to our manager. They didn't like our 'Smoking Velveeta' song."

"Maybe they didn't understand it."

Alex Z laughed. "I'm sure they didn't. It was complete nonsense. I was just searching for a rhyme for 'toking chiquita.'"

"Was *that* supposed to make sense?"

"Not that I could tell. But with the kind of music we play, nobody can hear the words anyway."

"Except lawyers."

Alex Z hunched his shoulders and spread his hands. "Who would've thought? I always picture them as having big mouths, not big ears."

Gage pulled up a chair, then gestured at one of the twin twenty-inch monitors on Alex Z's desk. "What did you find?"

"A lot of encrypted files. Some of the ones on the desktop were accessed early in the morning on the day Charlie got shot and some on the laptop and server right after he got back from the hospital."

"Did the burglar get into them on the day of the funeral?"

"He tried, but couldn't open any. The encryption system Charlie used kept a log of failed attempts."

"Is there any way to tell if he copied any of the files?"

Alex Z shook his head.

Gage scanned the dozen boxes of Charlie's software stacked next to the brick wall. "What program did he use?"

"FileLock. Pretty sophisticated."

"So you can't break in?"

"Nope."

"Viz'll talk to Socorro and get some ideas of the passwords he might have used."

Gage skimmed the directory on Alex Z's monitor. "What about a calendar?"

"No entries on the day he was shot."

"Billing records?"

"Nothing that day either, probably because he never made it back to the office. He went from the hospital to rehab to his bedroom."

Gage thought for a moment, feeling as blocked as the burglar and looking for a back way into what Charlie was working on that prompted the break-in.

"Can you get into his timekeeping program and get me his records for the last six months he worked?"

"I can't get into the program anymore, but I exported all the data before we shut things down at his house."

As Alex Z opened the database, he said, "Tansy told me he called you. You know what he wanted?"

"I'm not sure, but I know it wasn't to tidy up his practice. We don't do his kind of work around here. And he knew it."

Alex Z's fingers tapped his keyboard, and Palmer's records began emerging from the printer. He then pointed at the second monitor.

"You want me to keep working on the antitrust case or pass it off and focus on this?"

Gage glanced over at an unoccupied desk. "How's Shakir working out?"

"He's like a bat. He seems to do his best work at night. I can see why he didn't stay with the Federal Trade Commission. They want nine-to-fivers." Alex Z nodded toward Shakir's computer. "I've already got him working on the e-mail traffic during the conspiracy. He knows a helluva lot about price fixing and bid rigging. We're lucky you snagged him."

"Then turn the whole antitrust case over to him. Make Charlie's files your priority. We've got to figure out what he was up to."

Alex Z took in a long breath and exhaled, then shook his head. "Getting shot must've really rocked his world."

"Maybe. Maybe it got rocked before that." Gage reached for Charlie's time logs. "And we owe it to Viz to make sure it doesn't rock Socorro's."

CHAPTER 10

Tansy Amaro was waiting outside Gage's office when he arrived upstairs.

"Can I speak to you for a minute?" Tansy asked.

Gage directed her toward one of two wooden, straight-backed chairs facing his desk, and then asked, "What's on your mind?"

"Charlie Palmer." Tansy hesitated, eyes searching Gage's. "Well . . . maybe it's really about you."

Gage leaned forward in his chair and rested his forearms on the desk.

"I don't understand why you have such outrage for Charlie," Tansy said. "If it's because of Moki, don't. I made my peace with what happened long before we ever met."

"We don't know exactly what happened," Gage said. "And with Charlie dead, we never will."

Tansy shrugged. "Then maybe I've made my peace with never knowing. And . . . and I couldn't bring myself to put Moki through another trial. Doctors and psychologists testing and tormenting him again. He'd suffered enough. He may not recognize me anymore, but he still feels the pain of being treated like an object."

She paused again, her eyes losing focus. Gage followed her mind back ten years. Moki Amaro, beaten, not by thugs but by Hummer-riding drunk rich kids from Pacific Heights raised on gangster rap and delusions of turf. More than just beaten. Brutalized because he was a brown-skinned boy in hand-me-down sweats jogging through their upscale neighborhood. The four seventeen-year-olds had claimed self-defense. The lone prosecution witness, a city trash collector, fled the day before trial, and the judge dismissed the case. The person last seen by neighbors walking up the witness's front steps: a man who the prosecutor suspected was Charlie Palmer, but which he could never prove.

Tansy blinked and her eyes once again focused on Gage. He knew where the conversation was headed so he took the lead.

"In the end," Gage said, "it wasn't about any particular thing Charlie did, it was about everything he did. What he was. He had no respect for the truth, even as a cop. That's why he was the favorite of every politician caught with his hands in a lobbyist's pocket or in the pants of some young staffer. His so-called investigations were nothing more than blackmailing people into silence or suborning perjury—and that's what I believe he did to you and Moki. If the truth had come out, those kids would've gone to jail, their parents would be paying for his care, and you'd still have a nursing career."

Gage didn't have to finish his thought: If it hadn't

been for Charlie's crimes, Gage never would've met Tansy. A couple of years after the beating, Gage's father asked him to travel to the Rio Yaqui valley in Mexico to find out whether insecticide poisoning might account for the cancers of many of his immigrant Yaqui patients and the birth defects and learning disabilities of their children. Gage convinced a farmworker to help him steal samples from the fields and warehouses and smuggle them back into the U.S. A lab analysis revealed that the corporations farming the Yaqui land were using toxaphene, a compound of six hundred and seventy chemicals that had been dumped in Mexico after they were banned in the U.S.

The truth came too late for the man who'd helped him. Gage received a letter from his widow a month after he'd died of toxaphene poisoning. She wrote asking for help, not for herself, but for her niece, Tansy, who'd graduated from nursing school in San Francisco just before Moki had been attacked. Gage sought her out and after talking with her and with the prosecutor, he was convinced Charlie was behind the collapse of the prosecution of the kids who'd destroyed Moki's life.

There was no one in San Francisco other than Charlie who could have done it so perfectly.

Gage repaid the debt his father and his patients owed Tansy's uncle and tried to compensate for Charlie's crime by offering her a job that allowed her to both work and care for her disabled son. He even let her bring Moki into the office on days when she couldn't find a nurse's aide to stay with him at home.

But it was too late to reopen the case, even if Tansy had been willing, because the prosecutor's race against the statute of limitations had already been lost.

"And that's what Charlie did to a thousand other people." Gage jerked his thumb over his shoulder toward Pacific Heights where Moki had been assaulted. "Those kids grew up knowing their parents could buy their way out of anything by hiring somebody like Charlie Palmer."

Tansy fixed her eyes on Gage. "That's it, isn't it?"

"What?"

"When you hired me, I heard you left police work to study philosophy at Cal. I figured you'd be somebody who talked in theoretical concepts, whether for real or just to impress people." She grinned. "I had enough of that in the 1980s when graduate students would come out to the reservation thinking they could squat down with an old Deer Singer and he'd spit out their dissertations for them." She giggled, her face brightening. "There we were, in the middle of the godforsaken desert, trying to build cinder-block houses, and all they'd want to talk about was deconstruction."

Gage shrugged as if to say academics sometimes got lost in their jargon.

Tansy caught his meaning, but shook her head. Her grin faded.

"For you, it was never about abstract ideas, justice with a capital J and truth with a capital T. I've watched you. Everyone thinks you live in your head"—she tapped her chest—"but this is where you live. You understand heartache. That's what moves you. I've been told that's what the old people used to say about your father, and everything I've seen since I started working here shows me you're your father's son. I even can see it in Faith's eyes when she looks at you now."

She lowered her hand and fell silent. After a few seconds she nodded as though she'd found the just right words to express her thoughts, and said, "I'm thinking it probably would've been better if you'd been born a Yaqui."

"Why's that?"

"Because of the way your mind works. It's just like how we approach the world. It's even in our language. In English you say, 'I see the earth.' The emphasis is on the person seeing, the filtering through the mind. In Yaqui we say, *Inepo bwia vitchu*, I earth see. The emphasis is on us facing the thing as it exists in the world. It makes us a humble people."

Gage was quick to respond. "Too humble."

As a child, Gage had watched Yaquis traveling through Nogales from Mexico on their annual Easter migration, wondering whether they were like the Bedouins he was reading about in *Lawrence of Arabia*, except unarmed and nearly defeated, run out of Mexico by a government attempting to break their will and harassed by immigration agents and police at the border. They were only safe when they arrived at a patch of desert a six-year-old Apache schoolmate of Gage's once called a resignation, instead of a reservation. Gage remembered driving up to Tucson from Nogales with his father in the 1960s, when he went to stand with Yaquis at city council meetings protesting real estate developers encroaching Old Pascua village, a collection of dusty one-room shacks and shotgun brick houses founded by refugees fleeing Mexican government persecution.

"But we survived," Tansy said.

"Maybe the tribe should've gotten a cut from the Carlos Castaneda books," Gage said, finally offering a smile back. "And made some money selling tickets to watch him and that Yaqui shaman turn into crows and fly around the Sedona vortexes."

"Carlos who? I don't recall such a person dropping by, as a man or a bird. And the only vortex any Yaqui ever saw was a dust devil."

Gage shook his head in mock sadness.

"Lots of new age folks in San Francisco will be really disappointed to learn that."

"Not from me. When I see them heading my way, I pretend I'm a Navajo."

Gage had been the only one at the San Francisco Police Department who knew why they all called him Spike.

Homicide Lieutenant Humberto Pacheco, too short to play volleyball when he and Gage were growing up together, and now looking more like a mallet than a nail, lumbered through the entrance of the Fiesta Brava Taqueria on Mission Street a little after 1:30 P.M. Tan sports coat, brown pants, pale yellow shirt, and a blue tie painted with tiny footballs. He didn't pause to survey the interior of the storefront restaurant before heading toward a table in the far corner where Gage already sat. The rest of the tables were empty, the lunch crowd having already moved on.

Spike waved to their usual waiter, then dropped a manila envelope onto the table and sat down to the right of Gage, a plate of chicken in chili-laced cream sauce already cooling before him. A warming Coke stood next to it.

"Sorry I'm late," Spike said. "I got hung up at a

meeting with the chief. The mayor is pissed because some Japanese woman got mugged coming out of the St. Francis Hotel. Cut up pretty bad. He's worried about losing the Asian tourist business."

Gage set down his fork. "I've got an idea. Maybe he should hire the homeless to paint targets on the Nicaraguans and Sudanese so the crooks would know who he wants mugged."

Spike grinned. "Why didn't I think of that?"

"You did, you just didn't say it because you know the chief doesn't appreciate that kind of sarcasm." Gage pointed at Spike's plate. "You want it heated up?"

Spike mixed a little of the sauce with the rice, then tasted it. "No, it's okay." He tilted his head toward the half-eaten roasted *birra* in front of Gage. "You're still the only white guy I know who eats goat."

Spike dug into his chicken while Gage opened the envelope and thumbed through the thirty pages of police reports about Palmer's shooting.

"I appreciate you taking over the case yourself instead of leaving it with your underlings," Gage said. "Anything else besides what's in here?"

"There's also a ballistics check on the slug. A .38. Five lands and grooves, right twist. Could be just about any Saturday night special."

"What about the shooter?"

"Charlie gave us almost nothing to go on. The guy he described couldn't have been more average if Charlie had made him up."

"And that's what you think he did?"

"The uniforms at the scene pushed him real hard

for a description—a dying declaration in case he didn't survive. All they got was a cardboard John Doe. At first I thought maybe shock scrambled his brain, but it didn't get any better when I went to see him two days later. It was like he did some kind of statistical survey and came up with the mean . . ." Spike cocked his head and squinted toward the ceiling, then looked back at Gage. "Is it mean or median?"

"I think it's called the mode. Mode is what there's most of."

Spike smiled. "Mr. Salazar will be thrilled to know ninth grade math stuck." He took a sip of his Coke. "It's like Charlie came up with the mode, and then said, 'That's the guy.'"

"You have a theory?"

"I think he didn't want us to catch him."

"And do it himself after he got better?"

"Except he didn't get better. When I called Socorro last week, the doctor had just told him he'd recovered as much as he ever would. Might not get worse, but wouldn't get better. He was never gonna work again, that's for sure. Maybe never even get out of bed."

"That must be why he called me."

Spike shook his head. "I don't think so. He knew you're not a vigilante. He had to have guessed you'd be doing exactly what you're doing, not roaming the streets with a six-shooter."

"Then why didn't he reach out to you if he changed his mind and wanted to get the guy?"

Spike shrugged. "Maybe it has to do with one of his cases. Attorney-client privilege and all that."

He aimed his fork at the file. "You know what he was working on the day he was shot? He wouldn't tell me."

"A tax evasion case. Yachts. He was interviewing marine appraisers."

"Like those car donation scams?"

"But in the multimillion-dollar range. And knowing Charlie, he was probably trying to get one of them to commit perjury by testifying the appraisals were accurate."

Gage caught Spike's eye, then glanced toward the glass entrance doors. Two silver-adorned Jalisco cowboys entered, dressed in the style of their home state in Mexico. Silver belt buckles, silver toe tips on rattlesnake-skin boots, silver bands on their hats, and silver buttons and lapel points on their shirts. The men paused just inside the door and scanned the restaurant, then took a small table near the front window. One slid a black briefcase underneath, while the other pulled out a cell phone, punched in a number, spoke a few words, and disconnected.

"Must be door-to-door encyclopedia salesmen," Gage said, as a waiter delivered the men a basket of tortilla chips and salsa.

Spike slipped in a Bluetooth earpiece, punched in a number on his cell phone, and turned slightly away and passed on his location and a description of the Jaliscos. He rested his phone on the table, waited until the men were both looking down and reaching for chips, and then snapped a photo of them and sent it.

"It's just like riding a bike, isn't it?" Spike said.

"Don't you ever just want to get off it at least long enough to enjoy a meal?"

"Can't. It's like having the television on all the time in the back of your head."

"I used to think of it as white noise," Gage said, poking around in his *birra*. "Charlie used to alert to guys like that from a mile away."

"But that was more about like attracting like."

Spike reached into his coat pocket and withdrew a wallet-sized Mexican prayer card encased in plastic.

"My brother bought this for Faith at a shrine in Culiacán. He's still playing amateur anthropologist. He wanted to give it to her at your father's funeral, but it didn't seem appropriate."

He handed it to Gage.

"She still interested in Catholic *animas*?" Spike asked.

Gage nodded as he examined the image of folk saint Jesús Malverde, protector of drug dealers, overlaid on a painting of the Virgin of Guadalupe. He dipped his head toward the Jaliscos. "Those guys may need this thing a lot more than Faith."

"I'm sure they never leave home without one."

"They also don't leave home unarmed," Gage said. "Check out the front pocket of the guy on the right."

Spike's cell phone vibrated a couple of minutes later as the Mexicans ate shrimp cocktails from bulbous sundae glasses.

"*Hola, Mama.*" Spike spoke loudly, smiling at Gage. "*Estoy en la Fiesta Brava.*" He listened for fifteen seconds, then in a lower voice passed on the warning about weapons and disconnected.

"You know what else Charlie was working on?" Spike asked.

"Off the record?"

"I don't know. Tell me a little more."

"He was trying to recover the wallet of somebody who got robbed."

"Why off the record?"

"It was a government official."

"There's no law saying people have to report crimes against themselves," Spike said. "Off the record is okay."

"Brandon Meyer was mugged a week or two before Charlie got shot."

"No shit?"

"He wanted Charlie to get his wallet back."

"Why didn't Meyer report it?"

"I think he was afraid it would slop back on his brother."

"I don't get it. A mugging is a mugging. Happens all the time."

"But this one happened at night in the Tenderloin."

"The Tenderloin?" Even Spike wouldn't walk through the Tenderloin after sunset, and he carried two handguns and Mace. "What was the brother of a presidential candidate doing in there? That has *National Enquirer* written all over it."

"Meyer claimed he cut through on his way to a meeting, but I don't believe him."

Spike clucked. "You not believing an exalted federal judge like him. I'm shocked, simply shocked."

They watched the waiter deliver two Dos XXs to the Jaliscos.

"How'd you find out about the mugging?" Spike asked.

"From Socorro. Then Meyer called me to drop by, but only to make sure I didn't pursue it."

"Why didn't he just cancel the credit cards and forget the whole thing?"

"I don't know. He wouldn't tell me. Could be there was something in the wallet."

Spike grinned. "Like maybe a Viagra tablet and the cell number of a Tenderloin prostitute?"

Gage shook his head. "Unlikely. I'm not sure sex is his thing anymore. He gets off screwing over whoever shows up in his court."

Spike laughed. "Talk about a helluva photo op. That pale-butted pipsqueak bouncing up and down between the legs of some methed-up hooker in a skid-row hotel."

Gage cast him a sour expression. "I'm glad I already finished my lunch," Gage said, pushing away his plate. Spike was still grinning, now red-faced. "You better finish the thought before you explode."

"And Meyer working his little *pene*, yelling, 'Motion denied! Motion denied!'"

Spike laughed, stomach bouncing, until tears formed at the corners of his eyes. He wiped them with his napkin. "Man, what an image."

"Are you done ruining my meal?"

"I hope so." Spike rubbed his side. "I think I pulled a muscle."

One of the Jaliscos walked over to the jukebox, dropped in fifty cents, then punched a button. He returned to his table as an accordion blast began "El Corrido Contrabando," a ballad celebrating Amado

Carrillo Fuentes, Lord of the Skies, a Mexican who smuggled hundreds of tons of cocaine in 727s, then faked dying during plastic surgery and retired to Colombia.

"Is that song for your benefit?" Gage asked.

"No. They think I'm an insurance salesman. Just a guy selling term life." Spike grinned again. "When I'm really pushing life terms."

Gage shook his head. "You still get a kick out of this."

"That's why I can't bring myself to retire. It's even hard to think about it."

Spike's grin faded as his sentence trailed off. He paused, his face turned somber.

"Middle age is weird. You think about things you never thought about before. It hit me the other night that from the moment my father came across the border, he never felt at home again anywhere. Not in Mexico and not in Arizona, even after he became a citizen." Spike tapped the gold badge clipped to his belt under his jacket. "And I'm not sure I really felt at home until I got this piece of metal. Maybe that's why he wanted me to follow you up here. Kinda makes it hard to give it up."

Spike paused again, thinking, then his eyes brightened. "Well, that and Placita. She couldn't stand me hanging around the house all the time."

"She tell you that?"

"Straight out, the first time I talked about it. Then she reached for the phone and threatened to make her nephew give me a job driving one of his cabs—until I showed her a news article saying it was more dangerous than being a cop."

"But she'd made her point."

"Yeah, big time."

Spike pulled his case log out of the manila envelope.

"That's another thing." Spike skimmed down the chronology. "Charlie wouldn't tell me how he got over to Geary Street where he got shot, but I think he took a taxi. A Checker cab driver remembered dropping off somebody who resembled Charlie two blocks away about twenty minutes before it happened. Charlie denied it was him. But I think it was."

"So he didn't want to use a car that could be traced to him?"

"That's what it looks like."

"Sounds like you spent as much time investigating Charlie as you did whoever shot him."

"More. He was stonewalling. There had to be a reason, and it wasn't a no-harm, no-foul case. A few days after he was shot he got pneumonia and it seemed like he wasn't going to make it. Would've made it a homicide right then."

"What did the neighborhood canvass turn up?"

"We got a possible ID of Charlie at a coffee shop. Eyewitness IDs are bad enough, but this was one where the clerk had no reason to pay attention at the time. So I'm not sure what to make of it."

Spike tilted his head toward the two men, one of whom was opening his phone. The man held it to his ear, nodded, then snapped it closed. Thirty seconds later, a younger Hispanic man entered and pulled a chair up to the Jaliscos' table and set down a small black canvas duffel, stretched tight by its contents. He was dressed in Levi's and oversized sweatshirt and wearing wraparound sunglasses.

"Looks like they're going to do the deal right here," Gage said. "I wouldn't be surprised if there was heroin in that bag. They wouldn't need a briefcase of money to buy so few kilos of cocaine."

Spike punched redial on his phone, reported in to the surveillance officers driving down Mission Street toward the restaurant, then disconnected.

The three men kept casting quick glances around the restaurant, too often for Spike to risk another photo.

"They're bringing a dog," Spike said, sliding his phone into his jacket pocket. "He'll take a little sniff as they walk outside." He smiled. "Then off to the pokey." He pushed his plate away. "What're you working on besides Charlie?"

"The main one is a trade secrets case. Fiberoptic switches. My clients developed a switch—a kind of splitter—that tripled fiber-optic line capacity. FiberLink. The owners mortgaged their houses and borrowed from their retirement accounts to fund their research. Really nice people. The brains were two women who used to work at Intel. They came up with the switch on their own time, then brought in some friends to form the company."

"What happened?"

"One of their husbands smuggled out the design and sold it to OptiCom, which used it as the backbone for their bid to wire Western Europe, and they won. I chased him around Europe for a couple of weeks, then cornered him in Zurich. I brought him back and delivered him to the FBI."

"Why'd he do it?"

"Jealousy. He thought his wife was cheating on him."

"Was she?"

"I don't think so, but it still wouldn't justify what he did."

Spike looked over at an abandoned newspaper on the next table, an unopened business section lying on top. "How much was the European contract worth?"

"Billions and billions and billions. OptiCom's stock went through the roof. The world's biggest fiber-optic company doubled in value overnight."

"I'll bet their stock is going to tank when this hits the news. I mean really plummet." Spike smiled, then rubbed his hands together. "Maybe it's time for a little insider trading. I've been doing a little reading. Seems there's a way to make a lot of money if you know a stock is going to crash."

Gage smiled back. "Too bad you don't know of one."

"Yeah." Spike sighed. "Way too bad. I guess I'll have to keep making money the old-fashioned way. Slurping at the public trough."

Gage pointed at the envelope. "What's next?"

"Retrace my steps, see if I missed anything. But I'll lay off for a while if you're going to do something. You're probably in a better position anyway, what with the attorney-client privilege issues."

"That's fine. I'll make it quick. I need to make

sure whatever Charlie was up to doesn't snap back at Socorro again."

Spike and Gage both alerted to the Jaliscos leaning back against the window next to them. The newcomer's hand was under his sweatshirt.

"Something's going sour," Gage said. "Maybe it's a rip-off."

The newcomer angled his chair away from the Jaliscos, giving himself a view of the rest of the restaurant. He glanced around, his eyes hesitating when they fell on the cook and the waiter behind the counter to Gage's left, then on Gage and Spike, as if counting the number of witnesses who'd have to be eliminated.

Gage caught the waiter's eye, then tilted his head toward the kitchen. The waiter nodded his understanding: If two witnesses escaped there would be no reason kill the remaining ones.

The newcomer caught the motion and pushed himself to his feet. Seconds later all three dealers were waving guns at one another, then at the waiter, the cook, Spike, and Gage.

Spike slipped his right hand under the table and rested it on his gun while Gage rose with his hands up and eased toward the counter. Three barrels tracked his movement. The newcomer yelled, "Freeze, asshole." But Gage took a final step, coming to a stop in front of the cook and waiter.

The waiter pulled the cook to the floor with him and used Gage and the counter for cover as they crawled into the kitchen and toward the back door.

Gage lowered his hands and pointed at the weapons.

"Why don't you guys take your business outside?"

The Jaliscos swung their guns toward the newcomer.

Spike repeated Gage's question as an order. *"Tomen sus negocios afuera."*

He was now aiming his semiautomatic at the Jaliscos, his elbows propped on the table and using a double-handed grip.

"Just walk away," Spike said. "Nobody's gonna stop you."

The newcomer looked back and forth between Spike and Gage, but spoke to the Jaliscos: *"Estamos chidos."* We're cool.

The three looked at one another, then one of the Jaliscos reached down for the briefcase of cash, while the newcomer picked up his bag. They backed toward the entrance, then slipped their guns into their pockets as they turned and stepped outside into the glare of the afternoon sun—and into the sights of racking police shotguns.

Following six cars behind Gage as he drove up Mission Street toward his office, the Texan spoke into his cell phone.

"He met with a Mexican cop for lunch. Then a little fun and games with some narco-wetbacks."

"Could you tell what Gage was up to?"

The Texan snapped back: "You think I can read his mind?"

"Why didn't you get a table next to them?"

"And get caught in a crossfire?"

"What do you mean, crossfire?"

"It's not important. Anyway, it would've been stupid to go inside. Gage is like a bloodhound. His nose snapped toward those beaners the second they walked in the place. He would've sniffed me out in a heartbeat."

"Where do we stand?" Gage asked Alex Z the next morning.

Alex Z was hunched over his keyboard, his face inches from one of the monitors standing on his desk.

"I decrypted a spreadsheet using the name of Charlie's boat, but everything in it is coded except the numbers."

Alex Z pressed a couple of keys. A file opened. Gage saw subtotaled and totaled columns with dates at the top, and to the far left, a column of gibberish, a mixture of letters and numbers.

"What's your guess?" Gage asked.

"There are no negative numbers, so it's probably not money going in and then coming out again. So if it's really money, it's either all in or all out."

"How much?"

Alex Z scrolled to the bottom of the spreadsheet. "About ten million on this one."

"Maybe he was tracking financial transactions in a case. Have you tried decoding the label column?"

Alex Z scratched his head. "I was hoping you wouldn't ask that, boss."

"Stymied?"

"Yeah."

Gage smiled. "You'll figure it out. Anything else in there?"

"Lots and lots. I'm still trying to decode them."

Gage glanced down at a stack of billing records. Alex Z's eyes followed.

"I sorted those by case and by date," Alex Z said. "But there's not much there. About thirteen thousand outstanding, spread among three cases."

"I guess he really was closing down. Viz said Charlie used to clear about three hundred thousand a year."

Alex Z pointed at the printouts. "All he had going was the yacht tax fraud, an earth-moving accident that killed an oil executive's kid, and a dispute between Paramount and Universal over film rights."

"What about Brandon Meyer's mugging? Did he put time in for that?"

"No. But he kept all the receipts. Cab fare. Posters. Restaurant receipts."

"Restaurant receipts? From where?"

"Ground Up Coffee Shop on Geary. One from a week before he got shot and one just the day before."

Gage recognized the name. He'd remembered driving past it on his way from downtown out to the Presidio. It was a few blocks away from where Charlie had been shot and from where Spike suspected a Checker cab had dropped him off.

"Look and see whether he saved any Ground Up receipts from other visits," Gage said. "Maybe it was his regular place to meet people in that part of town."

"Already did. It doesn't show up at all in his accounting records, but neither do these two."

"Maybe was waiting to enter them until the case was over," Gage said.

"It would be the first time. I checked the tax fraud and the other cases. He entered the costs the same day he spent the money."

"Could be that he was getting a little lax since he was near the end of the career, then got shot and trapped inside his body."

Gage scanned the spreadsheet displayed on the monitor.

"Why would Charlie encrypt this and code it too?" Gage asked. "One or the other should've been enough." He reached for the mouse, clicked twice, opening the hidden document properties, including the author and the company that created it.

"He didn't put this spreadsheet together," Alex Z said, taping the author field on the screen. "Who is CEB?"

"Or what is CEB? It's also listed as the company."

"I wonder whether CEB sent it over coded, then Charlie encrypted it for extra security."

"Maybe," Gage said. "How many encrypted files are left?"

"About thirty. Plus two encrypted folders. I have no idea how many files are in those. I haven't been able to decrypt his password file yet."

"Print out whatever you can and have Tansy put them in my safe." Gage settled back in his chair and stared at the screen. "This is all very interesting, but—"

"But it may have nothing to do with why Charlie was shot."

"Exactly. Charlie had a lot to hide. We could uncover a dozen different schemes, but still never find out which was the one that ended with the bullet that cut him in half."

CHAPTER 13

"ou Toby?" Gage asked the twenty-five-year-old steaming milk behind the granite counter at Ground Up Coffee Shop.

"That's me," Toby answered, looking up at Gage. "Is this about the car accident? I talked to the adjuster yesterday."

Gage shook his head. "A customer." He pointed toward the front window. "And about something that happened down the street."

"Sure. I got a break in ten. You want something to drink?"

"Decaf."

"Cappuccino? Espresso? Mocha Macchiato?"

"Just a decaf coffee."

Toby grinned. "You must be from out of town."

"Thirty years ago."

Toby waved off Gage's money and said he'd bring the coffee to his table.

Gage grabbed a *New York Times* strung on a three-foot wooden dowel from a wall mount, then took the rear table in the narrow café. A few minutes later, Toby delivered the coffee and sat down.

"So what's up, Decaf?"

Gage pulled a photo of Charlie Palmer from his suit pocket.

"You remember a cop coming in here a few months ago asking about this guy?"

Toby took the photo. "Sure. Different picture, but I think it's the same guy. Got shot or something, right?"

"Yeah."

Toby set it down. "He doing okay?"

"He didn't make it."

"Sorry to hear that." Toby paused and shook his head, then pointed at Gage's coffee. "You want sugar or something?"

"No thanks."

Gage took a confirmatory sip.

"What's your part in this?" Toby asked.

"I'm a private investigator."

Gage handed him a business card.

"Graham Gage," Toby said, reading it line by line. "I heard of you. This guy's family must have big, big bucks."

"Not so big."

"I didn't mean that. I'm happy to help out. No charge."

Toby inspected Gage's face. "How come you don't look like a PI?"

"How is one supposed to look?"

"You know, grizzled. And not so tall. You look like a guy who thinks for a living, not somebody who mixes it up in back alleys."

"Mixes it up with whom?"

Toby shrugged. "The bad guys, I guess."

Gage smiled. "I'll go look for some after we're done and let you know how it turns out."

Toby picked up the photo again. "I think this is the same guy who was in here, but I'm not sure." He rocked his head side to side. "Maybe I'm just remembering the other photo."

"Assuming it was him, was he alone?"

"Assuming it was him, no. I was thinking about it a while back. I have a really vague recollection Mr. Comb-Over was with him. A white guy, early sixties, gray hair—what there was of it."

"Has he been here more than once?"

"Yeah. You don't forget a hair felony like that." Toby rested his palm on top of his head, then waved his fingers. "The kind that flaps in the wind."

"When was the last time you saw him?"

"Last week. That's what got me thinking. I'm off Tuesday and Wednesday, so it must've been Thursday or Friday . . . I think Friday."

"Driving or walking?"

Toby turned and squinted toward the front window. "Driving. He needed change for the meter. An early eighties Toyota Corona."

"You know your Toyotas. They haven't imported that model for over two decades."

"My dad owned one for like twenty years. I'll never forget it." Toby grinned. "It was the first place I got laid. Except Dad's was white. Comb-Over's was brown."

"Anything distinctive?"

"Just what you'd expect with a car that old. Faded." Toby closed his eyes. "No hubcaps." He opened them again. "At least on the passenger side."

"What about the plate? Regular or personalized?"

"Don't know." Toby pointed at a parking space directly in front of the store window. "He had that spot. All I could see was the side of the car."

"Can you get it for me if he comes by?"

"I'll call you right when he walks in the door. But . . ." Apprehension clouded Toby's face. "But he's not the shooter is he? I don't want—"

"No, he's just the beginning of the trail."

Toby held up Gage's business card. "You want me to tell him to call you if he comes in?"

Gage shook his head. "I think I'd rather he doesn't know I'm working on this. It'll give me a chance to deal with him fresh."

Landon Meyer found himself pacing as he read over the updated FBI background reports on his nominees, Starsky and Hutch. They both had told the truth when he'd grilled them in August. They'd remained as clean as they were at the time of their appeals court confirmation hearings less than a year earlier. And both had done as they were instructed. Neither had made any public statements except from the bench. Each had avoided sarcasm and hyperbole in their usually dissenting opinions. Landon had read each one himself before they were filed to make sure. No verb stronger than "disagree," no adverb more rabid than "respectfully," no adjective more extreme than "learned," and no noun more pejorative than "colleague."

Landon recalled fuming all through the Ardino confirmation. Not only had Ardino left fifty typhoonlike speeches in his wake, but his fifteen years of opinions had blown the door open to the Democrats' exploration of nearly every major constitutional issue facing the Court: presidential power, the death penalty, torture, the role of international law, and the legacy of *Brown v. Board of Education*. It also hurt that Ardino's forced and ominous smile engendered queasiness even among his supporters. The good news was he knew how to play the political game that was at the heart of confirmation hearings. The bad news was he appeared to be playing. His weeping wife fleeing the hearing room even seemed to Landon to be a stunt.

Not this time. Not with Landon as Judiciary Committee chairman.

Starsky and Hutch were going to play it straight and their wives were going sit behind them as poised and gracious as Laura Bush. If they didn't, they'd be doing a whole lot of crying for real, in private, in his office.

Landon walked to his desk and picked up the telephone. Committee staff lawyer Norvil Whithers answered on the first ring and arrived a few minutes later. He brought with him the list of lawyers appointed by the White House to Starsky and Hutch's murder boards. These teams of experts would question and requestion the nominees on every subject of potential interest to the senators on the committee until they had perfected sufficiently vague and mind-numbing answers that would cause the opposition to surrender, wearied of combat and defeated by obfuscation.

Landon directed Whithers to a seat in front of his desk, but kept pacing as he read the thirty-name roster: current deputies in the Justice Department, others who'd gone back to their national law firms, members of the White House staff, attorneys for the Republican National Committee, a general counsel to an oil company, two staffers from conservative think tanks.

"This is good," Landon said, coming to a stop behind his desk, "but I think we need a broader focus. Having smooth answers to hard questions won't be enough."

Whithers pointed at the list. "It seems pretty comprehensive to me."

Landon dropped into his chair, then drummed his pen on the edge of his desk.

"Let me ask you something," Landon said. "What are the first polls going to say when the president announces the names?"

Whithers shrugged.

"I'll tell you. The president gets the benefit of the doubt. Fifty-five percent in favor. Thirty against. And fifteen undecided"—Landon smiled—"because they don't have a clue what the Supreme Court really does."

"Sounds about right."

"But after the Democrats scare the hell out of the public and the media beats up the nominees a little?"

"It'll probably flop the other way." It was Whithers's turn to smile. "With fewer undecided because more people will realize how these nine little dictators control their lives."

Landon glanced at a photo on his bookshelf showing him standing before a group of reporters, digital recorders and microphones extended toward him.

"Liberals make fun of FOX News," Landon said, "but there isn't one of their regular viewers who can't name at least five members of the Court and six members of the Cabinet and who don't know what an oil depletion allowance is—and none of them will be among the undecided."

He looked back at Whithers.

"There's no question the Democrats will want to filibuster the nominations," Landon said. "Starsky and Hutch will have to use the hearings to reach out to the public through the television screen like they were George Clooney and Brad Pitt, and flip the numbers back by the time they reach the full Senate. Make a filibuster seem like treason."

"But these guys are judges," Whithers said, "not actors."

Landon smiled again. "They will be when I'm done with them."

Landon picked up his telephone as the door closed behind Whithers.

"Brandon? . . . We need to go Hollywood with Starsky and Hutch . . . I don't know how much altogether . . . Let's start with fifty thousand for acting coaches and a million for media to go after the opposition and see how far that gets us."

H e's here," the late morning caller whispered. "He's here."

"Who's he?" Gage asked, leaning forward in his desk chair.

"Mr. Comb-Over. At the table by the front window."

"Hold on."

Gage pressed the conference call button on his landline, then punched in a cell phone number.

"Viz, start driving to the thirty-two hundred block of Geary Street."

"Toby?" Gage asked.

"Still here."

"I've got a guy named Viz on the line. Was Comb-Over walking or driving?"

"Driving," Toby said. "At least there's a brown Corona that looks like his parked across the street."

"What's he wearing?"

"Dark green sweater, baggy gray pants. A San Francisco Giants cap . . . I mean the cap is on the table."

"What's he doing?"

"He's waiting for me to bring over his coffee."

"Viz, how far away are you?"

"Fifteen, twenty blocks . . . Asshole." Gage heard tires skidding. "Not you, boss, some guy cut me off."

Viz's gunning motor filled the silence.

"I got around him."

"Toby," Gage said, "keep Comb-Over there."

"I'll make a show of brewing up a new pot."

"Viz. First get the license plate of the Corona, then set up to follow him."

"Shit," Toby said. "I gotta go. He just got up and is heading my way."

Gage spotted Viz's blue-green Yukon at Geary near Thirty-third Avenue as he pulled up to the corner of Thirty-second. Viz was parked facing west, four cars ahead of the Corona, at a meter in front of a Russian bakery. Gage slipped into a space next to a Chinese produce market.

"What's cooking?" Gage asked Viz over his cell.

"Nothing. He's just drinking his coffee. Lots of it." Viz laughed. "Like it'll grow hair on his head."

"You get the plate?"

"I called it in to Alex Z. It's registered to a John, normal spelling, Porzolkiewski . . . Por-zol-kiew-ski. Normal spelling."

"You win the spelling bee for today. Where's he live?"

"The car's registered to a P.O. box downtown. But Alex Z did some database searches and found a street address, a house on Seventeenth Ave about a mile south of Golden Gate Park."

Gage saw Viz lean toward his window and peer into the side-view mirror.

"Boss. Two guys in a blue Ford Explorer came charging up and pulled in behind you, three cars back. Neither got out."

"What do they look like?"

"Too much reflection on their windshield, but the guy drives hard like a cop. What do you want to do?"

"Sit tight until I find out whether they're tailing me or are here on something else."

"What should I do about Comb-Over?"

"If they're following me, let him go. I don't want them making a connection between him and us."

Gage put a couple of quarters into the meter, then strolled along the storefronts past Viz's truck. He took a right onto Thirty-third, walking by pastel stucco bungalows and two-story apartment buildings. When he neared the end of the block, he climbed the steps onto the recessed landing of a duplex, then called Viz.

"The passenger walked up to Thirty-third and peeked around," Viz said. "He crossed the street to get a view down the block, probably trying to see where you stopped, then went into that kosher market."

"What's he look like?"

"Late thirties, blond hair, six feet, plus or minus, Levi's, oversized plaid workshirt."

"Cop or ex-cop?"

"My guess he's ex. He's wearing the 1990s under-cover uniform."

"What's he doing now?"

"Pretending to take an interest in the after–Rosh Hashanah sale items in the window as he keeps an eye on the street." Viz chuckled. "I never would have guessed. He seems like a mayonnaise and white bread kind of guy."

"I've been up here long enough," Gage said, then walked back down the steps. "I'm heading your way. Hit me when he comes out of the market."

Gage's cell phone rang as he walked on Geary back toward his car.

"He's thirty yards behind you," Viz said, prompting Gage to duck into a liquor store to let the man pass. After buying a soda to make the stop seem authentic, rather than countersurveillance, he continued walking to his car.

"I'll drive back toward the financial district," Gage said, pulling into the street, "but I'll loop around and lead them by you first."

The Explorer remained five car lengths behind him as he passed by Viz and circled the block.

"I'm almost back to Geary," Gage told Viz. "Get ready. We'll be coming by you in about thirty seconds."

Viz turned his ignition, then asked, "Why are they following you?"

"My guess? It's either Charlie or an antitrust case I'm working on."

Gage paused in the intersection to let traffic pass, then turned onto Geary, driving east slow enough for the Explorer to catch up. He glanced over at Viz's Yukon. Viz was staring down toward his floorboard where he had anchored a six-inch monitor fed by a camera hidden in his oversized side mirror. He controlled it by a joystick attached to his steering column.

"Got 'em," Viz said.

"How's the reflection?"

"Son of a bitch."

Gage saw Viz jerk his hand up to cover the left side of his face as the Explorer approached, then lower his head as if he was reaching for something on the floor.

"What is it?"

"A scumbag named Boots Marnin is driving."

"Who's he?"

"Ex-DEA. Started about the same time as me."

"Did he see you?"

"I'm not sure."

"Why scumbag?"

"He got indicted for taking kickbacks from an informant he put on the payroll. About two hundred grand." Viz sat up after the Explorer passed. "Boots would get a lead on where some dope was and feed the information to the informant. He'd then use the guy as his snitch, seize the dope, and apply to Washington for a reward for the informant—"

"And they'd divide up the money."

"Right. Until he got caught."

Gage watched his rearview mirror as he drove. The Explorer was gone. "What's going on?" Gage asked.

"Boots dropped out. He pulled into the Jack in the Box lot."

"I don't see anybody close enough behind who could stay with me." Gage looked ahead. "I think they may have someone in front of me. Maybe the brown Ford Taurus. It has a hesitant feel about it."

Gage watched the Taurus slow, then pull into the curb lane. Gage took the hint and passed it. The Taurus kept slowing until it was half a block behind Gage, then matched his speed.

"You're out of my view, even with the zoom," Viz said. "Where are you headed?"

"Down to the marina, then along Fisherman's Wharf to see if any other cars are involved."

"What about Comb-Over?"

"We're going to have to let him go for now."

Gage checked his mirror again. The Taurus was still matching his twenty-nine miles an hour.

"So, how'd Boots get caught?" Gage asked.

"His partner figured out the informant couldn't be in two places at the same time, comatose from an OD in the county hospital and in the Hip Sing Tong basement watching China white heroin being cut. Boots got two years in the federal pen. Out eight years ago. I thought he went back to Texas. I'm surprised to see him around here."

"Call Alex Z. Give him everything you've got on Boots and the license plates of the Explorer and Taurus. Then head back to the office and get the van. Call me when you're ready and I'll lead him up the Embarcadero so you can get behind him."

"I think you're reading him right, boss, he was always too arrogant to look over his shoulder. That's why he got caught."

"Have somebody else drive so he doesn't spot you."

"How long should we stay with him?"

"Until you're sure you know where we can find him when the time comes to kick in his door."

hat rhymes with Porzolkiewski?" Alex Z said as he walked into Gage's third floor office.

"Don't tell me you're trying to work it into a song," Gage said, looking up from his desk.

"Just practice. I'm thinking if I could find a rhyme for a name like Porzolkiewski, I could find one for anything."

Gage checked his watch. Six forty-five P.M.

"Isn't it past going-home time?"

"Sorta. We've got the first of a week of gigs at Slim's tonight. I figure I'll keep working until we have to go set up. Shakir the night owl will be here, too. I'm letting him work from 6 P.M. until 3 A.M."

Gage's phone beeped with a text message. He glanced at it. It was from Viz telling him he'd run the surveillance car license plates by Spike. They were both stolen.

Alex Z sat down in a chair across from Gage. He slid a binder across the desk and kept a matching one for himself.

"That's what I've got so far on Comb-Over," Alex Z said. "Pretty tragic life. Wife died of cancer. Son died in an explosion over at the TIMCO refinery about fourteen years ago. Kid was an engineering student at Cal, working a summer job when it happened."

"I remember it. Some other workers were killed, too."

"Porzolkiewski came to the U.S. from Warsaw when he was eleven years old. Lived with an aunt in Chicago. I don't think the American dream turned out to be what he'd hoped. He now runs a market-slash-sandwich shop on Turk Street. It's on the bottom floor of one of those skid-row hotels. The Milton."

Alex Z pointed at the binder. "It's all in a probation department presentence report. It's the second tab. He got busted for aggravated assault. He beat up some homeless guy who tried to steal an egg. One of those hard-boiled ones they sell over the counter. The public defender got him a no-time deal. Just restitution to SF Medical for them treating the victim, and they made him take anger management classes."

"What kind of business owner gets a public defender?"

"The kind who's not making any money, or at least not much. He was supposed to pay them a couple hundred dollars after the case was over, but he never did. I guess the PD doesn't send out bill collectors."

Gage flipped to the TIMCO tab. The first

document was the wrongful death complaint filed by the families of the dead workers. He skimmed through it.

"This is pretty vague," Gage said. "Like they filed the complaint before they knew exactly what happened, before the root cause investigations were even completed."

Gage turned to the twenty-five-page, single-spaced court docket, then jumped to the end.

"It was dismissed," Alex Z said. "No trial. No settlement. The judge ruled it was just a workers' comp case because they were working within the scope of their regular duties and because it was just an accident."

"So they had no standing to sue."

Alex Z nodded.

Gage flipped to the next tab, a medical malpractice suit.

"What about this one?"

"He settled for fifty-five thousand. The doctors gave his wife one course of the wrong chemo for pancreatic cancer, but the experts agreed she would've died within a year anyway."

"Which means after he paid his lawyer, the experts, and the deposition costs, he didn't net anything." Gage looked up at Alex Z. "How'd you find out about the settlement amount? The insurance companies usually insist on secrecy as a condition of agreeing to pay out."

"The clerk forgot to pull out the judge's notes before she gave us the file."

"But those are sealed."

"Somebody had already gotten to it. They slit open the envelope, probably with a razor. You could hardly tell."

"Charlie? Maybe before he met with Porzolkiewski at Ground Up?"

"No way to tell. They don't keep a record of who checks out files."

"What about the TIMCO file? Any tampering?"

"Not that I could see, but we've only gone through the first and last volumes. There are fourteen altogether. I've got two people on it and expect them to be done tomorrow."

Gage thumbed farther into the binder. "What are these code violations?"

"Just the usual ones low-end food service businesses get. A few health citations. And one electrical. I guess there was a fire in the kitchen. Too many appliances plugged into the same outlet. And one for blocking the back door with supplies."

Gage closed the binder, then gazed through the brick-framed casement window at a tugboat guiding a Hanjin container ship through the San Francisco Bay toward the Port of Oakland. A week earlier, a similar monster had crashed into the supports of a two-hundred-foot-tall crane. Six workers injured. Four million dollars in damage. Even before the sun had set, competing news conferences displayed blame already shifting in tides of legal argument.

"Who represented TIMCO?" Gage asked, reaching again for the binder. He turned to the first page of the docket. His eyebrows rose as he read it aloud:

"Anston & Meyer."

"Marc Anston was the attorney of record," Alex Z said.

"Was Brandon in on any depositions?"

Alex Z nodded. "Lots and lots."

"Porzolkiewski's?"

"Big time."

From just inside the entrance, Gage scanned Stymie's Gym in East Oakland at five forty-five the next morning until he caught sight of trial lawyer Skeeter Hall in a corner struggling under an Olympic bar. Gage tossed down his gym bag and slipped around the back of the weight bench to spot him.

"Breathe out, Skeeter," Gage said, looking down at his grimacing face, "or you're going to bust a gut."

Air exploded through Skeeter's clenched teeth.

Gage helped him guide the bar onto the crutches at the top of the roller tubes, then walked around and sat down on the next bench.

"Two twenty," Gage said. "Not bad for a sixty-five-year-old."

"Sixty-four," Skeeter said, sitting up. He wiped his face with the bottom of his sleeveless sweatshirt, then swung his leg over the bench to face Gage. "What are you pushing up, youngster?"

"For reps? No more than one ninety. I don't put these old joints at risk anymore."

"What could you do if you did?"

Gage grinned. "Two twenty-one."

"Smart-ass. You want me to spot you?"

"Just some information."

Skeeter glanced up at the wall clock above the entrance. "Isn't this a little early in the A.M. for gumshoeing?"

"I'm not a gumshoe. I'm a modern PI. This is called multitasking."

Gage reached into his gym bag and handed Skeeter a water bottle.

"Thanks." Skeeter flipped the top open and took a sip. "What task concerns me?"

"You remember the TIMCO case?"

"As if it was yesterday." Skeeter's mouth went tight. "Those assholes."

"You mean corporate assholes in general, or this particular one?"

"This particular one. I've never seen a company try to torpedo its own employees that bad. You got four dead guys, three of them with kids. One with a great engineering career ahead of him . . ."

"Porzolkiewski."

"Yeah . . . Porzolkiewski . . . Tom Fields helped me out on the case, may he rest in peace."

"Fields is dead?"

"Heart attack at Pebble Beach. Eleventh hole. A family history of heart disease and he was seventy pounds overweight. Did it to himself. A waste." Skeeter took another sip. "You know that kid Porzolkiewski was a paraplegic, right? A rookie cop chasing after a stolen car drop-kicked him out of a crosswalk. No lights. No siren. He was nineteen. A student at Berkeley."

"Looks like nothing came easy in that family."

"The kid used to haul himself up those huge fractionating towers hand over hand."

Gage understood the technology, so didn't ask for an explanation. Crude oil was heated at the base of the tower and the rising product was separated out by boiling point and then siphoned off.

"Forearms like piston rods. He was trapped a couple of hundred feet up when the thing blew." Skeeter put the bottle down on the bench beside him. "It was a chain reaction. A pressure release valve failed on the line carrying kerosene. It sprayed onto a generator they were using to run scrubbers to clean a drain. Set the thing off. The fire ran up the tower, then exploded. The diesel line blew. The gasoline line blew. A firestorm. None of the guys could get down. They were like marshmallows on a stick. It still makes me heartsick to think about it."

Skeeter lowered his head and rubbed his temples. His eyes were wet when he looked up.

"It was a tough case to lose . . ." Skeeter's face hardened. "Except we didn't lose it. It was stolen."

"What do you mean?"

"We . . ." Skeeter paused, as if finding himself halfway down a trail he had no idea why he was taking, and it was heading toward a cliff. "Why are you interested?"

"I'm not sure about the why, but I can tell you the what. I'm trying to find out more about Brandon

Meyer's role in the case and I'm especially interested in Porzolkiewski's father."

"Interesting guy. Sounds born in the USA, no accent at all, but underneath he was a starry-eyed immigrant. The American dream and all that, but the explosion turned it into a nightmare. I go by his shop whenever I have an appearance in federal court. Every time I walk in I'm surprised he's still there. I thought he'd have blown his brains out by now."

"He took it that hard?"

"It wasn't the money. It was losing his wife and kid, and plain old corporate betrayal. The company hired a PR firm before the fire was even out, got a lot of mileage saying how they were going to help the families, how they'd get to the cause of the explosion, how everybody would be taken care of, scholarships for all their kids. They even had Porzolkiewski appear with them at a press conference, televised around the world. I guess they were trying to reassure the folks at their foreign drilling operations and refineries. At the same time, their insurance carrier is lying in wait to attack, setting up to blame one of the dead guys, a pipe fitter—"

"To make it a workers' comp case so the company wouldn't be liable and wouldn't have to pay out."

"Exactly."

"I imagine four dead guys would've been worth a lot of money once the jury got a peek at the autopsy photos."

"That's what we figured, too, but after we met Porzolkiewski and got a sense of him and his kid and what they'd been through, the case stopped being about money for us."

"What was Meyer's part in it?"

Skeeter tugged at the right shoulder of his sweatshirt, pulling it closer to his neck, then did the same with the other. Biceps and triceps pumped, skin tight.

"Can't say."

"You mean you don't know?"

"I mean I have a trial starting in his court next week. I'm not even going to speak his name outside of the courtroom until the case is over." Skeeter extended his open hands. "You know what happened the last time I appeared in front of him? I'll tell you what happened. He screwed us all through trial and we lost. And we can't appeal until this next trial is over because it means pointing the finger at him."

"For what?"

"You know how he cuts off witnesses, then rephrases what they have to say? That's what he kept doing all the way through the trial. And every time I'd object, he'd tell me to move on. Even if I got to ask the question again, the punks on other side would jump up and make some bogus objection and he'd sustain it. Every time. Chopped us off at the knees."

Skeeter stood up, hands on hips. He glared down at Gage.

"You know what we found out when we interviewed the jurors afterward?" Skeeter jabbed the air. "You know what the critical evidence was for them? What they talked about in the jury room? The exact testimony that made them find against us?"

"Meyer's restatement of what the key witnesses said."

"That asshole. His version of the real testimony was a complete fiction, the whole thing constructed so the other side would win the trial."

"But you can't appeal based on jurors' thought processes. You need actual jury misconduct."

"I know. A couple of the jurors now realize what happened. They'll help us. I'll find something when this next trial is over. It's a class action stock fraud. I've got half a million dollars invested in it. Slam dunk unless he screws us."

"Then you'll talk about Meyer's role in TIMCO?"

Skeeter ripped off his lifting gloves, threw them into his gym bag, then reached down and yanked it over his shoulder.

"Who's Meyer?"

The manila envelope Tansy delivered to Gage's office late in the afternoon turned out to be a whole lot thicker than he expected.

"This came by messenger," she said, approaching his desk. She pointed at the handwriting on the front after setting it down. "What does 'Graham Gage: 221 pounds' mean?"

"I suspect it means I'm in for some heavy lifting."

Gage heard the floor squeak as someone inside crept toward the front door of the tiny shingled bungalow along Seventeenth Avenue in the flatlands south of Golden Gate Park. He leaned in toward the door as a hot afternoon wind gusted up the street and rattled leaves on the sidewalk. Another squeak. The curtain behind a wood-framed window to the right fluttered, then came to rest. Finally, a squeak close to the threshold. Gage watched the pinprick of light in the peephole vanish.

"Mr. Porzolkiewski?"

"Who is it?"

"My name is Graham Gage."

"What do you want?"

"I'd like to talk to you about TIMCO."

"Ancient history."

"Two months ago isn't ancient history."

"What does two months ago have to do with TIMCO? It was fourteen years ago."

"That's when you talked to Charlie Palmer."

Gage heard the floor squeak twice in the silence that followed, as though Porzolkiewski had rocked back and forth.

"Mr. Porzolkiewski?"

The floor squeaked again.

"Mr. Porzolkiewski?"

"I think you better leave now."

"Can I give you my card?" Gage said, hoping that would get Porzolkiewski to open the door.

"Just leave it."

"I'd rather hand it to you. I don't want it to blow away."

Gage reached into his shirt pocket and withdrew a business card, then held it up in front of the peephole. He heard the scrape and click of a dead bolt, then the rattle of the loose door handle as Porzolkiewski turned it. Gage could see the left side of Porzolkiewski's face when he opened the door a few inches and reached out his hand. Eye moist and bloodshot, in a deep socket surrounded by pale and droopy skin. He looked as though he'd once been a boulder of a man, but had been eroded by tragedy.

"I'm sorry about your son," Gage said, handing him the card.

"Lots of people were sorry. Didn't bring him back."

A Siamese kitten darted through the open door. Gage reached down and picked it up. Porzolkiewski slipped the card into his pants pocket, then stretched out his palm to receive the cat, but Gage cradled it on his left forearm, holding it hostage. Porzolkiewski dropped his hand to his side.

Since Porzolkiewski hadn't denied talking to Charlie, Gage took a shot: "I really just came for the wallet."

Porzolkiewski's face didn't react. "I don't know what you're talking about."

"Look. If Meyer wanted to press charges, he would've. There were fifty-six depositions in the TIMCO case. You were with him at more than thirty."

"I wasn't *with* him. I was against him."

"He was against you is more like it. In any case, he knows who you are. Lawyers tend to remember people who dive at them from across a conference table."

"I don't have it."

"Where is it?"

"I gave it to somebody."

"Palmer?"

Porzolkiewski glanced away for a second, then nodded.

"He said if I gave it back, I'd never be bothered again. They didn't want any trouble because it would slop back on Landon Meyer's presidential campaign."

That explanation made no sense. Palmer never came at people without some kind of leverage to move them the way he wanted, and Porzolkiewski's glancing away told Gage he wasn't a good liar.

"You mean he promised you your probation wouldn't get violated and you'd stay out of state prison."

Porzolkiewski shrugged. "Something like that. Palmer said they could get me for robbery. But that's not what happened. I didn't steal the wallet, it just fell out during the scuffle. The little putz Meyer ran away. Just left it on the sidewalk and I picked it up."

"A Good Samaritan."

"Sort of."

"What was the scuffle about?"

"You mean did I go hunting for him?"

"No. I wasn't assuming anything. It was just a straight question."

"I was on my way to the night drop at the bank. Meyer was coming the other way. I blocked the sidewalk just to see what the asshole would do."

"And that was?"

"His eyes started darting around, but there's no place to go. Stores closed, too much traffic going by. So he just stopped in his tracks, and then turned around and started scurrying away like a rat. I kind of lost it and went after him."

"When did you give the wallet to Palmer?"

"He called me one morning. I met him that afternoon."

"At the Ground Up Coffee Shop?"

Porzolkiewski's eyes widened. "How do you know that? Palmer tell you?"

"I found the receipt."

"I didn't figure he'd tell you about the meeting."

"Why not?"

"That's for me to know and you not to find out."

"You ever see him again?"

"No. And I never will. I saw the obituary. Good riddance."

Gage extended his hand holding the kitten. Porzolkiewski opened the door the rest of the way, accepted it, and then rubbed its cheek against his own.

"You open the wallet?" Gage asked.

"I'm not a thief."

"That's not what I meant."

"I was curious."

"Anything unusual?"

"For a human being or for a scumbag like Meyer?"

"Either."

"Isn't he married?"

"Thirty-some years."

Porzolkiewski smirked.

"There was a condom in there. New. I could tell by the expiration date. I sell them behind the counter. Twice as many as sandwiches. Lots of guys from the financial district slip into the Tenderloin for a nooner with a hooker."

"Maybe you should have a daily special. Half a sandwich, a cup of soup, and a condom."

"I hadn't thought of that." Porzolkiewski finally smiled. "Maybe I can franchise it like McDonald's and KFC."

"Why didn't you call the *Chronicle*? At least embarrass him."

"Because it would turn into a chess game I couldn't win."

Gage imagined lawyers ganging up on a man who'd seen more than his share of pinstriped suits.

"In Poland they say *Kowal zawinil, a Cygana powiesili*. The blacksmith was guilty, but they hanged the Gypsy—and I didn't want to be the Gypsy."

"Anything else in the wallet?"

"Driver's license, credit cards, about seven hundred dollars, frequent flyer cards, a couple of scraps of paper, stuff like that. It was so thick, I figured it made him taller sitting down than standing up."

"You make copies?"

Porzolkiewski looked away for a moment, then he smirked again, this time calculated. "You think I'd waste the paper?"

"I think you're not an idiot."

"There was no need for copies. It wasn't like I was going steal his ID and order a bunch of iPads. I told you, I'm not a thief."

"Porzolkiewski isn't coldblooded enough to shoot Charlie down in the street," Gage told Faith when he arrived at their hillside home in the East Bay late that night. They stood in the kitchen, her in a robe, him in Levi's and a sweatshirt and cutting on a smoked ham. Faith leaned back against the counter, her hair hanging loose. "But he lied to me about seeing Charlie only once."

"How do you know?" she asked.

"First. There's no way Charlie would've telephoned Porzolkiewski and asked him whether he robbed Meyer and whether he wanted to give back the wallet. He would've either showed up at his house and pushed his way in, or followed him somewhere and corralled him."

"And second?"

"He flinched at the wrong times."

"I'd have flunked you in Anthro 101," Faith said in mock disapproval. "Flinching isn't considered evidence at UC Berkeley."

"Unless it's a lab rat."

Faith shuddered. She was on the university committee tasked with ensuring the humane treatment of research animals.

"Anyway, investigating isn't a science." Gage raised a cupped hand, then blew on his fingernails. "It's an art."

"So Van Gogh, what's next?"

"I'm not sure, I'm waiting for inspiration."

Faith untied her robe.

He raised his eyebrows and smiled.

"I'm suddenly inspired."

The screech of slammed brakes, the squeal of skidding tires, and the crunch of metal on metal propelled Shakir Mohammed out of his chair and toward his second floor office window facing the midnight street. Overhead halogen lights illuminated two cars jammed together nose to nose. A man lay sprawled on the pavement next to an open driver's door.

Seconds later, a fist pounded on the back door and a man yelled, "Please, help! Please, help!"

The plea drew Shakir two steps at a time down the stairs. Four jabs at the alarm pad and he pushed the door open.

The first punch caught him under his rib cage.

The call shook Gage and Faith awake at 2 A.M.

"Boss." Alex Z's voice was shaking, choking, verging on tears. "It's about Shakir."

Gage sat up.

"What happened?"

"He's hurt. Really hurt. The ambulance is here. I'll ride with him."

Gage called Viz as he and Faith drove toward San Francisco Medical Center.

"Looks like some crooks faked an accident to trick Shakir into letting them in. Head down to the office. Make sure the police don't get into anything they shouldn't. If you can't control them, call Spike."

Twenty-five minutes later they walked into the emergency room teeming with the night's sick and damaged, the air a miasma of sweat and pain and fear. Alex Z sat in a plastic chair, staring at the cell phone in his hand. He looked over as they worked their way down the crowded aisle.

"I called his parents in Boston," Alex Z said, then glanced at his watch. "They'll take the first flight out they can get seats on."

"What are the doctors saying?"

"Nothing. They won't talk to me because I'm not family."

Faith sat down and reached her arm around Alex Z as Gage strode toward the reception station. He scanned the on-duty board behind the receptionist as he approached. He stood by the counter until he was certain the clerk was ignoring his presence as she made notes in a chart, and then said, "I'd like to speak to Dr. Kishore."

"I can't call her," the woman said, eyes still down.

"I'm her brother-in-law. There's a family problem I need to talk to her about."

The woman finally looked up. "Yeah, and I'm Mother Teresa."

Gage glared at her. "You want to make the call or roll the dice?"

He'd never understood why, but the phrase seemed to unnerve people more than an actual threat.

The woman snorted, then picked up the phone and punched a three-number extension.

"There's a guy here to see Dr. Kishore." She smirked at Gage. "What's your name, brother-in-law?"

"Graham Gage."

She repeated his name into the receiver.

Ten minutes later, Dr. Ajita Kishore walked through the ICU double doors, still wearing her surgical scrubs. She smiled as she approached Gage. It wasn't the first time they'd talked in that hallway.

"How was the flight from Mumbai?" Kishore's British-Indian tone was droll.

"Quick."

"What can I—"

"Shakir Mohammed."

Kishore's smile died. "I didn't work on him myself. I only saw the before and after. Somebody really beat on him. We had to remove his spleen and sew up a puncture to his left lung. Forty stitches on his face. He'll remember this night every time he looks in the mirror."

Gage exhaled. At least Shakir would live to remember it. He nodded at Alex Z, who clasped his hands together.

"He arrived in a lot better shape than your friend Jack Burch," Kishore said. Gage had first met Kishore when the international corporate lawyer was gunned down in a gangster's attempt to contain a securities fraud investigation. "And his recovery will be a lot quicker."

"When can I talk to him?"

"It'll be a couple of hours." Kishore glanced back at the double doors. "I've got to get back inside. I'll make sure someone calls you if anything changes."

Gage turned as Faith and Alex Z walked up after Kishore returned to the ICU.

"He'll be okay," Gage told them.

Alex Z hung his head.

"It's my fault. I shouldn't have left him there alone. He's too new."

"What happened?"

"I don't know. I stopped by on the way back from our gig at Slim's to check on him. The back door was open. But not like somebody busted it. I found Shakir in his office. Tied to a chair. Unconscious. Soaked with water." Faith reached up and covered her mouth as the same horrifying thought entered each of their minds: The burglars had knocked out Shakir, and then tried to revive him in order to interrogate him further; maybe they even succeeded.

Alex Z dropped his head into his hands and started to cry. He wiped his eyes on his sleeve and said, "Sorry, boss." He swallowed hard. "And there's something else. His and my computers are missing."

Shakir gazed from his ICU bed at Gage and Alex Z. It had been seven hours since the surgeon had finished putting him back together. Faith had gone back across the bay to teach a morning class.

Gage could see only Shakir's eyes, the bottom of his nose, and his mouth. The rest of his face with its dark, delicate features was wrapped in bandages. Two IVs fed into his arms. One for saline, the other for morphine.

Gage took his hand and sat down next to the bed.

"Tell me what happened," Gage said.

"Car accident . . . pounding on back door . . . I thought injury . . . men rushed in . . . wanted files."

"Could you recognize them again?"

"Masked."

Shakir tried to lick his lips. Gage wet the sponge end of an oral swab and moistened Shakir's mouth.

"Voices?" Gage asked.

"One . . . New York. . . . One . . . kind of Southern."

"Why'd they beat you up?"

"Security code for . . . for the storage room."

Gage looked at Alex Z, who shook his head. He hadn't given Shakir the number. No matter how or how long they tortured him, they'd never get it.

"What files?"

"Charlie Palmer's."

"Did they get your computer password?"

Shakir nodded. "I'm sorry. My computer, too."

Alex Z spoke up. "No problem. Everything is replaceable. We have backups on the server." He looked down at Shakir. "Did they get your file encryption key?"

A flicker of a smile appeared on Shakir's bruised lips.

"No."

* * *

Gage and Alex Z stood in the hallway outside Shakir's room.

"Stay with him," Gage whispered. "The nurse has notified the detectives he's awake. Tell Shakir it's okay to talk about the antitrust case, but play dumb about what else you two were working on. Otherwise this thing might spin out of control. I don't want to see Brandon Meyer's name on the front page of the *Chronicle* tomorrow."

Gage turned as footsteps came to a stop behind him. He faced a man who appeared to be a twenty-five-year-older version of Shakir and three inches shorter. His eyes were red, his brown suit was rumpled, the oversized knot of his tie hung an inch below his collar, and his fists were locked at his sides.

"You . . ." The Middle Eastern–accented voice caught. Behind him a woman stood twisting a handkerchief in her hands. A black hijab framed her face. "You . . . you did this."

"It was my fault," Gage said. "I didn't do a good enough job of teaching him our security procedures. I hope you and your wife will forgive me someday."

Shakir's father didn't respond, just stood there looking up at Gage.

His mother stepped forward and asked, "How is he?"

"He has a long road ahead of him, but the doctor says he'll be fine."

"Can we . . ."

Gage nodded, and then Alex Z opened Shakir's door and Gage followed them inside.

* * *

When Gage returned to the waiting room he spotted Alex Z sitting with a thirty-year-old uniformed Filipino cop. He first thought the officer was trying to pry information from Alex Z, but then noticed the officer's eyes were vacant, his slim body was rigid in his seat, and his hands were folded in his lap.

Alex Z caught the motion of Gage walking toward them and rose. The officer followed.

"This is Rodrigo, he's . . ." Alex Z glanced toward the ICU where Shakir's parents remained. "He's Shakir's partner."

Rodrigo shook Gage's hand, then shrugged, his face pained.

"Shakir's parents don't know," Rodrigo said. "His father couldn't deal with it." He took in a long breath, then exhaled. "And he's a hard man. He'd never let Shakir see his mother again."

"You work swing shift?" Gage asked.

"How'd you guess?"

"It explains why Shakir wanted to." Gage read Rodrigo's nameplate: R. Balatico. "Your name is familiar. You have a relative in the department back when I was there?"

Rodrigo shook his head.

"He was on the news a couple of months ago," Alex Z said. "The armored truck robbery outside of Macy's at Union Square."

Gage smiled. "It didn't cross your mind to duck behind a car when those crooks came running out of the store?"

Rodrigo blushed, then tilted his head back to emphasize the six-inch height gap between him and Gage. "I figured I was a small target."

"Not for a shotgun."

Rodrigo sighed. "So I realized in my nightmares for the next week."

Gage reached out and gripped Rodrigo's upper arm.

"Be careful," Gage said. "There's a guy down the hallway who needs you."

Boots Marnin stared at the two computers standing together in the corner of his Mariner Hotel room, thinking life was a whole lot simpler when you could get everything you wanted by sticking a gun in your target's ear. Now most of the guys who made the big bucks at his end of the market never left their keyboards, they just hacked their way in, mined for information, then sold it on contract or to the highest bidder.

I'm a forty-year-old dinosaur.

He inspected his alligator-skin Tony Lamas, then smirked at the irony.

Maybe it's survival of the fittest after all.

He reached for his cell phone and scrolled to a number. The man on the other end of the line didn't answer so much as grunt.

"It's me," Marnin said. "I got it."

"Palmer's computer?"

"A couple of Gage's. Everything from Palmer's was copied over to it. A kid decided to cooperate and told us."

"What about Palmer's?"

"We'd need explosives to get to it."

"Then let's cross that bridge when we come to it. First we need to find out what kind of records Palmer was keeping. We can torch Gage's place if we have to."

"Where should I—"

"Evergreen Security in San Jose. We got an ex-NSA guy down there who can break into anybody's hard drive. Somebody'll meet you in the parking lot."

"I don't know why they're going through all this. Why don't they just wipe the slate clean and start over with a new team? Couple of bodies. Done in an afternoon—and their mistakes buried with them."

"That would be sheer genius. You know the last time somebody got away with killing a federal judge?" He paused. "I'll tell you. Never."

Gage sat alone at his breakfast table, drinking coffee, and reading Skeeter Hall's fourteen-year-old file about the refinery explosion: the Richmond Fire Department reports recounting the recovery of the nearly incinerated bodies, the OSHA investigation showing that the root cause of the explosion was a failed pressure release device, the depositions of the TIMCO International Petroleum officers and refinery managers, and, finally, the deposition of John Porzolkiewski and his repeating over and over, "Money won't bring my son back." And Brandon Meyer, then the TIMCO lawyer, demanding, "What do you want?" And Porzolkiewski answering, "Nothing. I want nothing."

Gage next examined the court file, the transcript of the Superior Court Judge's Order of Dismissal, an apologetic:

> My hands are tied. This is simply a workers' comp case. The people of California made a trade a generation ago. In exchange for

guaranteed compensation, they waived their right to sue their employers in the event of their own injury or the death of a loved one.

The Plaintiffs have failed to prove the exceptional circumstances required by law. Even the minimal threshold, showing *prima facie* that management had created unsafe working conditions, has not been met by the Plaintiffs.

Notwithstanding how horrendous the consequences may have been, the Occupational Safety and Health investigation is dispositive: This is simply a matter of "accidents happen." Maybe even an accident waiting to happen. Nonetheless, this incident appears to be precisely what was envisioned by the Workers' Compensation Law.

Case dismissed.

Clearly, Gage thought, John Porzolkiewski didn't believe OSHA's claim that this was an accident that just happened. What he surely believed was that the root cause of his suffering wasn't a faulty valve and a spark, but Brandon Meyer—and that he wasn't acting alone.

Five minutes after Gage left the Sacramento Delta home of Ray Karopian later that afternoon, the retired OSHA inspector drove to a pay phone two miles away. But like a shoplifter in Home Depot, he noticed a thousand eyes but not the ones actually watching him.

"A private investigator was just here about

TIMCO," Karopian told the man at the other end of the line.

"What did you tell him?"

"You think I'm an idiot? You think I suddenly made up a new story after all these years?"

"Okay, okay. Take it easy. What's his name?"

"Graham Gage from—"

"I know where he's from."

"How do you—"

"I don't have time to talk about it. Call me if he comes back. And don't use your real name."

Viz and Alex Z were sitting at Gage's conference table when he arrived at the office from the Sacramento Delta.

"What's going on with Shakir?" Gage asked Alex Z, after he sat down.

"Dr. Kishore came by to see him this morning when I was there," Alex Z said. "She seems satisfied with his progress. She grinned at me just before she left and asked when your return flight to Mumbai was." He made a show of scratching his head. "I didn't have a clue what she meant."

Gage shrugged, then smiled. "I'm sort of like her brother-in-law."

"I still don't get it."

Viz reached over and squeezed Alex Z's shoulder, "Don't worry kid, I think this is one of those times where we're just gonna have to go with the flow." He then pointed at Gage's TIMCO file. "What did the OSHA man say?"

"That the pressure release device on the valve failed and the whole thing blew apart. Kerosene splashed down onto the scrubber motor and a spark set off the fire. They never even found all the pieces."

"Then how do they—"

"They pulled one off another line afterward and concluded that's all it could've been."

"What about the plaintiff's experts?"

"They couldn't come up with anything definitive to counter it."

"What about maintenance records?" Alex Z asked. "When was the last time they inspected the valve before it blew?"

"About a month. They did the annual turn-around, shut the tower down and inspected—" Gage caught himself. "Makes me wonder how well they inspected it."

"I'm no expert in workers' comp law," Viz said, "but that would still be just a screw-up on the part of some worker. How would that implicate management in creating dangerous working conditions?"

"It doesn't, but it's a place to start." Gage looked at Alex Z. "They deposed a welder in the shop, Wilbert Hawkins. He testified he inspected the release valve, but didn't see anything wrong with it. He went off to work in an oil field in Pakistan. Find out where he is now."

Viz pointed at Skeeter Hall's file. "What do you think the case would've been worth if the judge hadn't dismissed it?"

"Skeeter thinks TIMCO would have settled for ten million dollars, but he could've taken it to trial and got thirty."

"*If* they could have gotten the case to a jury."

"Yeah," Gage said. "If . . ."

* * *

Alex Z appeared at Gage's door two hours later, shaking his head.

"Hawkins never came back from Pakistan, boss. It's like he evaporated."

The strap of Jeannette Hawkins's yellow-flowered shift slipped off her shoulder as she pulled open her front door. Her half-exposed left breast lay sagging against her chest like a flag at half-mast. She shifted her Budweiser bottle into her left hand, hoisted up the strap, then looked up at Gage standing on her porch.

"I paid it already," she said.

"I'm not—"

"I paid the car note. Leave me alone."

Gage glanced over at the 1993 faded red Ford Fiesta parked on the hard-packed front yard of the hillside bungalow in north Richmond. He then took in the cracked concrete leading to the sagging front steps and the tan paint peeling from the weathered clapboard siding. The front right corner of the roof was covered with a blue tarp. Cigarette butts littered the porch like spilled popcorn.

"I'm not here about the car," Gage said. "I'm looking for your husband."

"*Ex* . . . Ex-husband . . . Ex-son-of-a-bitch husband." She inspected Gage. "Who're you?"

Gage reached into the pocket of his brown corduroy workshirt and pulled out his business card. She accepted it in her veined hand, but ignored it. Instead she stared at his shirt.

"That a Carhartt?"

He nodded.

"Son of a Bitch used to wear Carhartt every day over at TIMCO. Like a uniform." She squinted at Gage. "You're not from TIMCO, are you? I already got my check. I don't figure I have to keep saying thanks in person."

Gage pointed at his card in her hand. "I'm a private investigator."

"Big deal." She looked down at it, then extended it in front of her to allow her fifty-plus-year-old eyes to focus. "Anybody can make one of these. You got some ID?"

Gage reached into his front jeans pocket, withdrew his ID case, then flipped it open, displaying his California private investigator's license. She grabbed for it, but he pulled it away. "Sorry. No touching." He didn't want to wrestle with her to get it back.

"Why do you want to talk to Son of a Bitch?"

"It's about something that happened a long time ago," Gage said. "You know where he is?"

Jeannette lifted the beer to her mouth and took a sip while peering at him with narrowed eyes. The bottle made a popping sound when she pulled it away.

"What thing that happened a long time ago?"

She said the words in a tone communicating that other than Son of a Bitch running off, only one thing of any significance had ever happened in her life, and she had only been at the edge of it.

"Over at the refinery," Gage said.

"Can't help ya, pal. He's gone, gone, gone."

"As in dead, dead, dead?"

"Naw, just dead gone." She grinned, then eyed his left hand. "You married?"

"You looking?"

"Does pork fat come off a pig?"

Two Harley-Davidsons downshifted up the short hill; the syncopated chugging of their V-twins vibrated the house. Gage turned to see black Hell's Angels vests disappear over the crest.

"You wanna come in?" Jeannette asked.

Gage smiled. "You're not going to try to seduce me, are you? My wife won't let me go out and play anymore."

Jeannette winked. "We'll see."

Gage followed her as she backed into the house. It smelled of beer, cigarette ashes, and dog pee, the odors Gage went to sleep with as a rookie cop the night after his first day on the job. It couldn't be washed off and stuck to those old wool uniforms like epoxy. That was one of the reasons he'd decided to wear a cotton shirt and Levi's.

She pointed to the couch. "You can move those newspapers."

Gage was surprised. He hadn't taken her for a reader, and she wasn't. They were months-old *Auto Trader*s she apparently used to shop for the Fiesta.

"You wanna beer?" she asked, walking toward the kitchen and stepping over a Slurpee cup.

"Sure."

Gage watched her open the refrigerator, pull out two Budweisers, then twist off the caps. She headed back with the two bottles and handed one to Gage. He lifted it toward her, then took a sip.

As she lowered herself into a green upholstered Barcalounger, her shoulder strap slipped off again. She left it there, then peeked over at Gage and grinned.

"It do anything for you?"

Gage shook his head. "I'm not allowed to look."

She pulled it up.

He took another sip, then waited for her to take one.

"You know where he is?"

"Sorta. He's in one of them rag-head countries."

"You know which one?"

"I'm not good with geography. My son is though."

"Is he around?"

"Nope. County jail."

"How come?"

"Got wrongly accused of touching a little girl—at least that's what he says. But I don't believe him about that any more than I believed his father about anything."

"Has Wilbert called lately?"

Jeannette's brows furrowed. "Wilbert?"

She said the name with such puzzlement Gage thought for a half second he'd misremembered Hawkins's first name.

"Wilbert?" She laughed. "I've been calling him

Son of a Bitch for so many years I almost forgot his name was Wilbert." She shook her head, a smirk twisting her mouth. "What a stupid name for a guy born in Marin County."

She squinted toward the tan phone hanging on the kitchen wall.

"Yeah, he called three years ago. On my daughter's thirteenth birthday." She snorted. "He should've spent the money on child support."

"Where is she?"

Jeannette stared at the clock on the mantel of the trash-filled fireplace. "Let's see, she got off work at Wendy's about a half hour ago, then she was going to pick up my pills at the Walgreens . . . Let's see . . ." She tapped her finger against her chin as if thinking through her daughter's after work route, then looked back at Gage. "I know exactly where she is. She's screwing her thirty-six-year-old biker boyfriend in the garage he calls an apartment."

Gage glanced up at framed baby photos of the children on either side of the clock, innocent eyes gazing out at the wreckage their lives had become, and then changed the subject.

"Did Son of a Bitch leave an emergency number?"

Jeannette lowered her bottle to the armrest. Her eyes slid from Gage's face to his Carhartt shirt, then held there. She breathed in and out like a kid gathering up courage to race across a railroad track just ahead of a train.

"Yeah, you can have it. I don't owe any of them shit. None of them suits from TIMCO ever sat down in my house and had a beer with me."

sn't this kind of a long shot?" Faith asked as she drove Gage toward the San Francisco International Airport. They were traveling south past the 49ers' stadium, dropping down to the gray stretch of freeway bordering the bay. The afternoon traffic crept along, more stop than go.

"Of course it's a long shot," Gage said. "But at worst it costs the price of a flight and a few days of jet lag."

Faith flicked on the radio to check the traffic report in order to decide whether to slip onto the frontage road and skirt the backup. It was tuned to National Public Radio broadcasting one of a series of interviews of leading presidential candidates. It was Landon Meyer's turn. She reached to change to the A.M. news channel, but Gage said, "Hold on. Let's see what he has to say."

"*I'd like to start with your first campaign for Congress, your victory over Democratic incumbent Nelson Hedges. It's still the closest race in California history.*"

"It stands as a lesson that every vote counts." Landon chuckled. *"Well, at least the last twelve."*

"Were you aware during the campaign that Congressman Hedges had been diagnosed with ALS?"

"I didn't learn about it until his announcement on the day he left Congress."

Gage shook his head. "Amazing guy. He's still keeping his promise even though Hedges has been dead for years. I'll bet he's never even told Brandon."

Hedges had called Landon to come to his hotel near Stanford Hospital at midnight on the day he was diagnosed. The two talked and prayed together until past midnight. Landon promised neither to disclose nor to exploit it during the campaign.

"Did you learn any lessons from that election, Senator?"

The night concierge had spotted Landon exiting the lobby elevator at 2 A.M., a step behind a familiar prostitute from a local escort service.

Landon had called Gage moments after the first extortion attempt eight hours later.

"Yes. An extremely useful one. Elections often turn on events the public never sees."

Gage discovered the night's surveillance tape missing. He tracked it to the apartment of the guard who'd been on duty, where it was hidden with a dozen other tapes of guilty public figures who'd been blackmailed, and innocent ones like Landon who'd been extorted.

"And they depend on people you've never met before, but who become trusted friends for life."

Faith pointed ahead to a stalled car on the shoulder a quarter mile ahead and the traffic clearing beyond it, then glanced over at Gage.

"There are just too many ifs to justify a trip half-way around the world," Faith said.

"They're either ifs or they're links in a chain." Gage switched off the radio. "Porzolkiewski is the key to Charlie getting shot and I'm pretty sure he's got a copy of whatever was in Brandon Meyer's wallet."

"Is this about Charlie or Brandon? For a while I was wondering whether you were being driven by self-reproach for not insisting that Tansy let you prove it was Charlie who subverted the prosecution of those kids. But now I'm starting to think it's really about Brandon."

"Brandon's a pipsqueak. Landon never should have gotten him appointed in the first place. Sometimes Landon is just blind to what he's really doing." Gage's voice hardened. "And it wasn't the first time someone in the Meyer family sacrificed the public good to a private one."

"That makes me think you might be looking for a way to turn this into your father's last revenge."

One of the first things Faith had learned about Gage's father was his fury at the Meyer family, once the General Motors of the arms manufacturing industry. As a combat surgeon during World War II, George Gage witnessed the consequences of their weapons sales to Germany, many made after the Nazis' criminal intentions were clear. Only the intervention of the secretary of state prevented the indictment of Brandon and Landon's grandfather in 1941 under the Trading with the Enemy Act.

"I'm not looking to punish Brandon for his family's sins," Gage said, "and I certainly don't want to hurt Landon. And I'm only interested in Brandon to the extent he's the link between Porzolkiewski and Charlie."

Gage fell silent. He watched a plane rise from the runway, then his eyes lowered to an unseeing stare at the dashboard.

"What?" she finally asked. "Porzolkiewski?"

Gage nodded.

"Your heart goes out to him, doesn't it."

He turned toward her. "What could be worse than believing somebody got away with killing your child? I don't think anything has felt real to him since the day his son died. The only thing now connecting him to the world is anger."

"You think he'll be able to see his way clear to cooperate with you when you get back?"

"I don't know. At least he didn't go running out of the coffee shop yesterday when I sat down at his table to tell him I was going to look for a way to reopen the TIMCO case. The most important thing in his life is finding out what happened."

"You mean confirming what he already believes."

"He's not the only one. I reread the superior court judge's order dismissing the suit. I know judge-speak. He said 'my hands are tied' and 'this incident appears' to be an accident—not *is*, only *appears*—and he said the explosion was 'maybe even an accident waiting to happen.' Which tells me he didn't believe TIMCO. It was just that Porzolkiewski's lawyers hadn't made a strong enough showing so the judge could've let the case go to a jury."

"I don't know." Faith shook her head, then glanced over again. "How can you be so sure Porzolkiewski will tell you what really happened with Charlie if you deliver on your promise? What if the truth about TIMCO isn't what he thinks it is? Accidents waiting to happen can still be just accidents."

CHAPTER 24

Jeanette Hawkins was wrong. Son of a Bitch wasn't in an Islamic country. Gage had recognized it the moment she'd handed him the yellowed slip of paper bearing the telephone number. He'd also seen the hand of genius: laundering a witness through Muslim Pakistan, then depositing him in its Hindu enemy.

It was the overripe end of mango season in southern India when Gage arrived at the Rajiv Gandhi Airport outside Hyderabad. Vendors were selling juice and sodas from carts bordering the parking lot in front of the arrivals hall. Between them and Gage as he walked out of the automatic doors was a mass of men in short-sleeved shirts and women in saris standing pressed up against a low metal barrier. A dozen taxi drivers swarmed him, grabbing at his forearms to lead him toward their cars. Porters wearing dhotis tied around their thighs and pulled up between their legs reached for his rollaboard. He shook them off as he scanned past the hotel placards held up by drivers bearing the names of arriving business travelers, but he couldn't find the face he was looking for.

Instead, the face found him.

Gage grasped that customs superintendent Basaam Khan was standing behind him when the drivers and porters backed away. He turned toward a stubby man in a crisp white shirt and brown slacks, then reached out his hand, smiling. "Babu."

Khan was the youngest child in a family of ten who'd stayed in India after the partition in 1947, when millions of Hindus fled from Pakistan and an equal number of Muslims fled in the opposite direction into India. He was among the forty percent of the population of Hyderabad who were Muslim. As the youngest son, he was simply known among friends and relatives as Babu. Sonny in English.

Babu pushed aside Gage's hand, then hugged him, his head reaching only the middle of Gage's chest. When they separated, Gage could see Babu had gained twenty pounds since they last worked together.

Gage pointed at his stomach. "Married life?"

Babu nodded, proud not only that his happiness was reflected in his body, but that his parents had allowed him to choose his own bride.

Babu took Gage's briefcase out of his hand, and then led him along the barrier and through the opening toward a white Ambassador taxi, a five-year-old four-door sedan of the lumpy style manufactured in the U.S. in the 1940s. The driver set Gage's rollaboard inside the trunk. Gage and Babu climbed into the back. The seat was coved by a clean, white sheet, pulled tight and tucked in.

They didn't talk about Wilbert Hawkins as they drove from the airport and along Hussain Sagar Lake, the city's main water supply, toward the hotel. There was no reason to share the purpose of Gage's trip with the taxi driver. Instead, they talked quietly and cryptically about their last case, a multimillion-dollar diamond theft out of New York when Babu was deputy superintendent of customs at the Hyderabad Airport.

Gage had tracked the diamond cutter-turned-thief from Singapore to Bangkok, and finally to Hyderabad, then hired a local lawyer to analyze the legal issues involved in getting a warrant to search the man's house. The judge decided Gage hadn't met the probable cause standards imported into the Indian criminal code from British common law because Gage had no witness to testify that the man had the diamonds with him.

The judge suggested Gage speak with Babu, who reviewed the evidence, examined the law, considered the various legal options, and then kidnapped the thief's wife and imprisoned her in the squalid, lice-ridden central jail until the man surrendered both himself and the diamonds.

All but a single twenty-thousand-dollar gem was recovered.

The insurance company hadn't objected to Babu deducting his commission, they just wished they'd had the opportunity to offer it first.

Gage hadn't objected either. He knew someday having an Indian cop in his debt would eventually pay off.

And that day had come.

Babu pointed toward the windshield. A hundred yards in front of them on the Tank Bund Road bordering the lake, a sash-wearing young Muslim rode a galloping white horse to his wedding. Babu then tapped his chest and smiled, indicating that he, too, had taken the same ride.

They lost sight of the groom as they turned into the tree-lined driveway of the colonial-era Viceroy Hotel.

Only when seated in Gage's seventh floor room overlooking the earth-toned city did Babu mention Wilbert Hawkins.

"He is still living in Gannapalli," Babu said. "I'm not sure he is leaving the village since he finished building his house." Babu spread his hands. "Why he is picking the second hottest district in all of India, I am not understanding."

"Probably because it's the last place anyone would think he'd hide."

Babu grinned, his head working a slight figure eight, the Indian head bob variously meaning *I understand*, or *Yes*, or *Maybe*. "That, and the women, no?"

The forty-minute drive west from Hyderabad toward Gannapalli in Babu's Land Cruiser took them from the cool world of offshore Web designers to the scorched farmland of those whose lives were measured not by digital clocks, but by the gestation periods of cattle and the growing seasons of rice.

Villagers dragged flat wooden carts piled with coconuts and potatoes toward the city, while others pulled empty ones back to the countryside. Cows and buffaloes grazed along the undivided two-lane road. Travelers waited for buses in whirlwinds of dust while breathing diesel fumes belching from aging truck engines, and the occasional monkey begged for food from laborers gathered under the shade of axelwood and laurel trees.

"Have you decided on an approach?" Babu asked as he turned north from the highway toward Gannapalli.

"You mean since there's no one to kidnap?" Gage said.

Babu pulled away, as if offended. "I am under-standing from you last time that investigation is an art, a matter of applying the correct technique at the proper time. I am not a one-trick horse." He grinned at Gage and asked, "Horse?"

"Pony. A one-trick pony."

"Yes, indeed, a one-trick pony."

Wilbert Hawkins didn't expect to find a white man sitting in his living room when he woke from his afternoon nap.

It hadn't been difficult for Gage and Babu to obtain entry. The low-caste ten-year-old servant girl had cowered at the sight of them fifteen min-utes earlier, then backed away from the front door, eyes down.

The stucco house stood three stories tall on the edge of the town of ten thousand people bordering rice paddies and mango gardens; the rice tended by girls and women with their saris pulled up to their knees as they waded the shallow fields, the trees swarmed by young men in dhotis and sandals.

And Babu had known right where to find the house.

Hawkins was still rubbing his eyes as he walked from the kitchen and through the dining room carrying a bottle of Kingfisher beer. He first spot-ted Gage's briefcase on the marble living room floor, then took two more steps before he froze as his eyes first widened and then narrowed on Gage sitting on a bamboo-frame cushioned couch to his right.

Gage recognized the remnants of the oil field

scrapper displayed in the fifteen-year-old photo his wife had provided. Sixty-three years of weathered skin hung on his thin body. Wire-rimmed, aviator-style glasses and a receding hairline framed his face. Skinny arms extended from the sweaty T-shirt encasing his pot belly.

Gage rose as Hawkins stepped into the room. Babu remained seated.

"What the hell are you doing in my . . ." Hawkins didn't finish the sentence. They all knew the answer.

Gage handed him a business card.

"TIMCO," Gage said.

Hawkins frowned as he examined it, then shook his head as he looked up.

"I've got nothing to say."

Having made his stand, Hawkins gestured for Gage to sit back down and settled himself into a lounge chair along the wall dividing the living room from the dining area.

Hawkins whistled, and a thirteen-year-old girl strode in from the kitchen, past the dining table, and into the living room as though she was the queen of the house rather than a servant. She was wearing a full sari of an adult woman, not the half sari of a teenage girl. She stopped in the doorway next to Hawkins's chair.

"Beer? Coke?" Hawkins asked.

Gage and Babu both nodded at Coke, then the girl went back the way she'd come.

"You guys got something else to talk about besides TIMCO, I got lots of time." He grinned. "That, I got a whole lot of. Information? Zip."

"Just to make sure we're on the same page," Gage

said. "I think you know what really caused the explosion at TIMCO."

Hawkins rolled his eyes. "You didn't have to travel all this way through this godforsaken country when you could've read that in my deposition."

Gage sat forward, then aimed a forefinger at Hawkins's face. "You lied during your deposition."

Hawkins's face flared. "So Porzolkiewski's lawyers said, but they couldn't prove shit."

Gage glanced over at Babu, then fixed his eyes on Hawkins. "I don't have time to screw around."

He opened his briefcase and took out an eight-by-ten photograph taken by Babu four days earlier. It was a view into Hawkins's bedroom on a night too hot to close the drapes.

Gage rose, took two steps, loomed over Hawkins, and then dropped it in his lap.

Just then, the girl walked up behind Hawkins carrying a hammered aluminum tray bearing two Cokes. She looked down at the photo, wild-eyed, mouth gaping open. The tray fell from her hands. The bottles exploded on the marble floor.

The photo showed her on top of Hawkins. Legs spread over his face, his penis in her mouth. She darted toward the front door. Babu leaped up, grabbed her by the arms, and swung her down on the couch in one motion.

Hawkins stared at the image, not bothering to wipe the soda spray off his face and arms. He finally looked up at Gage, forcing a smile.

"When in Rome . . ."

Gage reached down and yanked Hawkins up by his T-shirt, stretching it to its limits. Hawkins hung backward, suspended, gasping, flailing. Gage dropped him in his chair, then backed away, and locked his hands on his hips.

"You know how much time you could get for child molesting?" Gage said.

Hawkins looked past Gage toward the front door. "The police here won't do anything." Hawkins returned his eyes to Gage. His voice strengthened. "They don't care. I pay them not to care. Hell, girls around here get married at nine."

Gage shook his head. "Not here. In the States."

Hawkins straightened himself in the chair.

"There's no way India's gonna extradite me to the U.S. for coming over here to screw these girls. Brings in too much money. Bombay is the new Bangkok. Just check the Internet. The worst they'll do is tell me to lay off." Hawkins shrugged. "So maybe I got to pay off some prosecutor. So what?"

"Not child molesting here, you idiot. In Richmond. Your kids."

Hawkins's jaws clenched.

Gage walked over to his briefcase and pulled out a criminal complaint charging Wilbert Hawkins with molesting John Doe and Jane Doe, forged by Alex Z a couple of hours after Gage had left Jeannette's house.

Hawkins's eighteen-year-old son awaiting trial for fondling little girls. His teenage daughter screwing thirty-year-old men. It wasn't hard to figure out how it all started.

Gage tossed the complaint at Hawkins. He grabbed at it too late.

Hawkins picked the Coke-soaked pages from the

floor. Shaking hands jerked them around in front of his face, making it hard to focus his eyes.

He got the point anyway.

"Relax," Gage said. "Nobody knows where you are . . . except me." Gage pointed at Babu. "And him."

Gage reached into his pocket and pulled out a tape recorder.

"You're going to tell me what happened at TIMCO, who ordered it, and who sent you out of the country." Gage paused, then scanned the furniture, the marble floor, and the half-dozen girl servants now gathered at the kitchen door. "And how you're paying for all this."

As they were driving away from Gannapalli two hours later, Babu let out a sigh.

"I only was kidnapping a wife, but you . . ." He glanced over at Gage, then shook his head. "You crushed that man."

O f course there's a litmus test. Only fools think there isn't."

Senator Landon Meyer pulled the phone away from his ear, then glared at it as if it were the idiot, not the Republican National Committee member on the other end of the line. He spoke into it again: "There are a half-dozen litmus tests this time around: abortion, gay marriage, stem cell research, terrorism, assisted suicide, prayer in schools—you think I chose Starsky and Hutch for their good looks?"

Landon slammed down the phone.

Screw these people. I was elected senator in a Democratic state because of a litmus test.

It was called the death penalty, and he never let thoughts of that election drift too far from his consciousness for fear he'd begin to take the gifts of chance for granted.

As soon as Senator Doris Wagner called for a moratorium on executions, the election was over. Maybe not that day, but no later than the following one when a maniac murdered six students and two teachers at a Compton elementary school. The Democratic base began to collapse when African-American political leaders prayed for the revenge they called justice on the schoolhouse steps—that and a last-minute revelation that fifty thousand dollars wired into Wagner's campaign bank account early in the year had originated with Arab charities under FBI investigation for supporting jihadists.

Landon picked up the telephone again. His brother answered on the first ring.

The next morning Senator Landon Meyer, federal judge Brandon Meyer, and Senator Blanche Zweck, chair of the National Republican Senatorial Committee, sat on facing couches in Landon's office. Half-empty china cups of now cold coffee lay on the low table along with an oversized spreadsheet. Only forty-six senators were committed to vote for Starsky and Hutch, five short of confirmation. Forty-four against. Ten undecided, and seven of those up for reelection.

"I don't see it," Zweck said. "It's political suicide for at least four of the seven on abortion and the Patriot Act alone. Women and liberals in those states will gang up, and hard-line don't-trust-the-government conservatives will stay away from the polls. The cost of getting our own voters to show up would be astronomical."

"That's why Brandon is here," Landon said.

"We're talking maybe an extra twenty million dollars." Zweck shook her head. "There's no way we'll get it, not with a presidential election coming up. Too many of us are chasing the same money. Contributors are already feeling like punching bags."

"As I said, that's why Brandon is here."

Brandon leaned in toward the table. His crowlike eyes peered up at Zweck.

"If you can come up with five million," Brandon said, "I'll find the rest."

Zweck shook her head again. "The president needs this vote in a matter of weeks. He wants to push it through like a tsunami before the opposition gets organized. The swing senators aren't going to carry IOUs out on a limb that skinny. They'll want money in the bank. No way you're going to raise fifteen million dollars that fast."

Landon dropped into the high-backed black leather chair behind his desk after Zweck left the office, then looked over Brandon.

"Will you need to dip into our own money?"

"I don't think so." Brandon stood and stretched. He hadn't slept on the red-eye from San Francisco. "But so what if we do? You get Starsky and Hutch onto the Supreme Court and Duncan will bless you as the next presidential nominee. That'll save us fifty million in primary costs alone. Maybe more." Brandon smiled. "Call it an investment of real political capital."

"How long is it going to take to come up with what you promised Zweck?"

"A week, maybe. A little money committed to us slipped away a couple of months ago."

"How?"

"It's not important. We'll get it back in time."

"Fifteen million isn't small change."

Brandon gazed down through the office window toward the Supreme Court.

"Don't worry. We'll get it. We have no choice."

It was only after Brandon was halfway back to California that Landon remembered he'd wanted to ask him if he ever got his wallet back.

This time John Porzolkiewski opened his front door wide. He surveyed Gage, then shook his head and smiled.

"You look like hell."

"A little jet lag is all."

Porzolkiewski's smile faded.

"You got something new," Porzolkiewski said, "or are we just going to be like hamsters chasing each other around in one of those wire wheels."

"Something new."

Porzolkiewski shrugged, then stepped back. "Suit yourself."

Gage walked inside and found a living room reminding him of his grandmother's in Nogales in the 1970s, except for the cats rubbing their sides against his legs. Not a sofa, but a huge flowered davenport covered in plastic. Not wing chairs, but two brown leather recliners facing an old-style television in a console. He had the feeling that Porzolkiewski had preserved the room just the way it was on the day his wife died.

Porzolkiewski directed Gage toward a lace-covered dining table. He walked to the head and pushed aside his half-eaten chicken and rice dinner, then motioned Gage to sit to his left and sat down.

Gage reached into his suit pocket and set his digital recorder on the table between them.

Porzolkiewski held his palms up to Gage. "Even if I had something to say, which I don't, I wouldn't say it on tape." He folded his arms across his chest.

"It's not for recording," Gage said, "it's for playing."

Porzolkiewski's face brightened. It struck Gage that he was probably once a charming man.

"But," Gage continued, "I want to cut a deal. Part of what you have for part of what I have."

Porzolkiewski's eyes narrowed. "Why only parts?"

"Because if you knew it all, you might get a gun and kill someone."

"So I guess one part isn't you trying to get me to say I shot Charlie Palmer."

"For the moment, let's classify his death as a kind of suicide."

"Now I'm confused. I thought Palmer was the point of you coming by the first time."

Gage shook his head. "Not entirely."

"Then what is it you want?"

"Judge Meyer's wallet."

"I told you I don't have it." Porzolkiewski paused, and then pointed a forefinger at Gage. "I'll give you something for free. And it's really true. Two guys came by after Palmer did. They gave me ten grand and I gave it to them."

A piece fell out of the puzzle Gage had put together in his mind. Meyer already had his wallet back when he called Gage in. Gage shoved the piece back in a different direction. Maybe Meyer just didn't want to explain how he got it.

"How about copies?" Gage asked.

Porzolkiewski smiled. "Let's see your part first."

"If it accounts for what happened at TIMCO, will you give them to me?"

"If I believe it."

Gage didn't like making decisions when he was jet-lagged, but he had years of reading faces and he knew that underneath Porzolkiewski's anger was a very sad man.

He pointed at the recorder. "Wilbert Hawkins."

Porzolkiewski's eyes hardened as he repeated the name. "My lawyer hired a private investigator to look for him after the judge dismissed the case. He wanted to file a motion for reconsideration. But the guy disappeared . . . gone. Where'd you find him?"

"Can't say. That's one of the parts you don't get."

Porzolkiewski opened his mouth to object, and then closed it. He stared at length at the recorder. Finally, he said, "Okay."

"Portions are beeped out, like where he is. And this is not all of it, just what you need to know at this point."

Porzolkiewski nodded.

Gage turned it on:

"My name is Graham Gage. I'm a private investigator from San Francisco, California." I'm in BEEEEEEP talking

to Wilbert Hawkins. I need you to identify yourself for the tape."

"My name is, uh, Wilbert Hawkins. I was a welder at TIMCO fourteen years ago."

"That's the asshole," Porzolkiewski said. "I still recognize his fake Okie accent."

"How long had you been working at TIMCO before the explosion?"

"Nineteen years."

"My understanding is that there was a turnaround a month before the valve failed on the kerosene line on Fractionating Tower 2."

"Yeah, there was."

"Explain what a turnaround is."

"It's, uh, when we shut down the tower for maintenance. You know, take apart the critical components and then make whatever repairs are needed. Takes a couple of weeks."

"Tell me what happened when you examined the pressure device on the valve."

. . .

"Answer the question."

"I need a lawyer. Even a lawyer from BEEEEP."

"You're not getting a lawyer."

Porzolkiewski smiled.

"Answer the question."

"I . . . I took the valve apart and, uh, found the pressure release was corroded."

"You tell anybody?"

"*My . . . uh . . . supervisor. Then me and him went to the, uh, plant manager. The tower was old. Nobody made that valve anymore. It was gonna cost maybe fifty grand to make another one from scratch—and we'd have to replace dozens of them, all over the refinery. We knew from experience that this one going bad meant that all of them had gone bad. He needed the plant manager to make the decision 'cause it meant shutting down all the fractionators for a couple of months.*"

"*And . . .*"

"*And TIMCO would've lost millions of dollars. We had kerosene, diesel, jet fuel, and gasoline coming off those towers. Huge amounts. Big contracts from buyers already signed.*"

"*What did the plant manager tell you to do?*"

"*He talked to the big bosses in Dallas, then called me in . . . He . . . he . . . uh . . . told me to pull out the release device and . . . uh . . . weld over the hole and try to keep the pressure in the pipe down once the tower was back in service.*"

"*What happened?*"

"*We didn't keep it low enough. And with no pressure release . . . the . . . . uh . . . the . . . uh . . .*"

"*The what?*"

"*The whole valve blew.*"

Gage switched off the recorder and watched Porzolkiewski finish the story in his mind. Kerosene spraying down onto the scrubber, flames exploding back up the tower. His son and three other men incinerated because a hundred-billion-dollar company didn't want to lose a few bucks.

Porzolkiewski closed his eyes, then lowered his

head. Jaws clenched. Face flushed. Fighting back tears. Hands gripped together on the table. His whole body shuddered, then he buried his face in his palms. Muffled crying, almost hysterical.

Years of outrage had dissolved into immeasurable grief.

Gage reached over and gripped Porzolkiewski's shoulder. "I'm sorry you turned out to be right," Gage said. "I wish it had been just an accident."

A few minutes later, Porzolkiewski looked up, then wiped his eyes with the back of his sleeve. "I never . . ." He cleared his throat, then took in a breath and exhaled. "I never cried for him like that before . . . I guess I was always too angry."

Porzolkiewski pushed himself to his feet and walked into the kitchen. Gage heard him open the refrigerator, then the inside freezer door, expecting him to return with ice water. He came back carrying a Ziploc bag and handed it to Gage.

"This is what you want."

Gage removed a dozen eight-and-a-half-by-eleven folded pages. Gage laid them out. They warmed in the dining room air.

Displayed before them were photocopies of Brandon Meyer's life, in paper and plastic.

As Gage lay in bed that night next to Faith, too jet-lagged for sleep, he didn't regret traveling halfway around the world to obtain something that all along had lain hidden in a freezer just miles from his office.

Then an image came to him: Porzolkiewski weeping at his dining room table.

And Gage's last thoughts before finally drifting off to sleep were of a father's grief finally anchored—forever anchored—to the truth about the corporate murder of his son.

Senior Special Agent Joe Casey stood by the printer in the Federal Building office of the FBI, watching the last of the search warrant print out. He felt a moment of regret, wishing he could give Gage a heads-up that the sledgehammer he raised when he retrieved the jilted Oscar Mogasci from Switzerland was about to fall. He shielded the machine with his body, for other than himself, only one other special agent, the U.S. Attorney for the Northern District of California, and the head of Criminal Division of the Justice Department in Washington knew its contents. Even the team of FBI and IRS agents and forensic computer experts standing by in the warehouse staging area in San Jose didn't know where they would execute the warrant. Casey would only tell them OptiCom was the target after the judge signed it.

Casey checked the wall clock. Five forty-five P.M. He imagined the judge was also watching the time, and selecting from his repertoire of disagreeable faces the one he'd assume when Casey finally arrived. This judge wouldn't have been Casey's choice, but these kinds of cases were always assigned to that judge since he had the expertise to evaluate them.

He removed the search warrant and his affidavit, then turned toward the copy machine and dropped them into the feeder, stapling the collated copies as they came out.

As he walked toward the elevator, Casey glanced into the conference room and nodded to the two agents guarding Mogasci, sitting at the table, his head facedown on his folded arms like an eight-year-old child in school detention. The long linoleum hallway reminded Casey of the one he'd walked two weeks earlier after badging his way past the TSA booth at the San Francisco Airport to meet Gage when he arrived back from Zurich. He'd spotted Gage directing Mogasci toward the glassed-in booths like an owner shepherding a puppy who'd soiled the carpet in the living room. And Mogasci's expression told the world he knew he'd done wrong.

Gage had returned Mogasci's passport as they approached the Customs and Border Patrol window. Casey intercepted Mogasci on the other side and waited for Gage to pass through. Casey then badged them past the baggage screeners and out into the arrivals hall, where another agent was waiting to escort them to a Ford Expedition parked at the curb and guarded by airport security.

Only small talk between Casey and Gage accompanied the ride up Highway 101 toward Gage's Embarcadero office, and there wasn't much of that. They mostly stared at the smog suffocating the bay and eclipsing the afternoon sun, the gray sky seeming to capture the enormity of what was about to happen.

Gage had climbed out of the SUV in his parking lot, leaving behind a briefcase filled with the trade secrets Mogasci had stolen from FiberLink and the Swiss bank account records Mogasci had surrendered to Gage in his Zurich hotel room three days earlier. Also inside was a flash drive containing an incriminating call between Mogasci and the president of OptiCom that Mogasci hoped to trade with Casey for his freedom.

Casey shook off the memory, then glanced at his watch as he stepped into the elevator. Six P.M. He got off on the eighteenth floor, then knocked on the office door of the judge's clerk, who let him in. Her purse and coat were piled on her desk, a not so subtle reminder it was an hour past quitting time. She escorted Casey into chambers, where he found the judge sitting on a couch next to a window framing a view of the Marin Headlands and Golden Gate Bridge, the evening traffic bunched up on the deck.

The judge nodded, accepted the search warrant and supporting affidavit, then directed Casey to a side chair. Casey checked his pants pocket for his car keys. In fifteen minutes he'd be out of there and on his way south to San Jose. In twenty-five years, first as a police detective, then as an agent with the FBI, he'd never actually seen a judge read a search warrant affidavit all the way through.

A half hour later, Judge Brandon Meyer was still reading the fifty-five pages.

Another half hour after that, Meyer looked up and said, "I'd like to think about this overnight."

Fury mushroomed inside Casey. It was a righteous case. Probable cause up the wazoo. But all he said was, "Yes, Your Honor," and then rose and left chambers.

Casey's stomach twisted as he walked toward the elevator, wondering if he'd forgotten some element of the crime, some proof of federal jurisdiction, some link in the causal chain—and there was also the embarrassment of calling the staging warehouse to send the agents home because he couldn't get the goddamn judge to sign the goddamn search warrant.

Casey thought of Gage.

What was Gage going to think when he learned the judge he called the pipsqueak had tossed his clients into a judicial never-never land?

After notifying the U.S. Attorney and the search team of the delay, Casey drove the ramp from the garage underneath the Federal Building. He spotted Judge Meyer walking uphill toward the Tenderloin, head down in thought, oblivious to his surroundings, as if it was a regular evening stroll.

Going for a walk to think through a complex case made sense, Casey thought, *but wading through drug dealers and hookers while doing it was damn stupid*.

Casey was tempted to pull up alongside Meyer to warn him to head another direction, but then changed his mind.

Fuck him.

orning sunlight flowing into Gage's office illuminated the copies Porzolkiewski had made of the contents of Brandon Meyer's wallet. Gage had laid them out on his conference table and organized them by type: credit cards, medical cards, business cards, identification, phone cards, scraps of paper with telephone numbers, notes, lists of names, cash, receipts, and a slim address book.

Porzolkiewski had even photocopied the condom.

Gage knew Spike Pacheco would be thrilled. The only thing missing from Spike's mental re-creation of Meyer's adventure in the Tenderloin was the Viagra.

Gage reached for the telephone. Alex Z arrived forty minutes later, accompanied by a bodyguard who waited in the hallway.

"How do you like your new office?" Gage asked.

Gage had set up Alex Z in a loft on the Oakland waterfront. He wasn't going to take a chance that whoever pummeled Shakir would get him, too.

Alex Z smiled. "It's a block from the best Thai food in the Bay Area. It feels like a vacation home. I may not move back."

"Just be careful when you go out."

Alex Z glanced toward the door. "Him and his buddies cover me. I feel like a rock star."

"You are a rock star, at least in San Francisco."

Alex Z shook his head. "More nerd than star."

He leaned over the table and surveyed the photocopies. He grinned when he spotted the copy of the condom, then locked onto the page next to it. When he straightened up, Gage was already nodding.

"Why does a federal judge need phone cards?" Alex Z asked.

"Spike would say that he doesn't want calls to a hooker showing up on his cell phone bills."

Gage passed Alex Z copies of two pages from Meyer's address book displaying a mix of corporate and political telephone numbers.

"On the other hand, maybe it's just political paranoia," Gage said. "Fear the Democrats might snoop in on his cell phone calls and catch Senator Meyer's little brother engaging a little too deeply in electoral politics."

Alex Z skimmed down the list. "I take it you believe Meyer is secretly managing Landon's presidential campaign."

"Judge by day, Machiavelli by night."

"Why not? They're brothers."

"The appearance of a conflict of interest. The real money around here is in Silicon Valley and Brandon mostly handles complex civil cases like securities fraud, intellectual property, unfair competition. Executives in any company appearing in Brandon's court would wonder whether contributions to Landon's campaign might improve their chances. What they call a velvet cash register. One thing they know for certain is that they could improve them further by hiring Brandon's ex-partner for cases appearing in his court. And they do it case after case after case. They know it's hard for Brandon to look down from the bench at Marc Anston and rule against him."

Alex Z drew back. "And everybody knows this is going on?"

"Sure."

"Why don't the attorneys on the other side of Anston's cases recuse Brandon and ask for another judge?"

"You can't recuse federal court judges. Judges have to recuse themselves. You're stuck with whoever the clerk assigns the case to."

Alex Z looked again at the corporate telephone numbers.

"Does Landon know he could be getting money coming from a kind of extortion?" Alex Z asked.

"I suspect the possibility hasn't even crossed his mind. Their family fortune was built on conflicts of interest. During World War II, his grandfather was the majority shareholder of Longridge Arms at the same time he was serving in the War Department handing out contracts. Longridge went from a couple of thousand employees in 1939 to over a hundred thousand by 1943 and became the largest supplier of tanks and armored vehicles to the army—and he wasn't the only political family that went that route. The wealth of one of our former presidents came from his grandfather serving on the War Industries Board during World War I and giving his own company contracts for making guns and ammunition."

"What about Landon and Brandon's father, was he in on it?"

"He was sort of a transitional figure, like most other Cabinet members. Work in government for a few years, feed contracts to corporations that support the party, leave government to take positions in those same companies, build a personal fortune by exploiting political connections, then back into government at a higher level, then back into industry—but that's not Landon's game. For him it's all about the public good, not about cashing in later. He's a decent man. Always has been."

Gage smiled to himself.

"Remember during the first few years of the Iraq War, all those government officials talking in jargon about optics and metrics and boots on the ground?"

Alex Z nodded.

"Landon once pointed down at the secretary of state during a committee hearing, and said, 'Stop calling them boots. They're soldiers, human beings—our sons and daughters.' Then he paused for a beat and said, 'Boots, Madam Secretary, do not feel pain.' She flinched like a bullet was heading her way and looked like she was getting ready to dive under the table. The scene was almost Shakespearean."

"But I thought Landon was an ideologue. That's his reputation anyway."

"Only in the sense that he's not afraid to follow political ideas to their logical conclusion, even if it sometimes ends in nonsense. When he was first in the House of Representatives he introduced a bill to make it illegal for companies engaged in interstate commerce to use any language but English in conducting their business."

Alex Z laughed. "You mean if Pedro Gonzalez in California e-mails his brother's market in New Mexico to tell him the tortillas are on the way, he'd have to write it in English? That's ridiculous. Anyway the Constitution gives us a right to privacy."

"The problem is once you start from the premise that English is the national language, it's where an honest thinker can end up. The difference in Landon between then and now is he's learned not to try to turn every logical conclusion into legislation."

"What about his brother?"

"For Brandon, it's about power. I think that's why he became a judge. He was never going to match his father's fortune on his own, so he needed a kind of authority his father couldn't buy, at least directly."

Gage scanned the copies laid out on the table. His eyes came to rest on the list of telephone numbers.

"How about doing a little research?" Gage said. "Find out whether any of these corporations match plaintiffs or defendants in cases Brandon's old firm handled or match contributors to Landon's campaigns."

"No problem."

Gage continued examining the copies as Alex Z turned to leave.

"Of course—" Alex Z turned back. Gage was holding up the photocopy of the condom. "Maybe Meyer was desperate to get his wallet back only because he was worried about getting caught cheating on his wife."

Gage picked up his phone and punched in a number after Alex Z left.

"Skeeter, this is Graham."

"Hey, man. I was about to give you a call about Brandon Meyer."

"I guess you won your trial."

"How do you figure?"

"You said his name."

Skeeter laughed. "Not exactly. The other side settled just before the case went to the jury. Even Meyer couldn't save their corporate asses."

"Congratulations."

"Thanks."

"You work out yet today?"

"Nope. Early court appearance."

"How about meet me tonight at Stymie's?"

Skeeter laughed again. "We're finally gonna find out who lifts how much, partner."

t pisses me off." Skeeter threw his gym bag at the side of his silver Mercedes in the night-shadowed gym parking lot. "You blew past me like I'm the kid who gets sand kicked in his face."

"Don't take it so hard," Gage said. "You're ten years older than I am."

Skeeter shook his head. "Well, at least I'm better-looking."

Gage laughed. "We both know that's not true."

"Well, maybe once."

"Okay, you can have that."

Skeeter popped open his trunk and tossed the bag in. The glow of the neon sign of the auto repair shop next door revealed a sober expression when he returned to stand next to Gage.

"I'm not sure there's any way to reopen the Porzolkiewski case," Skeeter said. "I'll have some associates do the research and let you know." He slammed a fist into his palm and his voice hardened. "I knew Hawkins lied in his deposition, I just couldn't prove it, and I suspected Charlie Palmer had something to do with getting him out of the country."

"Why didn't you ask me to find out?"

Skeeter threw up his hands. "Don't you think I wanted to? Almost every time I've called in the last twenty years, you've been between nine and fifteen time zones away. And that's probably what happened back then."

"Sorry."

"It's not your fault. It's my frustration. But I'll tell you this . . . if I could connect the dots all the way to Brandon, I'd get his ass impeached."

"Don't we both wish."

Skeeter leaned back against his car. "I've been thinking about your talk with Wilbert Hawkins. What's he been living on?"

"A flat million-dollar payoff. It'll last ten lifetimes in India."

"What about his wife? Is she getting some of it?"

"Nope. He signed over his retirement to her. He only had nineteen years in, but he was vested and she lives cheap. Just beer and McDonald's."

"Any way to link the million to TIMCO?"

"Hawkins said the money went through a Caribbean account. Even if he could've remembered the name and the island, we'd never get the records, but we're going through Charlie's computer and all his files, not just for that but, for anything suspicious."

"That links to Brandon?"

"He's just one of the names. Charlie left lots enemies behind."

Gage joined Skeeter in leaning against the car, then folded his arms across his chest.

"Let me try something out on you," Gage said.

"Shoot."

"Just between us."

Skeeter nodded.

"Everybody seems to agree that some of Brandon's rulings are bizarre, but they're always solid enough to withstand appeal."

"He's a master of making a record that boxes in the Ninth Circuit," Skeeter said. "His main trick is to make uncontestable factual findings that force appeals court judges to frame the issues exactly the way he wants them to. But his so-called facts of the case are usually pure fantasy. Fan-ta-sy . . . that asshole."

Gage looked over at Skeeter. "You ever wonder if Brandon is taking payoffs?"

Skeeter whistled. "That's heavy."

"I know."

"You mean through Marc Anston?"

"He's the attorney of choice for nearly every company that either gets sued or criminally charged in Brandon's court. An inflated fee, then a wink and a nod and the money ends up in Brandon's bank account."

"Sure would explain a lot," Skeeter said. "But really hard to prove. Maybe impossible."

"You have a couple of associates you can trust with something like this?"

"What do you have in mind?"

"We're putting together a list of all of the companies that have appeared in Brandon's court. Maybe your people can analyze Brandon's rulings in those cases and can detect a pattern."

"I've got a couple of kids who can do it, but . . ." Skeeter raised his eyebrows.

"But you're wondering if they'll end up like Shakir."

"Yeah, I heard about what happened. How's he doing?"

"He'll be out of the hospital in a couple of days. I wouldn't worry about your associates. The guys who went after Shakir were after something secret, not something anybody can find in a court file—"

"But only if they knew what they were looking for."

"Right. If they knew what they were looking for."

F inally." Joe Casey leaned back in his desk chair, gazed heavenward, and spread his arms. "Thank you Lord and the skies above."

Judge Brandon Meyer had signed the OptiCom search warrant.

Casey called the agents to reassemble at the staging area, then walked from his office to the elevator. He glanced at his watch. Eleven-thirty A.M. Given the size of the OptiCom facility and the breadth of the authorized search, he knew he wouldn't be getting home until the following morning.

Meyer's clerk was standing at her office door as he approached, hand outstretched holding the warrant. She shook her head like she was watching a mudslide sweep away a hillside of houses.

"This is a big one," she said when he came to a stop in front of her.

Casey nodded as he took the warrant from her hand. "A multibillion-dollar bubble will burst as soon as the media learns we've shown up at their door. Watch the news tonight."

She pointed at the packet of papers. "Check the signature. The judge's hands were shaking when he signed it."

Casey figured he'd take a look later. "You know what the delay was?"

She looked over her shoulder toward the door to Meyer's chambers, then lowered her voice. "You're asking to search the whole facility." She cocked her head toward the end of the hallway. "You hear what happened to Judge Spurling last week?"

Casey shook his head.

"The Ninth Circuit slapped him silly in a drug case, ruling he let the DEA go on a fishing expedition. They ridiculed him, wondering in writing whether he'd never read the Constitution, then tossed the whole indictment. It's got all the judges nervous. Judge Meyer went over your affidavit line by line, making sure there was specific probable cause for each place you want to search."

Casey felt a wave of annoyance, not because Meyer was second-guessing him, but because the first thing he'd always think about after a judge signed a search warrant was whether a defense attorney would later find a way to get it tossed. It pissed him off. Mostly because it got him second-guessing himself.

"I don't care if it gets suppressed," Casey said. "These gals are going to get their invention back, and OptiCom isn't going to make a dime off their sacrifices."

It was hours after daybreak when Casey walked into his silent Peninsula home. His kids were long grown and out of the house. His wife was at work. The cat was on its neighborhood prowl and the dog had already begun its first nap of the day. He went into the kitchen where his vacationing neighbor's bug-eyed goldfish swam in anticipation to the surface of its small bowl, then hung there in disappointment as Casey passed by the counter on his way to the refrigerator.

He felt like drinking a beer, but pulled out a V8, then glanced over at the kitchenette where a *San Francisco Chronicle* lay spread out, along with a bowl of cereal, a spoon, the TV remote, and a note from his wife.

> *I waited as long as I could. Have a snack,*
> *then get some sleep. XX*

He traded the juice for milk, then sat down at the table and reached for the television remote and located CNBC. An OptiCom stock trading chart filled the screen. A female voice-over announced that the SEC had suspended trading after the share price crashed on the news of the raid.

A male voice chipped in,

"*By my calculation, Chelsea, it would be a loss of . . . let me see . . . three point two billion dollars.*"

"*Do you think it'll recover?*"

"*Of course. As soon as OptiCom cuts FiberLink in on the European contract, the price will regain most of its value.*"

"*When will it happen?*"

"*My guess? In about an hour—if there's anyone with half a brain left running the show at OptiCom.*"

* * *

Casey stared at the television as he decided whether to eat or sleep. It regained his attention with crashing music and an explosion of red and yellow with the words "News Alert" pulsing at the bottom of the screen. The woman appeared next to an inset box displaying a profile of President William Duncan.

"We've just received word the president is planning to announce his nominees to fill the soon-to-be-vacant Supreme Court seats."

Casey felt a wave of tiredness, even relief, glad as always that his part of doing justice was merely to return things to the way they were, not remake the world to match somebody's political imaginings. He flicked off the television, then returned the cereal to the box and the milk to the refrigerator, and went to bed.

President Duncan emerged from a side door and strode to the podium in the East Room of the White House; trailing him were alias Starsky and Hutch, his nominees to the Supreme Court. All three met with a racket of applause from staffers, party leaders, and members of Congress that overwhelmed the collective gasp from the press.

Starsky was forty-two-year-old Judge Phillip Sanford from the D.C. Circuit Court of Appeals.

Hutch was thirty-nine-year-old Judge Julian Heller from the Fifth Circuit, covering Texas, Louisiana, and Mississippi.

Landon Meyer watched on television from his Dirksen Building office. He smiled as the cameras panned the audience, the faces of the White House press corps, feeling themselves the victims of a mechanized assault, transforming from shock to awe. He understood what they thought they were seeing: two white males who melded the extremes of their personal religion and their personal politics into a determination to remake the country in their judicial image.

But that wasn't what Landon saw, and what he knew to be the truth: Their religion was the country's religion and their politics were those of the Founders, and it was the melding of the two that had once shaped a great nation and would do so again. He remembered the last political discussion he had with Gage up at his cabin, wondering aloud why conservatives had stopped reading American Christians like James Fenimore Cooper and had turned instead to foreigners like the Russian atheist Ayn Rand and why they were blind to how it distorted their thinking and caused them to bow to a metaphorical Atlas instead of to a real God. These two new justices would restore both the law and the culture.

Landon refocused on the screen. He found himself worrying that Duncan would engage in a rant that would expose the desperation that had characterized their meeting in the Oval Office. But he didn't. His comments were standard and respectful toward the constitutional process of confirmation, treating the coming hearings as part of a legislative flow, not the flash flood Landon knew it would be.

Neither the president nor the nominees answered questions. The two offered obligatory thanks to the president and appreciation for the support they'd received from their wives and colleagues, and then stepped back in turn.

It was over in three minutes.

Landon's cell phone rang. It was Brandon.

"Turn to NBC," Brandon said. "James Bissell just keeps repeating the same thing over and over. It's hilarious."

Landon changed the channel.

"A gauntlet has been thrown," Bissell was saying, *"President Duncan's entire legacy hangs in the balance."*

Landon knew those words would echo for a generation.

"It's not clear to me how the Democrats can oppose nominees they confirmed less than a year ago—but they will because they have no choice. It's as if the president laid a trap back then, only to spring it now."

"Did you hear that?" Brandon said. "Laid a trap. Duncan couldn't lay a trap without lopping off an arm. Congratulations, Landon. Brilliant move."

"The next step," Bissell continued, *"is the Senate Judiciary Committee. Landon Meyer is the chairman. I have no doubt he was consulted in advance, but still, the task of moving these nominees through to confirmation will give him the fight of his career."*

An inset box appeared on the screen showing a reporter standing with the White House behind him.

"It makes you wonder, James, whether Justices Martinez and Fairstein are sitting in their living rooms wishing they hadn't decided to retire. If confirmed, these two nominees will roll back nearly everything they've accomplished in the last thirty-years. It's only a question of how long it will take."

The reporter paused, then skimmed his notes.

"You also have to consider what effect this will have on Landon Meyer's campaign for the presidency. He may

win this battle for President Duncan, but lose his own war for the top job."

"It's hard to say. New Hampshire is still months away. That's a lifetime in American politics."

Dark clouds pressed down on the city and a light rain fell as Gage walked up the steps to Socorro Palmer's Russian Hill Victorian. He glanced toward the eastern hills and saw the morning sun still shining on his neighborhood, but not for long. It had been there during dinner on his deck looking across the bay and over San Francisco that Faith told him she'd called and convinced Socorro it was time to talk about Charlie and his final days. Gage had wanted Faith to come along with him, but it was midterms at Cal, so she had tests to grade and final papers to read.

Standing at the front door, Socorro seemed thinner, her eyes dark and sunken. In her saggy sweatpants and loose fleece pullover, she gave him the impression she hadn't left the house since the day of the funeral.

Even though Gage had planned to go into his office afterward, he wore Levi's and a sport shirt, a way of communicating that he was more a friend visiting than an investigator questioning.

Socorro was her mother's daughter. Her first words were "Have you had breakfast yet?"

Gage nodded as he stepped across the threshold, and said, "But coffee would be fine."

She led him to the enclosed back porch where a carafe and two mugs stood on a table between the same green wicker chairs they'd sat in the last time. She poured for both of them and they sat down.

Gage pointed at the telescope in the corner. A dust rag was draped over the crossbar of the tripod. An open packing box lay on the slate floor next to it.

"Getting that ready for your son?" Gage asked.

Socorro nodded. "It's about all they shared. Camping in the Sierras above the city lights, looking at stars." She sighed. "The sad thing is that the only real connection between them was made through little specks of rock millions of light-years away."

They sat in silence for a long moment, the raindrops tapping the roof above them.

Finally, Gage asked, "How have you been holding up?"

He already knew from Viz that a truthful answer would be: *It's been the worst time in my life.*

"I'm getting along," Socorro said. "You know how these things are."

"Faith and I were thinking we'd like you to spend a weekend with us up at the cabin, maybe a change of scenery would—"

She cut him off with a shake of her head. "I don't think I'm ready." She looked back at the kitchen, then toward the flower garden. "Somehow I feel like I'd be abandoning him and . . . and there's kind of a mystery in this house that has to be solved."

"A mystery about what? The burglary?"

"About who my husband really was." Her voice was flat, as if the words were born of a nighttime resolution. "My brother told me you spoke to someone who Charlie might've harmed in some way. A man named John Porzolkiewski. He said when the time came you'd tell me about it." She fixed her eyes on Gage. "The only way I'll ever understand Charlie is by knowing the kinds of things he did."

Gage thought back on his conversation with Faith as they'd walked to their car after the funeral. Maybe Faith had been correct. That Socorro had been blind—perhaps by choice—to the life Charlie had lived. And he wondered what would be the psychological consequences of now coming to see and to accept who Charlie had been from the beginning, even as they'd held hands or shared a dessert on their first date.

"Are you sure you're ready for this?" Gage asked.

Socorro reached under her chair and withdrew a manila file folder. She opened it on her lap. The top page was a retirement account summary of cash, bonds, and equities. She handed it to Gage. His eyes followed the column of figures to the bottom: two and a half million dollars.

"From the little I know of his practice," Gage said, "this seems about right."

She handed him another folder. Inside was a letter from AmeriWest Annuities to Charlie saying he and she would be receiving income of thirty thousand dollars a month, effective six weeks earlier. A three-hundred-and-sixty-thousand-dollar-a-year annuity meant Charlie had probably purchased it for about seven million.

Socorro didn't wait for Gage to comment on it, instead she asked, "Where did he get the money?"

"You mean, what did he do for it?"

She nodded.

Gage flipped the folder closed and handed it back. She accepted it as if he was handing her a lab test revealing that she had cancer.

"I'm not sure I'm the best person to do this," Gage said. "There's a lot I don't know about his work."

"How about start with Porzolkiewski and his son."

The solidity and resolve in her voice pushed Gage past his internal resistance. He described the trail leading from Jeannette Hawkins in Richmond, to Wilbert in India, then back to Porzolkiewski and his descent toward hysteria on hearing the truth about his son's death.

Tears formed in Socorro's eyes, but her face remained determined, so he pushed on.

"And Charlie covered it up by paying off the OSHA inspector, packing up Hawkins after his deposition and taking him first to Pakistan, and then a few months afterward to India."

"India? Why India?"

"Because . . ." Gage hesitated to say the words to the mother of a daughter, but she wanted the whole truth and seemed ready for it. "Because that's where the girls were."

"Young girls?"

"Very young."

"Did Charlie know about that?"

Gage shrugged and said, "I have no idea," and then turned the conversation back to TIMCO.

"Basically, they paid out a couple of million dollars to Brandon Meyer's firm, Charlie, the OSHA inspector, and Hawkins to save thirty million in a civil judgment and prevent the prosecution of the plant manager and corporate officers for manslaughter."

Socorro reached out and touched his arm. "I need to go see Mr. Porzolkiewski. I need to apologize for . . . for us."

"That's not a good idea. I didn't tell him about Charlie's part in it. I was afraid he'd use it as a bridge to Brandon Meyer and walk over it carrying a gun. He's—" Gage caught himself. He wasn't going to tell her he was almost certain Porzolkiewski shot Charlie.

"He's what?" Socorro wiped her eyes.

"He's . . . a very angry man."

She drew back. "You don't think he'd go after Brandon?"

"He might—despite there being no evidence linking Brandon to what Charlie did. It could've been someone else in Brandon's firm. Maybe just a deal between TIMCO and Charlie directly without the firm involved."

"Did Charlie . . ." She searched his face. "Did Charlie do this kind of thing a lot?"

"A lot? That I don't know." Gage knew he did, but she only needed to know about one other. "There's a woman whose son was beaten up in Pacific Heights."

"Tansy? The woman who answered when Charlie telephoned."

"Yes, Tansy."

"Is it because of Charlie that she works for you?"

"Indirectly."

They fell silent, listening to the rain, watching flower petals beyond the screen bounce as drops struck. Socorro's aging golden retriever ambled in and rested its head in her lap. She petted it without looking down.

Gage picked up their cold coffees and emptied the cups into the kitchen sink. He returned and refilled them from the carafe and sat down.

"Do you know what was on Charlie's mind when he called me?" Gage asked, looking over at her.

"He wouldn't say," Socorro said, gazing out toward the garden. "But my guess is regret. I think for the first time in his life, he understood what suffering was. I think it's why he broke down when he heard Moki's name."

Socorro paused and her eyes went blank.

"All those years as a police officer," she finally said, "he was oblivious to what it meant to be a victim. I mean he said the right words in the right tone. Sympathy. Understanding. But he didn't mean them."

She blinked and then looked over at Gage.

"I noticed the change in him about a week before he died. Brandon called. They argued about something. When Charlie hung up his face was white, like he'd suddenly found himself at a cliff edge, looking down. He seemed defeated afterward."

"Could you tell what the argument was about?"

"Specifically, no. But generally about trust. Something had broken down between them. That, and somebody had been chosen to do the work Charlie used to do. Something important had to be done and Brandon was tired of waiting for Charlie to get better."

"What exactly was Charlie doing?"

Socorro shrugged. "I don't know. But not doing it left him feeling abandoned."

She lowered her gaze, seeming to finish a thought in her head, then nodded and reached into her sweatpants pocket. She pulled out a folded check and held it out toward him.

"I need you to find out where Charlie's money came from."

Gage shook his head. "I can't let you hire me."

"I'm not. The people whose lives he ruined are hiring you. I merely wrote the check. Even if money can't remake the past, at least they can learn the truth of what it really was. That's what you did for Mr. Porzolkiewski."

He accepted the check from her. Fifty thousand dollars.

"I'll charge my expenses," Gage said, "and give you back the rest."

Gage folded it and slid it into his jeans pocket.

"And there's one more thing." Socorro pulled out another folder from under her chair. "Charlie left an insurance policy with the children as beneficiaries."

"From who?"

"A company I hadn't heard of until Charlie showed me the paperwork. It's called Pegasus Limited. It's in the Cayman Islands."

"How much was the policy for?"

"Two million. One for each of them."

"Has it been paid out yet?"

"I haven't notified the company of Charlie's death. I'm not sure I want them to have the money if it's . . ."

"Tainted?"

"Yes, tainted."

Socorro rose from her chair. She wobbled and reached a hand toward the armrest. Gage stepped forward and put his arm around her waist, then guided her to a sofa in the living room and laid an afghan over her. She stared up at the ceiling and closed her eyes.

"There was something else I was going to tell you," she said. "But my mind has gone blank. I can't think."

"When was the last time you ate?"

She opened her eyes again. "I don't know. I guess yesterday."

"Or the day before?"

She forced a smile. "Maybe."

Gage walked into the kitchen and fixed an omelet and brought it to her. She was sitting up when he returned.

"I know what it was," Socorro said. "The key." She pointed at the low table by the front door. "It goes to a storage locker. It was in an envelope with the rental agreement." Her brows furrowed. "I didn't even know Charlie had it."

"Have you gone inside the locker?"

"No. I just found the key last night."

age telephoned San Francisco corporate lawyer Jack Burch as he drove from Socorro Palmer's house. He'd skirted around downtown and the financial district and was working his way toward the Embarcadero. The light rain had heavied and fog wisped along the pavement and grayed the storefronts.

Burch's chewing couldn't disguise his Australian accent.

"Early lunch?" Gage asked.

"Late dinner."

"Where are you?"

"Moscow. It's nine-thirty."

"Why didn't you tell me you were going?"

"It was last minute. Got here yesterday." Burch paused, then laughed. "Maybe it was this morning. It's hard to tell. I'll have to check my calendar."

"What's—"

"Bloody bullshit is what's up. Why an American microchip manufacturer wants to do a joint venture with a Russian company instead of just thumping them out of existence is beyond me. But that's what they want and that's what I'll give them."

Burch was the point man for dozens of the Fortune Global 500 not only because he was a brilliant legal strategist, but because he had the personal authority that allowed him to land in the midst of negotiations with enough force to flatten out the kinks even in the most complicated international deals.

"You think you can FedEx me some Alka-Seltzer?"

"Sure. How much?"

"Ten pounds—but enough of my whining like a stuck donkey. You need something?"

"Have you ever heard of a company called Pegasus Limited in the Caymans?"

"Pegasus . . . Pegasus . . . I don't think so. Let me call you back in a couple of minutes."

Gage's cell phone rang as he drove along the pier-bordered waterfront toward his office.

"I called a colleague who works the corporate governance end of things on Grand Cayman," Burch said. "Pegasus Limited is a part of the Pegasus Group and handles insurance."

"Captive?"

"Exactly. Offshore self-insurance, but only for U.S. corporations. Big ones who need coverage beyond the losses allowed by their domestic carriers."

"Do they have an office there?"

Burch laughed. "According to him, only inside a mailbox. He has no idea who operates it or from where, or even if they're still in business. He said the name hasn't come up for a few years. He'll send someone over to the Company Registry to find out if they're still active."

Gage disconnected and called Alex Z in the Oakland loft.

"Would you run the name Pegasus Limited in Charlie's accounting records?"

"No problem, boss."

Gage heard Alex Z's keystrokes in the background.

"Are you sure it's called Pegasus?" Alex Z asked.

"Socorro showed me a Pegasus Limited insurance policy."

"Sorry. He didn't pay anything to a company called Pegasus Limited. Ever."

"How about search just on the name Pegasus?"

A few clicks later, Alex Z had the answer.

"Nada."

Boots Marnin was sick of sitting in his Mariner Hotel room in downtown San Francisco. The room service food was lousy. The view toward the cubicled offices in the building across the street was depressing. He'd seen every porn movie on the adult channel a half-dozen times. The highlight of his day was when the Filipina maid came to clean. She was a little chubby, but beggars can't be choosers, and for forty bucks he didn't figure he could expect much.

Walking along Market Street turned his stomach. Dykes, wimpy pale-faced computer nerds, paunchy lawyers, and loonies peeing in the doorways or passed out on bus benches.

The only good news was he got paid for doing nothing, now that he didn't have to try to follow Gage around anymore. He could've told his keepers it was useless, but they had to figure it out on their own, like everything else.

He'd never wanted to get back to Houston so much in his life. He salivated at the thought of sitting in one of those woodsy surf-and-turf restaurants along Galveston Bay, drinking beer and eating oysters, then cruising the bars for a little overnight entertainment.

But that was going to have to wait.

Boots checked the bedside clock. In six hours, he'd posse up with his buddy and drive south through the Central Valley to LA. And about time, too. He didn't believe for a minute the NSA guys down at Evergreen would be able to break into Charlie Palmer's files. He knew all along it would have to be done another way.

Dinosaur, my ass.

Boots pulled down the ski mask just before the student opened the door to her West Hollywood apartment. Her eyes glazed with sleep. Black hair ruffled and twisted. Hands clasping her robe lapels together over her chest. He clamped his hands over her mouth and against the back of her head before she could scream. He kicked the door closed after his partner raced past him to search the apartment. One bedroom. No roommates.

Boots jammed her down into a kitchen chair as his partner put a gun to her temple. Boots leaned in toward her, her black hair framing a vaguely Hispanic face.

"Don't scream if you want to be alive when we leave."

She nodded against the pressure of his grip.

He started to remove his hands, then clamped them tight again.

"You understand?"

She nodded again.

He still didn't remove his hands.

"I'm just gonna ask you some questions. Silly questions. They have to do with your dear departed dad. And you're going answer them."

She nodded again.

"You don't need to know why. Don't even think about why. Just answer them."

Boots loosened his grip. She took in a breath, eyes locked on the man with the gun.

"You can put it away," Boots told his partner. "We have an understanding."

Boots sat down while the other man leaned against the refrigerator. Boots dialed his cell phone, put it on speaker, and set it on the table. A male voice answered on the second ring:

"Go ahead."

"First," Boots said, "What is your dog's name?"

"My . . . my . . ."

The young woman choked on the words.

"Relax. I told you they were silly questions. Just answer them and we'll get out of here."

"You're not going to hurt—"

"Nobody's getting hurt, you or your dog, as long as you answer the questions."

"Buddy. His name is Buddy."

The sound of typing emerged from the cell phone speaker, then the male voice said, "Not it."

"What was your previous dog's name?"

"Pancho."

More typing. The voice again. "Not it."

"Where are your mother's parents from?"

"Guadalajara."

More typing.
"Nope."
"Your father's parents?"
"Pittsburgh."
More typing.
"That's not it."
"And before that . . ."

An hour later Boots was still asking questions, running out of ideas. He glanced into the living room. A photo on the bookshelf. The scene was familiar. Emerald Bay.

"Your folks own a cabin at Lake Tahoe?"
"Yes."
More typing, and then the voice said:
"It's not Tahoe."
"What's the address?"
"I think it's 10110 Martis Valley Road in Truckee."
Typing in short bursts.
"Nope. Not on any of them."
"No, wait. It's 11010 Martis Valley Road."
More typing: "We got it. We're in."
Boots disconnected the phone and put it in his pocket. His partner walked to the door. Boots stayed seated.

"Let me tell you what's going to happen. You're going back to bed and pretend this was just a dream. You're not going to tell anyone—ever. You say one damn word and we'll feed your mother and brother to the sharks. Got it?"

The young woman nodded, mouth open.

"The only reason you're still alive—the only reason—is because it's less of a risk than killing you."

Boots smiled when he noticed a micro economics text on the coffee table.

"Let's just call it a business decision."

His smile died as he pointed his trigger finger at her forehead.

"Don't make me wish I'd added up the numbers a different way."

O f all the TIMCO corporate jets, Senator Landon Meyer most enjoyed the Gulfstream 550. It wasn't the largest. It wasn't the newest. He just liked the layout. The couches for taking a nap. The facing leather seats for reading or conversing. The hardwood mahogany tables, a bathroom better appointed than the one in his Senate office, and a galley better stocked than his liquor cabinet at home.

Staring out the window as the plane flew west from Washington, D.C., toward Silicon Valley, Landon didn't feel at all guilty about the corporate largesse. He reimbursed TIMCO for the expense, or at least what the Federal Election Commission would accept as the expense. More importantly, he didn't conspire with TIMCO or any other contributor to draft and enact favorable legislation, they simply shared a commonality of worldview that he molded into federal law.

Landon let his gaze travel around the Western-themed cabin interior with photos of the Texas oil fields in the 1920s, horse-drawn wagons, cattle in the distance. Suede fringed throw pillows. Bucking bronco painted dinner plates.

Did he like the TIMCO officers? No, not really. He never liked oilmen and their good-old-boy pretense. But that wasn't a consideration. That he didn't entirely trust TIMCO weighed on him, and for good cause, like the refinery explosion during his first senatorial campaign.

As far as unions and environmental activists were concerned, there was no such thing as an accident. There were only conspiracies.

Even now, Landon still felt sadness, even grief, for the victims and their families—and outrage. Not because of their desire for compensation—how else can a capitalist society measure loss—but because of the class action lawyers and the greedy clients they'd recruited from the neighborhoods surrounding the Richmond refinery. He still couldn't see what the big deal was about residents sheltering in place for a few hours while the smoke cleared. Small sacrifice for the money TIMCO brought into their community. Despite that, they demanded millions of dollars, two thousand dollars a household.

Landon glanced down at the Government Accounting Office analysis of a revision of the federal workers' compensation law to set limits on payouts. It reminded him that the only useful thing that came out of the tragedy was an example and an argument for tort reform.

But what had damaged him was the TIMCO executives' sixty thousand dollars in personal contributions paired in his opponent's commercial with photos of the burning refinery and with demands for better regulation. And it cost him six hundred thousand dollars in television time to buy back the voters' goodwill.

It was a good thing Brandon came up with enough money in the final days to pay for the media blitz vilifying his opponent for her disastrous reversal on the death penalty and for her acceptance of the jihadists' campaign contribution.

Anyway, Brandon had said the explosion really was just an accident, and Landon had no reason to doubt him. Brandon had even given him a copy of the OSHA root cause analysis, and Landon had distributed it to the press.

End of story—except for a lingering dark mood, the kind horror movie watchers carried with them as they left the theater and novel readers felt after closing a book.

And, staring at the TIMCO logo stitched into the leather seat across from him, he knew it would always linger.

Brandon was standing by a Lincoln Town Car parked on the tarmac at the San Jose Jet Center when the Gulfstream rolled to a stop.

My earnest little brother, Landon thought as he climbed down the stairs. *Always looking so perfectly earnest.*

He wondered what Brandon looked like on the bench, and was certain it couldn't be called earnest.

Brandon took two steps forward and shook Landon's hand. The chauffeur had the rear door open by the time they started for the car.

"What's first?" Landon asked as the limousine rolled toward the airport exit and the on-ramp to the freeway heading south.

"The first meeting is at two o'clock down at Conner Micro. The group is calling itself Silicon Valley Executives for Regulatory Reform."

Landon thought for a moment, then chuckled.

Bewilderment replaced Brandon's earnestness. "What?"

"Who made up that name?"

"I did."

"Better ask me first in the future. The acronym sounds too much like 'sever' or even worse, 'severe.' In either case, it'll invite sarcasm on the cable news shows."

Brandon squinted into the distance, then asked, "How about just Executives for Regulatory Reform? Like 'ear,' as in we listen."

"I think that'll come out 'err' like in 'error.'"

Landon noticed Brandon looking down and shaking his head. "Don't worry, little brother, we'll come up with something."

Brandon raised his head and smiled.

"Before we descended into acronym hell," Brandon said, "I was about to say I made reservations at Chez Nous. They'll give us a private room so we can talk a little strategy while we eat. And I'll wait there while you go lean on the contributors."

Landon looked at his watch.

"I think I'd like to stop and see Janie," Landon said. "It's been a while since I've been home."

"How about next time? We'll be cutting it too close."

"We can talk on the way."

"But—"

Landon's uncompromising expression cut Brandon short. He punched the intercom. "New plan. 910 Oregon Avenue, San Mateo."

The driver took the first exit, swung under the freeway, and headed north.

"How's your progress been?" Landon asked.

"Just short of ten million in pledges in the last week."

Landon's head swung around. "Ten million? How's that possible?"

"I had a lot of chips to play."

"What? You threaten to put people in the federal penitentiary if they didn't contribute?"

It was Brandon's turn to laugh. "Criminals rarely have any money. Despite all the talk about drug kingpins, dope dealers really don't do all that well. Turns out most of them sleep on their mother's couches."

"So we're only talking about another five or so in the next three weeks?"

"But it'll be a lot harder. People are tapped out, or are at least having trouble reaching the bottom of their pockets." Brandon grinned. "Makes me want to give them sort of a political wedgie and bring their pockets up a few inches."

Landon laughed and shook his head. "People will be shocked to learn Machiavelli has a sense of humor."

"Let's not tell them." Brandon pointed at Landon's watch, then bit his lip. "We really don't have time to stop."

"We'll make time."

"They've kept up the lawn nicely," Landon said, getting out of the limousine at the curb. He then pointed along the walkway. "Wasn't there a tree here? A poplar or something?"

"I don't remember," Brandon said.

"You mean you haven't been here since we came out together last time?"

Brandon shrugged. "You know how it is. There are only so many hours in a day."

Landon wasn't surprised, but wondered how their parents raised sons with such different attitudes, different feelings, maybe even different loyalties, toward family.

He felt himself well up as he cut across the grass and his heart ached even before he spotted her headstone: *Jane Meyer, Born 1956—Died 1960, Now with God*.

Landon stared down the marble slab, remembering the collision.

Or at least thinking he was remembering it.

He'd told the story so many times in speeches over the years, drawing so many different lessons as his political needs shifted, he wasn't sure of the truth—except that a drunk driver had killed his little sister.

Even as a child he'd understood exactly what had been taken from him, from his parents, from their grandparents. From Brandon, he wasn't so sure.

One thing Senator Landon Meyer knew with

certainty, and without regret, was that he'd been the first six-year-old in human history who believed in the death penalty.

Five minutes later, after a brief prayer, Landon took in a long breath and said:

"Let's go get some money."

oots is gone."

Viz was standing at Gage's office door.

"When?"

"Day before yesterday. I've been going by his hotel like you wanted. I talked up one of the maids after I hadn't spotted his van for twelve hours. She told me." Viz grinned. "She turned red and got all fidgety when I described him and pointed out his room. I think she was doing more than cleaning."

"You get her name?"

"Her tag said Rosa M. Full name, Rosa Montijo."

Gage walked to the kitchen after Viz left and poured himself a cup of coffee. He collected an empty banker's box from the supply room, then walked down the flight of stairs to the basement. He punched in the code numbers that had nearly cost Shakir his life, then went inside.

Boxes containing fifteen years of case files he and Viz had collected from Charlie Palmer's storage locker were stacked along the wall.

Gage lined them up along the floor, year by year,

and then lifted up the first in line and set it on the worktable.

He examined his hands, already grimy with dust, then searched around the room for a rag or paper towels. There weren't any. He wiped them on his Levi's, figuring it was the least damaging kind of dirt he was about to paw through.

He flipped open the box and sat down.

Seven hours later Gage noticed the time, surprised to find it was four o'clock, now broken free from his immersion in Charlie Palmer's life, or at least those parts leaving a paper trail.

Reflecting back on his moods as he'd examined the files, Gage found he hadn't felt anger so much as indecision, struggling to focus, wondering what he was trying to do and who his client really was.

Socorro?

Tansy?

Maybe even Porzolkiewski?

Every person who didn't get justice because Charlie played God and took their lives in his hands?

He knew that Faith would say: *You can only do what you can do.*

He decided to start with the easiest one.

Or perhaps, the hardest.

Gage walked upstairs. Tansy wasn't at her desk.

Gage hated the song. Hated it the first time he heard it. It sometimes played in his mind as he drove Highway 101 toward the bedroom communities south of San Francisco and looked up at the rows of little houses strung together like pieces of hard candy, striping the hillsides. He thought of the lyrics describing little boxes and ticky-tacky houses all looking the same. Lots of people knew it. Hardly anybody knew who'd first sung it. Gage did. Pete Seeger had been his father's favorite folksinger. He could still recall the album it was on, recorded during the 1963 *We Shall Overcome* concert at Carnegie Hall.

Gage remembered his father humming it one day as they'd walked to the plaster-covered adobe building housing his one-person medical practice in Nogales. Gage had just passed his thirteenth birthday. On Saturdays he raked the front yard, watered the cactus, and collected the tumbleweeds desert winds had rolled onto the property.

Gage recalled stopping on the sidewalk and telling his father, "Maybe that's all they can afford."

His father had turned toward him and said, "You're right, son." His father gazed for a moment at the distant mesquite and saguaro-covered foothills, then said, "I think there may be a lesson in this. Sometimes even the most decent among us don't listen to what they're really saying."

His father never hummed the song again and Gage never heard it again, except when his mind played it for him.

The song had faded by the time Gage had walked up the front steps of Tansy's tiny Daly City bungalow and rang the doorbell.

Tansy peeked out of the front window and then opened the door.

"How's Moki doing?" Gage asked, after she invited him.

"Okay. Some muscle spasms. It scared the aide so she called."

Gage spotted Moki sitting at the dining table coloring with crayons. Twenty-four years old with the mind of a child. Maybe not even a child. Children can recognize their mothers, if only just by instinct.

Tansy directed Gage toward the couch, then sat next to him and looked down at the file in his hand, Moki's name printed on the yellowed tab.

"It was Brandon Meyer's old law firm that hired Charlie to work on the side of the punks who jumped Moki," Gage said.

She shook her head. "They didn't represent anyone. You can look. I've got a copy of the whole court file in the closet."

"They didn't represent anyone, they represented everyone. They were the invisible hand behind the case that got rid of the witness."

Tansy's eyes went wide. "Got rid of . . ."

"Not that. Just out of town, way, way out of town. Charlie set him up in a condo one of the kids' parents owned in Cabo San Lucas. Until today, I had suspected Charlie of threatening the witness into fleeing. The truth is Charlie just paid him off."

"Where is he now?"

"Dead. Had a stroke a year later. He might've survived if he'd stayed in the States and was living close to a first-rate emergency room. He died of pneumonia a month afterward. I found his death certificate in Charlie's file."

Tansy bit her lip. "Poor man."

"What?" Gage threw up his hands. "Poor man? He was a disgusting human being."

"But pneumonia is a horrible, horrible way to die."

Gage started to answer, then caught himself. He examined Tansy's soft, round face and sympathetic eyes. She would've made a magnificent nurse.

He watched her drift off in thought during the quiet moments that followed.

"I didn't realize until now," Tansy finally said, "that despite what I told you, I hadn't really made peace with never knowing exactly what happened. I just stopped laboring over it in my mind." She glanced at the file. "How much money did Charlie make for doing it?"

"Nothing."

"Nothing?"

"As far as I can tell. His accounting records don't show any entries under that case number. Maybe he—"

Pegasus. Maybe the money was wired to Pegasus.

Gage wished he had known the name in India so he could've prompted Wilbert Hawkins's memory of the account that had wired the million dollars funding his escape.

In any case, Gage knew he needed to think it all through before he told Tansy.

"Maybe the payment was combined with something else he was working on," Gage said. Tansy's eyes flickered. He knew that she knew he was thinking something different than what he was saying. "Or something like that."

G ot it, boss."

Alex Z could barely dribble a basketball, but the enthusiasm blasting through the phone told Gage he'd just performed a slam dunk.

Gage was driving up the Embarcadero Freeway from Daly City back to his office, just about to the off-ramp toward China Basin and AT&T Park.

"There's no way anyone could have found it, no matter how much time they spent searching his computer."

"Except you," Gage said.

Alex Z laughed. "Of course."

"How did you do it?"

"Charlie named the file Med-USA and stored it among his medical records." Alex Z paused. Expectancy seemed to vibrate through the telephone line. "Get it?"

"Get what?"

"Med-USA."

"No. It doesn't mean anything."

"Remember the day I started searching Charlie's computer?"

"Sure. I walked into your office, tossed a paper airplane over your head . . ."

"My earrings."

"Earrings? Greek mythology?" Gage tried out versions in his mind. Med USA. Med-USA. MedUSA. "Medusa?"

"Bingo. Pegasus was the winged horse that emerged when Perseus cut off Medusa's head."

"Snakes."

"Snakes and money. Lots of snakes and money. Millions and millions and millions of dollars over fifteen years."

"What about the first spreadsheets you found? The ones with the coded columns?"

"I think they're bogus. Decoys for whoever might come snooping."

"Then why are you certain Medusa is real?"

"Because there's a million-dollar transfer from Pegasus to Andhra Bank in Hyderabad the same week Wilbert Hawkins disappeared."

Gage thought back on his conversation with Jack Burch.

"Where's the Pegasus bank account?" Gage asked.

"Cayman Exchange Bank."

Gage didn't like hearing the name. The bank had turned up in too many offshore financial scams over the years. Never convicted, but like most banks on the Caymans, often suspected.

"Can you tell where the money came from?"

"No. I think that's on another spreadsheet. I haven't been able to decode it yet."

"But you'll figure it out?"

"I'm not walking away from this computer until I do."

Bethel Island in the Sacramento River Delta.

Gage had gotten stonewalled the last time he drove out to confront the retired OSHA inspector, Ray Karopian. But that was then, when he had only vague questions about Karopian's investigation of the TIMCO explosion—

And this was now.

Viz followed Gage from San Francisco over the Bay Bridge then north, almost to where the Sacramento River flowed into San Pablo Bay. What had once been rolling hills grazed by cattle was now a commercial corridor of malls, fast-food restaurants, townhouses, and apartments.

Gage and Viz headed east on Highway 4 past the just-within-commuting-distance bedroom communities, condo complexes, and meth labs.

Hot, dusty, and windy.

They could see the TIMCO refinery spread out between the freeway and shoreline, its forest of two-hundred-foot fractionating towers operating around the clock, distilling crude oil into usable fuels and company profits.

Gage continued north after Viz pulled into a service station at the main Bethel Island intersection. He cast a glance toward False River, then hung a left along the waterfront to Karopian's three-story, clapboard-sided home. The house was set back from a wide street paralleling the shore. A third of an acre. Mature trees. Gage was still surprised at how little a million and a half dollars had bought before the economic collapse, even in Middle of Nowhere California.

He spotted Karopian working on the thirty-five-foot Bayliner tied to his private dock extending from the grass-covered levee, and remembered thinking last time it was an awfully big boat for such a slim stretch of water.

Karopian didn't turn until Gage's dress shoes thunked against the metal surface of the dock. Thin, balding, a rich, end-of-season tan. A walking JCPenney window display: Izod shirt, Dockers pants, and Sperry Topsiders.

"This is private property," Karopian said. "You need an invitation."

"I have one, you told me to come back if I had more questions." Gage smiled. "I guess you didn't mean it."

Karopian dropped his rag into the bucket at his feet, then stepped onto the transom platform and to the dock.

"On reflection," Karopian said, "I decided I wasn't thrilled with your attitude."

"I apologize. A kid in my office had just been beaten up."

Karopian's wincing face displayed fear, like that of a man who'd just made a wrong turn into oncoming traffic.

"Be . . . because of what?"

"That's what I'm trying to find out."

"I don't beat up people." Karopian stretched out his skinny arms as evidence.

"I didn't think you did."

"Then why are you out here again?"

"I came to tell you what happened in TIMCO."

Karopian's face darkened beneath his tan.

"I know what happened in TIMCO."

Gage nodded. "I believe you."

"If you believe me, then answer my question."

"I came back because what you know and what you wrote in your report were two different things."

A female voice yelled from behind Gage.

"Is everything all right, dear?"

Gage didn't turn around. Karopian waved to her, putting on a boyish smile. When it faded, Gage guessed she'd returned inside the house.

"I guess you two have been married a long time," Gage said.

"Thirty-five years."

"It shows. She can tell when you're about to pee in your pants."

Karopian's face darkened another shade.

"I'll make a deal with you," Gage said. "I'll tell you what happened and you just nod if I'm right." He paused. "Even better, try to look surprised."

Gage held his hands out like he was holding the valve.

"What happened was that somebody welded over the pressure release device and the weld didn't hold."

Karopian didn't look surprised.

"I examined every fragment we recovered," Karopian said. "I didn't find any fresh welds."

Gage felt his heart thump. *Gotcha.*

"The valve exploded right at the pressure release device," Karopian said. "So it had to have been what failed."

"You find all the parts?"

"You're not listening to me. That's what blew apart." Karopian's hand shot out toward the west. "For all I know the pieces flew all the way to San Pablo Bay."

Gage stared at him without answering. Karopian looked away.

"I think you need to try to reconstruct the thing in your mind," Gage finally said. "Maybe you'll come to a different conclusion." He turned, and said over his shoulder, "You've got my card."

age called Viz as he again drove along False River.

"He's panicking," Gage said.

"Did you tell him you knew Charlie's Pegasus company was the source of the money that went into his house?"

Viz was parked at the service station near the phone booth Karopian had used after Gage's first visit.

"I decided there's no reason to let the other side know we've gotten that far. Anyway I didn't need it to push him over the edge. Are you set up?"

"About fifteen yards from the phone. Where you gonna be?"

"Meet me at the fruit stand outside of Oakley."

A half hour later, Viz drove up to where Gage was sitting at a picnic table in the shade. Gage reached into a paper bag on the bench next to him and handed Viz a Coke when he sat down.

Viz slid over an iPod.

"How'd you get it?" Gage asked.

Viz smiled. "The parabolic microphone you bought me." He pointed at the new roof-mounted light rack on his Yukon. Black protective covers were fitted over two of the headlight-sized fixtures. One concealed the mike. "I have a little remote control in the cab." His smile widened. "You bought that, too."

Gage slipped in the earbuds, then pressed play. The first sound he heard was the Delta wind swirling into the phone booth, then footsteps, then the rustling of clothing, then a metallic snap, then tapping. Then a voice: Karopian's.

"It's me."

. . .

"Gage came back. He knows what really happened."

. . .

"How should I know? Maybe he . . . Oh shit."

Gage gave Viz a thumbs-up. Karopian must have just remembered he'd referred to "fresh" welds. Gage hadn't used the word, never even hinted about when he believed the pressure release had been welded over. The use of the word was Karopian's inadvertent admission that he'd known that the corroded pressure release device had been welded over, and it had been done just before the explosion. He therefore had known it had been the new weld that had failed.

"Nothing . . . I just bumped my elbow."

. . .

"Look Anston, I don't know what else he knows. That's where he left it."

. . .

Another thumbs-up. Marc Anston, Brandon Meyer's old law partner. The link Gage was looking for and the reason for his long drive out to the Delta.

"No. I didn't tell him anything except the party line."

. . .

"What's the statute of limitations on this stuff?"

. . .

"Then there's nothing he can do to us?"

. . .

"Slander. That's right. It would be slander if he said something."

. . .

"Yeah. I'll let you know if he comes back."

Gage removed the earbuds and handed the iPod back to Viz.

"Marc Anston is too smart a lawyer to think the statute of limitations has run on this," Gage said. "Unless he's forgotten he conspired to cover up a corporate murder."

age's cell phone rang as he walked into Skeeter's office to pick up his associates' research on Brandon Meyer's cases.

"I didn't do it," the caller said. "I'll take a polygraph."

Gage mouthed the name *Porzolkiewski* to Skeeter sitting at his conference table going over the reports.

"Didn't do what?"

"Karopian."

"Did what to Karopian?"

"I don't know." Porzolkiewski's voice rose in exasperation and panic. "I told you I didn't do it."

"Back up."

Gage heard Porzolkiewski take in a breath.

"The widow of one of the other men killed in the explosion called. She lives in out in the Delta. It was in the local paper. Karopian's wife found him dead late last night. Lying on his dock."

"Did the article say what happened?"

"No. They're doing an autopsy. But they're

guessing it was a heart attack brought on by heat stroke. Out in the sun too long."

"But you're thinking he must've been murdered," Gage said, "because you felt like murdering him yourself."

"Not just me. There are three widows and their kids who have just as good a motive as me."

"Where were you yesterday evening?"

"Home. I got back at about six o'clock."

"Back from where?"

"I didn't do it."

"That wasn't my question."

"The Delta. Near Big Break. She called me last week and asked me to help her pick out some shrubs at a nursery."

"Isn't that something she could've done herself?"

"Well, we sort of . . . kind of . . . made friends over the years."

"What time did Karopian's wife find the body?"

"The newspaper said ten o'clock. She last saw him during the morning. She spent the afternoon at one of the spas in Calistoga with her girlfriends. They had dinner in Napa."

Gage glanced at Skeeter's wall calendar.

"I'll check into it," Gage said. "Fax or e-mail me a chronology of where you were every minute during those hours. And give me a call if the police pay you a visit."

Porzolkiewski sighed. "You'll be the first."

Skeeter grinned after Gage filled him in, and said, "Maybe you scared the asshole to death."

Gage didn't smile back.

B oots Marnin drove by Jeannette Hawkins's house twice before he figured out which one it was. The first time he missed it because he'd failed to spot the faded plastic numbers against the peeling paint on the porch support. The second time he spotted both the numbers and a recycling bin overfilled with beer bottles.

He decided to postpone his visit until it was last call.

Marnin drove back through Richmond, past dope dealers, taquerias, full garbage cans, empty storefronts, and a couple of cops kneeling on the back of a homeless man in front of a shattered flower shop window. He crossed under the freeway, then slipped two blocks down a divided commercial street to Gold Rush Western Wear. The owner's exaggerated Texas accent was way too loud and he was way too friendly, but Boots got out of there in twenty minutes with a fresh pair of Wranglers and a George Strait button-down white shirt. He checked himself in the motel mirror just before he headed out that night. He even gave himself a little wink and a nod. He looked like he was just about to walk on stage at Nashville's Gaylord Arena.

The next morning Jeannette couldn't remember much of what happened.

The handsome man at the door. A gentleman. Cowboy hat held against his chest with both hands. Golly-gee-whiz shy. His father was an old buddy of Son of a Bitch from the navy.

That's what he'd said, anyway.

Come on in. Sure he'd have a beer.

First she got jealous when he stared too long at her daughter running out the front door, no bra, boobs bouncing under her father's faded AC/DC T-shirt. But then she got turned on when he looked back at her, a you're-my-type-honey smile on his face.

Man, what he would've thought twenty-five years ago when I had tits like that.

He was already gone by the time sunlight falling on her eyes woke her up. She rolled over, sort of expecting to see him, but there was just a slight depression in the pillow.

Must've been a light sleeper.

She was hoping for a nice note, nothing flowery, but something anyway, even just a phone number, but she didn't see anything.

She slid out of bed and steadied herself using the night table before shuffling to the bathroom. She examined herself in the mirror.

I look like shit. No afterglow on this broad.

She inspected the dark splotches under her eyes.

What did that cowboy want with me?

Something about Son of a Bitch. Hadn't seen him for years.

Yeah, he called. Couple of years ago.

Anybody come by trying to find him?

Some PI a while back. I got his card somewhere.

Jeannette took a pee, slipped on yesterday's shift, then walked into the kitchen. She decided on coffee instead of beer. She didn't need the hair of the dog, she needed something to jog her memory.

She dumped a little too much Folgers Instant into a cup, added water, then set it in the microwave. Took her a couple of tries to set the time. Twenty seconds. Twenty minutes. Twenty-two seconds. But finally she got the numbers punched in right: two minutes. She watched the cup through the fractured glass, wondering if she was irradiating herself, thinking for the millionth time maybe she ought to get one of them gizmos to find out if the thing was leaking microwaves and giving her cancer.

Maybe later. She didn't fear death much when she was hungover. In fact, it kinda seemed like a good idea.

She didn't wait for the beep. One-fifty was long enough. She pulled it out. *Shit.* Tasted like coffee grounds. She'd forgotten to sweeten it. She ripped open a couple of McDonald's sugar packets, then dropped in the contents and jiggled a spoon in the cup.

Another sip.

That's better.

She stood there, staring out the kitchen window at the rusted swing set in the backyard.

That's funny. Cowboy didn't even know Son of a Bitch got a dishonorable discharge. It's the kind of thing people talk about.

She turned back toward the living room. She smiled again. This time a bitter one.

Maybe his daddy liked fondling them little Okinawan girls just like Son of a Bitch.

Her eyes swept toward the telephone hanging on the wall. It seemed different. Not the phone. The wall around it. A blank spot.

Something's missing.

namaste."

"*Namaste* to you too, pal." Wilbert Hawkins pointed at a plastic lounge chair on the veranda. "Have a seat."

Prasad Naidu, deputy superintendent of the Gannapalli Police, glanced toward the central district, then shook his head. "I think we should sit inside."

Hawkins followed Naidu's eyes, and then scanned the street. A half-dozen buffalo were walking the dirt track, heading home from the fields on their own, and beyond them a group of men had collected at the bus stop, some looking sideways in Hawkins's direction. He grabbed his beer from the low table, then led the deputy superintendent into the living room. Naidu shut the door behind him and sat down. He wore a long-sleeved, dark green uniform pressed like folded paper. No gun on his black belt. No badge on his shirt.

"An American is asking where you are living," Naidu said.

Naidu's accent was heavy, sometimes sounding to Hawkins like comical gibberish, but not now.

"Same one?" Hawkins asked.

"Different."

"By himself?"

"With a Telegu language interpreter from the U.S."

"Did he say who he was?"

"He said he is working for the American consulate in Chennai and is coming here to check on your welfare. No one is believing him. Half the population has applied for visas, so they know the consulate only uses local translators."

Hawkins felt his stomach tighten. "What are people saying about me?"

"Playing dumb. He is not handing out money, yet. I think he is afraid they will figure out he is not for real once he does."

"But they'll take it."

"Yes, they will take it."

Hawkins rose. He walked into the hallway, then up the stairs into his bedroom. He returned two minutes later with an inch-high stack of hundred-rupee notes still stapled together like he had received them from the bank. Two hundred dollars U.S. He handed them to Naidu.

"Tell him I'm in Hyderabad for a few weeks," Hawkins said. "Say I needed hernia surgery."

"He'll be wanting to see your house."

"Bring him by. Walk him around the place like there's nothing to hide. That way I can get a peek at him."

* * *

Boots spent a jet-lagged, frustrating day trying to weasel information from a dozen different Hyderabad hospital clerks until he found a friendly one at the Deccan Infirmary, one who smiled at him and told him the doctors had recommended "Mr. Wilbert" have his surgery at the Parvatiben Gujarati Hospital in Chennai.

He felt like kicking himself. Hawkins had been no more than ten miles away from where Boots's flight from the U.S. had landed at the Chennai Airport, and not twenty hours down clogged and dust-swirling roads first to Gannapalli, then to Hyderabad, and back.

Twelve hours later, after speaking to the Deccan Infirmary clerk, he knew he'd been had: nobody at the Parvatiben Gujarati Hospital had ever heard of Wilbert Hawkins. And five hundred dollars in bribes had gotten him records proving they were telling the truth.

Boots felt like slitting a buffalo's throat.

Another guy trying to find him.

When Hawkins had peeked out of his upstairs window toward the dirt track running in front of the house, he had a nauseous feeling he wasn't so sure anymore who the good guys were. He knew who they used to be. Back then it was easy to tell. They gave him a million dollars and a first-class plane ticket to Karachi, then to Hyderabad.

But everything turned upside down when Gage appeared in his living room, and he still hadn't found his feet.

First he thought he'd call the good guys to find

out who his more recent visitor really was and what he might be up to. But he didn't know any of them anymore. He didn't even know who still worked at TIMCO. He'd never met any of the lawyers. He'd heard of Marc Anston, but never saw his face. And Charlie Palmer was dead.

Hawkins walked downstairs to the kitchen and grabbed a Kingfisher beer from the refrigerator. The five regular girls were sitting at the dining table giggling, painting their palms with henna and drinking mango juice through plastic straws. They knew he was worried so they went silent when he entered and didn't even look over to see if he wanted sex. Usually, he'd catch the eye of one or two, then jerk his head toward the door. It took them a while to learn what that meant since Indian men avoided using the insulting gesture, but now it was second nature to the girls. This time he walked past them through the kitchen and out to the back sleeping porch.

Hawkins stared at the monkeys sitting on the brown stucco wall. When he'd first arrived in India he thought they were cute; now they just seemed like big red rats. He couldn't even sit outside and eat anymore because of them begging or grabbing food off the table. Damn annoying.

Annoying. A face appeared in his mind, along with an answer. The only way the visitor could have figured out where he lived was from Jeannette. He hadn't talked to anyone at TIMCO for eight years, maybe more; at least since he moved from Hyderabad to the countryside. And he believed Gage when he said he'd keep his location a

secret because he knew Gage still needed him—
maybe.

But all Jeannette had was a telephone number.
Without his cop friend from Hyderabad, Gage
never would have found him. And if it was police
coming to arrest him on the criminal complaint in
Richmond, they'd have been Indian, not American, and the first thing they'd do was stick out their
hands for a bribe to go away.

Then the truth rose up before him: If the good
guys were still the good guys, they would've called
and just asked him if Gage had come by. Hawkins
wouldn't have told them, but he figured they'd ask.
Try to take his temperature. See if they needed to
send somebody out to snip off a loose end.

Hawkins set his beer down and returned to the
kitchen and picked up the telephone. He woke up
the person at the other end of the line and told him
the story.

"What did he look like?" Gage asked.

"I guess you could say he looked like a younger
George Strait. Same build, but a little taller."

"Does the name Pegasus mean anything to you?"

"Peg-a-sus . . . Peg-a-sus . . . That's it. That's who
sent me the money . . . Shit. You didn't tell Jeannette
about the money, did you?"

"No reason to. And don't call her yourself until I
tell you it's okay. I don't want anyone else figuring
out where you are."

Gage also didn't want Hawkins to figure out that
the criminal complaint was bogus.

"If I were you," Gage said, "I'd hightail it. The
George Strait–looking guy is named Boots Marnin.

There's no doubt he's on his way back to Ganna-palli, and I don't think it's to drink a beer with you on the veranda. Now that you've ducked him, he knows for certain you've got something to hide."

ld law partners. Thursdays, 11:45 A.M. at Tadich Grill in the San Francisco financial district. None of the waiters and none of the other regulars gave it a second thought after all these years.

Countless attorneys had been cut off mid-closing argument, even in mid-sentence, FBI agents had been left waiting outside chambers with search warrants to be signed, and juries left sitting with verdicts held over, all so Brandon Meyer could make it to lunch on time.

Marc Anston leaned a little closer toward Meyer sitting across the cloth-covered table. His Putin-like head gleamed in the light from a pendant fixture above, while his wireless glasses reflected the one suspended beyond the next table.

Looking back at him, Meyer felt, as much as saw, the familiar. A thin, old-money face, twelve years older than his, containing eyes that never stared or peered or gawked or leered or squinted. They only gazed, taking in, never projecting out. They were eyes formed by years of cold war intelligence work beginning in Moscow after Yale Law School and ending in Afghanistan in the 1980s.

"Gage knows about TIMCO," Anston said. "All we can figure is that he found Wilbert Hawkins and applied some pressure."

"What about the money trail?"

"We have to assume Hawkins told him about the million, but Gage didn't say anything about payoffs when he confronted Karopian."

Brandon took in a long breath through his nose, then breathed out, eyes fixed on Anston's. He interlaced his fingers and rubbed his thumbs together.

"What about Palmer's hard drive?" Brandon asked. "Anything?"

"Nothing. Our people searched every which way. There's no mention of Pegasus anywhere."

Brandon shook his head. His voice rose. "There has to be. He threatened to e-mail the spreadsheets to CNN."

Anston raised a palm toward Brandon. "Take it easy."

"It just pisses me off. That little punk takes a look at the grim reaper, then goes to jelly." Brandon pounded his middle finger on the white tablecloth. "None of us got into this for money."

"Except Palmer."

"And that's what's biting us in the ass," Brandon said. "He never believed in the cause in the first place. And once he realized money was no good in heaven or in hell—wherever he thought he was going—he caved. It's a damn good thing he had the seizure before he spilled it all to Gage."

"You know Gage," Anston said. "Is there any way to get him to back off?"

Brandon shook his head. "But we don't need to. Hawkins can't take Gage beyond Palmer, and Palmer's dead. Karopian knew how you fit in, but he's dead, too. Another lucky break."

Anston half smiled. "And Gage is in way too good a shape to have a seizure or a heart attack."

"What do you mean?"

Anston's smile faded. "Nothing."

"But what if he finds out about the Pegasus companies and all the accounts?"

"It won't make a difference. He'd have to go one step farther to connect them to us, and the Cayman Exchange Bank is never going to give up those records."

Both Anston and Brandon leaned back as the waiter set down their seafood sautés and remained silent while he topped off their water glasses.

"New subject," Anston said as the waiter walked away. "How did we do with OptiCom?"

"Should be around ten million."

"Ten?"

Brandon nodded. Big smile. "It's a multibillion-dollar company. Ten is nothing. Hardly a blip, and no one will be able to trace it to us. I'll find some way to suppress the evidence as soon as the defense files a motion to do it. I'll make a record so strong the U.S. Attorney won't even bother appealing. In the end, it's a no-harm, no-foul case. OptiCom pays a little money for FiberLink's switch as part of a civil settlement and everything is back to just the way it was before."

"How much more does your brother need?"

"For his campaign or the Supreme Court nominees?"

"One thing at a time. The nominees."

"I don't know for sure. We got pledges of about five in Silicon Valley during his last visit. It really depends on how big Landon's promises have to be to get his colleagues' confirmation votes once he gets the nominations out of the Judiciary Committee."

Anston fixed his eyes on Brandon's. His voice was low and hard.

"He's going to have to do whatever it takes. If Reagan had the guts to put up a fight in 1987, we'd have gotten Robert Bork instead of that wimp Anthony Kennedy. That lunatic cited European law more often than the U.S. Constitution. And I don't want to wait another twenty-five years for those idiots in Washington to get it right."

Anston stiffened as a two-term member of the city council passed by their table, a transsexual with the body of a linebacker, encased in a short-cut pant suit.

Anston shook his head as he stared after her.

"I hate this fucking town."

This really is like a ball of snakes," Alex Z said to Gage in his loft overlooking the tourist shops and seafood restaurants on the Oakland waterfront. "There's no way we'd have seen it if we hadn't been looking for it."

They stood facing a six-foot-by-eight-foot sheet of posterboard displaying a flowchart and chronology of the TIMCO and Moki Amaro cases.

"Walk me through how they did it," Gage said.

Alex Z picked up a yellow fluorescent marker from the worktable behind him and started at the left side of the chart.

"A million dollars showed up in the Pegasus Limited account after Meyer's firm got hired by TIMCO. It was later wired out to Hawkins. Then after the superior court ruled it was just a workers' comp case, TIMCO transferred another two million into Pegasus—"

"The fee for Anston and Meyer making the case go away."

"But I don't see anything that could have been a payoff to the judge who dismissed it," Alex Z said.

"I don't think there was one," Gage said. "If he'd been paid off, his decision would have been a lot more definitive than it was. He had to dismiss the case on legal grounds because the plaintiffs couldn't shake Hawkins or Karopian."

Gage scanned the complex chart. "Is that it for TIMCO?"

"It pops up again after Meyer was appointed to the bench. A TIMCO subsidiary got cited for toxic dumping into San Pablo Bay. The general manager was charged in federal court."

"Meyer's court?"

"Bingo. According to Skeeter Hall's research, Meyer forced the U.S. Attorney to knock it down to failure to report a spill, rather than an intentional release. No jail time. Just a fine."

"And the payoff?"

"A TIMCO subsidiary wired two hundred thousand into Pegasus a week before sentencing, and another two hundred a week after." Alex Z shook his head. "No one seemed to have noticed that TIMCO was a client of Meyer's old firm."

"Wouldn't make a difference," Gage said. "Meyer wasn't the attorney of record in the explosion case. That's all that counts in conflict of interest rules for judges."

"Makes you wonder whether Meyer is paying off clerks to direct the cases he wants into his court," Alex Z said.

"Possible," Gage said, "but untraceable. The payoffs would have been small and paid in cash, not hundreds of thousands of dollars wire transferred into offshore bank accounts." He pointed at the chart. "What about Moki?"

"That's even easier." Alex Z highlighted a series of lines. "Charlie's spreadsheets show four separate two-hundred-and-fifty-thousand-dollar payments into Pegasus."

"One transfer from the parents of each of the kids?"

"That's what it looks like. And a day later, four hundred thousand gets wired to the witness in Cabo San Lucas."

"So Charlie got rid of witnesses in the cases Meyer handled when he was a lawyer," Gage said, "and Judge Meyer got rid of cases that landed in his court."

Gage sat down and picked up the Pegasus spreadsheet.

"The problem," Gage said as he examined it, "is we have no way to connect Meyer directly to Pegasus."

Gage skimmed down to the bottom.

Alex Z pointed at the last line. "There was about nine million dollars in the account before Charlie closed it a week before he died. But I can't figure out where it was transferred."

Gage leaned back and crossed his arms over his chest. "I know where. Socorro showed me a Pegasus insurance policy. Two million dollars for each of their children. And another seven million went into an annuity for Socorro."

"You mean he stole it?"

"Either that or it was his cut for a career of criminality."

"Is that why they broke into his house? Trying to find where the money went?"

"At this point there's no way of knowing." Then a question came to Gage in an image of a writhing Charlie Palmer during his final moments. "It makes me wonder whether Charlie's death really was from natural causes."

Gage kept Lieutenant Spike Pacheco company on a wooden bench outside San Francisco Superior Court Department 23 while he waited to be called in to rebut defense claims at the tail end of a homicide trial. Gage surveyed the long marble-floored hallway, normally packed with defendants, attorneys, and the relatives of the in-custodies, but not at four o'clock on a Friday. It satisfied him there was no one close enough to overhear their conversation.

"Somebody who was trying to trace the money wouldn't have murdered Charlie," Gage said. "That would guarantee they'd never get it back."

Spike jerked his thumb over his shoulder toward the courtroom.

"You know what that scumbag in there told me after he murdered his wife and tossed her off Devil's Slide into the Pacific Ocean? 'I just wanted her back, I just wanted her back.' What did you beat into my brain when I got promoted into homicide? Don't look for reasons, look for motives, for what really drives people, because the reasons killers give can be nonsensical."

"And that's what's been nagging at me. Porzolkiewski. He's got the motive, triggered by bumping into Brandon Meyer on the street. Maybe it pushed him over the edge. First he shot Charlie when he came to retrieve the wallet and later got inside his house to finish him off. Then he figured from what I told him that Karopian was in on it and had been paid off to submit the false OSHA report on the cause of the explosion, so he went after him."

"Somehow."

"That's the problem. We've got a truck load of motive, but no suspicious cause of death. Porzolkiewski wasn't even on Bethel Island when Karopian died, and he sure was in a hurry to tell me he wasn't."

"Did you check?"

"He admitted to being about ten miles away from Karopian's house earlier in the day, but claimed he was at the Ground Up Coffee Shop on Geary at about the time of death. I talked to a couple of employees. He was there all right. He's known to most of the people who work there."

"What about the day Charlie died?"

"No idea. I made a deal with him. In exchange for copies of what was in Meyer's wallet he got to listen to part of my tape of Hawkins's confession. I didn't ask him anything about Charlie, not even about the shooting. I'm still not sure I know enough to ask him anything in a way that'll get an answer that would make a difference."

The courtroom door swung open next to them.

The DA stepped out. "The judge needs a five-minute break," she said, "then you're on."

Spike nodded and she walked back inside.

"How about taking a long shot with a little of the county's money?" Gage asked.

"For what?"

"Another toxicology analysis. The only way Porzolkiewski could have killed Karopian is by remote control."

"And you figure he might've done the same thing with Charlie?"

"And doing the tests here is a lot cleaner than getting the local cops in a tizzy out on Bethel Island."

Gage's cell phone rang the next morning as he was sitting at the conference table in his office puzzling over a printout of Charlie Palmer's Pegasus spreadsheet.

"The medical examiner just sent me the results. He feels like an idiot."

Spike wasn't laughing.

"What was it?"

"It's called sodium monofluoroacetate. Nobody would've thought to do a tox screen for poison in a case like Charlie's. It's banned in the States, but it's used in Canada to kill wolves. They put it in a collar around a cow's neck and when the wolf attacks he gets a mouthful. Let me read what the ME e-mailed me: white powder, no taste, no odor, attacks the cardiovascular and central nervous systems simultaneously. A tenth of a gram is all it takes to kill a human being."

"So you could put it in someone's coffee—"

"And the victim would think it was Splenda."

"What does it look like in action?"

"Seizures, convulsions, and cardiac arrest."

"Sounds horrendous."

"And there goes Porzolkiewski's alibi if it shows up in Karopian's blood, too," Spike said. "It can take as long as twenty hours to show itself."

Gage rested an elbow on the conference table, then ran his hand down the back of his head.

"It's hard to imagine John Porzolkiewski as a cold-blooded murderer," Gage said. "A manslaughter, heat of passion, enraged enough to shoot Charlie down in the street—that I can see. Sneaking into Charlie's house, lacing his juice or sticking a needle in him—I don't see him doing it. Or to Karopian either."

"We'll find out. I just called the Contra Costa County Sheriff's Department. Bethel Island is their jurisdiction. Usually they just find the bodies of dead meth dealers out there, and never find the killers. They're drooling over this one. They'll have the tox results by this time tomorrow."

Gage felt himself losing control of the investigation. In another forty-eight hours, the links—proven or not—among Porzolkiewski, Charlie, Karopian, and Meyer's former law firm would be front-page news. Reporters would be pawing through the search warrant affidavit and the police reports, the "what ifs" becoming "and thens." Unless . . .

"I'm worried about publicity," Gage said.

"You're not the only one."

Gage's mind wound its way through a forest of

dangers, then he had a thought about how to skirt around them all:

"I've got an idea of how to conceal what we're doing. Use me as a confidential informant and get an order sealing the search warrant affidavit for my safety."

Spike laughed. "Won't that be a little embarrassing when it comes out? People thinking you turned wimp."

"I'll take the risk."

There was a pause on the other end of the line.

"I've got a better plan," Spike finally said. "I'll just say there's an ongoing investigation that would be compromised. A little bullshit about CIs, pending search warrants, and means and methods. Judges like that kind of crap. It makes them feel important. And I'll get the DA to lean on the judge for a gag order if it looks like the case might break open. Judges like that, too, since it makes them the center of the media coverage. Nobody gets to talk except them."

John Porzolkiewski wasn't paying attention when the chubby Hispanic in the outdated brown sports coat walked into his Tenderloin store. His eyes darted back and forth between the two homeless men huddled by the beer display cooler on the opposite wall and the three high school girls giggling at the latest issue of *Penis Envy* at the front of the porn-lite magazine rack.

He still wasn't paying attention when the Hispanic man stopped in front of the counter behind which he was standing, when he pulled a single piece of paper out of a leather folder, and when two uniformed officers stationed themselves by the front door.

The words, "I'm Lieutenant Pacheco of SFPD. I have a warrant to search your store," finally broke through the auto-pilot haze of decades running a skid-row market.

Porzolkiewski reached out to accept the paper from Spike's hand. He spotted the words "Search

Warrant" in bold letters on the top, then shook his head and looked up.

"Busting my place apart because of some health code violation? What do you expect to find, plague?"

Porzolkiewski's eyes locked on a spot past Spike's left shoulder, then he threw his arm forward, jabbing his finger at the homeless men.

"Put that back and get out of here."

Spike glanced over and spotted the top of a silver and black King Cobra forty-ouncer protruding from a grimy army-jacketed armpit. The two patrol officers grabbed the homeless men, patted them down, removed four cans of malt liquor from their coat pockets, and pushed them out the door. Spike pointed at the girls, then toward the entrance. They slipped the magazine onto the rack, and slinked past him and out to the street.

Porzolkiewski was staring down at the search warrant when Spike turned back, his hands shaking and his eyebrows furrowed on what seemed to Spike to be a permanently sad face.

"I need you to keep your hands in view and come around the counter," Spike told him.

Porzolkiewski backed up a half step, then glanced under the countertop.

Spike pulled his coat back and rested his hand on the butt of his semiautomatic.

"It's not that," Porzolkiewski said. He bent down, reaching under the counter.

Spike yanked out his gun. A double-handed grip aimed it at Porzolkiewski's forehead.

"Don't do it."

Porzolkiewski looked up at the barrel just inches away, then toward Spike's face.

"What are you doing? It's not like I killed someone."

"It's exactly like you killed someone." Spike jerked the gun up an inch. "Back away."

Porzolkiewski straightened and stepped back. Spike skirted the counter, spun Porzolkiewski around, and pushed him up against the condom and hard liquor shelves. He reholstered his gun and snapped on handcuffs. He then gripped the chain linking the two cuffs with one hand, grabbed the back of Porzolkiewski's shirt collar with the other, and guided him around the counter toward the door. A uniformed officer waiting on the sidewalk took Porzolkiewski by the arms, leaned him over the hood of a patrol car, and patted him down.

Spike pointed at one of the patrol officers waiting in the store to execute the search warrant and said, "Check for a gun under the counter."

The officer crouched down, grunting as he moved items around on the two shelves.

A woman entered wearing a white disposable hazmat suit and pushing a cart bearing a portable chemical vapor detector. Black rubber boots encased her feet and neoprene gloves protected her hands. She breathed through a respirator attached to the plastic face shield of her hood.

Spike watched Porzolkiewski struggle against the handcuffs as the woman came to a stop in front of the cash register.

The officer stepped back.

"No gun, Lieutenant."

"Then what the . . ."

The officer reached down and pulled out a box. "This." He tilted it toward Spike.

Spike shook his head. "I nearly shot this guy over a Siamese kitten. What is it about these psychos? Poison two men to death, then almost give it up over some pound-worthy animal. It's like some 1950s B-movie."

He nodded at the woman, then said to the patrol officer:

"Let's get out of here and let her do her work."

G age wasn't surprised he didn't recognize the deputy on the other side of the bulletproof window on the seventh floor of the Hall of Justice. It had been over twenty years since Gage had been a regular visitor booking murderers into the jail. And like a snake that sheds its skin, it was almost a new sheriff's department. Only a few from Gage's generation were left, now in the upper ranks.

The deputy accepted Gage's PI license as a ticket inside, then activated the locks on the barred gate and the sliding metal door.

Gage stepped into the hallway and signed in on the visitor's log. He heard a baritone voice call out his name from behind the booking counter to his left. He looked over to find its source: a sixty-year-old freckled face below a bald head. It was a sergeant from the old days, now wearing a captain's insignias.

Gage walked over and stuck out his hand.

"I used to know a guy who sort of looked like

you," Gage said. "We called him Red, but I don't see the red anymore."

Red shook his hand and smiled. "Your day will come. You ain't gonna keep all that hair forever."

Red glanced at the sign-in sheet across the hallway, and asked, "Who you here to see?"

"John Porzolkiewski."

"The poison guy?"

Gage nodded.

"Weird dude."

"Weird dude?" Gage laughed. "Haven't you been out of this place in the last thirty years? No one says 'weird dude' anymore. That went out with 'put a cap in his ass' and 'what's up bro.'"

"Okay, forget the dude part. He's still weird. He didn't say peep other than 'I want my phone call' after Spike hooked him up at his market. He never even invoked. Spike says he read him his rights and the guy just stared back like a beached whale."

Gage looked down the hallway through a gate separating the visiting rooms from the rows of cells facing each other fifty feet away. He could see hands and forearms extending from the cells, some resting on flat cross pieces, others gesturing. Mostly brown and black. A staccato of hard voices, knife-sharp cackles, and assaulting laughs reverberated against the concrete and steel.

"He's not in main line." Red jerked his thumb toward the other end of the hallway. "We put him on suicide watch last night."

"You have a shrink talk to him?"

Red shook his head. "No point if he's not gonna talk back."

* * *

"I didn't do it," Porzolkiewski said, just as Gage crossed the threshold into the interview room.

"Then what were you doing with a pound of sodium monofluoroacetate in your storeroom?" Gage pulled back a plastic chair and sat down across the table from him. "That's enough to kill everyone who works at TIMCO."

"I never saw it before."

"It was on a shelf. Eye level."

"In a bag of flour. I don't open every bag of flour to see what's inside. Those cops planted it. Brandon Meyer and Marc Anston must've paid them off."

"Spike Pacheco isn't buyable."

"Then it was the hazmat woman." Porzolkiewski folded his arms over the front of his orange jump-suit. "You going to vouch for her, too?"

Gage shook his head. "I don't need to."

He pulled out the timeline Porzolkiewski faxed over to attempt to prove his innocence after the newspaper reported the discovery of Karopian's body.

"I went out to talk to the woman you visited in the Delta. You told me *she* called you. She told me *you* called her. You put yourself within ten miles of Karopian on the day he was murdered, then lied to me about why you were there."

Porzolkiewski stared at the page, face rigid.

"I also talked with Karopian's wife," Gage said. "She hasn't touched the boat since he died. SFPD and Contra Costa County sheriff's deputies are dusting the cabin for prints right now."

Gage dropped the chronology on the table. "What do you think they're going to find?"

Porzolkiewski looked up. "So I went to see him." He smirked at Gage. "It didn't take a genius to put two and two together. I figured out what else was on the recording you played for me. No one would've believed Hawkins unless Karopian had backed him up with the OSHA report. He had to be in on it. I wanted to see the look on his face."

"No, you wanted to see the *last* look on his face."

Porzolkiewski gripped the edge of the gray metal table.

"I . . . didn't . . . kill . . . the guy."

"I know. That was the poison's job. Just like with Charlie Palmer. You're lucky it's too late to recover fingerprints from his house. I'm sure his wife has cleaned up the bedroom, but then again . . . maybe not."

Porzolkiewski rubbed his hands together on top of the table. Lips compressed. Eyebrows narrowed. A bouncing left leg caused his body to vibrate. He scratched his head, then rubbed his nose. Gage sensed him trying to dam something inside himself, hold it back.

Then the floodgates broke open.

"I didn't go to Palmer's the day he died. It was three days earlier, and I didn't go there to kill him. I went there because I felt bad about . . . about . . ."

"Shooting him in the first place?"

Porzolkiewski's voice hardened. "I'm not going to talk about that or somebody'll plant a gun in my house. Look. I . . . didn't . . . kill the guy. Some-body's setting me up."

"How come everything you say to defend your-self sounds like a confession?"

Porzolkiewski rose and glared down at Gage.

"What a waste of time."

He took a step toward the visiting room door, looked out through the wire mesh window for a passing deputy, and began pounding.

While walking down the front steps of the Hall of Justice, Gage realized he had the answer he came for: Handing Porzolkiewski the truth was just like putting a gun in his hand.

It was a good thing Porzolkiewski didn't know where Wilbert Hawkins was living.

Gage heard something grate in the back of his mind like misaligned gears: Boots.

Was there a connection between Porzolkiewski and Boots Marnin? How did Porzolkiewski know to send Boots to India to find Hawkins, and how did he get hooked up with Boots in the first place?

But what if there wasn't a connection between Porzolkiewski and Boots?

Then what?

G age called Spike at SFPD Homicide after an hour working through Charlie's records with Alex Z. He knew he wasn't seeing something in the mass of data lying before them, but he didn't yet have the means to recognize it.

"What happened at Porzolkiewski's arraignment?" Gage asked.

"Nothing."

"What do you mean nothing?"

"He wouldn't say a word. Refused to enter a plea. Refused to talk to the public defender. The judge sent him off to the funny farm. Smart move on Porzolkiewski's part. He's just delaying the inevitable, but smart move anyway."

"Are you going to ship him off for trial first in Contra Costa?"

"We were until he admitted to you he went to Charlie's. Now the case here is as strong as the one there. Might as well do this one." Spike chuckled. "You ought to keep visiting the guy. Every time he opens his mouth he digs himself in a little deeper. What do you think he's doing?"

"He's just like all the shrewd crooks," Gage said. "Build your defense around what you can't deny and what's sure to be found out anyway."

"Well, I've got something else he won't be able to deny." Gage heard Spike shuffle papers on his desk. "I just received Porzolkiewski's cell phone records. It has calls to the Mariner Hotel where Viz had followed Boots Marnin. Four calls during the week after Charlie got shot. We can't trace them to his exact room, but the jury won't care. If Marnin had worked a little smarter in India, there could've been a third body."

The gears caught again. Porzolkiewski had claimed he sold the wallet for ten thousand dollars to two men claiming to represent Meyer. Maybe the calls to Boots were the negotiations, and maybe there was evidence to confirm it.

"Have you gone over everything seized from Porzolkiewski's house?"

"Not yet. The prize was the sodium monofluoroacetate from the store. In fact—more shuffling—"the evidence sheet shows the officers only took flour containers from the house and cleaning powders from the garage." Spike paused. More shuffling. "Beyond that, only some indicia to prove in court he had control of the house: telephone and electric bills, and his wallet."

"Porzolkiewski's wallet? That doesn't sound right. He would've had it with him at the store."

More shuffling. "There's a wallet listed on his jail property sheet, too. Let me call you back."

* * *

Spike called back fifteen minutes later.

"You may want to drop by. I've got two wallets sitting on my desk and one of them doesn't belong to Porzolkiewski . . . and there's some really strange stuff in it."

L unge and parry. Lunge and parry.

Landon Meyer felt a yawn rising, and forced it down. To the millions of viewers watching the confirmation hearing of Judge Phillip Sanford, Landon knew he appeared serious and senatorial, even presidential.

In fact, he was bored.

"May I have another five minutes, Mr. Chairman?"

Landon looked down the curving dais at Democratic senator Andrea Quick and nodded.

"With no objection."

The seventy-year-old Quick fixed her eyes on Judge Sanford. Her coiffed hair was as frozen in place as her belittling stare.

"Let me understand where your argument takes you, Judge."

Sanford gazed up at Quick; his elegant features and earnest expression had been a form of armor no other Democrat had been able to penetrate.

Landon smiled to himself. Jimmy Stewart

couldn't have appeared more wholesome and invincible; then his internal smile faded as he wondered why there were no actors like that anymore, nor even an America like the one Stewart lived in. But then he felt a wave of uncertainty, wondering whether that old America could be restored by someone as young as Sanford, experienced in law, but not in life.

"Doesn't your free speech argument lead us down a road toward the eventual overturn of entirety of McCain-Feingold and every other piece of legislation restricting corporate contributions directly to political candidates and—"

"Madam Senator—"

Quick wagged a finger at Sanford. "Don't interrupt me, young man."

Sanford's face reddened, then he grinned like a schoolboy trying to deflect a teacher's discipline.

"I was about to say . . ." Quick reddened, too, then stiffened.

Landon watched the slow recognition sweep across the room that Sanford had derailed her train of thought.

Quick scanned the notes her staff had prepared.

Lunge and parry, Landon said to himself. *Lunge and parry*.

"With all due respect, Madam Senator, I'm not sure it's appropriate for me to comment on a matter that may come before the Court."

Sanford had rescued her from the embarrassing moment by suffocating the issue, and everyone in the audience and watching on television or online had recognized it also.

By Landon's count, it had been the twenty-third

time he'd executed that question-strangling maneuver.

Landon understood the confirmation hearing wasn't about Sanford alone. It was also about how effectively the Democrats could take shots at President Duncan. For them, Sanford was both a nominee to be defeated and a surrogate to be whipped, but so far the rawhide had been missing its target and snapping back into the Democrats' faces.

But, in a way, Landon felt as though the whip's popper was just missing him or maybe just pricking him, for it reminded him of an internal tension that had vibrated within him since college. Was the conservatism he believed in composed of tradition or of ideology? Was he an Edmund Burke defending what the country had been and therefore what must be, or a Thomas Hobbes creating a Leviathan out of the chaos of competing wills and constraining everyone for their own safety? Was he a man who believed that the American was at heart a yeoman farmer who should be left to plow his fields as he pleased, or was he a man who believed Americans were merely impulse-driven juveniles whose lives—from their bedrooms to their doctors' offices—must be monitored and managed?

Landon knew who Brandon wanted to be, but in the twinges of conscience he sometimes felt, he wondered about himself.

He thought of the summer intern who'd misunderstood his biblical reference to the Leviathan, and now wondered whether he'd somehow misunderstood it, too.

Quick looked up from her notes.

"Is there anything that might *not* come before the Court, anything you feel you *are* free to comment on?"

Sanford displayed a bland smile and shook his head.

"I'm sorry to say, Senator, we live in a litigious society."

"Where do we stand?" Brandon Meyer asked his brother as they sat in Landon's office in the Dirksen Building.

The Senate Judiciary Committee had just completed a party-line vote to send Sanford and Heller's nominations to the full Senate.

Brandon had flown to Washington to meet with members of the National Republican Senatorial Committee.

"About seven Democrats are only pretending to be undecided," Landon said. "And we have two of ours who are truly sitting on the fence. They're not sure whether they can buy their way back from an affirmative vote."

"So they've got fifty against and we've got forty-eight in favor. If we can swing our two, then we're at fifty-fifty and the vice president breaks the tie."

"It won't be pretty," Landon said, "but it'll be done."

Brandon examined his tally sheet lying on the edge of Landon's desk, then asked, "How much more will it take to bring over those last two?"

"There's a prior question," Landon said. "How do we get it to them?"

"You just tell me what they need. I'll figure out the rest."

just keep hearing this grating in the back of my mind," Gage told Faith as they hiked up the hill from their house toward the pine- and oak-lined trails of the regional park early on Saturday morning.

Gage hoped the perspective of distance and high places would help him discern a pattern in what seemed contradictory and incongruous.

"Maybe it's just Porzolkiewski lying all the time," Faith said.

"That's part of it, but not all. I've got this peculiar feeling I'm doing someone else's work."

"You mean helping someone frame Porzolkiewski?"

"You should've seen the way he broke down at the end of the recording of my interview of Wilbert Hawkins. I don't think he was faking."

"How do you know it wasn't just relief he'd killed the right guy? Maybe he had a lingering doubt about what happened, then you proved the company was guilty and Charlie was part of the cover-up."

The road jogged west just before the park entrance. They paused, surveying the bay from San Francisco north toward Mount Tamalpais in Marin County. Low fog still lay outside the Golden Gate, extending past the Farallon Islands twenty-seven miles out into the Pacific.

Gage's eyes settled on the Richmond refineries in the distance, miles of jagged metal fragments jabbing upward.

"Imagine the men watching the flames shooting up the tower toward them," Gage said, "trapped, helpless . . ."

Faith finished the thought. "Then imagine Porzolkiewski living it over and over in his mind for fourteen years. Like Sisyphus, condemned to pushing the boulder up the hill, then watching it roll back down time and again. Then you showed him he could pick it up and use it as a weapon."

"Maybe it would've been better if he'd never learned the truth." Gage closed his eyes and rubbed his temples. "But . . ."

"Something doesn't fit?"

Gage looked again toward San Francisco, first focusing on the Hall of Justice south of downtown, then making out Russian Hill rising above the incoming fog to the north.

"Why don't we cut this short," Gage said, "and go visit Socorro."

Viz answered Socorro's door, wearing a sweaty T-shirt, grimy with dirt.

"We were in the neighborhood," Gage said. "We thought we'd check on your sister."

"Come on in. We were just taking a break from

cleaning up the backyard. It got a little overgrown in the last couple of months."

They found Socorro in the kitchen, finally changed out of her saggy sweats into faded Levi's and an oversized plaid shirt, dropping ice cubes into a pitcher of tea.

She turned at the sound of their footsteps, then smiled and said, "Reinforcements have arrived."

Faith stepped forward and reached out to her hug her, but Socorro held up her hands.

"I don't think you want to be wearing mud and lawn clippings on your sweater for the rest of the day."

Socorro motioned toward the veranda.

"Sit down. I'll bring you out something to drink."

They walked out into air perfumed by the smell of cut grass and fresh earth, and then sat down in the heavy wicker chairs now arranged in a semicircle facing the lawn.

A minute later Socorro arrived and set down their drinks, and then smiled at them.

"So, what do you need to know?"

Faith blushed. "Can't people just drop by?"

"Yes, but Graham has the look." She settled into her chair and patted Viz's arm. "I first noticed it on my brother's face after he'd been in the DEA for a couple of years."

Gage put up his hands. "I surrender."

"So?"

"I'm interested in the last week before Charlie died."

"Are you still putting the case together against John Porzolkiewski?"

"I wouldn't call it that exactly, but basically that's right."

"He didn't come by when I was home, and Charlie didn't say he was here."

Viz caught Gage's eye. Of course he wouldn't say anything, there'd be too much to explain.

Socorro shuddered. "The idea of Porzolkiewski sneaking into my house and poisoning Charlie. I haven't been able to sleep. I just keep imagining it over and over." She lowered her gaze and shook her head and said in a grim tone of self-reproach, "If I just hadn't left him alone."

"You can't blame yourself," Gage said. "I'm not sure we even know when it happened or how the poison was given to him."

Socorro shrugged. There was nothing Gage could say to defend her against her self-accusation. He knew it and she knew it. So he moved on.

"Let's go back a little further," Gage said. "You told me Brandon called about a week before Charlie died and they argued about something that was supposed to take place and about Charlie being unable to do some work."

Socorro nodded.

"Anything else happen during that last week?" Gage asked.

She propped her elbows on the arms of the chair, then rested her chin on her interlaced hands.

"I'll try to work backward. He woke up feeling weak and had difficulty breathing. Not suffocating, just really labored. I called the doctor, then went to pick up a prescription for Amantadine." She glanced behind her toward the inside of the house.

"I gave the bottle to Spike when he came by yesterday."

She closed her eyes for a few moments, then opened them.

"Viz told me you were coming back from Zurich. I passed it on to Charlie and he said wanted to call, but he had trouble dialing the phone because of numbness in his hands. So I did. Then he broke down when he heard Moki's name. And about forty-five minutes later I heard a thump and I . . . and I went back upstairs . . . and . . ."

Faith reached over and took Socorro's hand. "It must have been terrible."

Socorro took in a breath, then shuddered again, tears now forming in her eyes.

"Maybe I gave it to him myself, in the Amantadine—"

Gage cut her off.

"That's not possible. Sodium monofluoroacetate doesn't act that fast. It takes at least two and a half hours and as long as twenty. If he woke up with respiratory problems, that means he probably got it the day before."

"The day before?" Socorro shook her head. "I don't remember anything special happening the day before. The physical therapist came by in the early afternoon, Jeffrey something, so I went shopping. I got back about three o'clock. Jeffrey told me he went to the store for a few minutes to buy some massage lotion he forgot to bring." She looked over at Gage, "Is that when Porzolkiewski snuck in?"

"I don't know," Gage said. "How can I get ahold of Jeffrey? What agency is he with?"

"Physical Therapy Associates over on Mission below Cesar Chavez Street."

Gage pulled out his cell phone, punched in directory assistance, then let the service connect the call. He handed her the telephone.

"Ask for his last name, tell them you want to send a thank-you note. Don't pressure them for an address. I'll find it."

Socorro obtained the name, hung up, and then repeated it as she handed the phone back to Gage.

"I'm sure it wasn't Jeffrey," Socorro said. "He was wonderful, a sweetheart, much nicer than the previous one. I was glad when she quit."

Gage slipped the phone into his shirt pocket.

"Let's go back a little further," Gage said.

"Nothing. Everything was routine. No one came to see him except the kids. They flew up on Friday night and went back on Sunday. I know they were upset seeing their father in the condition he was in, but they didn't leave his side. They even slept in chairs in his room." She paused, probing her memory, then said, "There was a plumbing problem the day before Charlie died, but I was with the plumber the whole time." Her eyebrows furrowed. "At least I think I was."

"You know his name?"

"I've got his business card." She walked into the kitchen, then returned with a glossy blue card with gold lettering: Sang Ngoc Pham Plumbing and Rooting.

Gage took it from her hand, examined it, and then shook his head.

ang Pham's first words as he crawled out from
under the house in South San Francisco were,
"Oh shit."

Gage reached down and grabbed Sang's arm
before he could slither back under, then yanked
him out onto the grass. Sang rose to his feet and
glanced around. His eyes hesitated when they found
his stepside van, but his dejected expression seemed
to be saying there was no point in running because
he'd have to come back for it and Gage would be
waiting.

"It's called the statue of limitations." Sang's Viet-
namese accent had faded a bit since they last met.
"My lawyer told me about it."

"*Statute* of limitations," Gage said.

"Yeah. Statute."

Two generations of police detectives in San Francisco knew Sang, his grandfather, his father, his five
brothers, and their sister—and the Phams made
sure they knew each of their enemies. The family
was a form of organized crime: gambling, extortion,

fraud, prostitution. Gage's last contact with them was ten years earlier, in connection with a year-long series of Silicon Valley high-tech burglaries in which Sang's role was to deliver the stolen micro-processors to off-brand server manufacturers.

Sang was the youngest and the lightweight among the siblings, less a danger to society than a burden on it.

"What exactly did you do?" Gage asked.

Sang stared at Gage, then smiled the subservient grin Gage suspected he reserved for white people to whom he was giving plumbing estimates.

"Oops."

Gage pulled the Sang Ngoc Pham Plumbing and Rooting business card out of his shirt pocket.

"How'd you get a plumbing license?" Gage asked.

"Felonies okay. Really." He shrugged "Bonding, maybe not."

"The card says licensed *and* bonded."

"Good intentions."

Gage pointed toward the concrete front steps of the lime green stucco house. They walked over and sat down.

Sang spread his hands, grinning. "What do you think? Really."

"About what?"

"My rental house."

"Who chose the color?"

"Nobody. It was on sale. It's good in Vietnam." Sang surveyed the earth-toned houses bracketing his. "Here, maybe not." He lowered his hands and let his grin fade. "But you didn't come to talk real estate investment."

"I wanted to ask you about Charlie Palmer."

"Who?"

Gage cast him a sour look.

"I don't know a Charlie Palmer, really. He deal in computer chips? I've been out of that business a long time, since I got out of prison. Really."

Sang seemed convincing. With or without all the "reallys."

Sang cocked his head and squinted toward the sky.

"Palmer . . . Palmer. I did a Palmer." He looked at Gage. "A woman with a Mexican name. Senora or something."

"Socorro."

"That's it. She had a clogged drain in the kitchen. And I cleaned out some roots in the line near the street."

Gage gave him another sour look.

"She needed it. Really. I didn't cheat her."

"Did anyone come to the house while you were there? Maybe an older guy, heavyset?"

Sang scrunched up his face in thought, and then shook his head and said, "There was just a young guy in a golf shirt who came down from upstairs. I remember because he wanted to use the sink to get a drink of water. I don't know if he was still there when I left."

"What was he like?"

Sang gave a limp wrist wave, then grinned.

"Like that."

Jeffrey Stark wasn't at all like that. He was all black leather, except his butt cheeks, which were pink and hairy, and he was a hard man for Gage to find, even with the DMV photo Spike had given him. Gage spent the evening searching for a twenty-five-year-old in a golf shirt, not realizing it was theme night at the Bootstrap on Folsom Street.

Gage wore slacks and a button-down blue shirt, trying to look like a closeted middle-aged suburban husband on the prowl. He was leaning against his car three spaces down from the club when Jeffrey walked out, led by a shirtless eighteen-year-old in a black vest and leather pants. The combination was absurd even by San Francisco standards and too early for Halloween. The kid looked like an elf leading a wolf.

Gage pushed himself off the car and stepped in their path as they approached.

"Mind if I hold the leash?" Gage said.

A heavy chrome chain hooked to a spiked leather

collar around Jeffrey's neck terminated in Elf's left hand.

Elf's eyes registered the ten-inch rise between his eyes and Gage's. It caused him to a come to a stop one step sooner than Jeffrey, who bumped into his back.

Gage took the chain out of Elf's hand and pointed at the Bootstrap.

"Maybe you should go back inside for a couple of minutes."

Jeffrey's eyes were red and his face was bleary from too much dancing, too much beer, and too much giving and receiving inside the jail cell arena, the service stalls, and the glory holes.

"I want to ask you about a client," Gage said.

Gage's presence registered.

Jeffrey struggled to put some words together. "I . . . I can't talk about clients . . . because of . . . because of HIPAA. Confidentiality and all that."

Gage glared down at Elf. "I asked you nicely."

Elf looked up at Jeffrey, who shrugged and said, "Go. I'll meet you when I'm done."

They watched Elf walk to the entrance and glance back. The opening door released a thumping blast of music and a flood of light as he stepped inside.

Gage gave the chain a tug.

"Hey man, that's not a—"

Gage smiled. "A leash?"

Jeffrey's eyes flared. "You know what I mean."

"I'm not asking about anybody's medical condition. I just want to know what happened at Charlie Palmer's house during the two days before he died."

"Who are you?"

"Graham Gage. I'm a private investigator."

"For who?"

"His wife."

"What do you want to know?"

"Just what I said." Gage tilted his head toward the club. "Didn't you get enough dancing inside?"

Jeffrey bit at his thumbnail. "Nothing happened during the last two days."

"The sun came up, the sun set . . . what do you mean nothing happened?"

"I mean nothing important."

"You remember a plumber coming by the day before Charlie died?"

"Yeah, that happened."

"How long was he there?"

"A couple of hours. He left before I did."

"Anything else happen?"

A transvestite wearing a pink empire halter dress came clicking down the sidewalk in high heels. She stopped next to them and smiled at Gage holding the leash.

"Mm'mm. Room for a third?"

Gage shook his head. "Sorry. We're monogamous."

She shrugged and moved on.

Gage looked back at Jeffrey. "I was asking what else happened that day."

"I don't remember anything."

"What about the day he died?"

"I didn't even go inside the room. There was nothing for me to do. He was already dead when I showed up."

Jeffrey put on a satisfied expression, like he was off the hook.

Gage circled back. "You remember anyone coming to visit Charlie?"

Jeffrey paused and then seemed to drift off.

Gage tugged the leash.

"Hey. I'm thinking . . . Yeah, a guy came by the day before he died. A Polish name nobody can pronounce. He claimed Charlie called him so I let him in."

"What did he look like?"

"White guy, big. Sorta stooped over. Had a comb-over. Silliest thing I ever saw. I don't know who he thought he was kidding."

"You sure it was the day before?"

Jeffrey nodded. "Positive."

The comb-over was missing.

"What happened?" Gage asked, as the deputy removed John Porzolkiewski's handcuffs at the doorway to the visiting room on the seventh floor of the Hall of Justice. Porzolkiewski's hair was clipped short all around and the saddle-shaped patch of skin on the top of his head was pale and bald.

Porzolkiewski settled into a chair across from Gage as the windowed metal door slammed shut.

"I got a look at myself in a mirror in the psych ward. It seemed kind of ridiculous all of a sudden."

"Staring at the death penalty can suck the vanity out of anyone."

Porzolkiewski drew back. "The what?"

"You haven't heard?"

"No one talks to me. They think I'm crazy."

"That's not their fault."

Porzolkiewski shrugged. "Maybe it wasn't such a good strategy on my part."

"I heard from Spike Pacheco the DA's death penalty committee is reviewing at your case, deciding whether to charge you with special circumstances. They're probably going to do it."

Porzolkiewski smirked. "You here to celebrate?"

"I'm here to finish the conversation you marched out of the other day."

"Why the renewed interest in my welfare?"

"I have no interest in your welfare, at least not directly."

"That's a start."

Gage flipped open a manila folder lying on the table. "Let's begin with the things you've lied to me about."

Porzolkiewski threw up his hands. "Not this again."

"This again." Gage fixed his gaze on Porzolkiewski. "Why did you lie to me about not having Brandon Meyer's wallet?"

"Because it was like having that asshole by the balls, that's why."

"How? It's just a wallet. Everything in it is replaceable. It's more like you were standing there gripping the crotch of an empty pair of pants."

Porzolkiewski smiled. "You should be a writer."

His smile faded and he seemed to disappear into a memory.

"My wife used to write," Porzolkiewski finally said. "Mostly travel articles after we went on vacations. A lot of times for the AAA magazine. I was reading through some of them a couple of weeks ago. I'd forgotten how much more she saw in the world than I did, and we were looking at the same damn things." Porzolkiewski peered at Gage. "You ever take a picture of something the same time as somebody else and your picture is shit and theirs is magic?"

"I don't even bother trying anymore. I just hand the camera to my wife."

Porzolkiewski folded his hands behind his head, and then stared down.

"What a sweetheart. What she ever saw in me . . . There is an expression I remember from when I was a boy in Poland. *Miłość spada znienacka.* Love comes unexpected, and that's how she came to me."

He dropped his hands to the table and looked up again. "I don't get it. Why are you here?"

"I went by your shop and talked to your night clerk."

"Suzanne."

"Suzanne. She said she filled in for you for an afternoon three days before Charlie Palmer died."

"Why'd you believe her, when you wouldn't believe me?"

"She showed me the delivery receipts she signed. Some of them were time-stamped by the food service companies."

"I told you I didn't do it."

Gage held his palms up at Porzolkiewski.

"I'm not ready to go that far," Gage said. "Once you knew the layout of Charlie's house, it would've been easy to sneak back in."

"But I didn't sneak back in. I didn't. There was no need to. The guy was a wreck. He fell apart the moment he saw me."

"You mean he was terrified, thinking you were going to finish him off."

"That's not what—" Porzolkiewski caught himself. "I'm not talking about that. It has nothing to do with why I'm in here."

"So what happened when you went into Charlie's bedroom?"

"He acted like he knew I'd be coming. Maybe he heard the physical therapist talking to me. It was weird. The therapist looked at me like he knew who I was."

Porzolkiewski paused, then shook away the thought.

"Who knows? Anyway, Charlie tries to say something, but gets all choked up, sort of gagging. I thought he was going to suffocate himself. The therapist came running in and propped him up to get him through it. He said I should leave, so I did."

Porzolkiewski patted his thigh. "I even had Meyer's wallet in my pocket. I was going to give it to him or trade it to him. But then I forgot about it until I got home that night."

"What about the ten thousand dollars you told me you got for the wallet?"

"It wasn't for the wallet. It was for not telling the media about what I found inside. Do the math. Meyer plus condom plus Tenderloin equals some really bad press, for him and his brother both."

"Who gave you the money?"

"I don't know his name. He had a Texas accent. Looked like that country singer, the one who always wears the pastel shirts and pressed Levi's. The guy who sang 'I Hate Everything.' I love that song. It's practically my anthem."

"George Strait?"

"Yeah, except younger and darker hair. And doesn't smile."

"What did you tell him about the wallet?"

"I said I threw it in the bay."

"Where's the money he gave you?"

"In the bank. I divided it up into six thousand dollars and four thousand dollars and deposited it. I didn't want the bank reporting a suspicious transaction to the feds. Ten grand in cash all at once."

"It *was* a suspicious transaction."

Porzolkiewski smiled. "But I didn't want them to know it."

Gage took a September calendar out of the folder. "Here's the test question. Did you go back to Charlie's house?"

"You going to walk out?"

"That's up to you."

"Yeah, I went back. The night before he died."

"You passed the test. The police neighborhood canvass turned up a neighbor who described your Corona right down to the missing hubcaps. A wreck like that in a neighborhood like Russian Hill is practically probable cause."

"But I didn't go inside the house." Porzolkiewski raised his right hand. "I swear. I didn't go in."

"I know that, too. The neighbor was watching you the whole time, cell phone already with 911 punched in, thumb poised to press send, just waiting for you to get out of the car. Until I talked to Jeffrey Stark—"

Gage felt the conflict between Stark's story and Porzolkiewski's, but wasn't ready to challenge him and maybe provoke him into marching out again.

There were things Gage needed to find out, even before he confronted Stark again.

"Who's Jeffrey Stark?"

"The physical therapist. I thought you'd driven over to see if Charlie was still alive."

"No. I wanted to go yell at him, make him confess. Looking pathetic isn't a confession, but . . ."

Porzolkiewski's voice faded and he pursed his lips.

"But what?"

"But then I saw his wife through the living room window. Is she Mexican or something?"

"Half."

"Anyway, I saw her sitting by herself, just staring. Made me think of my wife. It kind of took the wind out of me." Porzolkiewski shook his head. "I regretted it later, after he was dead. I figured I missed my chance to force him to tell the truth. I was still pissed off when you came by the house the first time."

Gage removed photocopies of a list of names, some in English and some in Arabic, and numbers on a scrap of paper and of both sides of a credit card, then slid them across the table.

"Why didn't you give me copies of these?" Gage asked. "They were found in Meyer's wallet when the police searched your house.

Porzolkiewski glanced at the pages.

"I figured I'd keep something for leverage if I needed it," Porzolkiewski said. "All these names and numbers must mean something. And the credit card didn't seem right."

"What didn't look right?" Gage already knew the

answer, but was more interested in how far Porzolkiewski had gotten.

"The expiration date. It was like the way my parents wrote them in Poland. Instead of writing the month, then the day. They did it the other way around. I think they still do it like that in Europe." Porzolkiewski tapped date on the card. "See? Instead of March 30, it's 30 March."

Gage pointed at the list of Arabic names. "You figure out what all these mean?"

"Other than it looking like he was involved with some kind of terrorists?" Porzolkiewski cocked his head toward Gage. "They make any sense to you?"

"No. But I'll find out." Gage changed the subject. "What are you going to do in court tomorrow?"

"It depends on whether you're getting me out of here."

"I'm a long way from that. You've lied to me too many times. You still could've done it or hired someone else. And you were in the Delta at the right time to poison Karopian."

Porzolkiewski's face flushed and he pushed himself to his feet.

"Not that again." Gage shook his head and pointed at the chair. "Sit."

Porzolkiewski glared at Gage, then dropped back down.

"It's going to take some time," Gage said.

"How much time?"

"I don't know."

"Maybe my next phone call should be to the *San Francisco Chronicle*."

"What are you going to say? TIMCO, the San

Francisco Police Department, a respected lawyer, and a federal judge conspired to frame you for murdering two people who you hated for covering up the unproven cause of an explosion that killed your son fourteen years ago? And combine that with your recent trip to the psych ward—"

"What do you want me to do? Just sit on my hands?"

"Exactly."

"What do I say in court?"

"Tell the judge you need a couple of weeks to hire a lawyer. He'll be so thrilled you're finally talking, he'll give it to you."

"Should I get one?"

"You guilty?"

"No. I'm not guilty."

"Then don't waste the money."

"It won't cost me anything."

"How do you figure?"

Porzolkiewski smirked. "A bunch of those media-hungry cable TV lawyers contacted Suzanne at the store. Any of them will represent me for free just to keep their faces on television. They're excited as hell. They all think I'm a serial murderer."

"Instead of what?"

Porzolkiewski paused for a moment, then shrugged and sighed.

"I guess that's up to you."

t's the White House calling," Landon Meyer's secretary announced over the intercom.

"I'll take it." He punched the flashing button. "This is Landon Meyer."

A female voice spoke, "Please stand by for the president."

Landon pulled up his sleeve, then watched the second hand on the 1958 Elgin Durabalance his father had left him. He could gauge the importance of the call by how long the president kept him waiting.

"Good afternoon, Landon."

Five seconds. The president was desperate.

"Good afternoon, Mr. President."

"Three weeks."

"I know, Mr. President."

"And New Hampshire is three and a half months away. You know what I'm saying?"

"Yes, Mr. President, I know what you're saying."

"Let's get out there and kick those last two butts in line."

* * *

Brandon picked up on the first ring. Landon heard a crash in the background.

"What's that?"

"A waiter dropped a tray. I'm at Tadich Grill with Anston."

"Where do we stand with my colleagues from Ohio and Massachusetts?"

"Hold on. Let me step outside."

Landon heard shuffling as Brandon rose, then footsteps, then street traffic.

"They each wanted a million," Brandon said, standing next to a parking meter in front of the restaurant. "Part for them, and part for PACs and 527s."

"Can we cover it?"

"Sure. We've got more than that from the Silicon Valley group. But the problem is how to explain a huge influx of money so far in advance of their primaries. They're afraid it'll seem like a payoff coming this close to the vote."

"It's not a damn payoff." Landon's voice rose. "They want to vote our way, they just don't want to pay the political cost."

"And what if Starsky and Hutch don't get confirmed? Then every dime will get reported."

"There's no turning back now. Get it done."

The big man sitting in the Yukon a block away punched off the recorder as Brandon slipped back inside the restaurant.

Half a conversation was better than none.

Matar	7.1
Makirab	9.6
Algenib	10.12
Enif	11.4
Homam	6.11
Baham	9.21
Scheat	11.3
Sad Al Naamah	1.30
021000089	
36148388	

Shakir Mohammed studied the photocopy as he lay propped on the rented hospital bed in his room in the Oakland loft. His laptop was resting on an over-bed table.

"Did you explain to your parents why you wanted to stay here?" Gage asked.

"I just said that since you were continuing to pay my salary, I should try to do something for it."

Gage glanced down at the chart. "What do you think?"

"They're Arabic words all right. *Naamah* is 'ostrich.' *Matar* is 'rain.'" Shakir smiled. "But I don't think that's the important thing." He turned his laptop toward Gage. Centered on the screen was a picture of the night sky.

"They're stars?" Gage asked.

"Exactly."

Gage inspected the photo. "I'm not much into astronomy . . ."

"Pegasus. They're the stars that make up the Pegasus constellation."

Gage shook his head. "I should have guessed. It was Charlie's only hobby." He pointed at the list. "And the numbers?"

"It's probably money. Seven point one million. Nine point six million."

"Why do you think so?"

"Because the first number below the column is the routing number for Citibank branches in New York City. And below that is the number for the Cayman Exchange Bank. It's on their Web site. It uses that account at Citibank to accept dollar deposits from U.S.-based customers."

Gage paused as the acronym floated around in his mind.

"CEB . . . CEB . . . hold on a second."

He walked over to where Alex Z was working in the next room.

"You have Charlie's spreadsheet handy?" Gage asked.

Alex Z reached for a stack of papers.

"No, on your computer."

Alex Z leaned over and bounced his mouse around the screen.

"Show me the author information."

A few mouse clicks.

"CEB, boss."

"Cayman Exchange Bank."

Gage was annoyed at himself for not catching on to it earlier, but then recalled that the bank was generally known in the trade as CXB and used that acronym as its logo.

Alex Z straightened up. "Why would a bank send a spreadsheet? Why didn't they just mail out statements at the end of the month?"

"Because that's what you get when you have a banker in your pocket."

Ten minutes later they had their first breakthrough in cracking the codes on Charlie Palmer's spreadsheet.

"The second column isn't money," Alex Z said, pointing Shakir's laptop screen. "They're dates: July 1st, September 6th, October 12th, November 4th, like that. And they match what appear to be money transfers on the spreadsheet."

Gage looked back and forth between the spreadsheet and the list of names.

"Maybe that means Meyer was tracking when the money arrived, or was supposed to arrive, and Charlie was doing the accounting. And the stars' names are codes for whoever sent it."

Alex Z scanned down the columns of figures. "But that only accounts for the money coming in, and we still don't know where it's from."

"This is what I want you to do," Gage said. "Go back as far as you can. Try to match all these names and dates to the cases Meyer handled as a lawyer and as a judge. And call Socorro and get whatever telephone bills she has. Maybe we can recreate what Charlie was doing from his call records."

Gage paused and shook his head, thinking of the constellation and of Charlie and of how he'd spent his life.

"I think ultimately we'll be turning from Greek mythology to Shakespeare," Gage said.

"What do you mean?" Alex Z asked.

"The fault wasn't in Charlie's stars, it was in himself." Gage looked over at the wall calendar. "And whatever that was, we've got to figure it out fast. A week before Charlie died he had an argument with Brandon about something that was going to happen soon."

"You think the nine million dollars he took for himself figures in somehow?"

"One way or the other."

"Then why aren't they coming after it?"

"Probably because it might expose their scheme. But it's only a matter of time. Then they'll be coming after it, real hard."

Gage headed toward the door. His final words told him he had a call to make. He reached for his cell phone as he started down the stairs to the street level.

"Is anything wrong?" Socorro asked.

"No," Gage said. "But I was thinking maybe you and the kids need some time away."

"Your timing is perfect. They have a break from school coming up, and we were talking about a trip together."

"Would you like to stay at my father's old ranch outside of Nogales?"

"That would be wonderful, but I thought you'd rented it out."

"Just the land for grazing. The house has too many memories to let anyone live there."

lex Z brought Shakir a cup of tea after Gage left and sat down on the edge of the bed.

"You doing okay?" Alex Z asked.

"I guess."

"You sort of faded out of the conversation."

Shakir shrugged. "I'm not sure I'm in the right line of work."

Alex Z pointed at the bandage on Shakir's cheek covering the stitches. "Because . . ."

"No, not because of that. I could've just as easily been mugged walking down the street from my old job."

"You mean you don't like working for Graham?"

"It's not that either. He treats everybody like an equal, never talks down, never snaps orders, never is afraid to admit he's been mistaken about something. I don't think I've ever had a job where my boss took me so seriously."

"Then what?"

"I . . ." Shakir took a sip of his tea, then held the

cup in front of his chest. "I don't think I can do what he does."

"What's that?"

"Hover."

Alex Z's eyes fixed on Shakir. "What do you mean, hover?"

"At the Federal Trade Commission, at least in the section I worked in, things tended to be black and white. You could spot telemarketing fraud or false advertising at first sight. And even if you were puzzled by something, you could make a call or do some research, and get it figured out by the end of the day. It was like there was always a solid place to put your foot down. But here it's not that way."

"I get you." Alex Z held his hand out, palm down, and rocked it. "It sometimes seems like Graham floats." He lowered his arm. "I've seen him work on a case, everything going every which way, him in three countries in four days, back home and gone again a week later. And he's e-mailing and texting and calling me. 'Can you find out this?' or 'Can you find out that?' Sometimes he spends months and months and months with everything in flux." Alex grinned and raised his eyes skyward. "Then all of a sudden we're standing on top of a mountain I didn't even know we were climbing."

Alex Z's grin faded, then he tilted his head toward their work area and asked, "What's this all about?"

"I guess it's about how these guys moved money through Cayman Island accounts."

"Beyond that."

"Brandon Meyer?"

Alex Z shook his head.

"Charlie Palmer?"

"Closer."

"Socorro?"

"Almost."

"Then what's it about?"

"Tansy and John Porzolkiewski's sons. The tragedy. Their suffering. That's what anchors Graham in the world. Once we fight our way through all the words and all the paper and all the money traveling through cyberspace, for Gage that's what's real and at the heart of everything we've been working on."

Alex Z looked away for a moment. "I never expected when I started working here that what comes to mind when I think of Graham is that he has a kind of tragic sense. It's something he carries with him, but it never seems to weigh him down or paralyze him. Maybe it's because of his mother dying from MS when he was young." He gestured toward the window facing San Francisco. "Ask Spike and Tansy about his mother's last years. Graham won't talk about it, but they may. Spike knows about it firsthand, Tansy knows from old Yaqui patients of his father." He paused in thought. "Maybe part of it was growing up along the border. In some places it was more like the 1860s than 1960s. His father helpless to save cotton pickers and copper miners dying from lung disease and chemical exposure. Sometimes kids can witness too much, too soon."

Alex Z noticed a seasick look on Shakir's face, revealing more than the vertigo of unknowing. "And that's what's really bothering you, isn't it? It isn't just the uncertainty, it's the cloud of tragedy that seems to envelop what we're doing."

Shakir's gaze fell on his now-cold cup of tea, then he sighed and nodded as he looked back up.

Alex Z pointed at him and asked, "You ever hear that line from Isak Dinesen, 'All sorrows can be borne if you can tell a story about them'?"

"Sure. A lot of those new age self-help books use it and I've seen it on a bunch of places on the Internet."

"You know how it ends?"

Shakir shook his head. "That's all they ever say."

"Graham told me once when I was trying to work it into a ballad. It goes something like 'At the end we'll be privileged to view and review it, and that's what's called judgment day.' "

Shakir's eyes widened, then he nodded again and said, "I see why they leave the last part out." Shakir shook his head, exhaling. "It seems to be saying that not just any story will do, not any life will do. But I'm not sure I can take that kind of pressure. I don't think I'm tough enough. I've struggled for two years looking to find a way to tell my parents the truth about me and Rodrigo."

"But you will."

"I think so . . . I hope so. We've been trying to gather up the courage."

Alex Z looked at Shakir as if at a younger brother.

"Remember this. Lots of people want to work with Graham, but he saw something in you and knew when the time came you'd see it in yourself."

"But how do you deal with feeling like you're out to sea?"

"My girlfriend, my music." Alex Z smiled and tapped the blue-line image of Popeye on his upper arm. "And an occasional tattoo."

P lay it again," Gage said. He was sitting in Viz's office lined with metal shelves crowded with computers, sound enhancement devices, monitors, and surveillance equipment.

Viz ticked the play arrow on his screen, and Brandon Meyer's voice came to life against the background of cars and buses passing on the street in front of Tadich Grill.

"They each wanted a million. Part for them, and part for PACs and 527s."

. . .

"But the problem is how to explain a huge influx of money so far in advance of their primaries."

. . .

"And what if Starsky and Hutch don't get confirmed? Then every dime will get reported."

"I wish I could've gotten more," Viz said. "Back in my old DEA days, I'd have tapped his line and gotten both ends of the conversation."

"If they were dope dealers."

"Yeah. But somehow whatever is going on here seems worse." Viz looked over his shoulder at where Gage sat. "What are they talking about?"

"My guess? The votes on the Supreme Court nominees."

"How come so fast? I thought that took months and months."

"They were confirmed for appeals court seats less than a year ago. They're known quantities. No need for lengthy FBI checks or extended committee hearings."

"And the Meyer boys are paying off some senators for their votes?"

"Not them. Their campaigns."

"Same difference." Viz pointed at his notes written on a piece of scratch paper. "I know what political action committees are, but what's a 527?"

"It covers a lot of things, but I suspect the Meyer boys are using the type that can raise all the money it wants but doesn't have to register with the Federal Election Commission and doesn't have to report where the money came from or where it went. Like the Swift Boat Veterans. Now a lot of contributors are going even further and are using super-PACs that sprang up after the *Citizens United* decision, but the public is getting suspicious of them so they might not go that way."

"And I take it the idea is to launder the money though these groups to hide the sources?"

Gage nodded. "That's how it looks. And it ties in with Landon's genius as a strategist. He would get an initiative on the ballot in each state that he could uniquely tie to the senatorial candidate he was backing—abortion, gay marriage, stem cell research—then would flood the 527s supporting the initiative with money whose sources he doesn't have to disclose."

"And Brandon's the bag man? I'm not sure a federal judge ought to be doing that."

"He's a federal judge who's spent his whole career doing what he shouldn't be doing—so stay on him."

Viz glanced at his watch. "He should be leaving court in a half hour or so." He smiled. "Maybe tonight we'll find out why he had the condom in his wallet."

"We know the why, we just need to figure out the who and where." Gage rose. "I called Socorro and offered her and the kids the ranch for a couple of weeks. I made it sound casual so she wouldn't get panicked."

"I spoke to her right afterward." Viz pointed north. "Why not your cabin?"

Gage shrugged.

"Was it because it's easier in the desert than in the forest to spot someone sneaking up?"

"It crossed my mind."

"Mine, too."

"I've got a security system with cameras covering the property," Gage said. "I'll have Alex Z link into them through his computer in the loft so he can keep an eye on the place."

age lowered the lid on his gas barbecue, then sat down in one of the four chairs surrounding the wrought-iron table on the deck of his hillside home. FBI Special Agent Joe Casey was seated in another, sipping a beer and gazing out at the bay.

"It's another world up here, isn't it?" Casey said. He pointed at San Francisco. "I thought you made a mistake when you bought this place because it meant having to look every day at a city where you worked so many homicides."

Casey surveyed the three-story glass-walled house, the four acres on which it sat, and the pines, oaks, and redwoods surrounding it, then nodded and said, "But it doesn't feel that way."

"It's a mystery to me," Gage said, "but somewhere between the time I start up the canyon and when I pull into the garage, the magic happens. Maybe it's because from up here I can see the whole, and not just the parts."

But that wasn't entirely true, for sometimes he dragged parts with him as he ascended the eleven hundred feet. And that was the reason Casey was sitting across from him now.

He glanced over his shoulder toward the house. "Most of all, it's because this place is about only one thing: Faith and me. And whenever we're here, it seems like the center of the universe."

They fell silent as they watched a young hawk ride an updraft and pass over, flying toward the crest of the hill behind them.

Casey sniffed at the aromas drifting over from the grill.

"Smells good," Casey said, "but you shouldn't be cooking my dinner, I should be cooking yours. Maybe all your dinners. OptiCom is the third case you've handed me in the last four years. The special agent in charge keeps wondering if I'm paying you off."

"He knows that's not true. He's seen your pay-check." Gage winked. "He knows you can't afford me."

Gage twisted the cap off a beer bottle and took a sip.

"Has Oscar Mogasci stopped trembling yet?" Gage asked.

"I don't know. I got the judge to release him on a no-money-down bail this morning and then I pushed him out the door. The idiot thought he was going to get the federal Witness Protection Program, but all he got was a Caltrain ticket back to San Jose."

"San Jose? You're not telling me his wife took him back after almost ruining her."

"Not his wife, his mother."

"I should've guessed it would be something like that," Gage said. "He struck me as a mama's boy. The only powerful woman he could stand to have in his life was his mother, so he had to try to break his wife when she'd become successful."

Casey tilted his head toward the kitchen window. His wife, a former FBI agent and now a supervisor of the nuclear detection unit at the Oakland Port, was huddled with Faith drinking wine and displaying pictures of her new niece.

"I should ask Illyse," Casey said. "She reads *Psychology Today* like it's the Bible. She says it helps her manage her underlings. Every month or so the magazine has what they call self-tests. I missed something she said last week so she gave me one to check my attention span."

"How'd you do?"

"On a scale of one to ten, I got a failed miserably."

"On purpose?"

"Of course. It's best to keep the bar as low as possible." Casey flashed a grin. "She made a point of failing it, too."

Gage returned to the barbecue, flipped over the steaks, and then laid a salmon fillet next to them.

"But enough about my disabilities. What's going on with the Charlie Palmer thing?"

Gage filled him in while he kept an eye on the grill.

"Now that I lay it all out in one piece," Gage said, "it sounds kind of outlandish."

"What part? The planting of sodium monofluoroacetate in some Tenderloin shopkeeper's storeroom? Naming the whole operation after a constellation?

Or maybe just the part about the shopkeeper cutting off his comb-over in the county jail?"

"Is that multiple choice?"

"Yes."

"Then the answer is all the above."

Casey shrugged. "It wouldn't be the weirdest crime I've ever heard of. Close, but not quite." He sipped on his beer. There was no reason to retrade war stories. "What can I do to help?"

"How difficult would it be for you to access the wire transfer database the government started gathering up after 9/11?"

"It's just a couple of keystrokes," Casey said. "You want me to put in the Arabic names and see what comes back?"

"That's all it would take."

"I don't need actual probable cause, but I'll need some articulable suspicion. Got any ideas?"

"Call it money laundering. That covers a host of sins."

"Not exactly a home run," Casey told Gage over the telephone the next day.

"A triple?"

"I don't think so, but maybe. You got your list of names and the spreadsheet?"

"Hold on." Gage retrieved both from the safe in the opposite corner of his office. "Okay."

"Let's go over a few and I'll e-mail the rest."

Gage heard keystrokes ticking in the background.

"The Pegasus wire transfer records go back about ten years," Casey said. "But none of the Arabic names show up until about four years ago."

"Start from the beginning."

Gage heard Casey tap a couple more keys.

"Ten years ago, May 16th. Two million came into Pegasus at the Cayman Exchange Bank, then a couple of months later . . ."

"Why the suspenseful pause?" Gage asked.

"So you can ask where the money went."

"Okay. Where'd the money go?"

"Five hundred thousand was wired to the client trust account at Brandon Meyer's old law firm."

"Helluva fee paid into a confidential account," Gage said. "What about the rest?"

"Broken up into chunks of a hundred or two hundred thousand, some wired to the States and some to foreign banks."

"Let me make a guess about the original two million."

"Take a shot."

"It was it an insurance premium?"

Casey laughed. "You got a camera hidden in my office? All the senders until four years ago were U.S. companies, and the details of payment line all read 'Insurance Premium.'"

"It's brilliant."

"What's brilliant?"

"The whole TIMCO payoff scheme was covered by fake insurance premiums and real legal fees. Their attorneys couldn't go to the board of directors and say they needed to pay off a witness, so they fudged up an offshore insurance premium payment to Pegasus. They could call it whatever they wanted. Coverage for international operations or supplemental insurance for domestic accidents."

"In a twisted sort of way, it makes sense. What's insurance anyway, except a means to manage risk?"

"And then the money got broken up and forwarded on to Hawkins in India and Karopian for his Bethel Island house. The rest came back to Meyer's firm as a legal fee."

"If that's true," Casey said, "the scheme is over. No money has been wired from Pegasus to Meyer's firm, or anywhere else, in the last four years."

"You mean it's all still in the Pegasus account at CEB?"

"I have no idea. The database only shows transfers between banks, not internal account balances."

"What about the Arabic names and the dates on the list in Brandon's wallet?"

"Let's take the first one on his list. Matar on July 1st."

"Hold on." Gage highlighted the transfer in yellow. "Three million?"

"That's it. The wire transfer's details-of-payment line shows Matar-GRID, but it doesn't say insurance."

"Any idea what GRID is?"

"Not a clue."

"Who's the sender?"

"It just says 'from a client.' The client's account is at the Bank of New York."

"I'm sure Charlie knew who it was from," Gage said. "It was his job to work with a private banker at CEB to keep track of the money."

Casey paused on the other end of the line. After a long moment he spoke, "It sort of makes you wonder whether Judge Meyer—"

"Was using Pegasus to receive offshore payoffs from companies appearing in his court?"

"Exactly," Casey said. "And somehow I don't think this is the first time you wondered that."

G age stood back from a chart in the Oakland loft on the following morning. Alex Z leaned against the worktable.

"How was Casey able to access the financial database?" Alex Z asked. "I thought it was just for investigating terrorism."

"I didn't ask, but I imagine running searches on the Arabic names was his ticket in. Anything even vaguely Islamic is still accepted as probable cause, especially when it's connected to offshore money coming into the U.S."

Alex Z stepped up to his whiteboard chart showing Anston's clients, Judge Meyer's cases, and the deposits into Pegasus that appeared on Charlie Palmer's spreadsheet.

Gage and Alex Z turned at the grunting of Shakir rolling his wheelchair toward them.

"I thought we agreed you wouldn't get out of bed on your own," Gage said. "You could hurt yourself."

Shakir smiled, then wiped sweat from his forehead with his sleeve.

"I didn't want to miss any of the action, especially since my name was referred to as probable cause."

"There isn't much action at the moment," Gage said, "except our mental wheels spinning. But there will be." He turned back toward the chart. "How about you guys add the wire transfers and company names Casey found to this? See what patterns show up." He nodded toward Shakir. "Sort of like a constellation."

"No problem, boss." Alex Z grinned at Shakir, then looked back at Gage. "I did a little extra research. Did you know Meyer's nickname at Yale was Mach One?"

"Like in Machiavelli Number One," Gage said, "or the speed of sound?"

"That I don't know."

"Why is it important?"

Shakir laughed, then winced and reached toward his bandaged stitches.

Alex Z stepped over to his laptop. A couple of keystrokes and a click of his mouse later, a Web site burst onto the screen showing a statue of the Hindu god Krishna under a banner reading "Pacific Coast Institute of Tantric Sex."

He next typed "MachOne" as the user ID and "YaleForever" in the password field. He then entered the site and navigated to the account data.

He pointed at the last four digits of a credit card number: "It's Meyer's Cayman Island card."

"How did you find this?"

"I didn't. Somehow Charlie Palmer did."

"Any evidence he was blackmailing Meyer?"

Alex Z shook his head. "It may have been too late. The last activity on the account was a year ago."

"What did he buy?"

Shakir stirred in his chair and muffled a giggle.

"An hour of mentoring by what they call a trained guide," Alex Z said.

"I take it that means a prostitute for the new age elite?"

"The owner of the institute has a half-dozen arrests in San Francisco. It looks like she took her business inside about five years ago to keep herself out of handcuffs."

"Or into fur-lined ones." Gage glanced at the monitor. "He spend money on anything else?"

Alex Z grinned.

"Yeah, boss. A man's strap-on penis extender."

hole in the wall. A very long wall of thirty windowless doors spread along the third floor walkway of an L-shaped strip-mall office building in Las Vegas. The tan stucco structure looked to Gage like a 1950s motel with the swimming pool filled in and paved over into a parking lot.

Gage scanned the brown plastic nameplates. A generation of dust had settled into the corners and edges of the white etched letters: Las Vegas Commercial Insurance, West Valley Real Estate, PCC Accounting, and AAA Corporate Services of Nevada, Inc.

As he opened the office door, Gage wondered who Phillip Charters would be today.

Charters peered up over his wire-rimmed reading glasses at Gage. He was a plus-sized Danny DeVito with a full head of blondish-white hair, and with no surprise on his face or in his voice, asked:

"How's this sound?" Charters pointed at a State of Nevada Articles of Incorporation form lying on his desk. "Charter Aggressive Growth Fund."

"I think you'll need to get your stockbroker's license back," Gage said.

"No problem. I just won my appeal." Charters grinned. "Faulty jury instructions. I'm good to go again." He flicked a finger at Gage. "You had lunch?"

"You mean lunch or . . ."

"Food, just food. I promise."

Charters tilted his head and raised his eyebrows toward the Desert Agate Gentlemen's Club as they angled across the parking lot toward the Hometown Restaurant.

"You trying to get me to go in," Gage asked, "or is that just pride of ownership?"

"Pride of ownership." Charters spread his hands in front of him, eyebrows still raised. "Get it?"

"Get what?"

"Agate."

"I still don't get it."

"I wanted to call it Get Your Rocks Off but the city wouldn't let me."

"Is this what you do all day?" Gage shook his head. "Of course you do. You never turn it off."

"If I had to take a guess, that's why you're here."

Charters sucked in his stomach as he slid into the booth in the café, then laid his furry forearms on the table. His yellow and red flowered short-sleeve Hawaiian shirt stretched tight across his chest.

Gage made a show of doing a double take as Charters signaled to a waitress across the dining room.

"That's not . . ."

"My old secretary. What could she do? She had

to roll on me. She couldn't do jail time, not with three young kids to take care of. I told her to do what she needed to do."

Gage smiled at Charters. "And all this time I thought it was great investigation on my part."

"It was. None of those accountants and lawyers had a clue about what I was doing until you told them. Even worse, you figured out she was the weak link in my operation." Charters sighed. "Unfortunately, she trusted you."

Gage rose as the waitress approached. She appeared younger than she had five years earlier when she'd testified against Charters in his trial for offshore investment fraud.

"You look gorgeous, Linda," Gage said.

Linda stood on her tiptoes to give Gage a kiss on the cheek. "Thanks."

She reached into the front pocket of her black skirt and withdrew an order pad as Gage sat down.

"Crime was like a time machine turning me into an old lady at thirty-five. It's a good thing you put Phil out of business. I couldn't take the stress." She looked down at Charters. "I don't know how he handles it—"

"*Handled* it. I'm retired."

She smiled. "Actually I do know." She poked Charters's stomach. "He eats. If he wasn't a criminal he'd weigh a hundred and twenty pounds, instead of three-twenty."

Charters laughed. "I was born weighing more than that. A world record."

She dipped her pen toward Gage. "I know what Phil wants. How about you?"

"Burger and fries."

"One order, or two like him?"

"One, and coffee."

Charters fiddled with his wedding ring as she walked away, then asked, "To what do I owe this unexpected visit?"

"You're what I call uniquely situated."

"Situated? I'm crammed in here like sausage in a bun."

"Situated. Not seated."

"Oh. How am I situated?"

"Between Marc Anston and the Cayman Exchange Bank."

Charters shook his head. "If they got a connection, it ain't through me."

"Then how did you get hooked up with Anston after you got indicted?"

"Is this gonna get me into a jam?"

"I'll keep you out of it."

"I don't know if I should say anything. I'm not really comfortable playing the role of the good citizen."

"Linda seems to be playing the part well."

"Maybe I'll make her my role model." He pointed at a waitress leaning over a table to set down lunch orders. "But I'm not sure they make those short skirts in my size."

Linda walked up with a pot of coffee and filled their cups. She smiled at Gage and said, "Just like old times."

"I hope not."

She glanced at Charters. "Now that I think about it, me too."

* * *

Charters stirred sugar into his cup, then raised it toward Gage.

"Thanks."

"For what?"

"For stopping the government and the civil lawyers from grabbing the place I bought for my mother. It would've crushed her to lose her garden. She even knows the scientific names for all the plants, her little babies."

"They all thought you were hundred percent a crook," Gage said. "I convinced them you were only ninety, and the clean money was invested in her house."

"Why'd they give in?"

"The paper trail you left behind was too complicated for them to figure out."

Charters grinned. "Man, I was good back then."

"No, you were mostly bad back then."

"Well, thanks, anyway." Charters took a sip. "Let's see, where were we?"

"Anston."

"Ah, yes. Anston. Genus: *Legalis*, species: *Rodentia major*. When you started hounding my accountant in the Caymans I knew right away it was just a matter of time before you knocked on my door. I flew down there to see the attorney who set up my companies. You remember him, Leonard Quinton. He and I needed to get together and . . . uh . . ."

"Coordinate your stories?"

Charters laughed. "Yeah, that's a good way to put it. At my trial the U.S. Attorney tried to make it sound more like obstructing justice."

"He succeeded. It was count four and you got convicted of it."

"Hey, I won the appeal. That means I'm innocent." Charters took another sip of coffee. "Anyway, while I was in Grand Cayman I asked Quinton who I should use when I got indicted. He told me to hire Anston."

"Anston's not a criminal lawyer."

"But he's a partner in one of the judge's old law firms. Even though Brandon Meyer didn't get assigned the case, I figured it couldn't hurt. Who knows what goes on back in the judge's chambers? Maybe Anston gets Meyer to put in a good word for me at sentencing time."

"Did you get your money's worth?"

"In the long run." Charters smiled. "Well, the money made a long run."

"You mean you paid Anston offshore."

"Still at the top of your game, aren't ya? But that's his problem, not mine. It's not my fault if he didn't declare the income and give Uncle Sam his share."

"You remember where you sent the fee?"

"I didn't have to send it anywhere. The money just got transferred from one of my accounts at Cayman Exchange Bank to another one controlled by Anston. Quinton took care of it."

"You remember the name of the account the money went into?"

Charters narrowed his eyes and bit his lower lip, then shook his head. "Quinton would know."

"You ever hear of a company called Pegasus?"

Charters slapped the table. "That's it. Pegasus." He grinned like he'd been caught by his wife staring at a waitress's breasts. "I thought about doing one of those myself."

"Doing what?"

"A fake insurance scam."

"How do you know it's fake?"

Charters clucked. "I thought you were at the top of your game. You should've already . . ." Then he smiled.

"Let's just say I thought it was some kind of tax gimmick," Gage said, "but I hadn't figured out the details. That's why I'm here."

That wasn't the whole truth, but Gage didn't want to risk scaring Charters off by telling him that money transferred into Pegasus might have been the reason for a burglary at Socorro's and what had brought him to Las Vegas was fear for her and her children's safety. The longer Charters believed Gage's investigation only concerned tax evasion, the better.

"They did a riff on one of those old tax shelters," Charters said. "First, the clients would wire fake insurance premiums to Pegasus, then it would wire the money back as loans to buy yachts or cars or vacation homes." He hunched his shoulders, and reached out his hands. "Offshore captive insurance has been the best tax scam ever." He pointed at Gage. "You ever deal with Stone & Whitman in New York?"

Gage shook his head.

"They set up the ones for TransCont Trucking and Universal Tractor and a bunch of other giants. But Anston's genius was to make it available to the little guy." Charters laughed. "You know, the one-billion-dollar company, not just the ten-billion-dollar company."

"What was his gimmick?"

"Rent-a-captives, like Pegasus. Anybody could send premiums. Pegasus would bank the money, wait a couple of months, then ship it back into the States. It was sweet—swee-eet. Insurance premiums got tax deductions going out, and the money coming back in as loans was tax free."

"Like those old fake offshore consulting schemes."

"But way better. Because when you hire a consultant you're supposed to get something in return. A marketing plan or an advertising campaign. And the IRS can come by and ask to see what you paid for. But with insurance? It's a . . ." Charters cocked his head toward Gage. "What do they call those things in outer space that sucks everything in?"

"A black hole."

"That's it. Insurance is just a black hole people throw money into. Everybody knows it."

"How did Anston get his cut?"

"And Meyer. The firm was Anston & Meyer back when it all started. Anston was the tax expert, but in the deep background. Meyer was out front. He's the one who brought in the customers." Charters lowered his voice. "In order to get into the deal, the client had to do two things. One was to buy a legal opinion letter from Anston saying the tax shelter was legit and the other was to pay the accounting firm. And they always used the Big Four to make it all look like it was on the up and up. The opinion letter alone cost a butt load. A hundred grand."

"And he used the same one over and over."

"Exactly. Plus he got ten percent of the money the client saved on taxes each year by using his gimmick. They save a million, he gets another hundred thousand. It was like an annuity. And the same thing for the accounting firm. Except they got half a mil up front in addition to their percentage because they managed the whole thing and were on the hook if the IRS came knocking."

"You know how many of these Anston and Meyer did?"

"If I had to guess, maybe a couple of hundred. Thirty or forty million dollars a year, could be a helluva lot more. And most of their fees were paid offshore."

"How did Anston & Meyer move their fees back into the States? I don't see them telling clients how to evade taxes, then pay them himself."

"How Anston & Meyer did it, I don't know." Charters leaned forward. "But I'll tell you about a guy I know. He had real cool deal. Every month he'd have the Cayman Exchange Bank pull fifty grand in cash out of his account and hand deliver it to Citibank, right across the street in George Town. Citibank would treat it as kind of an advance credit card payment. That way my friend could spend all kinds of offshore money in the States and nobody would know. And no one knows where the money is from because Citibank credit cards all look the same."

"Almost."

"Yeah, almost."

"Your . . . uh . . . friend still doing it?"

Charters grinned. "Naw. He switched to debit cards, harder to trace the transactions."

Linda walked up, placed down their orders, then folded up the check and stuffed it into Charters's shirt pocket.

"Graham's is on the house, but you gotta pay."

Charters bit his lower lip as he watched her work her way back toward the counter, then exhaled and said, "I should've divorced my wife and married that girl."

"True love or only so she couldn't testify against you?"

Charters bit into a French fry. "Both."

"Did Anston and his people ever get investigated?"

"Yeah, because they made the same stupid mistake everybody else did. They'd send the money offshore and it would bounce back into the States from the same company. It was too obvious they controlled the money the whole time. IRS didn't like it. Didn't qualify as an arm's-length transaction. So Quinton—oops." Charters offered a weak smile. "I hope you knew that already."

"Let's say I did."

"You're keeping me out of this, right?"

"Right."

"Okay, let's say somebody like Quinton figures out a way so it doesn't look so obvious." Charters leaned in again, stretching his arms out on either side of his plate. "He sets up a regular finance company somewhere in the Caribbean—"

"So the premiums go into the insurance company, then to the finance company, and then back to the States as loans?"

"Boom. Boom. Boom. And the IRS is blind to

the whole thing . . . Beautiful. Just beautiful. And there are about as many Americans who understand how offshore insurance works as there are people who understand how a black hole does what it does."

"When did they add the third step?"

"About six, seven years ago."

"Is that how Anston got hooked up with Quinton?"

"I don't know. I just know they're hooked up somehow."

"So how'd you get onto this trail?" Charters asked Gage as he pushed his plate away and wiped his mouth with his napkin.

"I'd rather not say."

"Let me guess. We talked about Anston. We talked about Quinton. We talked about Meyer. We talked about Cayman Exchange Bank. Let's see . . . let's see . . . whose name could be missing?" Charters smiled. "Who could it be? Maybe Charlie Palmer? My dear investigator. Or, shall we say, Anston's dear investigator, may he rest in peace."

"Why 'my dear investigator'?"

"I paid him fifty grand for nothing."

"Why?"

"Because Anston told me to. He said we needed some investigation done. I think I just paid for Palmer's summer vacation in the islands. I never got any benefit from it. He didn't need to go down there and talk to people in Quinton's firm or at the bank. By the time you and the FBI were done, everybody knew what happened and it wasn't like I had a defense."

"I take it you paid him offshore, too."

"Yeah. It was to Pegasus."

Charters took a sip of coffee, then said, "I don't know where you're going with all of this, and I don't want to know. But I'd be careful if you're thinking about taking on Anston. The way his mind works scares the hell out of me."

Charters set his cup down.

"Anston figured it might help if I started going to church in case he wanted to put on a character defense. You know, get some minister to come in to say how I wouldn't cheat people or, if I did, it was unintentional or maybe the devil made me do it. Anston took me with him one Sunday to get me hooked up with a preacher. The sermon was about the Book of Job, and the suffering God had inflicted on the guy. Real graphic. Skin lesions and flesh falling off. I felt like throwing up.

"As we're driving away, Anston gives me this matter-of-fact look and says about the spookiest, most megalomaniacal thing I ever heard a man say. He says:

"'The minister has it all wrong. The real lesson of the Book of Job wasn't that God tortured Job and killed his wife and his kids and destroyed all his animals and crops. It wasn't that at all.' Then Anston does a long pause, and says, 'It's that Job made God come to *him*.'"

I hate this place," Boots Marnin complained in his third international call to Marc Anston. "Everything is filthy and noisy. I can't even sleep at night, between the imams calling the rag heads to prayer and horns honking and those goddamn Bollywood soundtracks blaring out of sidewalk speakers. And every day there's another idiotic Hindu festival for some god who looks like a mutant animal."

"Then find Hawkins and get out of there."

"What do you think I've been doing? You know how big Hyderabad is? Seven million dirty, sweaty, smelly people."

"Are you even sure he's there?"

"Positive. Some girl in his house overheard him tell a cop in town that's where he was going."

"Why do you believe her?"

"Because I gave her enough money to buy her folks two of them Brahma bulls and told her I'd come back and slit the throats of the cattle *and* her parents if she was lying to me."

"How are you going to find him?"

"I'm hoping he'll come to me. I hired some ex-cops to watch the *dhabas*. They're food shacks along the highway where the hookers work. It's the only place around where you can get teenage girls easy, and that's what he's into. Sometimes two, three at a time. Costs him about seventy-five cents each. Sneaking out to the *dhabas* is safer than bringing his own girls from Gannapalli. They might talk to neighbors and give him away."

"And when you find him?"

"My guess is he'll have a heart attack the moment he looks at me."

"Get it done. I need you back here. We're going to have to do something about Gage. He's been co-zying up to Porzolkiewski. Been to see him a couple of times."

The mob of Indian truck drivers surged like an amoeba as the fighting cocks jabbed and clawed and pursued one another in the trash-strewn dirt patch behind the row of food stalls and shacks along the Hyderabad Highway.

Despite the setting sun and the gray-brown haze of the dusty road, Boots Marnin caught flashes of rooster wings rising above the screaming men. He was hunched low in the rear sleeping seat of the trac-tor cab parked to the east, hiding his face from the drivers passing by and from the prostitutes trolling for customers.

The circle surged again as the cocks tumbled toward the legs of the men standing close to the rear of the nearest shack. Boots heard the thump of sweaty backs slamming against the wooden wall as the men dodged the razor-sharp spurs cinched to the roosters' legs. They re-formed the circle as the birds rolled the opposite way, toward the mango trees bordering the lot to the north.

Diesel fumes pumping out from the dozens of trucks parked around him once would have reminded Boots of his father's garage, but now they merely choked him and engendered not thoughts of Houston, but fantasies of escape. The only break came in the form of the wind-driven odor of reused coconut oil, deep-fried samosas, chickpea balls, burned wheat *chapattis*, and cumin and coriander and turmeric and a dozen other spices that made Boots want to reach for a gun. For the few days of his surveillance, Boots would look at the cows wandering along the highway or grazing in the fields, then daydream about a T-bone steak. Now the thought turned his stomach because he knew the meat would taste like India.

Boots heard a cheer and saw triumphant brown hands raise the victorious cock above the crowd. He then watched men separate into groups and exchange rupees before wandering back to their trucks or to the small wooden tables spread along the front of the *dhaba*.

The skies darkened as he watched them eat, then disappear into the shacks, and drive off twenty minutes later, making room for a continuing stream of other drivers stopping to eat at the tables or screw on the dirty cots or sleep in their trucks.

Boots leaned forward toward the ex-cop sitting in the driver's seat of the tractor cab.

"You sure this the right place?" Boots asked. "We've been here a long time."

"I am still believing this is the only *dhaba* he is visiting along the Hyderabad Highway."

They sat without speaking for another hour watching trucks, cars, and vans arriving and leaving, men cooking rice and lentils in stainless steel pots over open gas flames, women chopping vegetables and mincing herbs.

The ex-cop tapped Boots's shoulder, then pointed at a yellow, canvas-topped auto-taxi pulling to a stop along the side of the nearest shack.

The taxi *walla* remained seated inside the three-wheeled, open-sided vehicle while a potbellied man slipped out the far side, into the shadows along the wall, then disappeared around the back of the shack.

"That is Mr. Wilbert, yes?" the ex-cop said.

"We'll find out soon enough."

Wilbert Hawkins, beer in hand, bald head illuminated by the shack's dangling lightbulb, pants around his ankles, stared down at the naked teenage girl on her knees before him. He grabbed her hair and rocked her head back and forth—

Then flinched at the sound of the wooden door scraping the dirt.

"Close that thing," Hawkins yelled. "I got this one."

But the door didn't close.

Hawkins glared into the darkness at an unmoving charcoal gray figure framed in black.

"Who the . . . ?"

The man stepped forward, but his head and torso remained in a shadow that cut him off at the knees.

Hawkins's eyes alerted to the pressed Levi's, then

widened in terror as they fixed on dusty alligator-skin boots poised at the threshold. His scream choked in his throat as his erection died in the girl's mouth.

"Did he have a heart attack when he saw you?" Marc Anston asked during Boots's call from India.

"Not immediately."

"What about the body?"

"The Indian police will have it cremated."

"Do they know who he is?"

"No. Just a white guy who could've been from anywhere and collapsed while getting a blow job. Dead men don't have accents."

"How much did Gage find out?"

"Gage knows Hawkins got a million dollars from Pegasus. He knows TIMCO understood from the get-go why the valve blew. And he knows Hawkins believed you were behind Palmer—but dead men don't have beliefs either."

"Any way to control the fallout?"

"Not easily," Boots said. "Gage made a tape."

"So removing Gage won't solve our problem."

"What are you going to do?"

"Gage has been telling pieces of what he knows to too many people," Anston said, "but I'm not sure any of them would be able to put it together but him." He fell silent for a few seconds, and then said. "We need to go after Gage's weakness."

"What's that?"

"He's like a bloodhound. We just need to keep dragging the scent down the wrong path."

"Why not just take him out?"

"Gage is too well connected. And his pals Joe Casey and Spike Pacheco would never let it go. Especially Pacheco. He's like a Gila monster. You'd have to cut off his head to separate his jaws."

ook Quinton," Gage said, "we've got two dead people linked through Pegasus. Charlie Palmer and the OSHA inspector."

Cayman Island barrister Leonard Quinton, QC, pressed his fingertips together on the top of his desk in his office overlooking Hog Sty Bay in George Town, Grand Cayman. He looked back at Gage with the dead-eyed gaze of British ex-pat lawyers trained to keep secrets.

"That's no concern of mine," Quinton said. "I'll tell you the same thing I told you when you were here chasing after Phillip Charters. What companies do is their business, not mine. That would be like Citibank telling their clients what they can and cannot buy with their credit cards."

"Good analogy." Gage reached into his black leather folder, then pulled out a sheet of paper and slid it across Quinton's Victorian mahogany desk.

"That doesn't mean anything to me," Quinton said.

"Look at it more carefully."

Quinton slipped on his horn-rimmed glasses, then picked up the page.

"I don't see the relevance. I've never had the pleasure of the acquaintance of a person named Brandon Meyer. More importantly, I don't control to whom Citibank Cayman issues credit cards."

"But you do control how the money flows."

Quinton slid the page back across the desk.

"You're attributing powers to me that I don't possess."

"I've analyzed Charlie Palmer's telephone records. He didn't make a financial move without a call to this office. Never to anywhere else on the island. Not to any other lawyers. Not to any other accountants. Not even to the Cayman Exchange Bank."

"That will not advance your investigation. We manage dozens of companies. You saw their names posted outside. Which one do you suppose he was calling?"

"Do you really want to travel down this road again?"

"It's not my decision. Cayman Islands law limits what I'm allowed to reveal about companies, clients, and accounts. Unless you have some legal authority, there's really nothing more I can say."

Gage reached into his folder, withdrew Charlie Palmer's death certificate and a power of attorney signed by Socorro, and set them on the desk.

"This is all the authority you need to disclose information about Pegasus."

Quinton glanced at them, then shook his head.

"U.S. documents have no authority in the

Cayman Islands. They're merely pieces of paper. You'll need to make a visit to the U.S. embassy to have them certified. You do realize, of course, the embassy with jurisdiction over the Caymans is in Jamaica." He studied his watch. "Just an hour flight, but this late in the day . . . And you do know inheritance laws can be particularly complicated. It may take quite some time, perhaps many years, for this to work its way through our courts, and I'm not sure what you're looking for will be there to be found."

Gage watched Quinton adopt a posture of self-satisfaction: a half smile, shoulders squared, head tilted upward, eyelids lowered. Gage felt like smashing in his face, except he believed he'd gotten at least one of the answers he came for: Charlie Palmer didn't own Pegasus.

"That's a round-trip to nowhere," Gage said.

Quinton didn't react, except to say, "Then let me propose something you can pass on to your client."

"Legal advice is always welcome."

"This isn't legal advice. It is merely a suggestion. She would be wise to settle on being happy her husband's investments—by whatever means they were made—paid off so handsomely, and leave it at that."

T he middle-aged Canadian wearing the Savile Row pinstriped suit stood by himself on the smoking terrace of the Silver Palm Bar. From just inside the entrance, Gage watched him turn and face toward Seven Mile Beach, his forearms resting on the white wooden railing, a cigar in his right hand, a half-finished martini in the other.

The early October sun had just set over the second day of the Offshore Trusts and Financial Instruments Conference at the Grand Cayman Sapphire Resort. It was the annual meeting of bankers, attorneys, accountants, and government officials who managed the money flows through and around the Caribbean. Its attendees had just flooded from the meeting rooms to the poolside bars and wine lounges and had eddied up to form their dinner groups.

Daniel Norbett was the only one drinking and smoking alone, just as Phillip Charters had predicted he would be. Norbett was the real reason Gage had traveled to Grand Cayman, as he had little hope that he'd learn much from Quinton. He was still surprised he'd come away with anything at all.

Norbett blinked as the breeze sweeping inland blew smoke into his deep-set eyes, then he moved the cigar into his left hand so the light gray stream would slip past his face. He took in a long breath and exhaled, eyes fixed on the cobalt blue of the horizon. He then shook his head, as if rejecting an internal command or disagreeing with an unspoken proposal.

Gage worked his way through the crowd toward the slumped figure, dodging tray-laden waitresses and the gesticulating arms of cigar smokers. He came to a stop next to Norbett, then joined him inspecting the nearly invisible sea. Norbett stiffened when he sensed someone next to him, then pasted a smile on his face as he turned. The smile turned to a grin when saw it was Gage.

"I didn't do it," Norbett said. "Whatever it is, I didn't do it."

It was Gage's turn to smile. "I know you didn't."

"Didn't do what?"

"Whatever it was you said you didn't do."

Norbett straightened up, stuck his cigar in his mouth, and then reached out his hand.

"I think we've had this conversation before."

"Three years ago, almost to the day. And you really didn't do that one."

Gage shook his hand, then glanced around for a cocktail waitress.

"Forget it," Norbett said, "let's get out of here." He ducked his head as he scanned the crowd. "I don't want to ruin my reputation by being seen with you."

"What about *my* reputation?"

"I'm not sure it's all that good with the offshore money laundering crowd anyway."

Norbett led Gage across the terrace and through the lounge to the hotel lobby.

"What are you hungry for?" Norbett asked.

"Up to you. My treat."

"I assumed it would be."

Five minutes later the cab dropped them in front of the Copper Falls Steakhouse.

Gage pointed up at the restaurant sign. "How come here?"

"A free martini with every entrée."

"I guess that means you get two."

Norbett winked. "Just what I was thinking."

Norbett raised his martini to Gage's soda water as they faced each other in the high-backed leather booth.

"To whatever." Norbett set down his drink, then folded his hands on the tablecloth. "So, what's whatever?"

"How's business?"

"You get right to the point, don't you? Since I got indicted in Miami last year, it's been lousy." Norbett pulled the toothpick out of his glass and sucked off the olive. "But I suspect you guessed that."

"I thought your case was over."

"It is. Dismissed."

"How come?"

"It was all a misunderstanding."

"And you clarified things for the government?"

"Let's say, we had some discussions and they were satisfied with my explanations."

Gage picked up his menu. He'd gotten the first bit of information he came for. What Norbett called discussions were what others called debriefing, snitching, and the suspicion he'd done so was probably the reason he was being treated as a pariah at the conference.

"What are you having?" Gage asked.

"I think the New York strip steak. I always liked New York, at least some parts."

"You mean the Bank of New York."

"They were good customers. Or at least their customers were good customers."

"They're not sending you their offshore trust business anymore?"

"They didn't like seeing their name and mine in the same *Wall Street Journal* article under the headline: 'Cayman Island Accountant Indicted in U.S. Tax Fraud Conspiracy.' "

Gage raised his glass. "To loyalty."

"Not much of it around anymore."

"Have you thought about going back to Toronto and starting over?"

"I'm too old, and I let my Canadian license lapse."

The waitress delivered a second martini to Norbett, then took their orders.

"You pick up any business at the conference?" Gage asked.

Norbett spread his hands and shrugged. "Did it look like I picked up any business?" He leaned back in his seat. "Okay. Enough foreplay. What are you on the prowl for?"

"Information."

"About what?"

"A group of companies run by Leonard Quinton."

"I haven't worked with Quinton for ten, twelve years. Even then I didn't get all his work. Most of it, but not all."

"You doing anything with him now?"

Norbett lifted his martini. "What were you saying about loyalty?" He took a sip, then set it down.

"I'm looking into Pegasus Limited," Gage said.

Norbett's eyebrows narrowed. "Pegasus?"

"Did you do the accounting?"

"For all the companies?"

"Any of the companies. I went to the Company Registry. There were three companies that made up the group—"

"Four."

"Four?"

"One is in Bermuda. That's where the insurance company finally ended up. They figured out it was better if the right hand didn't know what the left hand was really doing, or at least how they were doing it." Norbett smiled. "The bank account was here, but the company was there."

"Let me guess. Cayman Exchange Bank."

Norbett spread his hands. "Who else does Quinton use?"

They fell silent as the waitress delivered their salads and walked away.

Norbett stabbed at a piece of spinach and then locked his eyes on Gage's.

"How about we cut to the proverbial chase?"

Gage nodded. "What's your hourly rate?"

"For accounting?"

"For what we'll call research."

Norbett drummed the table with the fingers of his left hand. "I would say . . . maybe . . . ten thousand as a retainer and two hundred an hour."

"I take it the retainer would be nonrefundable."

"Call it catastrophic medical insurance. Because if anybody finds out . . ."

'm picking up drumbeats from all over," Brandon Meyer told Gage in his chambers in the San Francisco Federal Building the next day.

Gage had responded to Meyer's voice mail demanding he call back by dropping by an hour and a half after his flight from the Caymans landed at SFO.

"Good ears."

"I haven't had a thing to do with Pegasus since I left my law firm, and the worst anyone can say is that what we did was in a gray area of tax law." Brandon pounded his desk with his knuckle. "The IRS never even published a notice prohibiting the practice until two years after I was appointed to the bench."

"That's not the question the drums were asking," Gage said, from where he stood near the window overlooking the city and the Pacific Ocean beyond. "The question is whether you had anything to do with the payoffs to Wilbert Hawkins and Ray Karopian in TIMCO."

"And I assume the next accusation is I had something to do with the deaths of those two and recruited John Porzolkiewski to poison them." Brandon smirked. "That verges on the ludicrous."

"I'm not making that accusation. But I'm also not sure Porzolkiewski did it."

"There was enough probable cause to arrest him. Despite your rather jaundiced view of how some judges do their work, none of us would sign a search warrant unless the probable cause was convincing."

"Aren't you worried about *how* convincing the evidence might be? And who might be implicated?"

Brandon's face twisted with anger. "There'll be hell to pay if my name is in it."

"Your name isn't. Anston's is."

Brandon rocked himself out of his chair and walked over to the bar. He poured two fingers of bourbon into a highball glass. He didn't offer any to Gage. He took a sip as he turned back.

"You don't have a clue about the relationship between Anston and Palmer, do you?" Brandon asked.

"I know exactly what their relationship was."

"I don't think so. You think there was ever a time in the twenty-some years they worked together that Marc Anston called up Charlie and said, 'Get rid of the witnesses.' It's the same on both sides. You think any DEA agent has to skirt the law by telling a snitch to go search somebody's house and check if the drugs are there before the agent bothers to get a warrant? The snitch knows what to do."

"It's not the law that's rough, it's how some people practice it."

Brandon turned away and walked toward his desk.

"I don't know why we're talking about this," Brandon said. "You can't prove what Anston does has anything to do with me."

"We'll see." Gage rose to his feet. "Did you get your wallet back from SFPD?"

"Yes."

"Everything there?"

Brandon's face colored as he slid onto his chair.

"I believe so."

"Including the—"

"I said everything was there."

Gage persisted. "Including the Cayman Citibank credit card?"

"Yes, including the credit card."

"How do you pay the charges?"

"I don't believe it's any of your business."

"You're right, it's not my business, except to the extent it's paid for by money you and Anston received offshore for making TIMCO and other cases disappear."

"It doesn't make any difference where the firm received legal fees as long as it paid taxes on the income. And as far I know that was always done."

"I'm not sure anyone would call the money you got from TIMCO a legal fee."

"That's neither here nor there since I've received no compensation, directly, indirectly, or deferred since I left the firm."

"The money had to come from somewhere."

"Don't play naïve. There are few things judges may do to earn money beyond their salaries. Books, lectures, and investments. And I don't write books and I don't give lectures."

"Then why make the investments offshore?"

"Tax planning, man. What else?"

"There are lots of other possibilities."

Brandon held up a palm toward Gage. His face went dark.

"Don't even go there. I challenge you to find one instance where I profited from a decision in a case."

"Thinking back over the records, there seem to be lots of payments to Pegasus from companies appearing in your court." Gage waited a beat. Brandon's expression remained fixed. "Aren't you supposed to look offended now?"

Brandon waved away the accusation.

"The suggestion is too ludicrous. While I have no direct knowledge, I suspect you'll find they were clients of Anston. Remember, he's not a trial lawyer. He's hired to advise on corporate issues. It was between him and his clients if he suggested offshore insurance is a wise investment. Countless U.S. corporations are engaged in self-insurance and he happens to be an expert in the field."

"And your investment portfolio doesn't include any of those corporations?"

"Yes, it does. But you'll find I recused myself in each case involving those corporations. Check the dockets."

"Look, there's a reason why all these companies hire Anston to play trial lawyer, especially on cases in your court. They figure they'll get something for their money."

"That's a crock. He files motions, the other side responds, then I decide them on the merits. The Ninth Circuit has never reversed me. Never. I make every decision with twenty-eight appeals court judges peering over my shoulder. I don't control the entire game."

Brandon rose again, then put his shoulders back and glared at Gage.

"I'm starting to lose patience with this little exercise," Brandon said. "I have no need to explain my finances to you." He pointed at Gage. "And I'm warning you. Make any of your accusations public and I'll bury you. Anston will be more than happy to disclose whatever Pegasus bank records are required to show I didn't receive a dime since I left the firm."

Gage let the threat slide by.

"So Pegasus is Anston's company?"

"Does it make a difference who owns it? I don't know whether it was Anston's or Charlie's or somebody else's. I never inquired." Brandon paused and a half-smile came to his face. "Let's just say Charlie and I had sort of an investment club. In exchange for his managing the fund, I let him piggyback off my investments."

"Socorro doesn't seem to have any record, not even a clue, what were the investments that funded her annuity and the life insurance policies for her kids."

"That's not my problem. Charlie apparently chose not to include her in on his financial decisions any more than I include my wife in mine."

"He just walked out of the building," Brandon Meyer told Marc Anston in a telephone call a few minutes after Gage left his chambers. "I can see him crossing Golden Gate Avenue, heading toward the parking lot."

"What happened?"

"I conceded what I couldn't deny. The plan worked perfectly. He'll be spending the next month trying to prove you're paying me off through Pegasus for decisions."

"What about the credit card?"

"He's still hung up on it. Just like he was when he went to see Quinton."

"And TIMCO?"

"He's obsessed with tying it to me, and me alone. You could've driven Hawkins to the airport yourself and he wouldn't care."

"Are you sure he hasn't started to put it all together?"

"As sure as I can be."

The pattern is there, boss," Alex Z told Gage as they sat with Shakir around the worktable in the Oakland loft. "I can match up fifty cases involving companies that made offshore insurance payments to Pegasus and appeared in Meyer's court, some before and some after the money came into its CEB account."

Alex Z pointed at the list of company names. "Nearly every company was a defendant in some kind of civil or criminal action. Toxic spills, industrial accidents, insider trading."

"And at least some of them, like TIMCO, used Pegasus as a tax-deductible slush fund to pay off witnesses."

"That's what it looks like."

"But it doesn't get us anywhere unless it leads back to Brandon himself."

"There are a hundred other companies that bought insurance that didn't have cases in front of Meyer," Alex Z said. "That seems to suggest this was solely an Anston-operated scam. Tax or otherwise."

Gage thought back on his last meeting with Brandon and realized he was no longer sure what had been the judge's purpose, now troubled, wondering whether it was a defense or a deflection.

"Why not just narrow our focus?" Alex Z said. "Go after Anston and try to reopen TIMCO and Moki's cases? Maybe sic the IRS on the fake insurance scam?"

"Because everything that's happened began with the wallet. It's a link between Charlie and Brandon and led to Charlie's death. I'm sure of it. And Socorro won't be safe until we figure out why."

Gage scanned the list of Pegasus star names to which Alex Z had added the wire transfer information from Joe Casey.

Matar-GRID	July 1
Makirab-NDB	September 6
Algenib-BNIB	October 12
Enif-LLDD	November 4
Homam-CNIP	June 11
Baham-TPOO	September 21
Scheat-NEVV	November 3
Sad Al Naamah-MM	April 30

"Quinton referred to what Charlie was doing as investments," Gage said. "And Brandon said he and Charlie had a sort of investment club."

Shakir spoke up. "Sounds like they're trying to push you in that direction—"

Gage smiled. "Us." He pointed at Shakir. "You're in this, too, kid."

Shakir smiled back. "Thanks, boss."

"And they're succeeding in moving us that way," Gage said, "either because they're clean or because it's a dead end."

"It seems like a dead end," Alex Z said. "None of the acronyms match the names of any of the companies that appeared in his court or were part of the insurance scam. And we haven't been able to match them with the cases Anston handled."

Gage leaned forward, resting his elbows on his thighs and interlinking his fingers. He closed his eyes, thinking.

Finally, he opened them.

"Maybe they really did have a little investment club," Gage said, "and they're more than happy if we spend our time investigating it. There's nothing illegal about him and Charlie investing together." He glanced at Alex Z, and then pointed at the star list. "Did you compare those acronyms with Charlie's retirement account statements?"

"No match, even after we tried decoding them different ways. They're not stock symbols."

Gage shook his head. "We're not seeing something. It could be something as simple as Brandon not wanting it exposed in the press that he's using offshore money to make investments. It would remind voters that Landon is a child of privilege and not a regular guy."

"I don't know," Alex Z said. "We've had lots of wealthy presidential candidates who swaggered around like itinerant cowboys and golly-gee-whiz farmers and voters bought the act."

"Maybe times have changed." Gage rose and said to Alex Z, "Run GRID and the rest through the code-breaking program again. See if any meaningful words emerge unrelated to either cases or investments."

Gage stepped toward the door, then turned back and smiled as he pointed down at Shakir's forearm.

"I like the tattoo," Gage said.

Shakir grinned and held it out. "Mighty Mouse."

wish I could've delivered a clean victory, Mr. President," Landon Meyer told President Duncan in the Oval Office, "but it doesn't appear possible. The vice president will have to break the tie, assuming there's no filibuster."

Duncan rose from his desk chair and walked the few steps toward the window facing the South Lawn. He centered himself as though the pose would be memorialized someday as part of a Smithsonian retrospective on presidential decision making.

Landon almost turned his head toward the door to see whether the White House photographer had slipped in behind him.

"I don't see a filibuster in the works," Duncan said. "None of the Democrats would even mention the word on the Sunday talk shows."

"Still, all it takes is one and we'll have a constitutional showdown. It's one thing to filibuster a district court judge, another to filibuster a justice of the Supreme Court."

Duncan returned to his desk. He picked up the

telephone and pressed the intercom. He listened, and then said, "I need you in here."

Stuart Sheridan, Duncan's chief of staff, entered less than a minute later carrying a yellow legal pad, his pen already poised.

"We need some talking points," Duncan told him. "This nuclear option threat is sounding stale. We need something that'll turn a filibuster into a turd nobody'll want to touch."

Sheridan tapped the pen against the pad and closed his eyes, then he opened them and smiled. "Tyranny of the minority."

"Brilliant," Duncan said, grinning. "Tyranny of the minority. FOX News will go rabid on the Democrats with that one."

Duncan laughed, and then grinned at Landon. "Did you see the head of the Democratic National Committee on FOX last night?"

Landon shook his head. "I was at a fund-raiser."

"Hilarious. Every time they cut to a commercial, it was for Preparation H." Duncan slapped his hands together. "Hilarious. I'll bet Wyeth Pharmaceuticals didn't even ask for it. A couple hundred grand of advertising and it probably didn't cost them a dime."

Landon didn't smile in return.

Sheridan pushed through the awkward moment by turning the conversation back to strategy.

"After we do the tyranny of the minority," Sheridan said, "we'll send the vice president out to compare the Democrats to the Sunnis in Iraq under Saddam. A minority dictatorship."

"And then . . ." The excitement rose again in Duncan's voice. "And then we wait a couple of days and add something like: Why did we fight for democracy in Iraq only to lose it at home?"

Landon spoke up. "Isn't that somewhat excessive, Mr. President? The Democrats aren't traitors."

"We aren't calling them that. We're just making it a matter of majority rule."

"I'd be careful how far you push the analogy," Landon said. "The other side will surely point out it's only the vice president's vote that gives us the majority and we've used the filibuster ourselves a hundred times. And look at the polls. Less than fifty percent want the nominees confirmed."

"Plus a margin of error of four percent," Sheridan said.

"Or minus a margin of error of four percent. And how about the rest of the data? A majority favors abortion. Seventy percent of the public believes innocent people are being executed. Seventy-two percent want stricter gun control. And only thirty-six percent think you're doing even a half-decent job. We need to be careful about how we construct our talking points."

"You're not getting weak-kneed on this, are you, Landon?"

"No, Mr. President. Sometimes we have to do what's in the people's interest even if they don't recognize it at the time, and this is one of those moments."

Duncan looked over at Sheridan after the door closed behind Landon.

"Did you hear his speech to the Press Club yesterday morning?" Duncan asked.

Sheridan shook his head.

"I couldn't tell whether it was brilliant or just bullshit." Duncan opened a folder on his desk. "Listen to this: 'Conditional charity for the poor, not a free lunch . . . Return matters of governance to the states, reserve for the federal government matters of national character . . . A humble foreign policy aimed at retilting the trade balance, not at leveling every Islamic dictator.'" Duncan closed the folder. "Conditional charity? What the devil does that mean?"

"I think it means the poor eat at the Salvation Army instead of at the public trough."

Duncan laughed. "Once you translate it into plain English, it sounds like what every Republican president has been saying since Reagan."

Sheridan shrugged. "Saying and doing are two different things."

"Except I have a feeling if Meyer gets elected, they'll be exactly the same."

It was Sheridan's turn to laugh. "You mean he'll be a one-term president?"

"Better a one-term messianic Republican who knows what he believes than a one-term Democrat who navigates by polls and focus groups."

"G raham," Tansy Amaro said into the intercom, "Senator Meyer's office is calling."

"I guess the pipsqueak went running to his big brother," Gage said. "I'll take it."

Gage punched the flashing button on his desk phone.

"This is Graham Gage."

"This is Landon."

"Sorry, I thought I was speaking to your secretary."

"Since when do we have people running interference for us?"

"I assume you're running interference for your little brother this time."

"Interference?"

"He didn't call you?"

"This concerns him, but not because he called. It was something else. A call from a maniac in San Francisco."

"Which maniac?"

"The poisoner. Porzolkiewski. He called my office ranting about Brandon. That Brandon killed his son or covered up for the TIMCO people who killed his son. He threatened to go to the press. My secretary promised him I would look into it personally and I'd ask someone to visit him in jail by this time tomorrow."

"Why me?"

"Brandon said you've gotten to know Porzolkiewski."

"How did he find out?"

"He didn't say, but I need to put a lid on this thing. I can't have this kind of grief right now, assuming the media listens to him."

"Trust me. They'll listen to him. Maybe not now, but eventually. Do you know the DA's theory about the case?"

"Only what's been in the press. I heard a couple of reporters were trying to find a connection between Charlie Palmer and TIMCO, but I assume they gave up. The only story recently was about Porzolkiewski saying he wanted time to hire a lawyer."

"I'll tell you the answer, as long as you keep it to yourself."

"What about Porzolkiewski ?"

"I'll quiet him down."

"Okay. Just between you and me."

"I think Brandon and Anston have been involved in a few things that may slop back—"

"Maybe we should talk in person."

"Where?"

"I'll be in Des Moines tomorrow."

"What did you think you were going to accomplish?"

"I don't know," Porzolkiewski said, "I don't know what I was doing. Maybe it was a substitute for not having a gun to blow my brains out."

Porzolkiewski stared down at the table, as if embarrassed by his own weakness.

"Just listen to the noise in this place," Porzolkiewski said. "I don't understand why more people aren't committing suicide in here."

Only then did Gage's mind register the yelling and clanging that composed the relentless gray background noise of the jail.

Porzolkiewski finally looked up. "You're the reason I'm locked up in this joint."

Gage shook his head. "Like I planted the poison in your storeroom?"

"No. You got them to search for it. How do I know you're not in it with them?"

"In with who?"

"Brandon Meyer and Marc Anston. You sure as hell aren't doing anything to get me out of here."

"Tell me what I should be doing."

Porzolkiewski spread his arms. "How should I know, you're the investigator." He tapped his chest. "I'm just the schmuck who pushed his kid too hard."

Gage squinted at Porzolkiewski. "Now you're blaming yourself because he took the job at TIMCO?"

Porzolkiewski's shoulders slumped, and then he exhaled and said, "Now that you repeat it back, it sounds stupid."

Gage leaned forward, resting his forearms on the table.

"Look," Gage said, "everything in life could've

turned out differently. Just because you think back and one thing seems to have led to another, doesn't mean everything was inevitable and you're responsible. That applies to Brandon Meyer, too. And threatening his brother just makes you look like a paranoid lunatic."

Porzolkiewski rose and stared out through the wire mesh window of the visiting room door.

"This place is unreal," Porzolkiewski said. "It makes everything unreal. There's no way to control your thoughts, they just fly around with nothing solid to hold on to. Then they start to hook together in weird ways." He turned back toward Gage. "I don't know what I was thinking when I called the senator's office. Everything just seemed like a huge conspiracy."

"You want to talk to a psychiatrist?"

Porzolkiewski shook his head. "Jailhouse shrinks just want to drug people up because they know there's nothing they can do about this place and the way it makes you go crazy."

"Then let me give you a few things you can to hold on to when things seem to start spinning."

Porzolkiewski sat down.

"Lieutenant Pacheco is having toxicology tests done on every liquid or powder that was in Charlie's room. We're also checking out the background of the physical therapist. How he got hired by the agency and how he got assigned to Charlie. Spike says they're stonewalling, but we'll keep pushing. If we can prove he was planted there, the case here will look weaker and maybe we can get you transferred out to Contra Costa County. There's no law that says you have to go to trial in the county where you were first arrested."

"How does that help?"

"It's a quieter jail and close enough for your lady friend out in the Delta to visit you every day."

"They have conjugal visits out there?"

"Sorry. You'll have to get convicted and sent off to state prison for that."

Porzolkiewski winced. "I think I'll pass."

Thanks for bringing dinner," Faith said to Gage as they sat on the edge of the circular fountain near the Hearst Anthropology Museum on the UC Berkeley campus. It was at that spot decades earlier that an ex-cop chanced to offer a napkin to a graduate student who'd splashed coffee on her blouse just before her first meeting with her dissertation committee.

Between them now lay sourdough French rolls and paper take-out boxes of grilled vegetables, olives, mushrooms, and tuna salad. Both were sipping on sodas and watching students and staff flood from the buildings and separate into streams, some heading to the garages, some to the buses, some up or down the sidewalks to dorms or frat houses or the apartments surrounding the campus.

"How's Porzolkiewski?" Faith asked.

"Off the deep end."

"There's a student group here that visits prisoners. You want me to give them his name? Maybe some outsiders would keep him in contact with reality."

Gage shook his head. "I can't take a chance he'll start ranting about Brandon and TIMCO. Next thing you know one of them is running to the press, either because it would be a big story or because Porzolkiewski looks like the victim of a conspiracy. They're good-hearted kids and too likely to believe everyone is innocent. And once they get a glimpse of that hangdog face of his, they'll be marching on San Francisco City Hall. That's the same reason I told him not to hire a lawyer. I didn't want to lose control of the case."

"What do you think?" Faith peered at him. "Is he innocent?"

"I don't know. I can see him losing control and committing a manslaughter, but premeditated murder, I'm not sure." Gage opened the grilled vegetables and handed Faith a plastic fork. "On the other hand, he was on a mission for years trying to prove TIMCO lied about the explosion and that Brandon was involved. He was damn methodical about that."

"He had to have been furious when Brandon got appointed to the bench. It must have felt like a betrayal, like the devil being appointed God." Faith smiled at Gage. "As I recall, he wasn't the only one who felt that way."

"I don't know what Landon was thinking when he put in his brother's name. It was like opening the door to the henhouse and laying out a red carpet for the fox."

"But I thought you said you can't link any of the premium payments into Pegasus to any decisions he's made in cases."

"None of those companies really thought they

were buying insurance. Charlie Palmer didn't run an insurance company and the Pegasus money we've traced came back as payoffs to witnesses, not as payments on insurance claims."

A car backfire rocked Bancroft Avenue as it bounced off the concrete façade of the building behind them. They both glanced over to see smoke envelop an early-seventies Suburban as it rolled to a stop.

When it cleared Gage noticed a familiar brown Taurus with a man in the passenger seat. Unlike everyone else on the street, he didn't watch the spectacle. He kept staring down toward the bay. He was also too old to be a student and too tough to be staff or faculty.

Gage lowered his eyes. "Look away from the street."

Faith reached for the vegetables and made a point of picking through them. "What's going on?"

"I'll try to find out." Gage pulled his cell phone out of his shirt pocket and called a number in its memory.

Viz answered on the first ring. "What's up?"

"I'm in Berkeley with Faith, near her office. Boots Marnin just showed up across the street. When can you get here?"

"I'm at the Federal Building waiting for Brandon to come out. So about a half hour."

"We're by the fountain. Call me when you get close and we'll figure out a plan."

"How long did he hang around our house after Faith and I got home?" Gage asked Viz in a late night call.

"Couple of minutes, then he followed the ridge and took Snake Road down to the freeway. I think he's been to your house a few times, he drove those winding streets like a local."

"And after that?"

"He was all over the place. I couldn't tell whether he was doing countersurveillance or what. He hit about eight different restaurants and warehouses in San Francisco. Inside for fifteen or twenty minutes, then on to another one."

"Did he make you?"

"Me?" Viz's voice rose. "Make me?"

Gage laughed. "Sorry I asked."

message was waiting on Gage's voice mail when his plane touched down in Denver on the way to Des Moines to meet Landon Meyer.

"Boss. I listened to the recording Viz made of Brandon Meyer outside of the Tadich Grill and then did what you said. It looks like money from Landon's Silicon Valley group just showed up in the Ohio and Massachusetts senators' campaigns. Each got a million-dollar loan from a San Jose bank called Mann Trust. Three members of the Silicon Valley group are on the board. I'll e-mail you a list of all of the money I've traced."

Gage stared out his window as the other passengers deplaned, still stunned by the cynical opportunism of Landon Meyer, whose campaign he'd saved from internal sabotage just two years earlier. Gage tasted the bitterness of Brandon's snide comment about him believing in the purity of the process.

Since candidates couldn't accept contributions

directly from corporations, Landon had deposited the Silicon Valley Group money into Mann Trust, and then the bank used it to secure the loans to the candidates.

Nothing more or less than political money laundering.

"Thanks for flying out," Landon said. "It's not exactly a short hop from San Francisco to Des Moines, but I didn't want to talk on the telephone."

Gage walked across the thin blue carpet in the Super 8 Motel toward the east-facing window with a view of Interstate 35. The afternoon sun gave an orange glow to the aluminum-sided semis grinding their way along the highway.

"I figured you for the Savery Hotel downtown," Gage said. "Georgian Revival in the prairie." He turned and scanned the child-sized desk, the winter scene print nailed to the wall, the stain-disguising green, blue, and yellow kaleidoscopic bedspread, and the television bolted to the dresser. He then took in a breath infused with an overdose of air freshener. "A tenth floor suite, not a second floor walkup."

"This is Iowa. Folks here keep an eye on how you spend the money when you've got your hand out." Landon spread his arms to encompass the room. "Sixty-three dollars a night, including breakfast."

"Folks?"

Landon smiled.

"Of course. And I even eat at the Flying J Truck Stop."

"Country fried steak and mashed potatoes?"

"What else?"

"Sounds like the Heartland Inn across the street would have been a better choice."

"They were booked up. It's the start of pumpkin season, and everybody in Washington, D.C., who has even the faintest hope of becoming president is out here kissing babies and thumping squash."

"Just be careful you don't do it backward."

"Sometimes I'm so tired I can't tell the difference."

Gage glanced back toward the hallway. "Aren't there supposed to be a bunch of underlings from Washington scurrying in and out of here?"

Landon shook his head. "I've got one guy next door, but otherwise I use local people. They're not as efficient, but they help get the message across."

"Which is?"

"That I was never a Washington insider who got cash from Jack Abramoff and from the K Street gang leaning on people."

Gage resisted the urge to reveal what he had just learned from Alex Z. It wasn't the right moment to talk about money.

"How many times have you flown solo on the Iowa circuit?" Gage asked.

"Altogether? Ten in the last two years. I'm a helluva lot more popular here than I am in California."

"Especially after the Supreme Court nominations."

"I better win the presidency." Landon pointed west. "I don't think the people of the Golden State are going to elect me again."

"You've got four more years. Voters have short memories."

Landon shook his head again. "Not this time." He reached toward the automatic coffeemaker sitting on a tray on top of the dresser. "Want some?"

Gage nodded. Landon poured two cups, then directed Gage to a cloth-covered chair at a table next to the window. Landon sat down across from him.

"What were you going to say yesterday after 'I think you need to know what Brandon has been up to'?"

"You really think your cell phone is being tapped?"

"Politics is brutal these days and the technology can be bought on the Internet. That'll change if I become president, but there's nothing I can do about it now except be careful."

"Especially about Brandon."

"Only because he walks a fine line—"

"Between the legal and illegal?"

"No. Between his role as a judge and his role as my closest political adviser." Landon raised his palm toward Gage. "Don't give me that look. Abe Fortas was practically part of Lyndon Johnson's Cabinet. Roosevelt didn't make a move without checking with Justice Frankfurter. Scalia used to chat up Cheney during their hunting trips."

"At this point I'm more concerned about Brandon's role as an attorney."

"That's ancient history."

"Only as ancient as John Porzolkiewski."

Landon leaned back in his chair and folded his arms across his chest. "Maybe you better tell me how the sentence you began on the phone was going to end."

"How about I'll start over with the punch line."

"Shoot."

"Marc Anston hired an investigator named Charlie Palmer to pay off the OSHA inspector and a welder at TIMCO to cover up the cause of the explosion."

"Was Brandon involved?"

"I think so, but I can't prove it."

"I wouldn't be shocked by anything Anston did. He believes in winning, only in winning. But I don't think he would involve Brandon. He needed Brandon's coattails to build the firm. Owed him too much."

"It always struck me that their relationship was upside down," Gage said. "The younger man bringing business to the older. But I was looking at it from the outside."

"It was a difference in background and career path and temperament. Anston went from Skull and Bones at Yale to law school and then into the CIA for twenty years. He needed Brandon because he never developed the personality to become a rainmaker on his own." Landon chuckled. "You know where the Book of Genesis talks about 'every creeping thing that creeps upon the earth'? That's Anston, the creepiest. But he had a talent for offshore finance. That's part of what he did in the Agency, setting up surreptitious ways to fund covert actions."

Landon leaned forward in his chair. "Did you follow the Iran-Contra hearings?"

"Some."

"You know who set up the Cayman Island account used to funnel private contributions to the Contras?" Landon didn't wait for an answer. "Anston. By using 501(c)(3) organizations."

"As though they were charities like the Red Cross?"

Landon smiled. "Fund a war, get a tax break."

"What about the money from the Iranian arms sales?"

"He did those through Switzerland." Landon settled back in his chair again. "See? Anston was the perfect guy to set up the offshore TIMCO pay-offs. There was absolutely no reason to involve my brother in anything."

"I think he may have involved Brandon at least in this one. The payoff money for the OSHA inspector and welder came from a Cayman account somehow connected to Brandon."

"Is that true?"

"Are you asking whether it's true or whether anyone can prove it?"

"Both."

"I don't know," Gage said. "There's no way to force the Cayman lawyer who runs the company to disclose anything. But I'm at least sure Charlie Palmer managed it."

"For Brandon or Anston?"

"I don't know that either. Probably both. And I do know that TIMCO wired money to that company. It's called Pegasus."

Landon shrugged.

"About a million and a half went in and out of Pegasus to take care of the TIMCO witnesses," Gage said.

"That looks bad. I received money from TIMCO

executives in my first senatorial campaign, but it was—"

"Before the explosion. I checked."

"Why?"

"Why what?"

"Why did you check? You don't think I was somehow mixed up with what they were doing?"

"It crossed my mind."

Landon shook off the implication.

"So TIMCO is the reason for the mugging?"

"It wasn't a mugging."

"But Brandon said—"

"I'm pretty sure Brandon got into a scuffle with Porzolkiewski and the wallet just fell out of his pocket."

Landon narrowed his eyes toward Gage.

"So there really is a connection between Brandon and Porzolkiewski? Why did Brandon lie to me about what happened?"

"My guess is there was something in the wallet that would give away the scheme."

"Do you know what was in there?"

"I've seen it all," Gage said, "but I don't know what it all means. Some of it's a little bizarre."

"Like what?"

"A list of star names and dates that seem to match Cayman Exchange Bank transactions in Palmer's account."

"So Brandon has some connection to whatever Anston is doing."

Gage could hear Landon's breathing start to accelerate.

"I may have to get ahead of this one. If it's true

Brandon was involved in hiding witnesses and suborning perjury in TIMCO, I'll probably have to go to the press first and he'll have to take his chances."

"Not probably. You'll have no choice. It's all going to come out in Porzolkiewski's trial and it'll slop over onto you."

"I know that. But I can survive it. Robert Kennedy survived Ted Kennedy leaving that poor woman in the Chappaquiddick River. George W. Bush survived his brother's involvement in the savings and loan scandal, Bill Clinton survived Roger's cocaine conviction, Jimmy Carter survived his brother becoming a lobbyist for Libya."

"I see you've thought about this."

"With a brother like Brandon, you have to think about every possibility." Landon paused for a moment, then asked, "How much of this is in the search warrant affidavit?"

"You mean how much is going to come out before trial?"

"To be specific, between now and when the Supreme Court nominations go to the full Senate."

"Not as much was in the affidavit as I know now."

"But what you think you know is only what Porzolkiewski believes."

"I know a lot more than he does. And part of that is in the affidavit, but it's still sealed."

Landon rose and interlaced his fingers on the back his neck and paced back and forth between the bed and dresser. He finally stopped and lowered his hands to his waist.

"So that's how it started."

"How what started?"

Landon squinted up toward the ceiling. "Who said it?"

"Said what?"

"'Every empire was founded on a great crime.'"

"Is that what your presidency is supposed to be, some kind of empire?"

"You wouldn't understand."

"I'll tell you what I do understand—"

"TIMCO would have done that whether or not they'd contributed to my campaign. They didn't do it for me."

"But you were the beneficiary and I'm sure it was in Brandon's mind when he set it up."

Landon flared. "You keep saying Brandon, but your evidence says Anston."

"Do you really think anything went on in the firm that they didn't discuss during their lunches at Tadich Grill? My guess is that most of the strategy was hashed out over those crisp white tablecloths."

"But you can't prove it."

"No. I can't prove it."

Gage heard a cash register ring in his head. *Every empire was founded on a great crime.* He remembered Landon's shrug and silence when he'd mentioned the name of the offshore company.

He stared into Landon's eyes, and said, "You've heard of Pegasus."

Landon looked away, then back.

"It's called capitalism. The logical political conclusion in a capitalist society."

"No, Landon. It's called fraud."

Landon glared down at Gage. "You just don't get it."

Gage felt a shudder through his body. Landon was wrong. He got it. He got every bit of it and he said it aloud:

"All the money you're putting into these campaigns is from fake insurance premiums corporations paid into Pegasus."

"Why do you think they're fake?"

"None of those companies needed the extra insurance, and Brandon and Anston sure as hell never paid out any claims."

Landon drew himself up and squared his shoulders.

"First, it's not Brandon, and second, companies buy insurance year by year, whatever isn't paid out in claims is profit."

"Well, has Pegasus ever paid out on an insurance claim?"

"It's not insurance. It's international reinsurance. It only pays out once a company exceeds its domestic insurance limits."

"That's not an answer. The question was whether Pegasus ever paid anything out."

"I wouldn't know. It's not my company."

Gage then began to see Pegasus though Anston's lens: Pegasus was simply a political replica of the CIA front companies Anston set up in the 1970s to fund covert actions—

Except this time it wasn't the leadership of a foreign country that was at stake. It was all three branches of the U.S. government.

Then more came to him.

"And the millions you put into those campaigns to get the last two votes for the Supreme Court nominees came from Pegasus."

Landon shrugged. "Sort of."

"I had thought the money came from the Silicon Valley Group."

"How did you get that idea?"

"Somebody overheard Brandon talking."

"They got it wrong. That was just bundling individual hard-money contributions. I put all of it into my political action committee. I've got copies of the checks to prove it."

"But you've still got a foreign company at least indirectly contributing to a U.S. election campaign. That's a violation not only of election laws but the Foreign Agents Registration Act."

"Think again. They weren't contributions. They were loans that came through Mann Trust."

"It's still foreign money."

"U.S. banks are full of foreign money. You don't think foreign deposits aren't going into every bank in the U.S. that's loaning money to political candidates? Hell, foreigners even own some of those banks."

"What about money coming from Caribbean islands directly into campaigns?"

Landon shook his head. "It never does. Maybe into 527s and political action committees, even super-PACs, but never into any campaign accounts I'm associated with. That would be a crime. And the money is clean as long as the foreign account is controlled by U.S. citizens." Landon smiled. "You want to talk to our lawyer?"

"Not if it's Brandon or Anston."

"The National Senatorial Campaign lawyer. And we have an opinion letter from Stone & Whitman."

"I'm sure everyone on your side thinks it's legal."

"It's more than legal. It's exactly what I said. It's what you get when you combine free market capitalism with politics."

Gage shook his head and pointed at Landon. "Remember what happened the last time you took something to its logical conclusion?"

Landon stiffened. "I was just ahead of my time. The immigration issue wasn't ripe."

"And I'm not sure this one makes any more sense than that one did. Your political business model is leaving you not with profit but with debt. A whole lot of it."

"For a while, only for a while. We just consider it an investment."

"The way my people have added it up, your so-called investment in the form of loans to candidates and 527s is around forty-five million dollars just this year."

Landon half smiled and looked away. "A drop in the bucket."

CHAPTER 77

Landon really did eat at the Flying J.

Gage found a booth while Landon glad-handed his way around the restaurant. He'd ordered for both of them by the time Landon sat down.

"Where's the menu?"

"You don't need one," Gage said. "You already told me what you were having. Chicken fried steak."

An outstretched hand attached to a plaid-covered arm injected itself into their conversation. Landon shook it, then scooted out of the booth. A skinny, five-foot-two-inch truck driver swept his John Deere cap off his head and offered Landon a toothy smile.

"Just had to shake your hand, Mr. President."

Landon smiled back. "We're still over a year away from the election and there's no guarantee I'll win. Just call me Landon."

The driver fidgeted, flustered by the offer. "I'm not sure I can do that, Senator." He slipped his cap back on. "Sorry I interrupted your conversation, but I just had to tell you how much I support you and them two nominees. I'm tired—" The driver jerked his thumb over his shoulder toward the tables of truckers behind him. "We're all tired of judges makin' the laws. We elect you-all to make the laws and they're supposed to follow them."

"I agree with you . . ."

"Chuck."

"I agree with you, Chuck. And I'll do my best to get the nominees confirmed."

"Thanks a lot, Senator."

"Landon."

"Okay." The driver displayed a bashful smile. "Landon."

Gage was still shaking his head when Landon slid to a stop on the bench seat.

"How many times do you go through that every day?" Gage asked.

"As many times as I can."

Landon grabbed a napkin, then slid it under the table to wipe his hands.

"The funny thing is I always thought I was a solid person," Landon said, "all of one piece. But every hand I shake is attached to someone who wants me to be something else." He offered a weak smile. "Sometimes I feel like Frankenstein's monster." He glanced over at the tables of truckers. "These people don't have a clue. Courts will always make law. There's no such thing as strict construction or originalism, that's why I never use the terms. The Founding Fathers never could've anticipated the Internet or stem cell research or nuclear weapons. The Court's job is to maintain the national character as embodied in the Constitution, but applied to today's problems, and sometimes that means restoring or even remaking the law when Congress or some lower court goes astray. Precedent and *stare decisis* can't mean anything more than that or be any more restrictive than that. Not in the real world. That's the only way the Court could have gotten to the *Citizens United* decision. It certainly wasn't because prior justices were confused about what a person was. The world had changed since the Constitution was written and the Supreme Court—not the Founders—wanted to give corporations the same rights as persons so they could participate in the political process."

Landon thumped the table with his finger. "The Boston Tea Party wasn't just aimed at the Revenue Acts, but even more so at the all-powerful East India Company. The last thing the Founders would've done was grant corporations the personal rights of citizens. But times have changed and now we have statutory ways to control corporate lawlessness." His eyes went vacant as though the thought was continuing to develop in his mind, then he said, "At the same time, a ruling not based on precedent or that the Court refuses to allow to be used as precedent subverts the legitimacy of the court. That's why *Bush v. Gore* was a travesty—not because the decision was wrong—it was right—but because the court cowered in the face of its own reasoning and ruled that it could never be cited as precedent in any other case."

"Why not just stand up and say all that?"

"Because people don't like to be confronted by the

nauseating reality that we build the bridges we walk on to get where we're going and sometimes have to repair or rebuild them from the middle. Those who describe themselves as strict constructionists or originalists are engaging in self-deception. Did you see Justice Sunseri on CNN last week? The reporter asked him whether torturing enemy prisoners was prohibited by the Constitution as cruel and unusual punishment. He responded by asking her whether she would ever use the word 'punishment' to refer to torture." Landon smirked. "What a stupid question. Idiotic. If originalism really meant anything to him, he would've asked whether the *Founding Fathers* in the eighteenth century would've applied the word to torture, not whether she would in the twenty-first. She didn't write the Constitution, they did. I'd never before seen someone expose himself so completely as a fraud—and no one in the media caught it."

Landon's face flushed. "If your position is well founded, there's no reason to create a mythology to support it."

Landon paused, then shook his head as if shaking off a catcher's sign.

"The same with the Bible. Nobody could follow it word for word. I'm not even sure anyone knows what the original words were. If we tried, we'd be stoning people to death every day. Billy Graham's greatness wasn't because he could shout out passages like a nineteenth-century orator, but because of the way he interpreted them and wove them into a modern message of personal salvation." Landon grinned. "He spent his life as a Frankenstein's monster, too. Always a registered Democrat."

The waitress placed a basket of dinner rolls and their salads on the table and winked at Landon before she turned away.

"Apparently she can't see where Dr. Frankenstein made the stitches," Gage said.

"She must be blinded by my star power among the blue-collar crowd."

Landon bowed his head in prayer, then picked up a dinner roll and buttered it.

"How about your star power in Washington?" Gage asked.

"I guess that's going to be up to you."

"How do you figure?"

"I'm pretty sure I can survive a TIMCO scandal and—"

"You fly commercial this time?"

"I always fly commercial to Iowa. And because of our conversation today, whether your allegations are true or not, I won't be accepting TIMCO's largesse in the future." Landon nodded with pursed lips. "Helluva fleet they have." He set the uneaten roll onto his plate. "Let's put it this way. Washington, and by Washington I mean President Duncan, will bless me if I get his nominations—"

"His nominations? That's not what the press is saying."

"Okay, my nominations . . . through the Senate. And you, my friend, are the only person in the country who can derail them. If you leak any of your, shall I say, *suspicions* to the press—"

"If your campaign funding scheme is legal, what difference does it make?"

"The public wouldn't understand, at least right away. And people fear what they don't understand."

"You mean they'll think it's a corporate conspiracy to manipulate the electoral process, like the way many voters view super-PACs?"

Landon thumped a finger on the Formica table.

"The corporate conspiracy to manipulate the electoral process is called the liberal elitist media."

Gage rolled his eyes. "Not this again." He spread his hands on the table, "And now you're going to tell me it will be the fault of the media if the public comes to the conclusion that your brother's law firm—"

"Ex . . . ex–law firm—"

"—obstructed justice using a Cayman Island bank account later used to funnel loans to political campaigns?"

"I . . . no. If you put it that way, no. But that has nothing to do with me, and it's not the issue."

"Then what's the issue?"

"The issue is political."

"I'm not a political person."

"You're the most political person I have ever met."

"What party do I belong to? Who did I vote for in the last presidential election?"

"Not that way." Landon pointed at Gage. "Everything for you is a moral issue. If it's between you and someone else, it's called ethics. If it's between you and world, it's called politics."

It was true, but Gage had never expected to hear it as an accusation. Except he recognized that

Landon was dissembling, for by "political" he really meant "partisan," exploiting the double meaning of the word to conceal—maybe from himself—the degree to which his own ethics had mutated since his first campaign.

"I didn't realize I was a subject of your psychological analysis."

"I pay attention to people who have become dangerous. And, at the moment, you're the most dangerous man in America."

"To these nominations, maybe, but not to America."

"You don't get it." Landon started thumping the table again. "These nominations are the future of America, and I'm not sure you want to compromise that future because of some silliness by my brother—allegedly by my brother—fourteen years ago."

Silliness.

The word ricocheted around in Gage's mind as he stood in the boarding line at the Des Moines airport.

Four men incinerated on the top of TIMCO's fractionating tower wasn't silliness.

Obstruction of justice wasn't silliness.

Bribing an OSHA investigator wasn't silliness.

Paying off a witness wasn't silliness.

What happened to the Landon Meyer I used to know? Gage asked himself. *The Landon Meyer who prayed to a God he believed would someday judge him? He can't really believe God is on his side in this one.*

The man behind Gage tapped him on the shoulder and said, "The line's moving, pal. Put it into gear."

Gage closed the gap between himself and the woman in front of him.

It had all come too fast. Gage knew he hadn't asked all the questions he should have. Even when he was sitting across from Landon in the Flying J, he knew it. Landon's people had a decade to work it out, he only had a fraction of that time to grasp it.

He felt his stomach turn.

For a while, Landon had said about the debts his chosen candidates had shouldered during their campaigns. *Only for a while*.

And Gage then knew he needed to find out when that while would end, and where.

arc Anston glanced at his airplane ticket as he walked from American Airlines Admiral's Club at the San Francisco Airport toward his departure gate. He hated his first name. Not the sound. Seeing it in print. The spelling: French. Like a recurring nightmare. The language of the self-important. The self-delusional. A nation that had been defeated in just days by the Nazis during the year of his birth, and despite having been rescued by soldiers such as his father, proclaimed itself one of the victors at the end of the war.

Fellow students at Andover called him Frenchie, but that ended after three bloody noses made their way to the school nurse. And by the time he'd arrived at Yale, word had gotten around to not even try. Nonetheless, Anston grew up feeling like the kid in "A Boy Named Sue," and nauseated by the fact that it was a song written by a Jew and sung by a country hick.

Anston surrendered his boarding pass and walked down the ramp toward the first-class cabin. In a few hours he'd be at the Rocky Mountain Center for Corporate Responsibility in Aspen.

That, too, he realized as he stepped across the threshold into the plane, was a boy named Sue.

Anston climbed out of the limousine in front of the St. Regis Resort and took a long look at the brick façade. He knew it would be the last time he'd breathe the alpine air or be seen in public until he checked out two days later.

After tipping the porter, he inspected the three bedrooms of his sixth floor suite in the Residence Club. One had been converted into a conference room. The second into an office. He walked to the master bedroom and changed from his suit into slacks and a sweater, then inspected the stocked refrigerator in the kitchen and brewed a cup of tea. He had just settled onto the couch in front of the stone fireplace when three quick knocks on the door brought him back to his feet.

"Am I the first one here?" Preston Walters asked as he strode across the threshold.

With his magisterial white hair, tan face, and self-satisfied expression, Anston thought Walters appeared even more presidential than Landon Meyer—and felt annoyance that he was stuck dealing with politicians like Meyer because the American public was unlikely to ever let anyone step from a corporate suite directly into the presidency.

Anston nodded. "How was the flight?"

"Cramped." Walters made a show of shifting his shoulders. "I hate playing the part of the worthy corporate citizen by flying commercial. All I could think about was our new Boeing sitting in the hangar. Range of six thousand miles. You should see that thing." Walters grinned. "The best fifty million dollars of shareholders' money I ever spent."

"What are you calling this one?"

"The TIMCO Star."

"We'll get campaign finance before the court by the end of November," Anston said.

Eleven of the twelve industry lobbyists and corporate officers sitting around the oak conference table nodded.

The twelfth was staring down.

He looked up at Anston and asked, "Who's the plaintiff going to be? It can't be one of us." He scanned the other faces. "It's impossible to make hundred-billion-dollar companies seem like victims."

Anston smiled. "We already have plaintiffs."

"Since when?"

"Two years ago. *Mid-State Machinery Incorporated v. Federal Election Commission* and *Americans for Americans v. Federal Election Commission*. The first to extend the *Citizens United* decision and allow for direct contributions by corporations to political campaigns, and the second to bar any corporation with less than fifty-one percent U.S. ownership from contributing to any campaign of any kind through any means of any kind."

"And by any corporation, you mean those owned by the Chinese."

"Of course, just because they're allowed to buy our bonds and our companies," Anston said, "doesn't

mean we're going to let them buy our politicians."
He smirked. "We have the exclusive on that."

"Call it a corporate citizenship test." Preston
Walters laughed. "Or maybe immigration reform."

"We had to get these cases through the district
and the appeals courts to tee it up for our new guys.
Oral arguments will be right after Thanksgiving."

"When will they issue their opinion?"

"The second week in February."

"Why then?"

"Because twenty percent of the caucuses and
primaries will be over. Things will be so chaotic
nobody will be able to figure out who the real beneficiary is—our side or the unions."

"Except us."

Anston nodded. "Except us."

Walters looked at this watch. One fifty-five P.M.
"We better get down to the conference. That foreign bitch Madeleine Albright is giving a talk on
the ethics of globalization." He shook his head in
disgust. "It makes me want to gag."

Eight hours later, Anston tossed a log onto the fire
as Walters settled onto the couch.

"How did the interview on CNBC go?" Anston
asked, taking a seat in one of the matching side
chairs.

"Softballs. That's all he threw. He didn't have a
clue we spend a thousand times more on advertising
our good deeds than actually doing them."

"I saw the one on Peruvian reforestation," Anston
said. "I felt like nominating you for environmental-
ist of the year."

Walters chuckled. "We did an acre and played it like we did a forest." He picked up a glass of Scotch from the side table and took a sip. "What's your pitch to the group going to be tomorrow?"

"That we calculate each sector's contribution based on percentage of GDP, aiming at a total of five hundred million dollars."

"That means . . ."

"Energy has to come up with forty million."

Walters laughed. "Hell, I could raise half that myself by selling TIMCO's Gulfstream. But are you sure five hundred is enough?"

Anston smiled. "We don't have to buy the entire election, just add it into regular campaign contributions to reach the tipping point. Two hundred million to pay off outstanding loans and three hundred in new money."

"I don't know. I'm still worried about Landon Meyer. I'm not sure he can play down the cultural issues long enough. He's always chomping at the bit about abortion and gay marriage. He thinks they're wedge issues, but they've become mainstream. He just sounds manic."

Anston's smile disappeared. "I'm worried, too."

"And we've got over half a billion dollars riding on him. Unless we have him in the Oval Office to veto Congress's attempts to circumvent the Supreme Court, it's going to be a wasted investment." Walters pushed himself to his feet, then pointed down at Anston. "If TIMCO still has the EPA and OSHA breathing down its neck a year from now and if we're still blocked from Arctic drilling, and if anybody in the next administration ever uses the phrase 'global warming,' I'll be pissed. All of us will be pissed. Our shareholders don't give a damn whether the enforcement guys at the EPA and the SEC and the Federal Energy Commission are fags, we just want them politically neutered."

Walters walked over to the window and studied Ajax Mountain, pine green and ragged gray.

"Sometimes I think Landon believes he's a new Moses," Walters said, "the bearer of 'the Word,' with a vision of a distant holy land, a new City on a Hill. But that's not the Moses we need. We need the one who butchered his way across the Sinai to clear a path."

Walters turned back toward Anston. "Landon understands how his trip to the White House is getting paid for, right?"

"He doesn't fully understand how he's getting where he's going," Anston said, "but he knows who he'll owe."

"That's not good enough. I'm tired of renting these politicians, or leasing them for two, four, or six years from political action committees and 501s and 527s. The guys who run these organizations can pivot at any time, even the fiscal conservatives, and run headlong at values issues—gays and drug testing and stem cell research—and forget why we gave them the money. And the politicians will pivot with them and forget why we put them in office."

Walters raised his hand and jabbed the air with his finger.

"And I'm already sick of dealing through super-PACs and the greedy bastards who run them, and I'm tired of doing the idiotic non-coordination dance. I want to own these politicians outright and I want them to know I own them. I want to be the company store. I want them sucking on our tit so long and so hard they forget there's any other one."

This is Norbett."

"What's up?" Gage glanced at his watch as he pressed his cell phone to his ear. It was near midnight in the Caymans. He hoped he was about to get something useful in exchange for the ten thousand dollars he'd wired to Norbett.

"Pegasus Insurance stopped issuing policies four years ago," Norbett said.

Gage sat leaned forward over his desk. "That can't be right."

"It is."

"Maybe they just moved."

"Nope. I checked. I spent a little of your money on calls to the places they could've gone: Barbados, Gibraltar, Guernsey, Isle of Man, and Luxembourg. Zip times five. If you're going to run an insurance scam, those are the places you go to."

"No companies named Pegasus at all?"

"Every constellation is represented in every jurisdiction, but not a single Pegasus is registered to sell insurance—hold on."

Gage heard a door close in the background.

"Where are you?"

"Home. I don't want my wife to overhear this part. She may misunderstand."

"Misunderstand what?"

"I intercepted Quinton's secretary when she was leaving work yesterday. We had a little fling years ago when I was doing the accounting for the companies Quinton's firm set up." Norbett laughed. "It was a hell of a lot more than a fling. I was head over heels for that gal. She broke it off because of her kids. She felt a little guilty. I knew I'd have to break up with her anyway. She likes her martinis too much."

"Even more than you?"

"Hard to believe, isn't it? Especially the ones at Copper Falls Steakhouse, and they got her talking. She confirmed what I was thinking. The insurance premiums were wired to Pegasus in Grand Cayman, then bundled up and sent on to the Bermuda company, Pegasus Reinsurance."

"Was it actually wired forward or was it just transferred within Cayman Exchange Bank?"

"Just within the bank, so there'd be no wire transfer trail."

"How much money are we talking about?"

"That's the interesting thing. She thinks between two and four hundred million went that route."

"That's a lot of—"

"Not really. It was only twenty-five or fifty million a year over eight years. Annually, that's only a half a million or a million dollars for each company."

"Hold on a second." Gage retrieved Palmer's spreadsheet from the safe. "Go ahead."

"What I was saying was that Pegasus wasn't all that big by Bermuda standards. You ever hear about Patrick Memorial Hospital in Houston?"

"Vaguely."

"Quinton set that up, too. They had a hundred and fifty million dollars in a bank account offshore for self-insurance. Just one hospital. In a hundred years they wouldn't pay out that much in claims. It was just a huge tax dodge." Norbett laughed. "You Americans think you've reformed your health care system, but you haven't even come close."

"Did all the Pegasus money travel the same Cayman to Bermuda route?"

"I don't know."

"But you can find out."

"Absolutely. Copper Falls has seven kinds of martinis and you've only bought me four so far."

"Are you sure she won't go running back to Quinton?"

"You've met him. He's a little much, even for a British solicitor. He treats her like a colonial subject because she's Jamaican. She's got twenty years of resentment built up. She'll come through."

"Then see if she knows whether Quinton ever had a client named Brandon Meyer. I need confirmation."

"Brandon Meyer . . . Brandon Meyer. That name is familiar."

"How's that?"

"I don't know. It'll come to me. It was some kind of shell game. Started years and years ago." Norbett fell silent. "Give me a day or so. It'll come to me."

Something changed four years ago." Gage's glove thudded against the heavy bag in the corner of Stymie's Gym in West Oakland. Two left jabs, then a right cross. Two left jabs, then a right cross. Two left jabs, then a right cross.

Skeeter Hall sat on the floor propped against a wall, sipping from his water bottle. He wiped away the sweat dripping from his forehead with a towel.

"We've been doing some research," Skeeter said. "But it feels like we've just been flailing around."

Gage lowered his gloves and turned toward the lawyer.

"What Pegasus did was so novel there's nothing in the law addressing it," Skeeter said. "It's not hard money and it's not soft money, in fact, it's not really money."

"You're right," Gage said. "It's not money. It's debt. I told that to Landon, but he shrugged it off. He said the senatorial campaign attorneys researched how loans should be handled and claimed they're clean."

Skeeter looked down as though studying his shoelaces, then back up. "If this all started with TIMCO, maybe—"

Gage shook his head. "I'm starting to think I'm wrong about that. I think the tax scam was in place first and Anston just used it for TIMCO."

"You mean for a bunch of TIMCOs."

"We just don't have records going back to the start of the insurance scam because Palmer didn't get involved until witnesses needed to be paid off."

Gage turned back toward the bag, set his feet, and then popped the rectangular Everlast label with a straight right, jolting the hundred-and-thirty-pound bag.

Skeeter grinned. "Anston's lucky that wasn't his head. You would've separated it from his body."

Gage glanced over his shoulder. "I wish it was that simple." He lowered his gloves and turned toward Skeeter. "You know what Landon told me? He said I was the most political person he ever met—no, he accused me of it."

"You?" Skeeter chuckled. "Politics in this country is treating opinions as if they were hard facts and unwelcome facts as if they were just opinions."

"Kind of like criminal defense work?"

"That's why I don't do it. Even so, a wrongheaded jury verdict isn't a declaration of war." Skeeter nodded at Gage. "Seems to me you're completely antipolitical. Nothing seems to outrage you more than pretense." He grinned. "Maybe that's why you're an investigator instead of a lawyer."

"Not a good one at the moment. I feel like I've been walking down the wrong trail for days."

"Maybe you need to backtrack a little."

"We've done some. We reviewed IRS listings of illegal tax shelters and all of the private letter opinions and didn't find Pegasus mentioned by name in any of them. So it wasn't like the IRS came knocking on somebody's door asking about them."

Gage spun and punched the bag one final time. Then turned back toward Skeeter.

"Wait a second . . . wait a second . . ." Gage smiled. "Maybe they knocked, but nobody was there to answer."

Thirty-four years old, a lifetime's worth of money, and no chance of ever getting laid.

Kelvin Kim answered the door in flip-flops, shorts, an X-Men T-shirt, and wire-rimmed glasses. He tried to flatten his hair as he looked up at Gage standing on the landing of his creekside Tudor mansion near Palo Alto.

"Sorry to bother you at home on a Sunday morning," Gage said, handing Kim his business card, "but I didn't want people at your company wondering why I wanted to talk to you."

Kim peered up at Gage. "*I'm* sort of wondering."

"I need to talk to you about some insurance Rave-Tron Electronics bought a few years ago."

A call to Norbett after Gage left Skeeter at the gym had gotten him the names of some of Pegasus's Silicon Valley clients. His own research suggested RaveTron was the best place to start, and Kim was the CEO.

"I'm not sure I—"

"I've seen the records."

"I'm still not—"

"Bloomberg says you guys are planning an IPO in a few months. For you alone, probably a half a billion dollars is at stake. A little bad press about a tax fraud investigation might snuff it out."

"Our lawyer said it was legal—"

"How do you know what insurance I want to talk to you about?"

Kim pulled back as though Gage had drawn back his fist.

"Because it's the only one that ever worried you?"

"How do I know you're not the one who'll go running to the press?"

"Because I could do it now, and haven't. And because I'm less interested in why you started buying it than why you stopped."

Kim backed away from the door, then turned to let Gage pass by and into the long marble hallway. Gage waited for Kim to close it, then followed him past the two-story living room and through the French doors and onto the redwood deck. Kim directed Gage to one of four teakwood chairs surrounding a matching table. Gage adjusted the umbrella to shade their eyes against the midmorning sun reflecting off the pool, then sat down.

"We were kids when we started the company," Kim said. "We didn't know anything about taxes. I don't think I'd even filed a tax return before. I was just out of Caltech. The second year I owned the company, the bottom line on my 1040 was larger than all the money my father made in his whole life."

"What was Marc Anston's pitch?"

"It was the other way around, at least at the beginning. Somebody said we could make a lot of money by offering extended warranties on the electronics we sell and we went to Anston to set it up."

"And he told you a warranty is like insurance."

Kim smiled. "How'd you know?"

"And he told you that you could make a lot more money by setting up offshore."

Kim nodded. "Basically. The customer bought the warranty from us, and then we'd buy reinsurance. We keep a little money here to pay off claims, like when somebody's iPod crashed, but ninety percent of the money went offshore. We didn't have to pay taxes on any of it. Tens of millions of dollars a year."

Gage glanced back the house. "I take it some of the money came back to pay for this."

The county assessor records Alex Z had located placed the value of the property at four point two million. The recorder's office records showed Kim paid off the property a year after he bought it.

Kim reddened. "Anston said I could. And not just me. All the guys I started the company with did it."

"Sounds like a good scheme."

"Anston's a shrewd guy, about lots of things. He talked us out of going public years ago, said if we held the company close we'd make a lot more money down the road."

"Are you sure he didn't want you to go public for fear that a new board of directors might audit the books?"

"I thought about that." Kim shrugged. "But he was right in the end."

"How'd he get you to agree to use some of the offshore money for political contributions?"

Kim drew back. "Shit. How'd you . . ."

"You're not the only one."

"Anston told us we needed to spend some money to fight having to charge sales tax on Internet purchases. Not having sales tax gave us a real edge on brick and mortar stores."

"Did he tell you how the money would be spent?"

"No. He just said to trust him."

"And every year it was something else."

"Like clockwork. Eventually he just took money without asking." Kim spread his hands. "What were we going to do? Sue him?"

"Sounds like extortion."

Kim blew out a breath. "Sure felt like it."

"Then how'd you get out of it?"

"The IRS saved our asses. Can you believe it? Four or five years ago, Anston found out they were investigating us, so he shut the thing down. He was really pissed. Apparently he had a lot of clients paying money into the company—"

"Pegasus."

"Yeah, Pegasus. And he had to make the company evaporate. He kind of blamed us because we were the only one doing warranties. And blamed himself because we were the only dot-com in the group. The rest were all old line, old money companies. Dow thirty and all that."

"Did he explain what forced the issue?"

Kim squinted into the distance, then looked back.

"Once he complained about cash flow but I didn't understand what he meant." Kim smiled. "If other companies were paying in as much as us, cash flow should've been the least of his problems."

"Did the IRS ever come after RaveTron for back taxes?"

"Nope. Anston had that covered. First, he got a senator to call the IRS commissioner and tell him to lay off by saying we were young guys and the company grew too fast. It was a bunch of bullshit. He never said who it was, but I can guess."

"Who?"

"Landon Meyer. Because his brother used to be Anston's law partner."

"And second?"

"I'm not sure I understand it exactly, but Anston had some gimmick where we wired the insurance premiums to the Cayman Islands, but the money ended up somewhere else. We never figured that part out. And after we were a few payments into the scheme, we were afraid to ask."

"I take it the reason for the somewhere else was so the IRS would never be able to connect the money you paid for premiums offshore with the money that came back to the U.S. as loans."

Kim nodded, then gestured with his thumb toward his house. "Ex-actly."

"How'd you pick me?" Kim asked Gage as he poured coffee into oversized blue RaveTron mugs in the kitchen. "You could've knocked on a lot of doors. I guess you figured me for the weakest link."

"Just the opposite. I read over some of the press coverage you got when your early investors were pressuring you into going public years ago. You said you didn't want to become a gone-tomorrow dot-com millionaire. You wanted to build a real company." Gage leaned back against the kitchen counter. "You made a mistake getting involved with Anston, but you weren't the kind of person who'd take millions and leave investors with an empty shell. A lot of others did."

Kim handed Gage a cup. "Well, we sure screwed up in that tax thing."

"I think you're the only one of Anston's clients who looks at it that way."

Kim lowered his head, then swallowed hard and looked again at Gage.

"Do you happen to know what the statute of limitations is on tax fraud?"

"Sorry, but there isn't one."

nstead of walking directly to the redbrick St. Francis Yacht Club, Gage grabbed his binoculars from his glove compartment and found a spot along a stepped sea wall with an unobstructed view of the Golden Gate. It took only seconds to spot the purple sail on the sixteen-foot Australian Mosquito catamaran, then a slight turn of the focus to capture international lawyer Jack Burch, feet locked on the rail, stretched out against the harness, back brushing the whitecaps as he shot under the bridge. They hadn't spoken in detail since Gage telephoned him in Moscow.

Gage tracked Burch until he arrived near the spit of land on which the club stood and that formed the boat harbor, then he began the long walk across the parking lot to meet Burch near the dock entrance. Burch looked like a wet St. Bernard wrapped in yellow Gore-Tex as he came through the gate and reached out his hand. He pulled it back and inspected it.

"Maybe I better dry off."

Fifteen minutes later Burch emerged from the locker room and directed Gage into the restaurant and then to a table by the wall of windows facing the harbor. It was set for five: Burch, Gage, their wives, and Alex Z, whom Gage had invited to Burch's birthday lunch so he could talk to the lawyer about using his offshore connections to investigate the ownership of the banks Anston was using.

Gage nodded toward the marina after they sat down. Nearly all the slips were occupied. "How come the members aren't out on the bay?"

"Big awards banquet this evening for those who didn't drown themselves during the Hawaii race."

The waiter appeared and took their drink orders.

"Thanks for coming in early," Gage said, as he walked away. "I need to run a couple of things by you."

Gage reached for his wallet, took out a dollar, and handed it to Burch.

"Your fee to make this a privileged conversation."

Burch accepted it and held it up to the light.

"Looks legal. Maybe I'll frame it." Burch glanced around the restaurant in mock furtiveness, then slipped it into his jacket pocket. "I shouldn't be seen taking money in this place. What would the other members think?"

"I don't recall that being a guiding consideration in your life."

Burch spread his hands. "What does a man have, if not his reputation?"

"His integrity."

"Yeah, I forgot about that part."

"No, you didn't."

Gage leaned forward, resting his folded hands on the edge of the table. Burch followed suit.

"Excellent," Burch said, "a conspiracy."

"You remember when I called you about a company called Pegasus in the Caymans?"

"I was bloody jet-lagged in Moscow, not comatose. Sure. Captive insurance."

"It looks like it began as a straight-up tax fraud, then as a cover for bribery, and finally a way to launder illegal corporate campaign contributions."

"Who set it up?"

"Marc Anston, and maybe Brandon Meyer."

"After he was appointed?"

"Before. More than fourteen years ago."

"Was the political money for his brother?"

"At first I thought it was. Now it seems it was also used to push legislation through by secretly contributing to senatorial and congressional campaigns."

"How did they do it?"

"Loans."

"I thought loans had to be reported."

"They do. But nobody really examines them. I did some research. One senator loaned himself over a million dollars in an early campaign, but nobody paid attention until eleven years later when the Federal Election Commission noticed something hinky about how he paid himself back—"

"By taking out another loan?"

"From a different bank. And now I think Brandon and Anston are in a race against time because Landon needs to get his nominations through before anyone—"

Burch smiled. "Meaning you—"

"Maybe . . . figures it out."

"Because . . ."

"The two new justices will join with Sunseri, Thompson, Robins, and Ardino to roll campaign disclosure law back to the eighteenth century and open the gates on corporate contributions directly to political candidates."

"And then Pegasus pays off all the loans in secret?"

Gage nodded. "I read Sunseri's dissent in the *Massachusetts Environmental Action* case. He comes right out and says it. Limiting corporate contributions is the suppression of political speech, and forcing the disclosure of the contributors' identities is a violation of privacy. Once you start with the idea that a corporation is a person, and not just an artificial creation, you're forced to the conclusion that it has First Amendment rights."

"And poof." Burch made an exploding motion with his fingers. "The public will never again be able to figure out who's controlling the electoral process."

"I'd never realized Landon was that cynical. He constantly wraps himself in grand ideas." Gage leaned back in his chair. "You know what Brandon told me when I went to see him after Charlie died? He said Landon took St. Augustine and Thomas Hobbes to read on a flight to Beijing a few months ago."

Burch raised a hand like he was seeking his teacher's attention in class.

"I know one. From Hobbes. 'There is always war of everyone against everyone, and the life of man, solitary, poor, nasty, brutish, and short'."

Burch glanced around the elegant, bright-lit dining room, and at the San Francisco elite now collecting at the bar.

"Not so poor here, of course." Burch looked back at Gage. "I tried to read the *Leviathan* at Oxford, a long, boring book written in an archaic kind of English. I never finished it."

"Landon didn't either. I don't think he struggled his way as far as the chapter where Hobbes says corporations are 'like worms in the entrails of natural man.'"

"Maybe he just skipped that part while rushing to read the celebration of the all-knowing, all-powerful sovereign."

They ceased speaking as the waiter delivered their drinks. Scotch for Burch. Beer for Gage.

Gage raised his glass, "Happy birthday."

Burch raised his in turn. "Thanks, old man." He took a sip and set the glass down. "Who else knows about what's been going on besides you?"

"It's hard to tell."

"Landon?"

"I'm not sure he's ready to accept the reality." Gage said. "The question is whether there's any way the scheme could be legal?"

"From a tax perspective or campaign finance perspective?"

"Both."

Burch took a sip of his Scotch.

"Are they still doing it?"

"It looks like the tax gimmick ended four years ago, possibly because one of their clients got investigated by the IRS."

Burch nodded. "I remember that time very well. Everybody who'd been using captive insurance to move money offshore and then back in again tax free, was bailing out. The real crime wasn't making premium payments to an offshore insurer, it was that the money was returned right away to officers of the companies."

"But what if the money was returned to the U.S. and put in someone else's pocket," Gage said. "Maybe sent from an offshore finance company and into a U.S. bank, and then invested in CDs or time deposits and held there until they needed it."

Burch stirred the ice cubes in his drink with his fingertip.

"It wouldn't be a good idea from an investment perspective," Burch said. "They could make a lot more money elsewhere." He paused in thought, then said, "This reminds me of a group in Chicago. They sent about two hundred million offshore as insurance payments, then invested the money in mutual and hedge funds operating out of the Caribbean and made a killing, tax free. An illegal kind of 401(k)."

"Except Brandon and Anston's aim wasn't to make money," Gage said, "just to move it into political campaigns."

"But that's pretty risky from a bank regulator's point of view. Campaigns are notoriously bad at making good on loans."

"But there's no risk if the loans to the campaigns

are secured by the deposits Anston and his people made."

"So, basically, you think it's a money laundering scheme."

Gage nodded. "Say the bank pays them three percent interest on their deposits and they pay the bank five percent interest on the loans. Or even two percent and four percent. The two percent spread between what the bank pays them and what they pay the bank is the bank's fee for laundering the money."

"Brilliant. The bank takes no risk at all."

"And there's something more," Gage said. "I think they've put a lot more money into the banks they're using than they've taken out. I'll bet they have a couple of hundred million waiting to be tapped."

Burch stared down into his glass, shaking his head.

"Seems to me they found a huge loophole," Burch finally said. "Big enough to drive a trainload of money through." He looked over at Gage. "The question is whether it's sleazy enough for you to act on."

"That's sort of what Landon said to me."

"My guess is they're trying to turn your strength into a weakness."

"Which strength is that?"

"Your sense of fair play. Isn't that why Landon has called you every single time somebody has tried to sabotage his campaigns? It wasn't as if you were ever a button-wearing supporter."

Gage shrugged.

"And now you're on the other side, they know you won't do anything unless you're certain this campaign finance scheme is illegal and Landon was in on it."

"Certainty may not be an option."

Burch fell silent for a few seconds, then cocked his head and raised his eyebrows.

"You've got me wondering what they've been up to for the last four years, since they closed down the insurance end."

"I don't know. Maybe nothing. Maybe they had enough money. By that point as much as four hundred million had passed through Pegasus, maybe even more."

Gage sensed motion by the restaurant entrance. He spotted Burch's wife, Faith, and Alex Z walking toward them. Happy birthday smiles on their faces.

Gage took Alex Z aside after lunch as they made their way across the parking lot to their cars. One of Alex Z's bodyguards trailed behind.

"It's not long before the nominations come to a vote," Gage said, "and Pegasus is still a black box."

"What do you need, boss?"

"I need to know everything about who is really behind Mann Trust. If you need more help from Jack, just ask for it, but keep his name out of whatever you do."

"Sounds like you've got an idea how to shine some light inside."

Gage shook his head. "It's more like following all the trails to see where they lead. We're still years behind these guys."

"What are you going to be working on?"

"Porzolkiewski. There are some things I still need to look into."

"How is he?"

"Suicidal."

oots Marnin's cell phone rang as he sat beating on the steering wheel of his Econovan parked on the frontage road near the San Francisco Airport.

"I lost the fucker."

"What fucker?"

"The rocker. Gage's database guy. He's got a bodyguard who's the best countersurveillance driver I've ever seen."

"You still don't know where Gage hid him?"

Boots looked up at a Virgin Airlines flight rising into the sky, then down at the airport. "I know lots of places he isn't."

"Don't let me down on this one. We need to know where everybody is just in case, and we already have over two hundred grand invested in you."

"I've got Gage nailed down and I've got Palmer's wife nailed down and I'm sure the Muslim kid is staying with the rocker."

"How'd you get onto the rocker's tail this time?"

"A birthday party for Gage's pal Jack Burch at the St. Francis Yacht Club."

"Why didn't you stick a GPS under his car?"

"You think I'm an idiot? His security guy never left . . . son of a . . ."

"What 'son of a . . .'?"

"Nothing. I'll call you later."

Boots disconnected, tossed his phone into the console, then reached into the glove compartment and pulled out a flashlight. He jumped down from the van and flattened himself on the ground in one motion. He worked the beam on the underside as he scooted farther and farther under. He finally caught sight of a black two-inch-by-two-inch tracking device duct-taped to the undercarriage.

"Son of a bitch."

He reached into his jeans pocket for his pocket knife, then stopped.

Wait a second. A rope can pull in two directions.

He slid out from the under the van, climbed back in, and headed toward the San Francisco Mariner Hotel.

Rosa M. was slipping on her bra at nine-thirty the next morning when Boots reached over to pick up his ringing cell phone from the nightstand. Rosa's cleaning cart was parked near the door. Now that he got what he wanted, as far as he was concerned she was human wallpaper.

Boots recognized the caller's number.

"I was just heading out," Boots said.

"Don't bother," the familiar voice said. "Our guys down at Evergreen Security found the rocker."

Boots sat up. "How?"

"There were a bunch of Internet and commercial database searches about Mann Trust early this morning. Our people traced them to a DSL line going into a loft on the Oakland waterfront. We backtracked and found that the same computer had been researching Pegasus over the last few days."

Boots's eyes settled on his alligator-skin Tony Lamas on the floor of the open closet, once more feeling like a dinosaur.

"Do you have a place lined up just in case?" the caller asked.

"Yeah, it's perfect."

Tell me something I don't know," Marc Anston said, gazing over the Ocean Beach seawall toward the fog-filtered Farallon Islands.

Only the footfalls of an occasional daybreak jogger and the squawk of seagulls intruded on the rustle of the low-tide surf.

"That's the part that'll cost you." Daniel Norbett glanced down at his worn Ferragamo loafers, now dusted with sand. The Cayman Island accountant gave a little shiver, unused to the chill of Northern California mornings.

"How can I be sure you'll deliver?" Anston asked.

Norbett cinched his trench coat tighter, then laughed. "That's a stupid question. I protected your ass in my Miami case."

"I wasn't part of your case."

"But you were part of what Quinton was doing and I sent the U.S. Attorney off in another direction."

"Quinton doesn't seem to see it that way."

"Only because his ego blocks his view."

"I know, and it's the cost of doing business with ex-pat British lawyers. They're stamped out of the same mold. I hated dealing with those guys even back in the Contra days."

They fell silent as a runner stopped on the sidewalk behind them and bent to retie her shoe.

Norbett watched her straighten up. "And there's something else. I think Quinton and Brandon may have outsmarted themselves when they talked to Gage."

"By saying . . . ?"

Norbett waved a forefinger side to side in front of Anston. "You don't get that either without a little money up front."

Anston folded his arms across his chest, weighing the offer and breathing in the salt air. He hated dealing with snitches. Norbett might not have informed on him and Quinton in order to beat his last case, but he snitched on someone.

"How much?" Anston asked.

"Twenty-five thousand."

"I thought Gage only gave you ten."

Norbett jerked his thumb toward the multimillion-dollar condos spread along the Great Highway behind him.

"We're in another period of irrational exuberance."

Anston reached for his cell phone and punched in a number.

"Quinton, this is Anston. Transfer twenty-five grand to Norbett . . . That's what I said, to Norbett . . . No, not from Pegasus, you idiot, from one of your accounts, then reimburse yourself from Pegasus."

Anston handed the phone to Norbett. "Give him your account details."

Norbett read off the numbers from a slip of paper he'd withdrawn from his wallet, then disconnected.

"Sometimes that asshole doesn't think," Anston said. "Let's walk."

"I didn't tell Gage anything he couldn't figure out for himself," Norbett said, as they returned a half hour later to the same spot along the wall. "I kept pushing the insurance angle toward a dead end. And played dumb about Brandon Meyer. But it's only a matter of time until he catches on."

"What about the Jamaican woman? How do we know she won't blabber what she told you to somebody else?"

Norbett raised his palms toward Anston. "Don't touch her. I need her to keep an eye on Quinton. He doesn't seem to realize how big this thing is and how hot it might get if it explodes. He may melt."

"There won't be time for that to happen. I have a plan to contain things. I'll just need to move it along a little faster."

Anston watched Norbett climb into a taxi to the airport in the Cliff House Restaurant parking lot overlooking Seal Rock. Seagulls fought over food wrappers blowing across the pavement, flailing and squawking and tumbling in the air. It gave him a feeling of revulsion, just like Norbett, the snitch who pretended he wasn't, who pretended he'd protected Anston in his Miami debriefing, when he was only protecting himself.

Anston reached for his cell phone as the cab pulled away.

"You have somebody in the Caymans?"

"No," Boots said, "not the Caymans. But I got a guy in Havana. An hour flight."

"Our friend just leaned on me for money and I don't want to have to keep paying him off for the rest of his natural life."

"I take it the emphasis is on natural."

"Exactly. I'll tell you when."

ocorro piled her baggage at the front door, then walked into the den to retrieve a collection of DVDs to keep her company at Gage's family ranch. She smiled to herself when she realized the stack was absurdly tall. She calculated how many she could stuff into the pockets of her carry-on and left the rest piled on top of the audio stand. Her cell phone rang as she zipped up the last compartment. It was Faith pulling up in front.

Socorro slid her bags onto the porch.

"This is some pretty raggedy luggage," Faith said as she climbed the stairs.

"I know, but it's hard to get rid of. It's been too many places." Socorro pointed at the torn security tapes from a dozen countries crisscrossing the locks of the hard-sided Samsonite. "There's one from China right on top of the one from Taiwan." She smiled at Faith. "I think some Chinese customs agent was trying to make a political statement."

"It's not much of one unless your bag passes

through Taiwan again and the Chinese get a look at it."

"Not likely. We only went there because Charlie had some people to talk to. It was one of Anston's super secret missions. They paid for me to go along to make it appear we were just a couple on vacation. I think I was the cloak while he was the dagger. I still don't have a clue what we were doing over there." She paused and shook her head. "They say marriage is about communication, but Charlie always practiced radio silence."

Faith grabbed the suitcase, gave it a tug, and then added a second hand to lift it from the landing.

"Jeez," Faith said. "How long are you going for?"

"Why don't you take the carry-on? I'll get that."

Faith shook her head as she lurched down the steps. After reaching the bottom, she extended the handle and let the wheels carry the load down the walkway to her SUV. Socorro followed with the rest and helped Faith hoist the suitcase into the back. Faith glanced at the bulging carry-on as Socorro set it inside.

"That thing is about to burst," Faith said. "I'm not sure you'll be able to fit it into the overhead compartment."

Socorro locked her hands on her hips as she examined the lump of luggage.

"I'll cross that bridge later."

"When are the kids arriving in Nogales?" Faith asked as they drove south past the Opera House toward the freeway.

"They have a wedding to attend on Sunday.

They'll fly out afterward and stay through the week."

"How are they adjusting?"

"Charlie Junior seems to be doing okay. Sandy is . . . I really don't know how Sandy is. She's been . . . I guess the word is erratic. Sometimes she treats me like I'm really fragile and she seems afraid she'll say or do something that'll upset me. Other times, she becomes as demanding as a drill sergeant."

"How long has this been going on?"

"It didn't start until a week or two after Charlie died. She called early one morning, maybe five o'clock, asking if I was okay and if the dog was okay and then ordering me to go around the house to make sure the doors were locked. She even tried to order me—*order* me—to get an alarm system."

"Did you ask her what prompted the call?"

"She said she had a bad dream."

Faith headed toward short-term parking lot after following the sweeping flyway onto the San Francisco Airport grounds.

Socorro looked toward Faith. "You don't need to come in."

"It'll take you an hour to check your luggage and get up to the security checkpoint. I'll keep you company."

They found a parking spot and took the elevator down to the departure level of the domestic terminal. Check-in moved fast enough for them to have time for a cup of coffee before Socorro needed to join the security line.

"Are you thinking about writing again?" Faith asked, after they sat down at a table.

"I only have one book left in print. I don't even know what the children's market is like now. I'm not even sure I know how to speak their language anymore."

Faith smiled to herself as she remembered proofreading the first of Socorro's "Oops" series of children's books about a little girl who wiggled her way out of one jam after another, but learned a moral lesson each time.

"Your carry-on was so heavy I assumed you had a laptop and manuscripts in there."

"DVDs. I'm going to spend every day before the kids get there watching Fred Astaire and Ginger Rogers and Clark Gable and Claudette Colbert and every *Thin Man* movie ever made. All black and white, except for *An Affair to Remember*. For that one I'll be crying my eyes out in living color." She raised her cup. "To love in its many hues."

Socorro took a sip, and then asked, "How do you and Graham do it? All these years and you still hold hands. Who does that anymore? At least not at our age."

Faith didn't want to respond. She never wanted to give women advice about how to live, or present herself or Graham as examples, or recommend their lives to anyone.

How could she? She knew how many times she'd lain awake when he was working in Pakistan or Russia or Egypt or dozens of other countries, afraid for him, and him afraid for her when she was researching in deserts and jungles where medical care was days away and in China or India where sudden changes in political winds often swept the innocent away.

Faith took a sip of her coffee to avoid answering.

And all of this, though it was invisible to outsiders, had been earned by worry and sacrifice. They'd grown into their life together. It hadn't been guaranteed by their marriage vows or received like an inheritance.

What made it bearable was that they had each other and respected each other's need to do some good in the world where it was in their power to do it.

But how could she say all that to Socorro?

In looking at her now, Faith realized Tolstoy was wrong: Happy families aren't all alike. And the way she and Graham found happiness wouldn't be how Socorro would, if she ever did.

Faith glanced at her watch. "Maybe we should . . ."

Socorro gave Faith a hug just before arriving at the first security checkpoint. As she watched Faith walk away, Socorro's peripheral vision caught the profile of a familiar face at the rear of the line next to hers. She stared at the dark-haired man for a few moments, but couldn't resolve whether it was someone she knew or maybe an actor she'd seen on television. She shrugged, then turned and presented her driver's license and boarding pass to the security agent, and passed on through.

An hour later, Viz filled the doorway of the China Garden Restaurant in San Francisco, where Gage was eating lunch with Faith after she'd left Socorro at the airport. He spotted them in a far booth and approached, hat in hand. Faith scooted around the semicircular bench so Viz could sit down.

"I figured I better tell you myself, boss."

"What's that?"

"I lost Boots."

"What happened?"

"He found the GPS I planted on his van and stuck it under a FedEx delivery truck. By the time we figured it out, he'd slipped away."

"What about the hotel?"

"I talked to Rosa, gave her a few bucks and asked her if she knew why he moved out. She told me she started to throw away a newspaper one morning and he told her he wanted to keep the real estate section. Later she overheard him talking about an investment he was making, and the next day she saw he'd circled some listings. He took it with him, was gone for a few hours, and then came back and checked out. She doesn't think he's coming back. She looked real disappointed. I think she'd gotten used to the extra money."

N amaste."

The Indian accent carrying the words into Gage's cell phone was both heavy and familiar. Gage swung his legs over the edge of the bed and sat up. He looked at the alarm clock, the red letters glowing in the dark.

"You know what time it is?" Gage asked as he emerged from the gray haze of sleep.

Babu laughed. "Of course, five in the evening."

"I mean here."

"Twelve and a half hours earlier. As it should be."

"Which means?"

"It's time to get up."

"Not in California.

Babu paused. "You mean Americans aren't getting up at the same time as us? I am always assuming they did. You want me to call back?"

Gage glanced over at Faith. He couldn't see her face, just the moonlit outline of her head propped up on one elbow.

"Hold on a minute," Gage covered the mouth-piece. "I've got a new cultural insight for you. Babu seems to think everyone in the world gets up at the same time as Indians."

Faith shook her head.

"I'm sure that'll be the next cover story for the *American Journal of Anthropology*," Faith said, then dropped her head back onto the pillow.

Gage slipped on his robe and uncovered the mouthpiece.

"Hold on. I'll take this downstairs."

Gage stood at the kitchen counter in the darkness, looking toward the lights of San Francisco, his view framed by pines and oaks on the lower part of the property. It was still more than an hour before the sun rose, and the owl hooting in the branch over-hanging the deck seemed to be asking why Gage was already awake.

"The Hyderabad police found Mr. Wilbert's body in a mango grove behind one of the *dhabas* along the highway," Babu said.

Gage felt his muscles tense.

"Did you see it?" Gage asked.

"No. He was cremated right afterward. We use our limited refrigerated storage for food, not dead people. But the local police took photos beforehand. That's how I knew who he was."

"What killed him?"

"Natural causes."

"How do you know?"

"Because foreigners in India only die of natural

causes, even if the body shows signs of . . . of . . . shall we say . . . abuse? Our Ministry of External Affairs insists on it."

"How much abuse?"

"Maybe as long as a few hours. Some bruises had time to form and some wounds scabbed over, others didn't. My guess is that he was strangled in the end."

"Do the local police know who he is?"

"They suspect he's German because it's mostly them who come to India on the sex tours. More to Kolkata and Goa than to Hyderabad, but still . . ."

"How about encouraging them in that idea?"

"They'll find encouragement in anything that allows them to put the matter to rest."

Just before sunrise, Gage brought a cup of coffee to Faith, still lying in bed and watching the local news. On the screen was a repeat from a previous evening's news segment.

A self-satisfied President Duncan leaned forward in his chair toward the interviewer.

"Of course, we'll swear them in immediately after the Senate vote."

"What about a filibuster?" the reporter asked.

"The Democrats would look ridiculous if they tried. A third of the Senate and the entire House hit the campaign trail in a few months, and nobody wants to carry that kind of ugly baggage."

"Or is it merely that they don't want the same treatment if they take the White House a year from now?"

Duncan straightened his shoulders.

"That's not going to happen."

Gage handed Faith her cup, then sat down on the edge of the bed.

"I think we've lost TIMCO."

"Hawkins? Is that what Babu called about?"

Gage nodded. "Murdered."

Faith shuddered.

"Now we have no admissible evidence."

"Unless you can work back from whoever killed him."

"That's assuming the killing was related. For all we know, it was something else. Maybe revenge for Hawkins's mistreating a girl."

"But you don't think so."

"No. But we'll never know for certain. There's nothing left of the crime scene except dirt and rotting mangos, and nothing left of Hawkins except ashes."

"And Babu?"

"There's not much he can do. I'm positive the local cops he'd have to rely on have already been paid off by whoever did it."

Gage called Joe Casey as he drove toward his office.

"Can you find out if a Robert Marnin came through customs recently?"

"Hold on."

Casey came back on the line a few minutes later.

"He flew into Newark. Flight AI–191 from Paris a few days ago."

"Thanks."

Gage disconnected and slipped his phone into his shirt pocket.

AI–191. AI. Air India. A redneck like Boots Marnin

wouldn't fly Air India from Paris unless the flight originated in Delhi, Mumbai, or Kolkata.

Gage looked up from the Bay Bridge at the fog intertwining itself in the financial district. Then his mind cleared: Charlie Palmer, the OSHA inspector Karopian, and Wilbert Hawkins weren't killed for revenge.

They were chosen one by one because they were links in an evidentiary chain Gage had followed hand over hand; one that now had exploded into a thousand pieces, just like the valve that had set off the TIMCO firestorm.

Gage shook his head and exhaled. *At least there's no one left to kill.*

He drove on for a half mile, then found himself gripping the steering wheel.

Unless whoever was behind the killings stopped thinking like a lawyer.

Instead of taking the exit toward the Embarcadero, Gage continued on the freeway to the off-ramp nearest the Hall of Justice. After a couple of hours researching criminal files in the superior court clerk's office, Gage realized he was wrong.

There was one person left to kill.

T he Elf was leading a different Wolf when Gage pulled to stop on the one-way Folsom Street in front of the Bootstrap at eleven-forty that night. Apparently Jeffrey Stark, Charlie Palmer's physical therapist, hadn't taken all that well to the yoke.

Gage stepped out of his car as they came even with him. The overhead streetlight gave Elf's face a yellow pallor. His eyes widened and he dropped the leash.

Gage shook his head. "This isn't about you. I'm trying to find Jeffrey. His cell phone is disconnected."

"He fell behind on the payments so it got turned off."

"And I went by the place where he told me he was staying. Nobody answered the door all day."

Elf's eyebrows narrowed. "Why's everybody so interested in Jeffrey?"

"Who's everybody?"

"The company he worked for—"

"Physical Therapy Associates?"

"Yeah. They called me like six times in the last two days, real anxious to contact him."

"Why you?"

Elf glanced over at his Wolf. "He put me down as his next of kin on his application."

The Wolf glared at Elf, then stomped away.

"Sorry," Gage said.

"No problem." Elf tilted his head toward the club. "There's lots where he came from."

"Practically a candy store."

Elf's eyebrows went up. "You're not . . ."

Gage shook his head again.

"Too bad."

Gage smiled. "Anyway I think I'm a little old for you."

Elf smiled back. "I don't know. I've seen *Sabrina* like a hundred times. Audrey Hepburn and Humphrey Bogart. May and December."

"Sorry."

Elf shrugged. "So what's up with Jeffrey?"

"I'm trying to figure that out. Do you know why the company was trying to contact him?"

"A job, I guess. But I'm not sure why they ever hired him."

"Because of the identify theft convictions?"

Elf nodded. "The state revoked his license because his victims were all people he was treating. Mostly old folks recovering from hip and knee replacements."

"Then why did Physical Therapy Associates take him?"

"It's not like he applied. They came to him. Like out of the blue. A couple of days after he got out of jail."

"When did they last call you?"

"Three hours ago. I got tired of them bothering me so I told them about his new job working as a security guard at the MetroTowers construction site."

"Which shift?"

"Midnight until eight."

Gage checked his watch. Eleven forty-five. He pulled out a business card and handed it to Elf.

"I'll head over," Gage said, "but if you hear from him before I get there, tell him to go to a safe place and give me a call."

Elf peered up at Gage. "A safe place? What do you mean a safe place?"

Gage opened his car door.

"He'll know."

Gage made the half-mile drive to New Montgomery Street in two minutes. He squinted as he cruised the half-block construction site trying to see past the halogen lights flooding the perimeter. He caught glimpses of rebar rising from the unfinished below-ground parking structure and a latticed crane rising up fifteen stories, its mast topped by a horizontal jib. He finally spotted a brown modular construction trailer stationed along the alley behind the site. He parked on a side street next to a half-finished condo tower and retrieved a semiautomatic from a lockbox in his trunk.

Gage ducked in and out of the shadows until he reached the single lit window of the trailer, and then climbed the metal steps and stretched over the railing until he could peek inside.

The body in the chair was slumped over the desk. *Damn. Too late.*

He straightened up and checked the time. Eleven fifty-five.

This isn't right.

He smiled to himself, then leaned over again and tapped the window. Jeffrey Stark's head jerked up. He blew out a breath when he saw it was Gage, then pushed himself to his feet and opened the door.

"Man, you scared the hell out of me," Jeffrey said. "I thought you were my supervisor."

"What are you doing at work so early?"

"I kinda used up my welcome where I was staying, so I've been sleeping here before my shift."

A clunk sounded from the wall behind Jeffrey. Gage glanced over, then at the opposite window. A dime-sized hole was centered in the glass. He grabbed Jeffrey by the front of his uniform jacket and yanked him down to the floor. Gage heard a bone crack and a shriek as Jeffrey's shoulder hit the linoleum, then the rapid-fire clunk-clunk-clunk of slugs piercing the trailer.

Gage dragged Jeffrey behind the desk, fired three times to knock out the overhead lights, then punched 911 into his cell phone.

"Shots fired at New Montgomery near Mission. MetroTowers," Gage told the dispatcher. "We're trapped in the construction trailer."

The clunks then became methodical, as if the shooter was calculating how to place his shots for the best coverage. One slug ricocheted off the desktop, two hit the file cabinet.

Sirens in the distance brought them to a halt.

Jeffrey grabbed the edge of the desk with his good arm and tried to get up. He yelped as Gage pulled him back down and propped him against the wall.

"Let's pick a story," Gage said.

"As opposed to what?"

"You bird-dogging Charlie Palmer and conspiracy to commit murder."

"Murder?" Jeffrey's voice rose. "Murder wasn't part of it. I was just supposed to keep an eye on him and report in."

"To who?"

"I can't say."

Gage jammed his elbow into Jeffrey's broken shoulder blade. "Yes you can."

"Shit, man."

"I need the name."

"Mr. Botas."

"Is that a nickname or last name?"

Gage didn't tell him, but *botas* was Spanish for "boots."

"That's all I know. Botas. I never met him. Just by phone."

"He have an accent?"

"Texan."

"How'd you meet—"

Spotlight beams hit the side of the trailer. A voice boomed from a patrol car loudspeaker:

"This is the San Francisco Police."

"I can't go back to jail," Jeffrey said. "What's our story gonna be?"

"I'm investigating construction equipment thefts at a site down the street. I was canvassing the area. We've never met before."

"Are we going to meet again?"

"You want to keep on living?"

"What are you going to do with me?" Jeffrey asked Gage.

It was two o'clock in the morning and they were sitting outside the emergency room of SF Medical, waiting for the radiologist to examine the X-rays to decide whether a sling would be sufficient to immobilize Jeffrey's broken shoulder. An icepack was strapped over it.

"That's up to you."

"Right now I'm afraid to leave this place. What if the guy's waiting outside?"

"He probably is."

Jeffrey's gaze shifted toward the door. "Thanks. That's just what I wanted to hear."

"Tell me how you got hooked up with Botas."

"Shit. Is he the one who's out there?"

"Probably."

Jeffrey held out a trembling hand. "Look at this. Nobody's tried to kill me before."

"How'd you meet him?"

"Through somebody in jail. He knew somebody who knew somebody who knew somebody who wanted a guy to keep an eye on Palmer. They set it up with Physical Therapy Associates to hire me and place me at his house."

"Did you ask who arranged it?"

"The director just said somebody dropped by and offered to pay triple the going rate if they did it."

"What was this somebody trying to find out?"

"They didn't tell me. They just wanted me to cozy up to him. Dependent people tend to talk a lot. But I didn't have much time. I was only there a week before he died." Jeffrey drew back and winced. "Is that what this is about?"

"Yes."

"So the comb-over guy really did it?"

"Porzolkiewski."

"Yeah. Porzolkiewski."

"Maybe. Maybe not. Tell me the truth about when he came by."

"Sorry about that. Botas told me to say that Porzolkiewski showed up the day before Palmer died, not three days before."

"Did you ask why?"

"I tried to, but he cut me off. And he isn't the kind of guy you argue with."

"Did Porzolkiewski come back?"

"Not that I saw. But I was only there in the afternoons."

"Anything happen the day before Palmer died?"

"Aren't you supposed to be asking me about the day he died? I thought he was murdered."

"Just play along."

Jeffrey tilted his head upward and scrunched up his face. "Let me think." After a moment, he looked back at Gage. "Nothing except a messenger delivery from a pharmacy."

"What was that?"

"Oxycontin tablets I gave him."

"I didn't see the bottle."

"I . . . I . . . went into his bedroom and pocketed

it after they took him away. He wasn't gonna need it anymore and I figured I could make a little money on the side."

Gage had the urge to jam his elbow in Jeffrey's shoulder again. He now knew how Palmer had ingested the poison and imagined a couple dozen dead drug users scattered around San Francisco.

"You mean you sold them," Gage said.

"No. I didn't. Botas called me the night Palmer died. Somehow he guessed I took them. He told me to flush the pills and destroy the bottle."

"Did you?"

"Flush money down the drain? No way. I just told him I would."

"Where are they now?"

"I have a little stash of things where I used to stay. A guy down the hall let me use his storage locker in the basement until I find a new place."

"Did you give any to Palmer?"

Jeffrey's head snapped toward Gage. "Wait a second . . . you're not saying I killed him?"

"No. I think poison in the tablets did."

"Hey man, I didn't sign up for that." Jeffrey looked again at the door. "Shit. Then who's trying to kill me, Palmer's people or Botas?"

They were one and the same, but it wasn't something Jeffrey needed to know.

"Botas. You seem to be a link in a chain that needs to be broken."

Jeffrey leaned away from Gage as if he was afraid of being caught in a crossfire. "I'm starting to think maybe you're one, too."

you're in the crosshairs." FBI senior special agent Joe Casey's voice blasted through the phone at Gage the following morning. Gage imagined him stomping around his Federal Building office. "Because of what happened yesterday."

"How'd you find out so fast?" Gage was sitting at his desk searching online news reports to see how the shooting at MetroTowers had been reported. He and Jeffrey had been convincing. It had been reported as random shots, just an aggravated malicious mischief, and neither of their names had been mentioned.

"What do you mean, how did I find out so fast?" Casey said. "I was there."

"Then why'd didn't you do something?"

"They don't let me talk in court."

"In court?"

"Yeah, in court."

Gage laughed. "I think we're talking about different crosshairs."

"Don't laugh man, Brandon Meyer painted a

bull's-eye on your face yesterday afternoon. Mine, too."

Gage sat up. "What?"

"OptiCom is claiming you threatened Oscar Mogasci into implicating their executives and you tampered with the recording you made of the call between Mogasci and the OptiCom president. They've even got a declaration from the little punk. He says you held him hostage in Zurich until he said the right words."

"Why didn't you call me last night?"

"Orders. The head of my office and the chief of the Criminal Division of the U.S. Attorney's Office ordered me not to talk to you until they debriefed me. And it didn't end until past midnight."

"How is OptiCom going to get around the fact that they bought stolen designs?"

"They're claiming they came up with their own simultaneously with FiberLink."

"That's a crock. The material you seized during the search shows it's not true."

"That's the other thing. Meyer's making sounds like he's going to suppress the evidence."

"Let me guess. Based on false statements in the affidavit?"

"Yeah. And get this, that the search warrant was too broad."

"But he signed the thing."

"So what. His argument is that once you delete from the affidavit what the defense is claiming is false, what's left doesn't justify what he's now calling a fishing expedition."

Gage heard Skeeter Hall's voice in his head: *Asshole*.

"He's claiming you lied to him in the affidavit?"

"Not yet," Casey said. "But he will. And that you lied to him through me."

"Who's representing OptiCom?"

"Two lawyers from Kemper Stewart and one from Anston's firm to give them some extra leverage. Word is Meyer mentored him when he was a new associate twenty years ago and they stayed close after he became a judge."

"I should've guessed. This isn't about OptiCom."

"You bet your ass it isn't. It's about attacking your credibility in case you want to go to the media about TIMCO. Didn't anybody from the press call you after the hearing?"

"There were calls from the *Chronicle* and the *New York Times* and Bloomberg and a few others. I assumed they just wanted some background on OptiCom. I wasn't going to call them back anyway."

Gage heard Casey drop into his chair, then the sound of tapping keys.

"What are you searching for?" Gage asked.

"OptiCom's share price." The sound of Casey's fist slamming his desk reverberated though the phone line. "Son of a bitch. It's five points higher than where it was the day before we kicked in their door. The value of the OptiCom president's stock options just went through the roof. It isn't the wages of sin, it's the rewards of sin. I'll bet he made millions."

"What about FiberLink's claims?"

"Rumor is that OptiCom is going to buy them out and shut them up—I thought you said those women were straight shooters?"

"They probably had no choice. The cost of civil litigation would've wiped them out."

Gage leaned back in his chair. He imagined OptiCom's stock chart.

"What are you thinking?" Casey asked.

"Somebody who bought OptiCom stock the day after your search and after it dropped fifty percent, and then sold it this morning would've made an astronomical amount of money."

"You mean if he was certain the case was going to go away?"

"Exactly. Buy low and wait for it to go high—and who'd be in the best position to know that?"

"How'd you know it was going to happen, boss?" Alex Z hadn't bothered knocking. He stood breathless in front the desk holding a file folder. "Mann Trust just gave out another three point three million dollars in loans."

Gage pointed at a chair. Alex Z dropped into it, then scratched his head.

"There's just one problem. I'm not sure where the money came from. Just like you thought, the investment arm of Mann Trust bought a couple of million shares of OptiCom the day after the search, right when it hit bottom, but as far as I can tell, they never sold them. The three point two must've originated somewhere else."

The financial flowchart Gage had drawn in his mind fractured.

"That means our theory is wrong and there's no way to link it to Meyer."

"Looks that way." Alex Z withdrew a sheet from his folder, and reached it out toward Gage. "And you've got nothing to fight this. It just hit the Internet. It'll be on all the cable channels in a few minutes."

Gage took it and read the Reuters headline:

"FBI Agent Under Investigation for Perjury, Relationship with PI Under Scrutiny"

Tansy Amaro was weeping when she appeared at Gage's office door, shoulders shuddering, face buried in her hands. He walked around his desk and put his arm around her.

"Is it Moki?" he asked.

She shook her head and pointed at the television next to the corner safe. He walked over to his desk, picked up the remote, and punched the on button. It was already tuned to CNN.

News anchor Warren Jennings stared into the camera.

The screen-in-screen showed a satellite image of Mount Shasta in Northern California.

"As you just heard, Oregon senator Edward Light-foot's twin engine Cessna crashed into California's Mount Shasta at about ten-fifteen this morning, just forty minutes ago."

The satellite image was replaced by a close-up of the snow-covered crash scene. The word "Live" was pasted across the top of the screen in red letters.

"Mount Shasta is part of the Cascade Range and

rises 14,162 feet above sea level. It's a dormant volcano, having last erupted two hundred years ago." Jennings pointed at the image. *"The specific area of the crash is called Avalanche Gulch at about 8,000 feet—we're now receiving a feed from a KORE television helicopter above the crash scene. Let's listen in."*

Gage returned to stand next to Tansy as an urgent female voice emerged from the stuttering roar of the helicopter.

"There's no way anyone could've survived."

The camera scanned the mountainside.

"Debris is scattered for a half a mile."

The camera drew back. Antlike figures dressed in yellow and orange parkas picked their way across the snowfield toward the broken fuselage.

"A search and rescue team has just been lowered to the crash site."

Jennings spoke again.

"On the telephone from Klamath Falls, Oregon, is Republican Congressman Doyle Ludlow. Thank you for speaking to us at this difficult time."

Jennings didn't wait for a response.

"Do you know what Senator Lightfoot was doing in Northern California?"

"I can only tell you that during congressional recesses he would return to Oregon and fly major financial supporters around. One of his favorite trips was to follow the Hells Corner Gorge down into California and circle Mount Shasta. It's a spectacular sight. Sometimes—"

"Sorry to cut you off, Congressman. If you'll stand by a moment."

Jennings pressed his fingers to his earbud.

"We've just learned from the FAA that Senator

Lightfoot filed a flight plan in Klamath Falls for exactly that."

Jennings looked into the camera as a photograph of the congressman appeared on the screen behind him.

"You were saying, Congressman?"

"Even though Senator Lightfoot's parents moved from the Klamath Indian Reservation before he was born, he'd often fly into local airports and pick up Native American kids and follow the same route."

"Do you know whether any children were on this flight?"

"I have no way of knowing. But I do know Senator Lightfoot was a hero to them."

"For our audience who don't know Senator Lightfoot's background, could you give us a thumbnail?"

"He played football at the University of Washington, got an MBA, and then went into real estate. He was elected to the Klamath Falls City Council, then the state assembly and later to the congressional seat I now occupy. He was the first and last Democrat to hold the seat since 1940. He actually encouraged me to run to take his place when he decided to try for the Senate."

"But you're a Republican."

"Edward Lightfoot didn't believe public service should only be performed by Democrats. After the election, and even though he fought tooth and nail for my opponent, he let me stay with him in his D.C. townhouse until I found a place of my own."

Ludlow paused, then chuckled.

"Not many people outside of Oregon know this, but the senator's nickname in the late 1960s was El Camino."

"El Camino? Like the car?"

"For two years he traveled the country living in the back of his Chevy trying to unite the various Indian tribes into what later developed into the American Indian Movement. He started in the Northwest with the Klamath and Modoc and worked his way south to the Apache and Yaqui, then headed east. When I was a little kid, everybody, even the Indians, wanted to be cowboys when we played cowboys and Indians. By the time he was done, all the kids wanted to be the Indians." Ludlow chuckled again. *"It became damn hard to find a willing cowboy . . . People . . . people who—"*

Ludlow's voice cracked. He caught his breath.

"Sorry . . ."

Ludlow cleared this throat.

"People who didn't know him will never understand what a gem he was."

His voice cracked again, now on the verge of tears.

"Man, I'm going to miss that guy . . . I . . . I need to hang up."

Gage wondered how long it would take before Jennings felt that Lightfoot was dead long enough to talk about the impact on the Supreme Court nominations. Gage's guess wasn't off by much. Eleven minutes later, the screen-in-screen showed CNN's chief Washington correspondent.

"What effect will this have on the nominations, Jane?"

"Absolutely none. You have a Democratic governor who'll simply replace Senator Lightfoot with another Democrat, maybe even the senator's wife. She's very popular in Oregon."

A tally sheet of expected votes for the nomination appeared on the screen.

Gage's cell phone rang. It was Alex Z. "Are you watching the news?"

"Tansy just came in."

"They've got it all wrong."

"Who are they?"

"Jennings and his crew. I know. I checked the Oregon state Web site. The governor of Oregon can't appoint anyone to fill Lightfoot's seat."

"You mean it has to be done by election?"

"Exactly. And there isn't time between now and the confirmation votes."

"So the president doesn't need the vice president's vote any more to break a tie."

"And that pulls the nuclear option off the table," Alex Z said. "The Democrats' filibuster pitch was wholly based on a kind of separation of powers argument, that the vice president as part of the executive branch shouldn't be playing a due role in a matter like this. Now they don't have to—sounds to me like the Democrats should've made a different argument."

"I guess they didn't know Lightfoot's plane was going to crash," Gage said, then felt his hand tighten around his phone, fearing that there were those who did.

"Congratulations, Landon," President Duncan's voice was cheerful, gloating.

Landon Meyer turned off the sound from the FOX News broadcast in his Manchester, New Hampshire, hotel room and pushed himself to his feet.

"But Mr. President, Ed Lightfoot was—"

"Serves him right. You know what he called me last week?"

"No. I've been campaigning."

"A buffoon. He called me a buffoon."

Landon felt anger surge. *You* are *a buffoon.* "He once called me a fascist on the Senate floor. It's no reason to celebrate his death."

Maybe what the public thinks about politicians like me is right, Landon thought.

He felt himself cringe.

Silliness.

Why did I use the word "silliness" in talking to Gage in Iowa? Four dead refinery workers and I called it silliness.

Damn, what Gage must think of me now.

"He sure as hell would've celebrated mine," Duncan said.

"I don't think so Mr. President." *You son of a bitch.* "In fact, I'm sure he wouldn't have."

"Doesn't make a difference. The nomination fight is over. It's just a matter of counting down the last forty-eight hours."

Landon sat down on the edge of the bed, staring at the now silent cell phone. A wrenching, nightmarish image of Ed Lightfoot's mangled body invaded his mind: hands that no longer reached out, a face that no longer smiled, a heart now motionless in his chest. Landon tried to fight off the image, but felt himself well up, then his whole body shook with grief, with anger, and with self-reproach.

Silliness.

What kind of devil have I become?

You sure this isn't going to make things worse?"
Viz was parked three blocks from City Hall
on the route Brandon Meyer had walked on
the night of his scuffle with John Porzolkiewski.
"And isn't this going to turn you into a Charlie
Palmer?"

"Charlie Palmer would've gone public just with
the condom."

"I don't know boss, this is pretty close to black-
mail."

"You want to bail out?"

Viz laughed. "No way. Finding that asshole buck
naked on top of some hooker will be the highlight
of my career."

Judge Brandon Meyer emerged from the north door
of the Federal Building at six-fifteen, jaywalked
across the street, turned right up the sidewalk, then
headed into the Tenderloin. He'd changed from his
suit into a knit shirt and slacks. Out of his robes and

in a San Francisco Giants jacket and cap, none of the drug dealers and hookers on the street would recognize him.

"I still don't get why he'd choose the Tenderloin." Viz said.

"Think about it. There's not a person on the street who's not watching for police surveillance 24–7. They don't always spot it, but they start yelling when they do. And he sure isn't going to bump into a fellow member of the Opera Guild or the Yale Club up here at night."

Gage watched Brandon glance at a middle-aged, dark-skinned woman wearing a grimy overcoat pushing a grocery cart filled with cans and bottles. Brandon turned north on Larkin and fell in behind an obese hooker, his eyes fixated on her thong-cinched butt extending below a silver miniskirt.

"Take her, take her," Viz pleaded into his cell phone. "I want that picture."

The cart lady stopped to search the garbage can, then continued up the street.

"What about the one with the grocery cart?" Gage asked.

Viz laughed. "I know for sure she's not his type."

Gage started up his truck.

"I'll swing around and try to get a couple of blocks up the hill above him."

He skirted Larkin until he got into position, then Viz came on:

"He just turned left on Geary."

Brandon had disappeared by the time Gage found a place to park on the crowded street. He punched a number into his cell phone as he watched the cart lady slip into a recessed doorway. She answered on the second ring.

"Where'd he go?"

"The McCall Hotel," Tansy answered in an excited whisper. "This is a kick. Why haven't you let me do this kind of thing before? It's like being invisible." She laughed. "Except for the smell."

"Did he meet anyone?"

"No. He didn't even stop at the desk. He just walked right past and to the elevator."

"Good work. Why don't you go back to the office and get cleaned up."

"You sure you don't want me to hang—"

"No. Viz and I'll take it from here."

The thirty-something clerk behind the bulletproof reception window of the residential hotel glanced up at the sound of Gage's knocking. He leaned forward in his chair and put down a worn paperback on the desk. Gage saw it was Jean Paul Sartre's *Being and Nothingness*. Only in San Francisco, Gage thought, do hotel clerks read French philosophy.

The clerk reached for a registration card.

"You don't need that," Gage said. "I'm looking for someone."

The clerk offered a bucktooth grin.

"Everybody's looking for somebody, pal, but I can't help you, unless you got a warrant or something."

"We're not cops."

"Tough break."

Gage heard the hotel door swing open fifteen feet away, then stayed silent as a skinny sixteen- or seventeen-year-old girl in pink hooker shorts walked behind them and toward the elevator. Two men sitting on soiled couches along the opposite wall tracked her like homeless men watching a ladle of mashed potatoes heading toward their plates at the Salvation Army dining room.

Gage looked back at the clerk. "How much for her?"

The clerk shook his head. "She's taken." He pointed toward the rooms above. "Got a regular. Maybe you can catch her on the way out."

Gage shook his head. "Looks like jailbait to me."

"I wouldn't know. We don't check IDs."

"What about the ID of the guy in the Giants jacket who came by here a little while ago?"

The clerk's face hardened. "What about him?"

"You know who he is?"

"Yeah, asshole. His name is John-Doe-who-pays-his-rent-on-time."

"Hey, man," Gage said. "Don't get your back up. This isn't about you."

Gage reached into the inside pocket of his windbreaker, then made a show of looking at the clerk's paperback. He pulled out two hundred dollars and held it against his chest so the men behind him couldn't see it.

"You ever read Sartre's *Transcendence of the Ego*?" Gage asked, then set the bills in the tray at the bottom of the window. "You should buy a copy."

The clerk grinned and reached for the cash.

"Room 923."

Viz took his phone out of his pocket as they rode the elevator and set it to take video. He cupped it in his hand when they stepped out on the ninth floor. Television shows and muffled arguments reverberated down the hallway as they walked along the stained and cigarette-burned carpet. Gage put his ear to the door when they arrived at 923, but couldn't make out any sounds. He wondered whether they were a few minutes too early for the heavy breathing.

"Can you pop the door without kicking it?" Gage whispered. "Too noisy."

Viz braced his shoulder against it. He gave it a push, but it didn't budge. He straightened up. "It's too solid."

Gage nodded. Viz took a step back and then kicked the door just above the handle. The frame exploded and the door flew open. Viz rushed in, phone ready to take video.

Gage remained in the hallway, scanning up and down. He pointed at every face that appeared, then toward the inside of the resident's room. Each in turn ducked back inside.

Only then did Gage step into the room. A condemned man strapped to a gurney in a gas chamber couldn't have looked more terrified than Brandon Meyer.

Viz stood over him.

Gage reached for his cell phone.

"Joe, I'm at the McCall Hotel. You need to come over here."

"Is it about Meyer?"

"Yeah."

"I can't. The U.S. Attorney told me—"

"Forget what he told you. It isn't his career on the line."

Gage helped Brandon off the bed and into the desk chair. Brandon's body trembled. He bore the shell-shocked expression of men who get snagged in undercover john operations or pedophiles who walk into news camera lights in suburban juveniles' homes.

"Anybody else here?" Gage asked Brandon.

"No."

Gage pointed at the closed bathroom door and Viz started toward it.

"I told you," Brandon said, "there's no one here."

Viz glanced inside, then shook his head. The bathroom was empty.

Gage walked to the dresser and turned down the sound on the television. It was tuned to a news report about the pending confirmation vote.

A monitor on the desk showed an online stock trading Web site.

Flowcharts tacked to the walls tracked the money flow to Pegasus, then to Mann Trust, then to senatorial candidates. Next to them hung oversized spreadsheets titled "Confirmations" and "LM."

Bookcases of slim binders stood next to the window: fourteen bearing the name Pegasus, eight in the star names, two labeled TIMCO, and dozens of others in the names of Fortune 500 companies.

Gage walked over and pulled the OptiCom binder off the shelf. He leaned against the wall as he thumbed through it.

Finally, Gage said, "I had it backward."

Brandon didn't say anything.

"What do you mean?" Viz asked.

"He sold short. He held on to the search warrant long enough to borrow and sell a million shares of OptiCom stock. Then he signed the warrant, Casey kicked in the door and the stock price collapsed. That's when Brandon bought cheap shares to repay the expensive ones he'd borrowed. He cleared ten million dollars."

Gage glared down at Brandon. "Is that about right?"

Brandon still didn't say anything.

"The only question," Gage said, "is whether you're going to bring your brother down, too."

This time, Brandon responded:

"Landon didn't know anything about it. He didn't. He thought we were still doing it through insurance."

"What changed?"

Brandon lowered his head.

"I'm going to find out one way or the other," Gage said.

Brandon looked up again, his eyes darting about the room. They paused for a second on Viz blocking the doorway, then focused on the window.

Gage stepped in front of it. "Suicide isn't an option."

Brandon swallowed hard, then licked his lips.

"We had to stop because of an IRS investigation. But . . ." He took in a breath. "But Mann Trust was overextended and the bank regulators went after us for not keeping large enough cash reserves. They threatened to shut us down. The whole thing would have collapsed."

"You mean you own Mann Trust?"

Brandon shrugged. "In a way."

"You needed a few million dollars and right then a warrant to search a high-tech company came walking into your chambers."

Brandon didn't react.

"It's the star names," Gage said. "Each one was a predecessor of OptiCom. An agent would arrive with a search warrant, you'd sit on it long enough to make a trade, then cash in."

"I had no choice."

Gage shook his head. "You had lots of choices."

"You don't understand what was at stake."

Viz' cell phone rang. He flipped it open. "What's up?"

The color drained from his face. "When?"

He clenched his teeth. "I'm on my way."

He snapped the phone shut. "Socorro's disappeared."

Viz stepped toward Brandon, grabbed him by his suit lapels, and lifted him out of the chair. He held

Brandon up, feet dangling, then stepped toward the window.

Brandon's eyes turned wild.

"Gage. Stop him. You've got to stop him."

Viz held Brandon against the curtain. "If anything happens to my sister I'll break you in two."

"Viz, put him down."

Viz lowered Brandon to his feet, then backed away and turned toward Gage.

"Socorro left the ranch at nine o'clock this morning to go shopping in Nogales. She didn't come back. And she isn't answering her cell phone."

Gage could feel fury begin to rage, at Brandon, at Anston, and at himself. Instead of protecting Socorro, he had led her into a trap.

Gage fixed his eyes on Brandon. "Where's Boots Marnin?"

"Who?"

"Don't play dumb. Where is he?"

"I . . . I've never heard of anyone named Marnin. I'm telling you the truth."

Gage pointed at the desk chair and Brandon sat down, then he led Viz into the hallway. "Have you talked to her daughter?"

"Socorro called Sandy yesterday to say she was going shopping in town. Alex Z was watching the video feed this morning and saw her drive away. She was supposed to be back at the ranch by noon."

Viz glanced toward the elevator. "I better get out there."

Gage shook his head. "I know some ex-Border Patrol guys in Tucson. They're tough and know the area." He searched his cell phone contacts and connected the number. He introduced Viz, then handed him the phone.

Gage returned inside and pointed at Brandon. "I want Anston."

Brandon slumped in the chair. "No way. He's insulated himself. The paper trail seems to go to him, but once you look at it, it dead-ends with Palmer and with me. His intelligence training wasn't wasted. I'm the one who went to the Caymans to first meet with Quinton fifteen years ago."

Brandon's eyes darted toward the bookshelf.

"Are we talking about TIMCO now," Gage said, "or the campaign money?"

"Both."

Viz walked back into the room.

"I've got to e-mail them some photos of Socorro." Viz looked at Brandon, but spoke to Gage. "You going to be okay with this asshole?"

"Take off. Joe will be here in a few minutes."

Viz glared at Brandon, now shrunk back in his chair.

"You better hope she's all right. You've got no place to hide where I can't find you. No place."

Gage worked the fractured door closed after Viz left and then sat down on the bed.

"I thought we'd find a hooker in here," Gage said.

Brandon shrugged.

"Your wife will be relieved. Maybe she'll even visit you in prison."

They both alerted to a knock at the door. Gage

stood up, reached under his windbreaker, and rested his hand on his gun. He pulled the door open a crack, peeked through, then opened it the rest of the way and let Casey inside.

Casey surveyed the room. His eyes came to rest on Brandon. Gage filled him in on the scam and about use of the hotel room as a secret office, and about the urgency created by Socorro's disappearance.

"What do you want to do?" Casey asked.

"Number one is to get Anston before he can hurt Socorro."

"And number two is Landon?"

Brandon pushed himself to his feet.

"I told you. Landon had nothing to do with any of this. He doesn't know anything about it."

Casey pointed at Brandon.

"Sit down."

Brandon dropped back into the chair.

"Why not Landon first?" Casey asked. "Maybe go public. Try to freeze everything in place."

"Because then we'd never get Anston. Once this blows up, he'll know he's next and make a run for it, and he won't leave any witnesses behind—starting with Socorro." Gage felt his body tense. "If she's still alive."

Forty minutes after Gage called the Oakland loft, Alex Z and Shakir came through the hotel room door. Their bodyguards posted themselves in the hallway. They set up their laptops to catalogue everything in the office and copy the drives on Brandon's computers.

Gage swept his hand from the bookcases to the computer on the desk to the file cabinet in the corner, then turned toward Brandon.

"Walk us through it."

G age watched from inside the surveillance van parked a block west of the restaurant as a dinner crowd of black-suited men and women filled the entrance of Tadich Grill. Limousines were double-parked in front. Streetlights and neon signs shone down on pavement slick from an uneasy mist swirling down the street.

Brandon Meyer had difficulty working his way through the door. As he crossed the dining room, he saw Marc Anston set down his cell phone on the starched white tablecloth.

"Why are you sweating?" Anston asked as Brandon settled in his chair.

"I had to park six blocks away and I got a late start from court."

"That's not like you."

"I set off some fireworks at the OptiCom hearing. The chief judge came by to kibitz. I couldn't walk out on him."

Anston smiled. "We neutralized Gage. Nobody will listen to anything he says."

Brandon nodded. "And Casey, too."

Anston pointed toward the restroom sign and picked up the phone. "I've got to go the john."

Gage was seated on a metal chair bolted to the floor of the van. Shelves of electronic equipment stretched along the driver's side: receivers, bugging devices, two-way radios. Viz was stationed at the rear window, binoculars pointed at the entrance, and Joe Casey sat in his Ford Explorer in a yellow zone a block to the east.

"The restaurant is noisy as hell," Gage said to Viz after Anston left the table. "The wire on Brandon is picking up a lot of background sounds."

Gage kept the headphones pressed against his ears trying to hear through the conversations at adjoining tables, the clink of glasses, and the clatter of dishes, waiting for Anston to return.

Viz looked toward Gage. "I'm sorry about that Socorro thing. I hope it didn't get you in a jam with your pals in Tucson."

"No problem. I'm just glad she finally called."

"I should've told her we were watching the video feed from the ranch."

"It's not your fault. Neither one of us wanted to worry her." Gage adjusted the sound level on his receiver. "Did she say what she was doing?"

"Visiting some friends in Tempe. Then she stayed overnight because she was too tired to drive back and then her cell phone battery died. She's going to stay one more night and go to a play at the university."

"You didn't tell her about Brandon, did you?"

"No. She might've done something preemptive."

Gage peeked through the curtains separating the cab from the interior of the van. He looked through the windshield, scanning the cars and sidewalks and the office and store windows.

"You see anything we need to worry about?" he asked Viz.

Viz raised his binoculars and peered out the rear window. "There are a lot of people on the street, but no George Str—"

"Hold on," Gage said. "Anston's back."

"How do we keep Gage quiet after the Senate vote tomorrow?" Brandon said. "I can't keep OptiCom going forever and eventually Oscar Mogasci will roll back the other way. Casey will put him on a polygraph and he'll fold."

Anston leaned over the table. His voice turned hard. "I'm tired of Gage and I'm about an inch away from sending him the same way as Charlie Palmer."

Brandon's mouth went dry. He hadn't believed Gage the night before. It was too absurd. His voice fell to a whisper.

"You're insane. Completely insane. You didn't kill—"

"TIMCO was a domino. If it fell, everything would've followed. I had no choice. *We* had no choice."

"There's no 'we' in this."

Anston laughed. "What is it about judges? The second they're caught up in something themselves they forget what a conspiracy is. How many of those teenage Mexican wetbacks did you send to federal prison? You think any of them had a hand in any of the murders their narco-bosses committed? But you gave them prison terms like they'd pulled the trigger themselves."

"I never signed on for this."

"That's what they all say."

"What about Karopian?"

Anston shrugged.

"But Hawkins can show up any time—"

"That would be a helluva trick."

"You mean—"

"Why don't you grow up? You and your brother. Lives of pretending their hands aren't stained by their family's crimes."

"Crimes. What crimes?"

"Stop it, Brandon. Don't embarrass yourself. I saw it. All of it. The CIA doesn't throw away anything."

"I don't want to talk about this."

"Hundreds of thousands of lives have been lost defending the American way of life. A couple more is a small sacrifice to get where the country needs to go."

They glanced up at the approaching waiter.

Anston looked back at Brandon.

"Give the nice man your order."

"Why'd Brandon cut it off?" Viz asked Gage.

"He knows the recording will eventually make

the news. He doesn't want Anston talking about his grandfather's arms trafficking with the Nazis."

"It's not like he's gonna have a reputation left after today."

"I think he's still trying to protect Landon, and he's terrified by what Anston might say about Ed Lightfoot's plane crash."

Gage's cell phone rang.

"Brandon didn't tell you everything." Alex Z was breathless. "But we hit a home run, boss. Charlie Palmer set up thousands of straw contributors over the years. Not just fake companies, but dead people, homeless people, institutionalized mentally ill people. Did it all through the Internet—"

"And charged offshore credit cards for the contributions."

"Exactly. And scattered them all over the country so nobody would notice, then used the money to pay off the Mann Trust loans if anybody became suspicious."

"How much?"

"I don't know yet. But in the last five years each fake contributor put in between fifty and one hundred thousand dollars in small increments."

"Do the math for me."

"I would guess between two hundred and three hundred million dollars."

Anston took a sip of water after the waiter left, thought a moment, then asked Brandon, "Why the sudden interest in my side of things?"

"I keep getting chills up my spine, like I'm about to get blindsided."

"That's your lifelong problem. You never look around until it's too late, and your brother, too. I'm thinking we may need to change horses in the presidential race. I created him and I can dismantle him in a heartbeat. I'm not sure I want to blow our last couple of hundred million on somebody with what may be a genetic weakness."

Brandon didn't answer.

"You know what my wife calls me?" Anston said. "Machiavelli's Machiavelli. It's ironic that everybody reads *The Prince* when they're in college and thinks he was some kind of immoral genius. In fact, he was an idiot savant." He peered into Brandon's eyes. "You ever read Machiavelli's *Art of War*?"

Brandon shook his head.

"He didn't have a clue it was the rifle, and not the pike, that would determine the outcome of wars for the next three hundred years." Anston grinned. "See? The prince needed a Machiavelli, and Machiavelli needed somebody like me to fight his wars for him."

Viz recognized the gait before he spotted the face.

"Oh shit."

Gage's head snapped toward Viz.

"It's Socorro," Viz said. "She just slipped around the corner and ducked through the crowd into the restaurant."

Gage flipped open his cell phone. Joe Casey's number was set for redial.

"We've got a problem," Gage said. "Socorro just went in to confront Anston and Brandon."

"With what?" Casey asked.

Gage looked at Viz. "With what?"

Viz spread his hands and shrugged.

"What do you want to do?" Casey asked.

"It's up to Viz."

Viz turned toward the window and scanned the sidewalks and cars on the street. "I'm pissed she lied to me, but it's contained, and it took a lot of guts to walk in there and try to set things right—and for her that's what this has been about from the beginning." He locked on to the diners gathered at the entrance. "And they can't do anything to her with that kind of big-money crowd around her."

"Good evening, Judge. Marc."

They looked up.

Socorro made a show of glancing around the restaurant.

"You two really are creatures of habit. Don't you ever get bored with this place? Maybe you should try Mexican food sometime."

Her voice had a sense of self-satisfaction neither Brandon nor Anston had heard from her before.

Anston stood and extended his hand. Socorro didn't accept it.

"It's not that kind of visit."

She reached behind her and pulled an empty chair up to the table. She and Anston sat down. She was the only one in the restaurant wearing jeans, and the only Hispanic except the busboys.

Anston tried again. "To what do we owe—"

"Money," Socorro snapped. "You've got money belonging to other people."

Anston smirked. "You have it backward, my dear. You have money belonging to other people."

Brandon looked around the restaurant, then cut in. "I'm not sure this is the place to discuss this."

Socorro reached into her purse, pulled out a DVD, and set it on the table. Its cover showed Henry Fonda, arm extended in accusation.

"You're right," Socorro said. "Let's go watch a movie."

"I'm sure it's a fine film, but we have better things to do than spend an evening watching *Advise and Consent*, no matter how timely."

Socorro opened the case and turned its contents toward Anston. It was labeled *Charles Palmer Investigations, Meeting with Marc Anston re: Pegasus*.

Anston's eyes fixed on the DVD.

"I like what you've done with your study," Socorro said. "That Rothko hanging on the wall must've cost a pretty penny." She grinned. "Of course it did. I checked. One point two million. Sotheby's. Last year."

Anston reached for the case. She pulled it away. "Not so fast."

"What do you want?" Anston lowered his hand to the table and drummed his fingers.

"Little nervous there, Counselor?" Socorro said, closing the DVD case. "Don't you want to know what's on it?"

"If it's really from last year, then I know."

"What's on it?" Brandon asked, voice shaking.

Anston shook his head. "We're not getting into that. She may be wired. Like husband, like wife." He peered at her sweater, with his eyes coming to rest on her breasts.

She smiled. "You want to check? Unlike your

little amigo here, I doubt whether your bony little hands have touched anything like them in a generation."

"You surprise me, my dear. You sound like a different woman."

"One finally with power."

"Or with somebody behind you." Anston cast a glance toward the entrance. "Did Gage put you up to this?"

Brandon spoke fist. "He wouldn't . . ."

Anston's eyes shifted toward Brandon. "He wouldn't what?"

"He wouldn't . . ." Brandon knew panic showed on his face. He bit his lip, hoping it would fade. "He wouldn't send an amateur."

Anston paused, then nodded. "That's true." He looked at Socorro. "What do you want?"

"I told you, money."

"Sounds like extortion."

"It's not for me. It's for the TIMCO families and Moki Amaro's mother and for all the other families you cheated."

"If all you want is a little contribution to a charity of some kind . . ."

"I want all of it."

"Are you going to throw in the nine million Charlie stole?"

"Every penny."

"How generous." Anston eyed the DVD. "Why don't we get together at my office tomorrow to talk about it?"

Socorro's face went blank. In that instant, they all recognized she hadn't thought through what came next. And they all also recognized that was the difference between her and Charlie. She manipulated characters in children's books, while he moved real people in the directions he wanted in real life, and they all knew she'd been too impulsive.

Anston smiled. "You didn't expect me to pull out a checkbook right here and now, did you?"

Socorro returned the DVD to her purse. "Let's go type up an agreement." She looked back and forth between them. "And I want both of you to sign."

Anston caught Brandon's eye and nodded.

"That's fine with me," Brandon said.

"And don't try anything. I've hidden two other copies of this thing."

"And we get all three once you have your money?" Anston asked.

"I won't need them anymore."

Anston's cell phone rang. He pulled it from his coat pocket and glanced at its face. "It's my office. My secretary is working late." He connected, then listened and said. "Sure, I'll be right there. And check to make sure your assistant is standing by to do the thing we talked about."

"This has gone far enough," Gage said. "Let's get her when they come out of the restaurant."

"She's out of her mind," Viz said. "What was she thinking?"

Viz crawled past Gage, then into the cab and climbed down from the van. Gage slid to the rear and watched him cross the street. Viz walked down the block, then positioned himself against the brick wall ten feet west of the Tadich Grill entrance, on the route toward Anston's office three blocks away.

Gage heard shuffling as Socorro, Brandon, and Anston rose from the table.

"My car is just outside," Anston pointed at the crowd gathered in front of the reception station, blocking the entrance. "We'll have to go out another way."

Gage heard "excuse mes" and "sorrys" as they worked their way through the restaurant. Then a cacophony of sizzles, dishes clacking, and pots rattling.

Gage hit redial. "Joe, they're going out the back through the kitchen."

He then punched in Viz's number. "They're coming out on the Halleck Street side."

Viz sprinted west to circle the block as Gage pushed his way through the curtain into the cab and started the engine.

The passenger doors of the silver Lexus SUV were already open in the alleylike street behind Tadich Grill.

"I didn't know you had a driver," Brandon said.

Anston ignored the comment. "You sit up front. Socorro and I'll take the back."

The driver's face made Socorro uneasy, somehow familiar, and somehow frightening. She decided it was just nervousness, then climbed in.

The driver turned toward the back. "Everybody got their seat belts on?"

The Texas accent. That's it, Socorro thought, *he looks like that country singer.*

Boots started the engine and began rolling toward the intersection. He jammed down the accelerator when he spotted a huge man at the end of the block trying to see inside the SUV.

"Stop," Socorro yelled.

Boots reached into the console, pulled out a .38 revolver, and then passed it back to Anston, who pointed it at Socorro. "Shut up."

Brandon swung around in his seat as Boots charged down the alley.

"What are you doing?" Brandon's voice rose to a desperate squeak. "Let her go. My God, Anston, I'm a federal judge."

Anston didn't take his eyes off Socorro. "Not another word, Brandon. Not another word."

Then Socorro's voice: "Take your hands off me. Take your hands off me . . ."

Viz held his ground as Boots bore down, then dived and rolled when the SUV hit the intersection, turning and skidding until it was pointed south. It blew past Gage stuck at the cross street, trapped behind cars and by oncoming traffic.

Gage called Casey's cell phone.

"They didn't come out my way," Casey said.

"They went south. Boots Marnin was driving."

"You want me to call Spike?"

"Hold on." Gage conferenced in Viz. "You get a plate?"

"No. But I'm almost sure it's the same SUV I saw after the burglary at Socorro's."

Gage's phone signaled an incoming call. He switched to it. It was his office, where Tansy, Alex Z, and Shakir were standing by.

"A man just called," Tansy said, her voice wavering. "He told me to tell you that you can have Socorro back tomorrow night. If you call the police, he'll kill her. What's going—"

"I'll call you back."

Gage reconnected to Viz and Casey and passed on the message.

"It's my fault," Viz said. "I shouldn't have—"

"No, it isn't," Gage said. "Any one of us could've closed this thing down."

Gage punched in Faith's cell phone number. "Where are you?"

"At home. Is everything okay?"

"Things have gone sour. They've got Socorro."

"Is she—"

"She's all right for now. I need you to—"

"Hold on, there's a knock—"

"Don't answer it. Get out the back way. Take the trail down to Tully's place, but stay connected to me."

Gage put her on hold and called Casey.

"Contact the Oakland police, tell them there's armed burglary in progress at my house."

He reconnected to Faith. He heard her feet thudding on the narrow path, then caught his breath at the sound of crashing branches, fearing it was the crook catching up.

"Faith?"

He heard a distant explosion of wood and glass. He knew it had to be the crook kicking out the back door.

"Graham? I'm okay," Faith's breathing was heavy. "I slipped."

More footfalls on the dirt and then on wood, pounding on a door, and finally Tully, the ex-cop, asking Faith, "Are you okay?"

A quick, gasping explanation, "Burglar . . . broke in . . . chasing me."

Tully's voice came on the phone, "What's going on?" he asked Gage.

"There's too much explain."

"Shit, what was that?"

"What?"

"Sounds like he's found the trail and is on his way down. I'll handle him."

Gage heard a rustle had he handed the phone back to Faith, then the pump action of Tully's shotgun ripped the silence.

Five minutes later, Gage walked toward Casey and Viz in an underground garage near the restaurant. They looked at him, arms spread in expectation.

"She made it," Gage said. "My neighbor scared the guy off, but OPD got there too late to catch him."

"That means they were planning to kidnap Faith just to make sure you kept your mouth shut." Casey shook his head. "If we hadn't spotted them grabbing Socorro, they would've gotten her."

Gage took in a breath, then exhaled. It was the sort of trade none of them wanted to dwell on.

"Where do we stand?" Gage asked.

"Nowhere," Casey said.

The obvious hung in the air, unsaid. Anston

needed all the copies of the DVD, whatever was on it, and Boots possessed the techniques to find out where Socorro had hidden them—he'd proved it with Hawkins.

Gage leaned back against the van.

"What are they going to do?" He tried to visualize the moves. "Anston doesn't know we have Brandon and just wants to get through tomorrow. He's a survivor. He'll take one problem at a time."

Gage pointed at Casey and said, "I'll take your truck." Then at Viz. "You better ride in the back of the van. If Anston sees you . . ."

"Then my sister's dead." Viz shook his head. "Damn. I screwed up."

Gage reached over and gripped Viz's shoulder.

"We'll find her."

He lowered his hand and his mind searched for a lead.

Finally, he said, "You remember the night you followed Boots after I spotted him watching me and Faith at Cal?"

Viz jerked his thumb toward the van. "My surveillance log is in the laptop."

"You and Joe hit all those places. I'm going to go lean on someone."

The uniformed Secret Service agent waved Landon Meyer through the northwest gate onto the White House grounds. Ten o'clock and Landon still hadn't had dinner. CNN and other cable news reporters and their crews were packing up after filing their final stories for the night, all of them reporting on the same thing: the following day's full Senate confirmation vote.

Landon had thought about calling Brandon during the drive from the Dirksen Building, but he decided he wasn't in the mood for Brandon's kind of glee, not with Senator Lightfoot's death so heavy in his heart.

President Duncan and his chief of staff, Stuart Sheridan, both raised highball glasses toward Landon as he entered the president's study. Duncan pointed at the buffet along the far wall where a silver tray bearing decanters of bourbon and Scotch lay next to a matching ice bucket and crystal glasses.

Landon shook his head and took the only unoccupied seat in the room, an upholstered wing chair set at one point of an equilateral triangle.

Duncan tilted his head toward Sheridan.

"The brain trust here says you're ten points ahead of everybody else in New Hampshire, Republican *or* Democrat."

Landon's first thought wasn't satisfaction. It was a question that had bothered him since he'd arrived in Washington: Why were taxpayers fronting the salary of a political operative like Sheridan?

"Give or take three percent," Landon said.

Duncan smiled. "Ever the realist."

"The Supreme Court nominations may have hurt me a little."

"Americans have short memories. They'll have forgotten about them in a month. But if they haven't"—Duncan grinned—"just blame me. Everybody else does. And remember the old Nixon rule: Run to the right in the primary election and to the center in the general." He laughed. "Not everybody can do a Bill Clinton or John McCain and run in all directions at once."

Landon didn't respond. It was exactly what Duncan had tried and failed at. The Supreme Court nominees were his last chance to save his presidency.

"It may help if you make yourself scarce for the swearing-in tomorrow afternoon," Sheridan said. "A face in the crowd. Give yourself a little distance."

Landon grasped what Sheridan was really saying: Let Duncan be seen alone planting the flag to mark his legacy.

"Won't having the ceremony an hour after the

vote seem a little rushed?" Landon said. "Maybe we should wait a day and make it look stately."

"I want it to be more like a door slamming," Duncan said. "You can do it your way when you live in this house."

Landon's peripheral vision caught Sheridan stir in his chair.

"I wanted to talk to you about the campaign," Duncan said. "A deal is a deal."

"Thank you, Mr. President."

"But instead of making some kind of explicit announcement, I'll do it a little at a time. Each week the endorsement will get a little stronger. Sort of massage the base until it's lined up behind you."

"It'll collapse if we move too quickly," Sheridan said. "They like to see themselves as a voluntary army, not conscripts."

Maybe a deal wasn't a deal after all, Landon thought. It would be easy for political winds to blow away an endorsement written in sand. Impossible if it was etched in stone. He wondered what would be the quid pro quo that would bring out the chisel.

Duncan turned his body fully toward Landon. "I had a thought I'd like you to consider . . ."

The pause at the end of the sentence revealed Duncan's timing at its best. It forced Landon to ask, "What's that, Mr. President?"

"I'd like you to consider taking Sheridan on as an adviser in a couple of months. I'm the lamest of lame ducks, so there's not much for him to do around here after tomorrow."

Landon straightened. "I respect his abilities, Mr.

President, but I'm not sure how that would play in the media."

"That's not a problem. His wife has been diagnosed with a medical problem. He can resign for family reasons."

"I'm sorry to hear that," Landon said, looking at Sheridan. "I hope it's not serious."

Sheridan shrugged. "She'll get over it."

Rosa M. dropped her dishrag as her eyes widened at the man filling her apartment doorway. It was the look on his face. She drew back, cowering.

"*No me haga daño.*" Don't hurt me.

"I'm not going to." Gage flashed his ID. "I need some information."

She nodded once. Slow, hesitant.

"It's about a guy who stayed in room 527 of the Mariner Hotel a while back. A Texan."

Rosa's cheeks flushed.

"It's not about that."

Gage called Casey as he drove away. "It's somewhere South of Market. A warehouse. It was used as a marijuana grow room before it got busted by the DEA. She overheard Boots talking on the phone just before he checked out. She thought it was part of an investment deal he'd been offered. It has an inner plywood structure. Almost soundproof. Boots referred to it as cocoon. A perfect place to take a hostage. But she doesn't know the address, or even the street."

"We've already driven by a half-dozen ware-houses. Nothing."

"You have somebody in the DEA you can call to find out all the places they've raided?"

"I'll have the information by the time we hook up."

"How many of these grows have there been in San Francisco?" Gage asked as he read Casey's notes. They were parked under the freeway a block south of the California Supreme Court building.

"Dozens and dozens. The medical marijuana movement has been good for business."

"How many are South of Market?"

"Eight that have been closed down in the last couple of months."

"Map it out. I'll drive."

Gage climbed into the cab while Viz and Casey got into the back. Casey gave him the first stop and Gage headed south through the dark streets.

They hit six in the next forty minutes. They were nearly to the waterfront, four blocks from Gage's office. And there were two left on the list.

"Maybe we missed it," Viz said, lifting off his headphones. "I haven't heard a thing. Maybe they found the device on Brandon."

"We're in big trouble if they did," Gage said. "Joe, where's next?"

"Near the Flower Mart on Brannan."

Gage drove west from the bay, then south away from downtown. He hit Brannan Street just east of the deserted flower market, then drove farther west toward Gilbert. The commercial street was abandoned except for the generic homeless people curled up in doorways with their overfilled shopping carts parked next to them on the sidewalks. Gage slowed when he neared his turn, then crept along, searching the street, headset pressed tight against his ears.

Listening.

*S*ometimes you have to take one for the team."

The voice was faint and staticky, but recognizable.

"We got it," Gage said. "We got it."

Gage peered through the van's windshield as they crept along. The voices strengthened.

"Are you listening to me?"

Gage spotted the numbers stuck on the brown-painted brick front of the second warehouse from the next corner. The streetlight reflected off a red-on-white "For Sale or Lease" sign hanging above the trailer-wide roll-up door. He scanned the unlit windows filling the prongs of the sawtooth roof, then pulled around the corner and into a parking space.

Gage slipped though the divider curtain and into the back.

"Let's go," Viz said, reaching to remove his headphones and turning toward the rear door.

"Wait," Gage said. "We don't know what we're up against."

"What if . . . ?"

"Yes, I'm listening."

Gage pointed at Viz. "Just wait." He closed his eyes and concentrated on the voices.

"Why are you dragging this out, Brandon?"

Gage knew why. Brandon would keep talking and stalling, hoping Gage would pick up his voice in the ether. Brandon had read enough search warrants and took enough testimony to know the range of the device was at least two hundred and fifty feet, and he knew Gage was somewhere out there.

"I'm not," Brandon said. *"I just need time to think."*

"We need those DVDs. The time for thinking is over."

"But Socorro will never say anything. Will you, Socorro? You won't say anything?"

"No," Socorro said. *"Never. Just let me go. I have children."*

"See," Brandon said, *"you always have that threat. She can't be there all the time to protect her kids. Now she knows you're serious. And she needs medical attention."*

Gage reached out and grabbed Viz's shoulder. Casey locked on his arm.

"Let's not get her killed," Gage said.

"It's hard to think in here. It's like a coffin."

"The grow room is still there," Gage said.

"A plywood coffin. It's suffocating."

"Viz, get us a satellite shot of the warehouse."

Viz flipped open his laptop.

"Suffocating? Brandon, you look like you're about to vomit. A little blood make you queasy?"

Viz's hands shook as he typed the address into the SAT-View Web site. Seconds later he had the image.

Anston again: *"It all looks a lot different down here in the trenches instead of up on the bench. It's easy to be a tough guy in a black robe."*

"There are skylights up there," Viz said. "I can climb up the fire escape of the building behind, then drop down."

"You'll sound like an explosion when you hit the roof of the inner structure."

Viz glanced around the inside of the van. He reached for a fifty-foot coil of coaxial cable and held it up. "This is strong enough to hold me."

Gage nodded. "You head for the roof. Keep an eye out for Boots. And be careful, he may have called in someone to back him up. I'll take the front door." He looked at Casey. "You take the office window."

Gage slipped a handheld receiver onto his belt and pointed toward the rear of the van. Viz headed out first. After he called to say he'd gotten into position on the roof, Gage and Casey climbed out and walked down the sidewalk toward the warehouse.

"What's going on. First we had a trip down memory lane on the way over here, practically a geography lesson. Then an architectural review of this place. Jesus Christ, you talk like a maniac when you're panicked."

"That's not it." It was a new voice. A Texas accent.
Footsteps and scuffling replaced the voice.
Brandon yelled. *"Anston, let go of me."*

Gage heard the sound of Brandon's shirt ripping.

"You traitor. Boots, help me. You . . . whatever your name is . . . check the perimeter."

Then a yelp and a crash, and silence.

Gage yelled into his cell phone:

"Viz. Go, go, go."

He held his hand up toward Casey, who was poised with a garbage can raised above his head, ready to throw it through the office window and climb inside.

Gage pressed himself against the brick wall next to the warehouse door. He turned his head toward Casey and mouthed, *Wait*.

The metal door scraped opened an inch, then two inches, then three. The barrel of a 9mm semiautomatic appeared. Then a hand. Gage chopped down on it with the butt of his gun. The wrist cracked and the 9mm crashed to the sidewalk. Gage grabbed the arm, dragged the man through the door, and swung him headfirst into wall. Gage winced at the thunk of flesh and bone.

Casey set down the trash can and cuffed the man to a water pipe.

Gage ducked his head inside. Boots's Lexus SUV was parked just inside the roll-up door, next to the plywood grow room occupying most of the warehouse. Gage's angled view through the opening revealed a series of ten tables stretched across the room, each topped by an empty, full-length black plastic tub.

He slipped through the warehouse entrance, then edged toward the inner door. The smell of marijuana, long since seized by the DEA, but still infusing the plywood, filled the air. He peeked inside the grow room, then ducked back, everyone's places fixed in his mind:

Brandon was slumped against the right wall, holding his chest where the tape was torn off.

Anston was crouched behind Socorro, who was tied to a wooden chair by the left wall, his gun to her head.

Boots was poised behind a four-foot-tall grow table, pointing his gun at the ceiling, trying to track Viz's steps moving from north to south, waiting for the order to fire.

"Back off, Gage." Anston's voice was calm. Hard. He sounded like a thirty-year-old intelligence agent. Not a sixty-eight-year-old white-collar lawyer.

"I'm not coming in," Gage said. "Let her go. There's no point. We've recorded everything."

"Then you'll just have to give me the recording."

"And we've got Brandon's records from the hotel."

"That's Brandon's problem."

Gage heard Viz's boots hit the cement outside the structure behind Anston, who then fired through the plywood. Gage ducked inside. He heard Casey's footsteps behind him. He pointed to the right and dived left and rolled behind bags of potting soil stacked three feet high. He crawled farther toward the left as Casey took up his position in the right corner.

A four-by-eight-foot sheet of plywood exploded inward. Gage looked over and saw Anston falling into Socorro, whose chair toppled to the side. He then spotted the motion of Boot's handgun and his arm stretching over the grow table to target Viz as he ducked through the opening in the wall. Gage and Casey opened fire together, the bullets cutting through the plastic shells of the tabletop tubs. Boots grunted, then collapsed.

Viz spun away as Anston fired, then collapsed to the floor, reaching for his sister.

Anston alerted to the motion of Gage rising from behind the bags, turned his head and raised his gun just in time to see the flash from Gage's barrel.

asey slid along the right wall until he got close enough to see whether Boots was still alive, then reached down and took the gun from the dead man's hand.

Gage didn't give Anston a second look. He'd seen where the slug struck his forehead. He ran to where Viz lay shielding Socorro. Blood soaked through the upper right back of his shirt.

Viz rolled over and stared up at Gage. "Is she okay?"

Gage dropped to his knees between them. Socorro was lying on her right side, still bound to the chair, her face bruised and bloody. She nodded.

"She'll be okay. Hang in there."

Gage saw blood pooling by Viz's shoulder. He ripped open Viz's shirt, then reached around and pressed his palm against the open wound.

"Man, I never thought I'd die like this," Viz said, looking up at Gage. "It's too soon . . . I've got . . . I've got things . . ."

Gage locked his eyes on Viz's.

"You're gonna make it. You need to trust me. If you weren't, I'd say so. I wouldn't take that away from you."

"This is Graham."

"Let me turn it down," Spike Pacheco said.

Gage heard television voices fade in the background.

"I guess you just saw Landon on TV, too," Spike said.

Gage's world mushroomed outward from the carnage lying before him.

"Graham," Spike finally said, "you still there?"

"Yeah. I'm at Gilbert and Brannan. I just called 911 for an ambulance. You better get over here before your whole department shows up."

Spike shook his head as he surveyed the bodies of Anston and Boots. It wasn't the worst crime scene he'd been called to, but it was the only one that ever had a federal judge curled up in a corner, rocking back and forth like an infant.

"I'm not sure I can contain this," Spike said. "The media listens to our 911 dispatcher."

"Just try to keep things muffled," Gage said, "at least until seven o'clock tomorrow morning."

"Then what?"

"Speculate your ass off."

"What about Viz and the bruises on Socorro? How are you going to explain all that at SF Medical?"

"Casey knows what he needs to do. He'll think of something by the time the ambulance gets them there."

age turned on his cell phone and checked for messages as the United Airlines red-eye from San Francisco set down on the runway at Dulles International Airport at ten o'clock the next morning. He scrolled through the texts until he found one from Faith reassuring him that Viz and Socorro would be all right. He then activated the CNN Internet site. A reporter stood in front of the Gilbert Street warehouse, a microphone in his left hand and an open notebook in the other. The camera panned up toward the "For Sale" sign, then down again to the reporter.

"*Details are scarce and the crime scene is still being sorted out, but the story we're getting is terrifying. Apparently, Judge Brandon Meyer, the brother of presidential hopeful Landon Meyer, went with an ex-law partner, Marc Anston, and another investor to scout a possible site for a live-work loft development. Judge Meyer was spotted by a disgraced and deranged ex-DEA agent named Boots Marnin who pursued them into the warehouse. By chance, FBI special agent Joe Casey was*

*in the area on an assignment when he noticed Marnin
following Judge Meyer. It's still unclear what happened
inside, but the result was that Anston and Marnin now
lie dead and Judge Meyer has been taken to SF Medical
for what they're calling observation."*

"Does that mean medical observation?"

*"They didn't say. But one source claims he had some
sort of mental breakdown."*

*"I understand Judge Meyer and Special Agent Casey
had a recent conflict."*

*"Yes, Bob. The irony is overwhelming. Just a few days
ago, in open court, Judge Meyer all but accused Casey of
perjury in the OptiCom trade secrets case."*

Gage climbed into the black Escalade to find Senator Landon Meyer sitting on the rear bench seat.
The tinted windows shrouded the interior in near
darkness. Gage sat down next to him.

As the SUV pulled away from the curb, Landon
asked, "Were you there?"

Gage recounted the battle.

"And Brandon?"

"He'll recover, but he'll never walk out of federal
prison."

"That bad?"

"That bad."

Two hours later, Gage removed Charlie Palmer's
DVD from his laptop, closed the spreadsheets Alex
Z had copied from Brandon's computer, and flipped
down the screen. The click echoed in Meyer's
Senate office.

Landon's face was gray. He gripped the arms of

his chair to rise, then stopped as though afraid his legs would give out. He lowered his hands to his lap and exhaled.

"I know Palmer and Anston didn't talk about my first campaign on the video," Landon finally said, "but you don't think Anston was behind the killing of those poor children in Compton?"

Gage shook his head. "He just paid off some community leaders to sound like they were reversing their stand on the death penalty. He used Pegasus to funnel the money, like with the fake jihadist contribution."

Landon leaned forward in his chair, then hung his head.

"So every election was tainted . . . every single one."

Gage didn't interrupt the silence that followed, and didn't have an answer to the question that would surely come next.

Landon looked up, his face nearly bloodless, his fists clenched, his whole body rigid.

"Tell me . . . please God tell me they didn't kill Ed Lightfoot."

"ince Watergate," Landon told Gage, "everybody says follow the money and you'll find the source of the corruption. But it's not that simple."

It was an hour before the press conference. Landon had met briefly with his staff and sent them away to make the arrangements.

"I remember when I was young and heard my father railing about the links among organized crime and the Teamsters and Longshoremen's unions and the Democrats and asked myself how politicians could've let that happen to themselves. What were they thinking? How could they have been so self-deceiving? Now I know."

Landon opened his lower left desk drawer and withdrew a humidor of Cuban Cohiba cigars. He opened the box, selected one, and held it up.

"You know where I got these?"

Gage didn't answer.

"The vice president." Landon paused, then added,

"of the United States," a reminder of the decades-old U.S. trade embargo.

Landon reached into the drawer again, withdrew a half-empty bottle of Wild Turkey, and set it next to the box.

"You know what's wrong with the phrase 'follow the money'?" Landon unwrapped the plastic cigar casing. "I'll tell you what's wrong. It's no secret where the money comes from. Everybody knows from where and what it does." He looked over at Gage, and then said, "Remember years ago I wondered aloud why Americans had stopped reading James Fenimore Cooper?"

Gage nodded. It had been during a late night talk, up at his cabin. Landon pacing, struggling to understand the country and his place in it.

"It was because of a line of his that had stuck with me since college. He said it 'was the proper business of government to resist the corruptions of money, not to depend on them.' Now I know why we turned away from him. It was too much like looking into a mirror that revealed all our hypocrisies and self-deceptions."

Landon slipped the end of the cigar into a miniature spring-loaded guillotine and snipped it off.

"Picture this. Early May, late evening, sitting on the porch of the vice president's mansion. Me, him, and the head of the energy lobby, drinking Scotch and sucking on Cohibas. Male bonding. That's what my wife calls it. But this wasn't playing football in the park or catching bass on Lake Okeechobee or guzzling beer over boiled crayfish."

Landon paused, glanced around his office, and then asked himself aloud, "Where am I going with this?" He ran the cigar under his nose, drawing in the aroma. "Following the money.

"Three little criminals sucking on Cohibas. Federal criminals at that." He pointed at Gage. "I know what you're wondering. You're an investigator. You're wondering where the vice president got the criminal cigars." Landon smiled. "From the lobbyist, of course." He gestured again, not pointing, simply punctuating. "And where did the lobbyist get them? From the president of Hudson Wire and Cable. And where did president of Hudson Wire and Cable get them? At a meeting in Barbados with the managing director of Hudson's Cayman Island subsidiary that installed the electrical infrastructure for thirty-four hotels that were built on Varadero Beach in Cuba. And where did the managing director get them? From Fidel Castro's brother's son's sister-in-law's cousin who supervises the entire construction project.

"So there we were sitting on the back porch . . ." Landon paused, then clucked. "In case you're wondering, the sister-in-law's father is the leader of the largest anti-Castro group in Florida."

Landon rose, walked to the window, and gazed over Washington. "Given this introduction, you're no doubt imagining the lobbyist met with us to push for lifting the embargo. Not at all. And it's not because he supports it. It's simply irrelevant. Anti-Castro Cubans in the U.S. are no more than a bloc of votes to be delivered to politicians—on both sides of the aisle—who vote the right way on other matters.

"Hudson Wire and Cable makes tens of millions a year in Cuba, embargo or not. And one of those millions found its way into a political action committee backing me, and part of it has been set aside to get out the anti-Castro Cuban vote in Florida."

Landon spun toward Gage.

"You think Hudson Wire and Cable ever gave a damn about how many political opponents Castro imprisoned and executed over the years? Or how many innocent Chechens Putin murdered or Egyptian protesters Mubarak shot down in the street? Or Suharto's genocide in East Timor? Not a bit. As long as Hudson is free to pursue its interests in Cuba and Russia and Indonesia, it doesn't care. And people like me who took their money didn't choose to think about it."

Landon picked at a fingernail.

"But let's face it. The deaths of innocents are like fertilizer. Take China. Our Internet hardware manufacturers overlook political repression in order to sell them routers. Routers open the Chinese to the Internet. The Internet opens their eyes to freedom of speech and democracy."

Gage pointed at Landon. "You're starting to sound like Anston."

"That's exactly the problem, except Anston didn't believe in democracy, only in fertilizer."

Landon paused, then a half smile appeared on his face.

"There's a certain irony in all of this I didn't grasp until now. Brandon used to think of himself as my Machiavelli. What he didn't realize was that Machiavelli believed the first act of a newly formed republic was sacrificial. It must murder the prince—and I suspect it's something Anston never doubted."

Landon's eyes focused on the bookshelf behind Gage. "You know what St. Augustine says about original sin?" He looked back at Gage, but didn't wait for an answer. "He calls it an inescapable blindness in human action. We never really know what we're doing. And by 'we' I mean all of us. It's not just Republicans or Democrats. We're all coconspirators in our own self-deceptions. We create the most powerful industrial nation on earth, but only by funding oil-producing governments that want to destroy us. And then once in a while we wake up, have a moment of terrifying clarity, then run from it or go back to sleep pretending it was just a nightmare." He hung his head. "Worst of all, when we most think we're our own men, we're really just someone else's puppets."

Landon inspected the cigar in his hand as if he'd never seen it before, then threw it into the wastebasket next to his credenza.

"In all these years since you gave me Augustine's *Confessions*, it never crossed my mind he was talking about me."

Landon dropped back into his chair, his arms limp in his lap. His eyes went vacant and inward for a moment, then he squinted as though searching for something far in the past. He finally focused on Gage.

"You always knew how all this would end, didn't you?"

Gage shook his head, He hadn't known. He had no way of knowing. And he was certain that in his heart Landon didn't believe Gage knew. It was just that the floundering man still needed to believe that there was such a thing as perfect knowledge—both insight and foresight—with which he could have armed himself against the tragedy that now enveloped him.

"Maybe not specifically," Landon continued. "Maybe you couldn't have foreseen where I am now, but from that first day on the river, you saw the hazards below the surface"—he lowered his gaze—"and all I really saw was my own reflection."

Senator Landon Meyer paused at the threshold of the Senate Radio-Television Gallery, just out of sight of the video cameras focused on the door. He looked over at Gage.

"You know where I am in the New Hampshire polls?" Landon asked.

"Does it make a difference?" Gage asked.

Landon shook his head. "Turns out it never did."

He then stepped through the doorway into the floodlights. In three strong steps he stood behind the podium. He scanned the familiar faces before him, the sources of thousands of questions over nearly two decades. While they were always dissatisfied with his politically polished answers, he was always forgiven because of his charming delivery.

He glanced toward his wife standing behind him, thinking that she would have made a wonderful first lady. But he knew the voters would never forgive him for Brandon, and for his own blindness. She smiled at him as though they were alone in the kitchen reading newspaper cartoons over coffee or at the dinner table after he said grace.

As Landon's eyes turned back to the crowd, he caught sight of an NBC producer, eyes pleading for action, as if to say the networks weren't giving up advertising revenue only so the public could watch a senator gaze at his wife.

Landon glanced back at her again, then faced the cameras and removed his notes from his suit breast pocket.

"I have served as a United States senator for the last fourteen years and have sought to represent the people and the interests of the State of California."

He paused and scanned the standing-room-only crowd.

"What does that mean? To represent. To act for others."

He paused again.

"Who are the people? And what is in their interest?

"Does representation mean casting my vote to reflect the polls? Or does it mean voting my conscience that tells me what's right, what's wrong, and what's in the true interest of the country, regardless of what the polls might say? It means all of this and, as it turns out, a great deal more.

"I say these things as a preface to a story I need to tell not only to the people of California, but to the people of the United States, for I serve in the United States Senate, not the California state legislature. This story recounts how I became elected to that body, how it happened that I continued to serve in that body, and finally became a candidate for president."

Landon looked toward the rear of the packed room where producers and camera operators lined the wall.

"Cognizant as I am of deadlines, news cycles, and the short attention span of the press, I shall begin with a sound bite that can be quickly digested."

Landon stared at the NBC camera.

"Unbeknownst to me, I have been the beneficiary of both corruption at an unimaginable level and disgraceful political maneuvering that destroyed not only lives, but the reputations and careers of each of my senatorial opponents in turn."

The crowd condensed into a stunned mass. Not a gasp. Not a stir. Not a word.

"It began twenty years ago . . ."

Fifteen minutes later, the press had answers to questions none of them would have ever thought to ask, but not the one Landon posed when he began.

Landon thought about the president watching in the White House, knowing Duncan was as shaken as he was.

"Now," Landon said, "let's return to where we began. With the matter of how I'm to represent the people of the State of California, people who were deprived of the senators they would've chosen had the political process not been corrupted, but in whose interests I must act.

"I return, therefore, to one of my initial questions. What is that interest? Is it a matter of polls or conscience? Is it a particular interest relating to these nominees for the Supreme Court or a general one relating to how we are to be governed? It seems to me it is all of these."

Landon gripped the podium, shoulders square.

"The bottom line is this. I believe these two nominees are highly qualified to serve as justices of the Supreme Court of the United States. I recognize they hold views considered by many to be extreme. The fact is that in good conscience I share many of those views, and do not at all think they are extreme.

"Given the tragic death of Senator Lightfoot, and given that ninety-eight other senators have already announced their intentions, it would appear the confirmation of these nominees rests in my hands."

Landon paused, staring at his notes, then folded them and returned them to his pocket.

"But that's not true. In fact, these confirmations were never in my hands. They were in the hands of the people of California. Even before the nominations were made by the president, before the Senate Judiciary Committee held its hearings and sent them on to the full Senate. Indeed, even before the tragic events of last night. In truth, these nominations were in the hands of the people of California when they walked into their polling booths, when they marked their ballots or touched the computer screens.

"I firmly believe that had it not been for corruption and deceit, I wouldn't be in a position to decide whether these nominees become justices of the Supreme Court."

Landon took in a long breath and exhaled. It was

as if he was the only one in the room who breathed at all.

"An argument could be made, and I've made it to myself, that the appropriate course of action is to abstain from voting. The matter would then go forward as if I was not present, and the vice president would break the forty-nine to forty-nine tie."

Landon imagined the president leaning forward in his chair, praying that Landon had devised a way to salvage the nominations.

"But that would leave the people of the State of California unrepresented, with no one to stand in their place and act for them, in the most important confirmations in our nation's history. It is for that reason I will vote against . . ."

President Duncan pressed the mute button on the remote and stared at length at the screen, at the now-vacant podium in front of which a CNN reporter stood.

"Mr. President?" Stuart Sheridan asked.

"It's all down the tubes. Every bit of it."

"But we can nominate—"

Duncan shook his head. "Landon took us all down. The Democrats are going to own the nominating process."

"But . . ."

"We did everything right. Everything. How the hell were we supposed to know?"

A re you going to be there?" John Porzolkiewski asked Gage in the visiting room at the San Francisco jail.

Gage shook his head. "There's no reason. But are you sure you don't want a lawyer?"

"You know what you told me when I first got arrested? You told me not to waste the money."

"That was a different situation."

"It was worse than different." Porzolkiewski smiled. "You were the one who got me arrested, then told me to trust you to figure out what happened even though you didn't believe me when I said I didn't do it."

Gage smiled back. "It makes you look like an idiot when you put it that way."

"Thanks. That's a confidence builder an hour before court." Porzolkiewski glanced at the new indictment lying on the table. "Isn't it ironic? I got charged with going after the same guy twice. Two different ways at two different times. I wonder if it's ever happened before."

"That's all the more reason to let Skeeter Hall help you. It was his and his associates' research that helped us figure everything out and he'd like to do more." Gage tilted his head toward the waiting room beyond the two sets of security doors. "He's sitting out there with one of the best criminal defense lawyers in the city."

"I appreciate the offer, but I've got to do this alone."

"Except it's pretty complicated. Legally. Medically. The DA could still bring in an expert to testify that Palmer wouldn't have died from the poisoned prescription if he hadn't already been weakened by you shooting him. That would make you guilty of the homicide."

Porzolkiewski shook his head. "I'll cross that bridge if I come to it." He then hunched forward and stared down at the metal table. "You know, I'm not so different from the people who killed my son."

"You're a lot different."

Porzolkiewski rotated his head and looked up at Gage. "It's just a matter of degree." He dropped his head again. "I'd almost convinced myself I shot Palmer in self-defense. Right after it happened I wanted to believe he charged me after I wrestled the gun away. I imagined him bearing down on me and me turning my head and firing. But that's not true. He hit his head against the lamppost and was dazed. I could've just walked away."

Porzolkiewski pursed his lips.

"Then I told myself the gun went off by accident. That my hand was shaking so much I squeezed the trigger. I even acted it out in my cell, imagining myself in front of a jury."

"But the difference is that you never lied to anybody about what happened."

Porzolkiewski straightened up.

"Yes, I did. I lied to myself, and not telling the truth was a way of lying to Palmer's wife. She had a right to know. Every time I think of her tied up . . . and Palmer. If I hadn't gone to see Palmer, they never would've killed him."

"Don't even think it. There's no way you could've known what was really going on. In any case, not everything in the world is your responsibility."

Porzolkiewski drew back and said, "Seems like a strange comment coming from you. What exactly did you owe me in this thing? Nothing. You owed me nothing."

"I owed you the truth," Gage said, "the same thing you owed me."

Porzolkiewski laid his palm on his chest in an act of contrition. "I understand that now."

He reached to his left for an oversized envelope, then pulled out a stack of papers and slid them toward Gage. On top was a letter from FourStar Media in Hollywood.

"Five hundred thousand dollars," Porzolkiewski said. "That's what they want to pay me for my story." He pointed at the papers. "There's a contract underneath. All it needs is my signature."

Gage slid them back. "Why not? You're a hero to every parent who lost a child because of corporate greed. Your picture is everywhere on the Internet,

and on every television station and in every newspaper in the world."

Porzolkiewski shook his head and slid the papers
back into the envelope.

"I think I'll pass. This wasn't about me."

He propped his elbows on the table, then smiled
and arched his eyebrows.

"I've been wondering about the condom. Did you
happen to ask Brandon Meyer who his girlfriend
was?"

"He claims there was no girlfriend. He said he
found it on another judge's bathroom floor a couple
of hours before he ran into you. Brandon had to pick
it up, otherwise the judge would know he'd seen it."

"Because the other judge was the one with the
girlfriend?"

"That's his story."

"Sounds a little lame to me. Did you believe
him?"

"Is it important anymore?"

"I guess not." Porzolkiewski paused, then exhaled
like a man standing hands-on-hips gazing down
toward a valley trailhead after climbing to a moun-
taintop. He peered at Gage. "I never thought to ask
how you got involved in all this in the first place."

"A call from Charlie."

"What did he say?"

"He didn't have a chance to say anything."

"You know what he wanted?"

Gage thought back to Charlie's last day, his last
words, his desperate, pleading voice. For the first
time Gage understood the burden he'd carried since
those final moments.

"More than anything," Gage said. "I think he wanted me to finish out his life."

"The way he would've done it himself?"

Gage shrugged. "We'll never know, but this is how it had to be."

"I understand there's a disposition in this matter," Judge Louisa Havstad said, peering down at John Porzolkiewski, dressed in an orange jail jumpsuit and standing next to the deputy district attorney. The judge fixed her eyes on the prosecutor.

"Ms. Kennedy, do the People have any objection to Mr. Porzolkiewski representing himself?"

Kennedy shook her head. "No, Your Honor. I met with him yesterday and then again a few minutes ago, and I'm satisfied he's making a knowing waiver of his right to counsel."

Judge Havstad then surveyed the courtroom, the reporters packed into the front rows and the broadcast and cable video cameras in the jury box bearing down on Porzolkiewski. Her pale skin and tense stare, combined with the sense of expectation in the courtroom, gave the impression of someone fearing a dam was about to break.

"My concern is that the defendant's behavior in the early stages of his previous case was somewhat bizarre. I don't want to see this proceeding turn into a spectacle."

"I don't believe that will happen," Kennedy said.

Havstad turned her gaze toward the defendant.

"For the record, Mr. Porzolkiewski, is it your intention to proceed without counsel?"

Porzolkiewski nodded.

"You have to answer aloud so the stenographer can take it down."

Porzolkiewski reddened. "Yes, Your Honor. I want to represent myself."

"Have you read the *Faretta* case?"

"Yes, I have. The district attorney gave me a copy."

"So you understand that if you act as your own lawyer, you can't turn around later and appeal your conviction by claiming incompetence of counsel?"

Tension-cracking laughter broke out and rattled among the spectators. Havstad slammed down her gavel, and then aimed it at the bailiff.

"If anyone makes another sound during the remainder of this proceeding I want them hauled out of here and brought back tomorrow in handcuffs. Understood?"

Havstad looked again at Porzolkiewski.

"Did you hear my question, Mr. Porzolkiewski?"

"Yes, Your Honor."

"And the answer?"

"Yes. I understood *Faretta*."

"And is it your intention to plead guilty to count one of the indictment, assault with a deadly weapon?"

A murmur rolled through the courtroom. Havstad raised her gavel and glared at the audience.

"Yes, Your Honor."

"Before you do that I need to advise you of certain of your rights and of the consequences of such a plea . . ."

Gage sat by the window in Spike's office watching television reporters opining about Brandon Meyer's appearance before the federal grand jury investigating corporate tax fraud and campaign money laundering through Pegasus. He switched the TV off when Spike opened the door.

Spike hung his sports jacket on the corner coatrack, then dropped into his chair.

"Tough guy that Porzolkiewski," Spike said. "He didn't weasel. Didn't make any excuses. Just got up and told the story."

"You're okay with assault with a deadly weapon as the disposition, instead of attempted murder?"

"I believed him," Spike said. "He wanted to hurt Charlie, make him suffer, not kill him."

"What do you think Havstad is going to do?"

"Hard to say. It's two, three, or four years on the assault plus a consecutive three, four, or ten for using the handgun."

Gage rose and looked down through the window. News crews were gathered in semidarkness on the front steps, cameras were pointed at the bronze exit doors.

"I don't think she would've released him without bail," Gage said, "if she intended to max him out."

"Will he show up for sentencing next month?" Spike asked.

"He'll show."

Spike smiled. "You want to put some cash on it?"

Gage glanced over his shoulder. He didn't smile back. "Don't talk to me about money."

"I'm afraid you'll be talking about it for a helluva long time to come."

Gage shook his head. "Not so long. I talked to Jack Burch a few minutes ago. TIMCO has agreed to settle with the families of the workers. And the parents of the kids who beat up Moki will each put a half million into a trust fund."

"What about Tansy?"

"She didn't want anything for herself. She just wants to have confidence in the care Moki gets and to go back into nursing." Gage paused, imagining Tansy's empty chair, anticipating the heartache of her absence. "It's going to be hard to walk past her desk and not see her there."

"Who's going to clean up Anston's mess? The press is reporting there's about a billion dollars to be accounted for."

"That's up to the Justice Department and the Federal Election Commission. And Jack rounded up some lawyers who've volunteered to reopen all the old TIMCO- and Moki-type cases."

Gage felt a surge of both weariness and relief.

"I'm out of it."

G age brought Chinese take-out dinner to Faith and Socorro sitting at Viz's bedside at SF Medical, then drove back to his building. The sounds of urgent voices and ringing phones and churning printers faded as he climbed the stairs toward his third floor office. After the fire door closed behind him, only his soft footfalls accompanied him down the long dark hallway toward his door—

And a recurring thought. Joe Casey was wrong. Nothing could ever be returned to the way it had been. And whatever justice was, it surely wasn't that.

As Gage crossed the threshold, he saw his desk lamp cast a circle of light on a handwritten note lying against a slim square object wrapped in white cloth.

He walked over and picked it up.

Dear Graham,
    These are the songs that brought joy to my little angel so long ago.

Thank you, you dear, dear man.
Tansy

Gage untied the ribbon. Lying before him was a CD. Ten-year-old fingerprint powder etched the last places Moki had touched before running up the hill for the last time to gaze at the horizon.

He sat down and slipped it into his computer, and then leaned back in his chair. The drive whirled and clicked as he stared out toward the invisible bay, its shoreline marked by glimmering city lights. There was a long pause, then the beat of drums, the rasp of sticks, the rattle of gourds and, finally, rising from the weeping earth, the harp, the violin, and the flute.

On top of the enchanted world,
far down you are flying
west, where the sun falls,
beautiful, sparkling, and forever,
you go with the wind.

Acknowledgments and Note to the Reader

A s usual, friends gave generously of their time to help me figure out what I meant to say and get it on the page. They are: Denise Fleming, whose editorial knife is as precise as it is sharp; Carol Keslar, whose early insights went a long way; Dennis Barley, a great investigator and shrewd judge of the motivations of humans, both real and imaginary; Davie Sue Litov, who insists that it be on the page; Bruce Kaplan, the only writer I know who can start with the weather and get away with it; Seth Norman, meandering the meander; and Randy Schmidt, who helped with some of the weightier issues.

Thanks go to my cousin Bobbie Chinsky and Howard Somerville and my sister Diane Gore-Uecker and John Uecker, early adopters of Graham Gage and Harlan Donnally; Louisa Havstad, of such good character that I made her one; Glenn and Judy Pollock, who knew Gage back when and have the photographs to prove it; Trevor Patterson, a former investigator who was everything Charlie

510 • ACKNOWLEDGMENTS AND NOTE

Palmer was not; Cassie Patterson, a proud great-grandmother.

Thanks also for their enthusiasm, support, and good times: Lincoln, Gayle, and Haley Litov, Pauline Kaplan, Erin Kaplan, Erik Woods, Scott Sugarman, Chris Cannon, Bob Waggener, Paul Wolf, and Carl and Kathy Polhemus.

As always, the editorial, production, and design staff at HarperCollins did a wonderful job of making my work presentable to the reader: Emily Krump, who not only took on Graham Gage, Harlan Donnally, and me all at once, but asked all the questions a writer needs to hear from an editor; my publicists, Andy Dodds and Katie Steinberg, who had all the right contacts, and Stefanie Rosenblum of Planned Television Arts, who took me coast to coast; and to the sales and marketing people who have done such a great job of getting the books in places readers can easily find them. Thanks again to copyeditor Eleanor Mikucki, whose attention to both story and detail much improved the manuscript.

My wife, Liz, as always, made the book good enough to risk showing to others.

Like the other novels, in both the Gage and Donnally series, this one benefited from help I received in the course of my investigative work. Among those helpers were: Karnati Rama Mohan Rao, a legendary, gravel-voiced, wild-haired criminal defense lawyer in Andhra Pradesh, India. P. A. Kamaleswari of Hyderabad, a fine lawyer and advocate for Indian women and villagers, for whom caste is, in word and in deed, no bar. Banker "X" in Lugano, Switzerland who explained the art and craft of offshore deniability. And Police Superintendent "Y" whose display of a wad of currency told me that money would once again defeat truth and justice in South Asia.

Readers interested in the irreconcilable perspectives inherent in the notion of representation reflected in Landon Meyer's speech might want to look at *The Concept of Representation* (University of California Press, 1972) and *Wittgenstein and Justice* (University of California Press, 1972) by Hanna Pitkin. They suggest an approach to accepting seemingly contradictory claims not only about representation, but about what counts as having done justice.

Readers interested in the two strains of conservatism Landon Meyer finds competing within him, and the issues involved in reconciling them, might want to look at the work of the great British conservative political philosopher Michael Oakeshott, collected in *Rationalism in Politics* (available in various editions). It contains the famous and beautifully written essay "On Being Conservative," which is also available online.

The Yoeme (Yaqui) language quotes from the traditional Yaqui Deer Songs that begin and end the book are drawn and modified from "Maiso Yoleme/ Deer Person," Felipe Molina, Yoem Pueblo, August 21, 1984, in *Yaqui Deer Songs, Maso Bwikam: A Native American Poetry*, Larry Evers and Felipe S. Molina (University of Arizona Press, 1987, pp. 71 and 106). The phrase "the weeping earth" is from "The Elders Truth," a sermon by Miki Maaso at Yoem Pueblo on December 22, 1987 (transcribed by Felipe S. Molina and Larry Evers, *Journal of the*

Southwest, volume 35, number 3, Autumn 1993). I put together my own version of the song that ends the book.

The lines said by Alex Z beginning: "All sorrows can be borne if you tell a story about it" are paraphrased from Isak Dinesen, author of *Out of Africa*, quoted in Hannah Arendt's "Truth and Politics" in *Between Past and Future* (Penguin Classics, 1993). The concluding part of the line is: "At the end we'll be privileged to view and review it—that's what's called judgment day." A different version appears in Dinesen's *Last Tales*.

I hope I didn't offend any readers with Tansy's comments about Carlos Castaneda and his fictional Yaqui shaman, but like her, while growing up along South Sixth Avenue in Tucson, Arizona, I never saw an Indian fly—even as we raced with dimes in our hands from the sandlot next to my house past Vic's Trading Post to the legendary Le Caves Bakery on the corner.

New York **selling author**

JAMES ROLLINS

MAP OF BONES
978-0-06-201785-7
There are those with dark plans for stolen sacred remains that will alter the future of mankind.

SANDSTORM
978-0-06-201758-1
Twenty years ago, a wealthy British financier disappeared near Ubar, the fabled city buried beneath the sands of Oman.

ICE HUNT
978-0-06-196584-5
Danger lives at the top of the world . . . where nothing can survive except fear.

AMAZONIA
978-0-06-196583-8
There are dark secrets hidden in the jungle's heart, breeding fear, madness . . . and death.

DEEP FATHOM
978-0-06-196582-1
Ex-Navy SEAL Jack Kirkland surfaces from an underwater salvage mission to find the Earth burning and the U.S. on the brink of a nuclear apocalypse—and he is thrust into a race to change the tide.

EXCAVATION
978-0-06-196581-4
For untold centuries, the secrets of life have been buried in a sacred, forbidden chamber in the South American jungle. Those who would disturb the chosen must now face the ultimate challenge: survival.

SUBTERRANEAN
978-0-06-196580-7
A hand-picked team of scientists makes its way toward the center of the world, into a magnificent subterranean labyrinth where breathtaking wonders await—as well as terrors beyond imagining.

JR1 0211